MANDALA ROAD

Mandala Road

THAMES RIVER PRESS
An imprint of Wimbledon Publishing Company Limited (WPC)
Another imprint of WPC is Anthem Press (www.anthempress.com)

First published in the United Kingdom in 2013 by
THAMES RIVER PRESS
75-76 Blackfriars Road
London SE1 8HA

www.thamesriverpress.com

Original title: Mandara do
Copyright © M. Bandō 2004
Originally published in Japan by SHUEISHA, Tokyo
English translation copyright © Wayne P. Lammers 2013

A CIP record for this book is available from the British Library.

ISBN 978-0-85728-248-4

Cover design by Laura Carless.

This title is also available as an eBook.

This book has been selected by the Japanese Literature Publishing Project (JLPP),
an initiative of the Agency for Cultural Affairs of Japan.

MANDALA ROAD

Masako Bandō

Translated by Wayne P. Lammers

THAMES RIVER PRESS

1

Before sleep comes, the woman drifts into dream. As she makes her way about a garden, gathering herbs, she picks out dream forms in the glistening dew on the grasses at her feet and in the bright swirls of light rising around her. Her eyes, black as obsidian, dart after the elusive figures as she wanders on through the forest of eternity.

2

The morning the first oleanders came into bloom, Shizuka brought Asafumi a notebook that had belonged to his grandfather. It was the old-fashioned kind, bound with threads around the spine on the outside, with pages wider than they were tall. The threads were soiled, and the paper had grown woolly, its edges worn and dog-eared. Inscribed in thick black brushstrokes on the cover was the label "Medicine Kit Register," accompanied by the date: April 19, 1947.

His grandfather, Rentarō, had been a medicine peddler.

Beginning in the Edo Period, men from Toyama had travelled far and wide, selling medicines of every kind out of distinctive five-tiered wicker baskets they carried in large cloth-wrapped bundles on their backs. Rentarō's generation, born shortly after the turn of the twentieth century, had stretched their legs beyond Japanese shores – across the East China Sea to the Asian continent, to the countries and islands of the southern tropics, and even across the Pacific.

As a child, whenever Asafumi visited his grandfather's house, which always smelled of damp straw, a black-and-white photograph displayed on top of the tea cupboard used to catch his eye. It pictured seven medicine peddlers, all dressed alike in derby hats and knickerbockers as they stood in front of a cluster of mandala flowers. Behind the shrubs' large, white, trumpet-shaped blooms spread a palm grove that looked rather like a crowd of long-necked people with dishevelled hair. The peddlers stood with their gaitered legs braced firmly, as if determined to show the languorous tropical landscape around them that they meant business. Six of the men were obviously very young, no more than twenty or so, and the white, high-collared shirts they wore with coat and tie made them look as stiff as six-year-olds on their first day of school. The seventh man was older, obviously the leader, wearing round glasses and sporting a moustache; a gold chain dangled from his watch pocket, and he stared at the camera with every ounce of authority he could summon.

But spoiling any gravity the men conveyed were the massive cloth bundles tied to their backs, with two corners of the dark wrapping cloths knotted horizontally across their chests. The bundles were obviously of considerable weight, for all seven men stood with both hands gripping the fabric in front of their chests like begging dogs, their lips set firmly with the effort of remaining upright. Altogether, the heavy-laden band of peddlers from Japan looked more like a delegation from the Planet of the Toads who'd just arrived in a land of eternal sunshine. They were not merely comical; one actually felt sorry for them.

Rentarō had explained that the picture was from when he used to sell medicines in Malaya. Asafumi promptly began boasting to his playmates that his grandpa had gone all the way to the Himalayas to sell his goods.

There in the Himalayas they had trees with flowers like white trumpets, and lots of palm trees, too, he declared. There were flowers as big as washbowls, and some that were shaped like birds-of-paradise. They had trees that looked like they were in flames when they bloomed, trees that ran with white milk, and trees that produced all kinds of weird fruits and nuts. There was fruit that had jiggly, jelly-like stuff around the seed, and fruit shaped like a star; fruit that tasted like *gyoza* and butter, and nuts that tasted like lunch buns. His friends listened wide-eyed as he repeated what his grandfather had told him. When some smarty-pants pointed out that the Himalayas were covered in snow all year round and palm trees couldn't possibly grow there, Asafumi was unfazed. Just look up there, he replied, raising his hand toward the mountains. The Tateyama Range was always covered with snow, too, but their own town at the foot of the mountains still got plenty hot in the summertime, didn't it? And besides, he added, his grandfather had seen it all with his own eyes.

In his mind, he pictured the Himalayas as a land of endless summer surrounded by white-capped mountains. A place where strange plants were constantly in bloom and trees bent low with exotic fruit. If someone had asked him then where he thought heaven might be, he would have named the Himalayas without a moment's hesitation.

Asafumi was forever trying to get new stories out of Rentarō with which to impress his friends. But the old man's recollections invariably shifted from flowers and fruit to women, and once he got onto that topic, he'd get stuck there like a fly on flypaper and never move on.

"And the women of Malaya, they're really something else," he'd say with a faraway look. "So passionate, so frisky. Go to bed with them and it's like dipping your pecker in warm kudzu sauce. Pure heaven. Put your thing in once and you're a goner. There's no escape."

Forgetting his grandson was even there, Rentarō would toy with his teacup as he dreamily extolled the virtues of Malayan women, on and on, until finally he sank into a sea of memories and fell silent. Then nothing could induce him to speak up again. He remained submerged in the vast ocean of his past, lips clamped shut as tight as a clam.

Already past eighty by this time, his mind was beginning to fail. He might recall certain scenes and foods and women from his travels, but he could no longer identify which of the seven young men in the photo was him. When Asafumi went to get the picture for him, he would put on his reading glasses and hold it up for a closer look. Almost right away he would stab a shrivelled index finger at one of the figures and say, "That's me." But then Asafumi would point his own finger to confirm, "This one here?" and he'd say, "No, the next one over." Asafumi would ask again, "So this is you?" only to have him insist that he was the one on the end. Since the faces in the picture all looked pretty much alike, Asafumi himself could not tell, and in the end Rentarō went to his grave without ever reliably identifying which of them he was.

It was only after his grandfather had died and he'd gone on to junior high that Asafumi learned the difference between Malaya and the Himalayas. Reminded of the picture, he asked his parents about it, but it had apparently been mislaid in the confusion surrounding the funeral.

Sitting cross-legged on the veranda, he began turning the pages of the notebook labelled "Medicine Kit Register." The handwriting was in a style popular during the Meiji Era, with strokes like tangled vines, and he might as well have been trying to read Sanskrit. He managed to make out the name of Ōyama Village, along with several personal names, but the medicines and old-fashioned numbers that accompanied them were impossible to decipher.

The object he held in his hand was the vaunted Toyama medicine peddler's most precious business asset – his sales register. It was in notebooks like this that each peddler recorded the names and addresses of his customers – all the homes where he had placed his medicine kits, along with the makeup of the family who lived there, a running tally of what drugs they had used, and the payments received. Asafumi was aware that there were people who specialized in buying and selling these valuable registers.

He looked up at Shizuka, who'd been standing there watching him in her shorts, her bare legs planted on the ground like the two tips of a draftsman's compass.

"Where'd you find this?" he asked.

"In the shed," she said, pointing her chin toward the overgrown garden behind her.

Beyond the place where the purplish-pink oleanders bloomed stood a dilapidated shed that Rentarō had used for storage after moving into this house in retirement. Thinking of the lost photo, Asafumi asked if she'd seen anything else that might have belonged to his grandfather. She thought for a moment before giving her head a single quick shake sideways.

"I think I'll go and see," he said, stepping off the veranda and into a pair of sandals.

"There really wasn't anything else," she said, sounding a little peeved that he didn't seem to trust her.

"Yeah, I know," he said as he headed through the narrow opening next to the oleander bushes.

The slender, olive-coloured leaves ruffled, and the sweet smell of the freshly opened flowers swept his cheeks. He moved on through the fragrant air into the swirl of vegetation beyond.

The property on which his grandfather's old house stood wasn't actually all that big, but the garden was so thick with bushes and shrubs of all sizes that you felt you could easily get lost if you weren't careful. In the middle of it all, a single giant tree with a tall gray trunk spread its limbs overhead, and the ground was covered everywhere with a variety of grasses, herbs, and flowers. But besides the oleanders, the only plant Asafumi could identify by name was a fig tree. Otherwise, the yard was a dense tangle of unusually shaped leaves, vines, and flowers he'd never seen before, flourishing and declining in their turn. A few stepping-stones were visible among the plants, but there were no discernible paths, and years of neglect had allowed everything to become so overgrown, with roots and branches and leaves tightly enmeshed, that it was almost impossible to make one's way between one plant and the next. The single exception was the narrow track resembling an animal's trail through the woods that had been worn between the house and the storage shed, starting next to the oleanders.

Pushing through the branches pressing in on both sides, Asafumi made his way toward the small building that had become almost completely hidden in green ivy. Although they referred to it as a shed, it was in fact a proper post-and-beam structure of substantial size – with a slate roof to boot. He stepped through the door Shizuka had left standing open. A small window let in enough light for him to make out such things as a foot-warmer, a table fan missing a blade, bundles of newspapers and magazines, an ancient potbellied stove, and a battered old tea cupboard. Items left behind by the most recent occupants of the house appeared to be mixed at random with older objects from his grandfather's day, but Shizuka had obviously done some straightening up, for everything was now in a neat pile to one side. Coming in behind him, she reached around his shoulder to point.

"It was in that," she said.

Sitting on top of the tea cupboard was a rectangular tin box with rounded corners, just large enough to hold the notebook. Colourful yellow, purple, red, and white flowers decorated the outside, but patches of the paint were worn away, revealing rusty metal underneath. Neither the flowers nor the particular colours were recognizably Japanese. Thinking that it must originally have been a box of sweets from overseas, Asafumi lifted the lid to look inside. Except for the dried-out shell of an insect about the size of an adzuki bean, it was empty – just as Shizuka had said. He traced his finger around the rim of the rusting tin.

"I suppose Saya must have had it," he said.

Shizuka gave him an uncomprehending look. It suddenly occurred to him that he hadn't ever told his wife about Saya.

3

Beyond the undulating stretch of blue loomed the shadow of land. Aboard the repatriation boat, the Japanese returnees crowded the deck for a first glimpse of their homeland, jostling like ants on the remains of a night-laugher. Among them stood Saya, keeping a tight, sweaty grip on the hand of her seven-year-old boy as she gazed at the approaching dark landmass that was foreign soil to her.

After nearly a month at sea, the crisp, freshly laundered short-sleeved dress she'd put on in Singapore looked like a soiled washrag. Her hair, done up in a knot so as to hide its natural curl, had grown greasy, and her light brown skin was grimy, too. Her armpits reeked, and an over-ripe smell came from between her legs.

She could shade her face and figure, but she could do nothing about the female odours her body sent out from inside – smells that attracted the other sex. "This is to protect yourself in case you run into men on the rut," her brother had said as he slipped her the parting gift she now kept hidden in her hair – a tiny finger-hole knife with a hooked tip. It had been his own trusty companion until then. People carried such knives somewhere on their heads for the moment when they might need to slit an enemy's throat.

And it had in fact come in handy. One evening during the long journey from Malaya, a man she'd overheard talking about the clothing store he ran in Kuala Lumpur forced her into the shadows of a passageway. Saya quietly drew the knife from her hair, slid an index finger through the hole, and pressed it to his throat. With an edge that could make short work of the man's scraggly beard, one tiny flick of the blade would send blood spurting from his sagging chin as well.

"This one much harder and sharper than man-sword in trousers," she said in her slightly broken Japanese. The man began quaking as if he'd walked through a shower of leeches.

Holding her brother's knife in front of her, she slowly backed out of the dark and hurried back to her spot in the hold. After that, the fellow had settled for eying her from across the room with a mixture of lust and hatred; he never bothered her again.

Beneath a sky tinged with the colours of the rising sun, a blast from the ship's horn shook the air. Frightened, the boy pressed closer to her side. Because he spoke little Japanese, she had told him to keep quiet on the ship or they'd both get thrown to the giant alligators in the sea, and he had been surprisingly well behaved ever since. He communicated with her entirely by touch, making his desires known to her simply by the way he clung to her or gripped her hand. Saya released the boy's sweaty palm to wipe her own hand on the skirt of her dress before taking his hand in hers again.

Islands large and small hovered dimly in the violet-blue merging of sea and sky. The former Imperial Navy transport vessel, carrying nearly a thousand demobilized soldiers and more than two thousand civilians, spewed black smoke from its stacks as it glided slowly among the soft, tree-covered islands, its bow cutting through the calm waters of the Inland Sea toward a pier still veiled in morning haze. Small villages came into view here and there along the jagged shoreline on either side, with tiny fishing boats clogging their ports like clumps of seaweed. Saya knew the ship was headed for a much larger port named Hiroshima. She'd heard people near her in the hold saying that the city had been hit by something called an atomic bomb, which had destroyed everything as far as the eye could see in an instant and killed untold numbers of people. But she noticed no signs of any such catastrophe as the ship steamed past a small peninsula that reached out into the ocean like a bent arm and entered the port.

Boats tied up to a quiet pier formed a bold horizontal line along the edge of the water. A small steam-powered vessel abruptly broke from this line, kicking up a white wake as it made straight for the ship.

"It's coming this way! A boat's coming this way!" Excited cries erupted all around and the crowd pressed against the rail: a woman with a baby tied to her back and tears streaming down her face; a breathless man standing with his mouth agape; a child jumping up and down in an effort to see; soldiers in tattered uniforms, staring grimly toward the pier – some on crutches, others missing an arm. Looking like a ragtag army of homeless tramps with their grimy clothes and greasy hair, the assemblage of men and women on deck rippled with both thrill and apprehension.

Saya stared fiercely at the land before her across the water, glinting in the morning sunlight, as it continued to get nearer.

This was Japan. The country spoken of with such bitter hatred and anger back in Malaya. There was no way of knowing what lay in store for her here. It was like stepping for the first time into a part of the jungle where a leopard or a python or a scorpion might lie in wait at any turn, and the slightest rustling of leaves, the faintest sound on the ground, or the tiniest whiff of something in the air could be clues for staying out of danger. Every nerve in her body was on alert. She turned her head gently back and forth to feel the weight of the knife in her hair.

"The medicine man said a magic spell over it to help it cut down evil spirits," her brother had told her when he gave it to her. "Keep it with you, and it'll protect you from most any danger."

"But in that case, you need to keep it," Saya replied.

A broad smile spread across his brown cheeks. "Don't forget, my name is Kekah. I have the bite of a savage dog. Let any evil spirit come near me and I'll rip it to shreds with my teeth. So don't worry about me. Take it."

The next day he was found beaten to death on a back street in Kota Bharu, covered with mud – his eyeballs out of their sockets, his arms and legs bent at impossible angles. Saya wept as she buried him. She could not even give him her tribe's customary send-off by raising him to the top of the tree of the dead in the jungle.

The boat from the pier came alongside as soon as the ship dropped anchor. A rope ladder was lowered, and a Japanese man in civilian dress climbed aboard, accompanied by several white men in crisp military uniforms carrying batons. They exchanged greetings with the crewmen who stepped forward to receive them then moved quickly in the direction of the captain's quarters.

A low buzz surged through the throng of returnees on deck. Hey, did you see that? It's just like they said. The Allies have taken over the country. What's the world come to? Somebody said kids are bein' born with blue or red eyes. Look at those guys – tramping around like they own the place.

The sight of the Americans in uniform put a damper on the excitement that had been brewing. With many a nervous glance toward the captain's quarters, people began streaming back to their places below-decks. Saya and her boy joined the flow.

Down in the hold, the passengers had staked out swatches of space wide enough to sit and sleep in, with their baggage piled at the head, away from the aisle. Everybody promptly began packing away the things they'd had out during the journey – dog-eared pocket notebooks, eating utensils, clothing, and sundry other items. The long-awaited homecoming was at hand, and it seemed no one could bear to sit still.

Except Saya, who returned to her spot and simply sank onto her knees. The few belongings she'd brought along fitted into a single travel-worn suitcase she'd found at a Chinaman's second-hand shop in Kota Bharu, so she had no special packing to do. She just sat there in the semi-darkness of the hold like an animal crouching in the underbrush, watching the others put their things in order and listening to their impatient chatter. It had not been particularly difficult to get herself and her boy aboard the ship simply by pretending they were Japanese and blending in with the crowd, but she'd never had the first idea what they would do once they reached Japan. Her anxiety and agitation swelled. Sensing his mother's tension, the boy pressed harder against her hip.

"So where're you headed once we land?" came a voice from nearby.

It was the slant-eyed, hollow-cheeked lady in the next space over. The greying woman, dressed elegantly in Western style, had come aboard with an unusually large amount of luggage and laid claim to her spot with the air of someone accustomed to having her way. There were in fact a considerable number of unaccompanied women like her on the ship, as well as many others who were travelling with just their children, like Saya, but this woman stood out from the others. She sat with her mountain of luggage behind her as if ensconced in her own private fort, never joining in the tales of hardship that others around her exchanged, never deigning to get acquainted and share her background. The others responded by keeping their distance. In this respect, the woman in fact resembled Saya, who held herself apart in order to conceal her identity. Their ending up side-by-side might even have been a case of like kinds attracting. Each had sensed something kindred in her neighbour, and remained stiffly conscious of the other's presence throughout the journey – though, not unlike two monitor lizards circling each other in the swamp, even as each kept the other in her sights, neither of them had taken any step that would actually bring them closer.

Now suddenly, as they were preparing to go ashore, the woman had finally spoken to her and it caught Saya by surprise. She was equally surprised to discover that the woman had found time to change out of the clothes she'd worn throughout the journey into a crisp, clean outfit, as well as to smooth her hair with a comb and tie it neatly at the back of her head.

"Toyama." The name popped out before Saya even realized she was breaking her longstanding silence.

"Toyama?" the woman said. "That's an awful long way from Hiroshima."

What a stupid thing to say, thought Saya. However far it might be, distances inside a country couldn't possibly compare to the distance they'd already come across the vast ocean.

"Is he yours?" the woman said, eying the boy's curly hair and dark skin.

Saya nodded. The boy sensed they were talking about him and nervously put a hand on her thigh.

For several moments, the woman studied each of them in turn.

"A native father, I suppose?"

Since this was a repatriation ship, the woman naturally assumed Saya was Japanese. Many of the passengers had lived in Malaya or Indonesia for so long that they'd become darker in the tropical sun and could easily be mistaken for locals. Some had even begun to lose their fluency in Japanese, and more than a few had been born overseas to begin with. Even with her round eyes, thick lips, upturned nose, and slightly curly hair, Saya could pass for Japanese so long as she did her hair in a tight knot, wore Western clothes, and kept her mouth shut. But reflecting his tribal roots, her son had a wide nose, noticeably darker skin, and a distinct kink in his hair. He seemed to take after his uncle Kekah more than his mother.

"Father is Japanese."

The woman cast a dubious glance at the boy. "Well, I should certainly hope so," she said. "Coming home with a half-breed in tow would be like putting a great big sign on your forehead saying 'I slept with a savage.'"

Saya shot her an angry look and turned away. A glimmer of satisfaction crossed the woman's face.

"Don't get me wrong now. I'm not talking about you."

She lightly touched Saya's hand, resting on her knee. Saya shook it off as if she'd been stung by a bee.

The woman's eyes flashed. "I wouldn't go putting on airs if I were you. The kid's a dead giveaway that you're a badger from the same burrow as me. You're not pulling any wool over my eyes." She abruptly turned away and shifted back to the middle of her space.

A badger? What was that? Some kind of insect or plant? With the unpleasantness of the exchange still gnawing at her, Saya tried to think if she'd ever heard the word before, but she couldn't place it.

The group leaders now returned. During the trip, representatives chosen from each section of the hold had met to discuss rations and any other problems that arose, and they'd been summoned again in connection with arrival procedures. The passengers immediately directed their attention to them, eager to hear the instructions they brought.

The leader of Saya's group was a fortyish man named Miyata, who'd owned an import-export business in Sumatra. He wore glasses and had close-cropped hair. Though his clothes were very much in need of laundering, they were obviously of good quality, and he had the manner of a man accustomed to giving orders. His deep, resonant voice rang out as he began explaining.

"The men from the Repatriation Relief Bureau and occupation forces have just left. They found no particular matters of concern, and we've been cleared to go ashore. The landing boats will arrive shortly to begin shuttling us to Ujina Pier, so please make sure you're ready to disembark at any time."

"Hell, we've been ready since before we set sail!"

This energetic voice came from a man getting on past middle age, with bony, blue-veined knees sticking out beneath his shorts. His wife sitting next to him smiled wryly as she wiped her face with a hand towel. Nearby, a woman travelling with two small children nodded her agreement, grinning from ear to ear. The whole group bubbled with excitement.

Obviously feeling just as keyed up as the rest of them, Miyata went on: "Before we leave the ship, I'm supposed to collect the Returnee Questionnaires that were passed out when we first set sail. The information from these forms will be used to issue your Repatriation Certificates, so you need to bring them to me now."

The hold came alive with activity again as the passengers began searching through their luggage.

Saya opened her suitcase and got out the paper she'd received at the beginning of the trip. Her spoken Japanese was enough to get by on, but she couldn't read or write a single word; at a loss what to do, she'd simply put the form away blank. From what Miyata had just said, though, there was no avoiding having to fill it out. She stared at the lines of incomprehensible characters in growing distress. It was bound to mean trouble if she didn't find a way to get it done. She scanned the room. Some people were still double-checking their forms, while others were already turning them in. When her closest neighbour returned from submitting hers, Saya decided she had no other choice.

"Excuse me," she said.

The woman looked up from a suitcase the size of a goat into which she was pushing the last of her things.

Saya held the questionnaire out to her. "Please can you help me?" she said.

"Help you?" the woman all but snapped at her. Then seeing the pleading look in her eyes, she looked down at the blank questionnaire with a frown. "With what? Your form? Why should I have to..." She stopped. "Oh," she said, lowering her voice, "you can't write?" Her scowl softened. She took the sheet from Saya's hand and placed it on her lap, then retrieved a stub of a pencil from the small bag she carried looped around her neck and shoulder. "What's your name?" she asked.

Opening her suitcase, Saya dug out another wrinkled piece of paper and handed it over. She paid close attention as the woman read from it.

"Kim Suk-hwa?" she said, looking up. Saya looked back without saying anything. A growing smile accentuated the wrinkles along the woman's upper lip. "You mean to say you're Korean?"

Saya nodded. The woman turned back to the wrinkled paper and studied it some more.

"Born in Shimonoseki, 1912. Well, well," she mumbled as she bent over the form and began filling in the blanks, licking the tip of her pencil now and then between characters. "I'm from Amakusa myself, so you could almost say we're neighbours."

Saya kept a sharp eye on the woman as she referred to the paper to fill out Kim Suk-hwa's details. Could she have guessed that Saya wasn't actually Korean? The thought made her jittery inside. What if she suddenly pointed a finger at her and cried out for the entire hold to hear that she was neither Japanese nor Korean? She was terrified. But she also knew she couldn't let it show. Feigning calmness, she sat on her haunches, hugging her knees and watched the woman's every movement.

Here and there, those with questionnaires finished and submitted had launched into farewells. Some were exchanging addresses with friends they'd made on board. People who had thought only about themselves and heaped endless abuse on other passengers over rations and drinking water and use of the toilets during the long passage were all of a sudden acting as if they could hardly bear to part.

The woman raised her head. "Where did you live in Malaya?" she asked.

"Kota Bharu."

She gave her a searching look, but then quickly turned back to the form.

"What will your address be in Japan? Shimonoseki?"

Saya fished another scrap of paper from the bottom of her suitcase and handed it to her. It was a return address torn from the back of an envelope, its edges yellowing. The woman smoothed it out and read it aloud.

"Rentarō Nonezawa, 13 Tamaishi San-chōme, Senbashi, Toyama. This is where you're going?"

Saya nodded, her obsidian eyes gleaming.

4

As Shizuka emerged from the storage shed, the golden late-afternoon sun stabbed at her eyes. The light seemed to illumine each individual leaf in the garden with a sublime glow. A gentle breeze stirred a clump of leaves similar to a maple's. The illusion of countless fluttering hands reminded her of a scene she'd chanced upon when she was only eleven.

It began with an arm and hand spotted through a thicket of spring leaves. The hand moved slowly back and forth, and as it did so, a contrasting patch of purplish-pink colour began appearing and disappearing between the fingers. The patch of purple-pink seemed to grow larger with each stroke of the hand, almost like a magic trick. Before long it jutted out like a curved pillar of stone – a menhir erected among the foliage.

The object glistened sharply in the light, with another strong masculine hand gripping it at its base. Shizuka's eleven-year-old eyes moved from this hand to the forearm, then slowly up to the shoulder, but there the arm disappeared among the foliage and she could not see the face of its owner. Her eyes fell back down the arm. The hand was moving again. Harder. Faster. The arching pillar stood at the centre of a green cosmos. Every force in the universe seemed to be condensed in that single point, and her eyes were held fast by its pull, unable to look away.

The hand stopped. A thick liquid dribbled from between the fingers wrapped around its tip. The fluid ran down the fist and dripped into the greenery below. Her eyes traced the viscous drops as they fell, and by the time she looked up again, the menhir and hands were gone, leaving only gently stirring leaves.

"You know, I just don't get it."

Asafumi's voice broke through Shizuka's thoughts as she stood watching the motion of the maple-like leaves. She turned to find him emerging from the storage shed in his flashy, flower-pattern Bermuda shorts. What she had seen in that thicket all those years ago made her eyes instinctively gravitate to the point where his legs came together at his crotch.

"Don't get what?" she asked, quickly looking away from the bulge in his shorts.

"That register has to have been one of my grandfather's. But he should have given my dad everything he had when he turned the business over to him, so why would just the one notebook still be left here in the shed?"

"It was probably just an oversight," Shizuka said with a shrug.

Her opinion of Rentaro, Asafumi's grandfather, had taken a sharp nosedive the moment her husband had begun telling her about Saya. The man had gone all the way to Southeast Asia to peddle his medicines, taken up with a local wife while there, and then come waltzing home. The very term "local wife" made her blood boil, with its implication that women were nothing more than a commodity.

"Sales registers like that are the most important assets you have in this business. It's not the sort of thing he'd overlook. I definitely need to show it to my dad."

"I guess," Shizuka said, sounding none too enthusiastic about the idea. She started up the path toward the house. Showing the notebook to Asafumi's father would require a trip to his parents' house, which was something she had hoped to put off for as long as possible. A visit there meant addressing as "Father" the man who took his seat by the central pillar and talked of nothing but his salesman's travels, and "Mother" the woman who wielded her authority over the household with a quiet but deceptive benevolence. Calling them that, when she in no way thought of them as father or mother, felt somehow like an act of self-betrayal.

She stepped past the oleanders into the open space beside the small, single-storey house. The roof tiles were faded, the mortared walls stained, and the windows appeared slightly askew. The house had the appearance of barely managing to hold itself upright with its flimsy aluminium sashes as crutches, and the sight put her in a decidedly grey mood.

How could I have been so stupid? The words had echoed through her head over and over during the last two days, and this time she almost spoke them aloud. She glared at the mountain of packing boxes stacked inside the open veranda doors with a combination of bitterness and despair.

Slightly more than six months before, she and Asafumi had lost their jobs, both at the same time. Until then, they'd been light-heartedly brushing off all the recession talk as if it were a fire on the opposite side of the river, when all of a sudden their own company, a large confectionery firm, announced a series of major layoffs, with members of the Product Development Lab first on the chopping block. Had the two of them belonged to the section of the lab that was actually creating new products, like sesame chocolate bars, they might still have survived. But they were in basic research, studying things that had no direct link to revenue, such as the toxins present in broad beans or the comparative saliva viscosity of humans and cows, so they immediately got the axe. They felt little sense of alarm as they joined the ranks of the jobless, however, since they knew they had unemployment benefits to cover them while they took their time looking for the right new positions.

Liberated from the constraints of their previous daily grind, they enjoyed an extended break. They wandered aimlessly about Yokohama hand-in-hand as they had when they were first dating, they took long drives out to Okutama in western Tokyo and Lake Yamanaka near Mount Fuji, or went on overnight trips to the Izu Peninsula. In between, they flipped through recruitment magazines, put in appearances at the unemployment office, and scanned the wanted ads in the newspapers.

The days and weeks had flowed by as carelessly as water down the toilet until the month before, when they received notice that their unemployment benefits were running out. The freedom they'd revelled in gave way to panic. With the pressure on, they buckled down for a serious job search, but work calling for their kind of research expertise remained difficult to find. For one thing, just because they'd begun putting more effort into the job hunt didn't mean openings would suddenly materialize where none had been before. About the time they realized they could no longer afford their stylish apartment on a hilltop in Yokohama, Asafumi's parents suggested they should consider coming home to Toyama. The house his grandfather had used in retirement was vacant: they could live there, and he could join his father and brother in the family business.

Asafumi began saying it might not be such a bad idea, at least until he found something else. When he assured her that the place they would be living in was located quite some distance from his parents' home, and that it was a small, detached house with a very large garden, Shizuka thought it might be worth seeing what life in Toyama would be like. And so they had quickly packed up their apartment in Yokohama and arrived here just two days before.

But oh, what a difference between the advance notices and reality! Shizuka was crestfallen to discover that the cosy little cottage she'd been imagining, surrounded by a neatly landscaped yard, was in fact a dilapidated structure all but swallowed up by an untended, overgrown forest of a garden. Now she stood before the veranda and stared at the piles of cardboard boxes waiting for attention, wishing she could have them loaded up again and taken right back to Yokohama.

Slipping past her elbow, Asafumi stepped up into the house by way of the veranda and resumed his work on the sound system. With great deliberation, he went about plugging a growing tangle of wires into the speakers and various other components. Shizuka stepped out of her sandals to follow him inside, where she began scanning the labels scribbled in felt marker on the sides of the packing boxes to sort out which ones could go straight to the storage shed. Shoes, summer clothes, dishes, toiletries, handbags, sheets, paperbacks... She found herself marvelling at the prodigious assortment of possessions that made up a person's life.

Her thoughts drifted back to their busy days of preparing for the move, back in Yokohama. They had agreed to throw out or give away anything they didn't genuinely need, but every corner of their tiny apartment kept turning up items they couldn't bear to part with, one after another, as if by magic. A T-shirt from the Aikido club Asafumi belonged to in college. A ceramic plate so heavy it could serve as a boat's anchor, received as a return gift at a friend's wedding. A wide-brimmed hat like those worn by upper-class European women, bought at a discount import fair. A cricket bat acquired during the brief period when Asafumi had taken an interest in the sport. They both knew perfectly well they would never use or wear these things again, but they simply could not let them go. In each case they explained earnestly why they had to keep the item, and the other acquiesced. But the main effect of this exercise had been to make Shizuka realize she didn't really know why she was so attached to these relics any more than she could truly convince Asafumi that she should be. In the end, it was simply one of those things people didn't understand very well about themselves. That was what she concluded.

"One voice, one thought,
One way, one God…"

The crooning of a male vocalist suddenly filled the room. Startled back to the present, Shizuka craned her neck like a bird and found Asafumi crouched in front of the stereo with his back swaying to the music. He seemed to have gotten the sound system put together again without any special difficulties.

Her husband was one of those people who couldn't live without music. He liked to feed his ears a constant stream of audio from the time he got up in the morning until the moment he crawled back into bed at night – keeping the stereo system going when he was at home, and running his portable player on his way to and from the lab. If he could, he would have listened even during work hours, but his boss had disapproved of conducting research with speaker buds in ear, so he'd had to give it up for that part of his day.

When they first started dating, Shizuka simply thought it meant he was a music lover. But when she noticed how constantly he kept the sound going, even when they were making love, she began to think of it as more of an addiction. He simply couldn't sit still without music. It was as if he lived in a movie or television drama: nothing took place without a soundtrack in the background.

Accompanied by his current soundtrack, Shizuka began moving the mountain of boxes.

> "One voice, one thought,
> *One way, one God...*"

The singer repeated the words in a fluid, undulating voice.

> "One voice, one thought..."

Sheets... letters... sweaters. Shizuka removed the box marked "Sweaters" from the pile and carried it to the veranda.

> "One way, one God..."

As she sang along in her head, she gazed out over the garden where the branches of the oleanders swayed in the breeze.

> "One hand, one cock..."

She stared longingly into the shadows among the leaves.

5

On the night she landed in Japan, Saya saw her brother Kekah again. She hadn't seen him in quite some time. He stood close by, with a branch of white spirit flowers in his hand. The contours of his face and form were a bit blurred, but as always, she could tell it was him. The damp smell of the tropical jungle hovered about him. She could even hear the characteristic drone of the ear-ringing ferns her brother had been fond of.

In the dim, orange glow of a lamp, he lifted the branch of white flowers to his lips and shook it back and forth. The teardrop-shaped leaves fluttered with the movement, but when they came to rest again, he was gone. The smell of the jungle he'd brought with him vanished as well, and the din of returnees chattering and laughing all around the large *tatami* room washed over Saya again.

She had been in the midst of straightening up her suitcase in a dormitory at the Intake Centre of the Repatriation Relief Bureau. Her little boy was sprawled on the floor beside her, fast asleep, breathing peacefully. They'd been brought to this place after a supper of stewed vegetables, soup the colour of mud, and steamed white rice with grains as plump as well-fed maggots, and her fellow travellers were passing the evening hours remembering the many hardships that were now behind them. Safely in Japan and freed from the constant motion of the ship, Saya, too, could feel her tightly stretched nerves beginning to ease

Her brother had come to her a number of times after he was killed in Kota Bharu, but those appearances had ended once she was on board the ship, and it had made her sad, so seeing him again today came as a great comfort to her. A smile gathered on her cheeks as she looked back at the suitcase. The boy's underwear, her own loincloths, a needle and thread... As she rearranged their few personal effects, puffs of white powder wafted into the air, and it brought back the dizzying events of the day.

A small, dilapidated boat that looked as though a single large wave could pull it under at any moment had carried them from the ship to Ujina Pier, where to Saya's surprise they were greeted by a crowd of teenage girls in short-sleeved white blouses and navy-blue skirts waving their handkerchiefs and hats, crying out "Welcome home!" at the top of their lungs. The moment the travellers set foot ashore, the girls raced forward to help with their luggage, all but tearing their bundles and suitcases from their hands. Among the demobilized soldiers, voices could be heard saying out, "Look at that! A whole bevy of beauties!" and "Hey, there's some girls left for us after all!" It was hard to tell whether they'd really been worried about it or were merely joking.

At the entrance to the pier, a throng of people who'd come to meet the ship searched expectantly for the faces of returning

family members. With an American-style pop tune playing jauntily
somewhere in the background, a voice rang out over a bullhorn:
"We'd like to extend a hearty welcome home to you all! We've
been eagerly awaiting your return. Every person, every mountain
and stream of your beloved homeland has been waiting with us!"
Since they'd expected to find the country in a shambles when they
arrived, the returnees seemed uncertain what to make of the festive
atmosphere. Even Saya couldn't help feeling as if the spirits of the
jungle were playing tricks on her as she gripped her son's hand
and followed the crowd toward a row of wood-framed structures
belonging to the Repatriation Relief Bureau.

First they were led to a large, warehouse-like building for a customs
inspection, where they were told to line up and spread their luggage
open on the floor so the contents could be easily examined. Nurses
in white uniforms with white cotton masks covering their faces came
by with spray pumps, which sent a strong-smelling powder billowing
over the luggage like smoke, sometimes enveloping the people
standing behind the luggage as well. After them came the customs
officers, who went carefully through each person's belongings. The
sight of occupation soldiers in army caps and shorts standing guard
at key points around the hall with bayonet-fitted rifles created a
menacing contrast to the exuberant atmosphere on the pier.

As the fumigation and inspection proceeded, angry voices rose
among the travellers. A man with a large number of bags protested at
the confiscation of an ivory figurine. A woman cried out in distress,
"What do you mean, I can't keep my jewellery? How am I supposed
to live if you take these from me?" Saya was opening her own suitcase
for fumigation when she heard someone nearby yell, "You can't do
that. Those are mine!" It was her neighbour from the ship. The
officer was taking rings and bracelets and such out of a velvet bag
he'd found in her luggage.

"I'm sorry, ma'am, but for precious metals and fine jewellery, the
rule is one item per person," he said wearily, as she kept insisting that
she'd accumulated these things with the sweat of her brow and they
belonged to her.

A nurse with a spray pump reached Saya. There was a small,
sharp hiss, and a white cloud rose up in front of her. When her

boy started coughing from the fumes, she reached down to rub his back. A moment later the customs officer was squatting down over her suitcase.

"What's this?" he said, pointing to a white cloth bag.

Saya pulled the drawstring open to show him. The bag bulged with a jumble of seeds and nuts.

"To eat," she said.

The officer studied the contents dubiously for a while, but then waved his hand as if to say, "Okay."

"Do you have any cash or precious metals with you?"

Saya showed him the cash voucher she had kept constantly on her person ever since Singapore. It had been issued to her by Allied officials at the Japanese relocation camp in Singapore in exchange for a wad of Malayan dollars her brother had given her along with the finger-hole knife. The small stack of five- and ten-dollar banknotes adorned with rubber trees and coconut palms and "THE JAPANESE GOVERNMENT" inscribed across their face, a hundred dollars in all, had been transformed into this one thin scrap of paper. Every time she thought of those wrinkled bills, Saya's heart ached. She knew all too well the price her brother had paid to get that money for her.

The officer glanced at the document and said, "All right. You can go."

Closing the lid of her suitcase, she and the boy walked out of the customs building.

Their next stop was the quarantine station, where they had blood drawn and were examined by doctors before being inoculated and sprayed from head to toe with the same white powder used on their luggage. After that they were directed across some train tracks to the building they were settled in now.

Saya dug through her suitcase and pulled out the bag she'd been asked about at customs, roughly the size of a baby's head. Her claim that the contents were for eating had been only partly true.

The mixture of seeds in the bag ranged from tiny flat dots that looked like flecks of black dandruff to plump egg-shaped capsules the size of her fingertip. They were seeds of the plants she had grown up with in the jungle. When she'd made up her mind to go to Japan, she wanted to take along something that would remind her of where she came from. She was too poor to pay for a family portrait, or to buy expensive accessories and mementoes. But she could collect as many seeds as she wanted in the jungle without it costing her a thing.

She reached into the white bag and took out a palmful. Rainbow spring lily. Silvergold basket. Egret flower. Devil's bell. Bent root grass. The names of the plants they came from chased one another through her mind.

The medicine man had taught her that each one of these seeds held the spirit of the forest within it.

Saya was from a tribe known as "the jungle people" in Malaya. For centuries, they had made their home in the forest, moving about from place to place as circumstances required. The tribes all had healers who used plants and incantations to treat illnesses and injuries brought on by errant behaviour or the meddling of evil spirits. As a little girl, Saya had looked up to her tribe's healer as a figure of wonder. He was old and withered, little more than skin and bones, yet he was still as spry as far younger people. Venturing deep into the jungle, he would return with plants no one else knew anything about and give them to the sick. Saya and her playmates liked to follow him around and watch his every move, craning their necks to see as he named the herbs he picked and explained what each was good for – razor tongue for headaches; red spot for cuts; lost-in-the-night fern for colds.

Each time the members of her tribe left their makeshift palm huts behind to move to another settlement, the medicine man would prepare for their departure by sowing seeds of the plants they depended on for medicines and food. As he pressed them one by one into the ground in the spots where he knew each was most likely to thrive, he offered up a prayer that it might grow and flourish for the day when the tribe returned to that place in the jungle. Only then could they begin their journey. Through the forest they would go, every man, woman, and child carrying baskets filled with their belongings. They had to walk for many days before they reached their new dwelling place – crossing rivers, circling around marshes, sleeping under the stars.

When they arrived, it was invariably a site the tribe had used before, but the palm-leaf walls and roofs of their former huts would be caved in, the plots where they'd grown vegetables choked with weeds, and the jungle encroaching thickly overhead. Yet among all this rampant growth, the seeds the medicine man planted when they last pulled up stakes in that spot would also have sprung to life, their new leaves reaching for the sky.

It always felt to Saya as if they had circled right back to the place they'd come from only a few days before. She'd be convinced that many months or even years had gone by while the tribe was moving through the forest, and in that span their flimsy huts had fallen, the forest had reasserted itself, the vegetable patches had returned to nature, and the medicine man's seeds had grown into hale and hearty new plants. Yet when she looked at herself in the water, it still reflected the face of a child, not yet etched by age – which made her wonder if somehow she and her tribe alone had travelled outside the course of time during their journey through the jungle. She knew the huts were different huts, yet the feeling remained that they had simply come back to the same dwellings across a leap in time. That, to her, had been the medicine man's greatest wonder of all: he could manipulate time itself to make the plants they most needed grow.

She put her nose to the mouth of the white bag and drew in a deep breath. The seeds smelled of the earth after a freshening rain. Thick, moist air, redolent with verdure, filled her lungs. The whine of mosquitoes sounded in her ears. She saw the figure of the healer walking in front of her with a rattan basket tied to his waist, planting his staff on the ground and talking to the spirits of the jungle as he slid among the trees as smoothly as a snake. Beneath his frizzy, salt-and-pepper hair lay vast stores of knowledge. He handled the leaves and roots he gathered with the same reverence he showed the spirits, taking care not to damage them as he dried or boiled or prepared them in other ways for administering to the sick. Saya had dreamed of becoming like him herself. The dream remained with her until the day the red flower of womanhood blossomed between her legs.

"Hello again."

At the sound of a voice near her ear, Saya looked up to find the woman who helped her with the questionnaire crouching beside her. She had noticed this person keeping an eye on her and her boy ever since they'd landed. But upon arriving in this room, she had steered clear of them to settle in against the opposite wall, and Saya had thought she could relax. Now, with the woman approaching her again, her guard was immediately up.

She pulled the drawstring tight and pushed the bag of seeds back into her suitcase before turning to face her.

Saya's blank stare seemed to catch the woman off balance. "Remember me?" she said. "I helped you with your immigration form."

Saya nodded indifferently.

The woman frowned, obviously not pleased with the way this was going. She fingered her collar for a moment as she seemed to hesitate, then leaned close to whisper, "I know you're not really Korean."

Her heart skipped a beat. The woman had guessed the truth after all. But she knew she had to keep her composure.

"Don't talk nonsense," she said.

"You can drop the charade," the woman said. "When you run a P-house like I did, you see a lot of Korean girls and you get to know them right to the bottom of their honey pots. There's no way in hell you're Korean."

Saya froze at the word "P-house."

"Not to mention, I lived in Malaya for twenty-four years – long enough to know a native when I smell one. You might fool the idiots from the Repatriation Bureau, but I'm not falling for it."

"Leave me alone," Saya said coldly, slamming her suitcase shut. She felt the heat of the woman's eyes on her as she straightened the shirt she had thrown over her boy's stomach. What would happen if this person took it into her head to announce for all to hear that Saya was a fake trying to pass as Korean-Japanese?

Under the Japanese occupation, the people of Kota Bharu and the vicinity had lived in constant terror. Imperial Army units and the Kempeitai security police descended on villages throughout the State of Kelantan, beating the men, molesting the women, and ransacking homes as they searched for straggling British and Indian troops and any signs of anti-Japanese activity. Villages near the city sent their young women into the area's *nipa* swamps to spare them from the brutalities. Anybody suspected of being in the resistance was taken to the Kempeitai lockup and tortured. Virtually no one came back alive. Saya knew all too well how ruthless the Japanese soldiers could be.

Now she was in the very land those soldiers had gone home to, populated entirely by others just like them. Even if they were beaten in the war, what were the chances of their turning over a brand-new leaf barely a year later? What would they do to her if they found out she'd smuggled herself into the country under a false name? She could expect them to hunt her down to the farthest corner of the place, just as they'd done with the Commonwealth troops in Malaya. There'd been horrifying stories about how they killed the British and Indian stragglers they found. She braced herself for what the woman might say next.

"If you want me to leave you alone, I'm gonna need a little something in return."

She held out her hand with her thumb and forefinger formed into a circle. Saya's obvious failure to recognize the gesture was a reminder that she was dealing with a foreigner. Pursing her lips, she unbent her fingers and held out her open palm instead.

"I'm talking about money," she said. "I know you've got some. At least a little."

With a sinking feeling, Saya realized the woman had probably seen her showing the cash voucher to the customs officer.

"I wish I didn't have to do this," the woman went on, "but first the military scrip I'd been stashing away turns into scrap paper, and now they confiscate my precious rings and necklaces and all but a thousand yen of my cash. How's a body supposed to get back on her feet with a measly thousand yen? It's a bad joke."

Saya casually glanced about the room as she gave her hair knot a pat with one hand. Everybody appeared to be wrapped up in their own conversations, but she could tell people were watching them out of the corners of their eyes. She lowered her arm.

Noticing the movement of Saya's eyes, the woman said, "They told us we could exchange our vouchers for cash tomorrow. And even if you don't have anything to exchange, everybody's supposed to get a little something to tide them over. So the deal is, any cash you get, you hand it right over to me. Got that?"

Saya nodded.

"And don't even think of trying to back out on me, 'cause I'll go straight to the police."

The woman rose to her feet and returned to her spot against the opposite wall.

6

The platform at Ujina Station was jammed like the deck of the repatriation ship with jostling travellers. An attendant shouted into a bullhorn: "All passengers for Echigo and Hokuriku, please proceed to cars 13 and 14!"

With her suitcase in one hand and leading her fussy, sleep-deprived child in the other, Saya joined the flow of people moving in that direction. The platform where their repatriation train waited had only rafters overhead and no roof. The triangular lines stood out in dark silhouette against the deep blue of a sky just beginning to gray with the light of dawn.

The returnees had spent two nights at the Intake Centre, during which time they were offered a bath and warm, if somewhat scanty, meals. Now, laden with all they could carry on their backs and in their arms, they clambered aboard the train like a swarm of crabs. Each car had a capacity of eighty, and every adult was supposed to get a seat. But the belongings each person carried were of greater bulk than their owners, which meant that at least half of the available room was occupied by luggage. Women with their breasts bulging beneath the crisscross ties that held their babies to their backs had both their hands filled with luggage as well; after trying to juggle their child and other items on their lap, they often wound up sitting on one of their bags. In a seat by the window, Saya set her suitcase on the floor beneath her feet before lifting the boy onto her knees.

The locomotive spewed black smoke and the long train slowly started moving. Staff from the Repatriation Relief Bureau stood waving goodbye as the coaches slid by along the platform. Passengers leaned from open windows to call out their thanks. A fresh breeze blew in, quickly expelling the stuffy, sweaty air that had been building up inside.

Saya rested her head against the wooden seat-back and let out a long sigh of relief. The train was supposed to take them all the way to Toyama. She could finally relax.

She now carried a Repatriation Certificate identifying her as Kim Suk-hwa. When their group leader came back with the documents for everybody else, he told Saya she'd been summoned to the bureau office. Fearing the worst, she went as instructed and found herself standing in front of a young man with sunken eyes wearing a sweat-stained shirt. His first reaction was to stare at her and blurt out in surprise, "You're Korean?" Her chest thumped as if someone were pounding it with a fist from inside. She nodded nervously, while the man cocked his head and gave her a sceptical look. "You look more like someone from Okinawa than Korea," he said as he dropped his eyes to the document in his hand then mumbled, "Born in Shimonoseki, eh?" Fortunately, he was too worn out from having to deal with three thousand other repatriates to pursue the question further. He noted mechanically that there was a ship in port going to Korea for those who wanted to return to their homeland, and suggested she might want to take it. When Saya shook her head, he looked at the document again and asked, "Why are you going to Toyama when you're from Shimonoseki?" "My husband is there," she told him. He eyed her as if he didn't quite know what to think, and for a moment seemed about to say something else, but in the end he changed his mind and simply handed her the all-important certificate.

As she made her way back to the large *tatami* room, Saya recalled the man's expression. She thought she'd seen both puzzlement and sympathy in it. But she was so relieved at having her paper safely in hand that she did not dwell on it. For two long months at the Jurong Internment Camp in Singapore, another month confined aboard a ship steaming toward Japan, and a final two days at the Intake Centre after landing, she felt as if she'd been crawling along the edge of a precipice, but the danger was now past. She had successfully turned herself into Kim Suk-hwa.

Saya ran her fingers over the boy's curly black hair. He turned his head as if to say something, but when he saw her smiling, he broke into a smile, too, and buried his face in her chest. That morning's early departure had meant being woken before dawn, and he hadn't had enough sleep.

"I suppose in the end it was a matter of just too many things weighing on her conscience."

The voice belonged to a man in a faded blue cap sitting across from Saya. He had large, drooping bags under his eyes, and cheeks so saggy they looked as if they might fall right off his face.

"It's not hard to see," the woman beside him nodded. "No matter how good she might have had it during the war, she basically made out like a bandit, running a whorehouse that took advantage of the troops. Not to mention, she built the place with her own whoring money to begin with. She probably felt the whole dirty business crashing down on her head once she got back to Japan."

The woman was wedged in at an angle between the man and a large handmade rucksack placed on the seat beside her. There could be little doubt the two were husband and wife, given the way her body was pressed slug-like against his – so tight you might expect flesh to tear if you tried to pull them apart.

"The shame probably sank in when she set foot on home soil, and all of a sudden she realized she really had nowhere to go."

"Speaking of which, we're pretty much in the same boat ourselves. We've still got to figure out where and how we're going to make a new start of it."

The husband grunted in agreement, rubbing his chin with his hand. They both fell silent.

The train made its way among deserted rice paddies in the pale morning light. The plants looked spindly and uneven. In the distance rose colourless hills covered with fallen trees. Here and there stood wood-frame houses with broken siding, windows and roofs, their surrounding fences collapsed. In some places the damage had been patched up with boards or tarps, but elsewhere it remained unrepaired. The sight reminded Saya of a sick forest. One tree would become diseased, and as its leaves turned brown and the tree died, the disease would pass on to another. Before long all the trees in the vicinity would appear to be sick. This landscape looked a bit like that.

"I still can't get over that she did herself in the very next day after getting here, though," the husband spoke up again. "I mean, even if she was determined to die on home soil—"

"What I want to know is, why she had to slit her throat out behind the toilets like that. The person who found her said there was blood splattered all over the place – the grass, the wall, everywhere. Took a razor blade or something to her jugular, I guess. She obviously wasn't thinking of anybody but herself, right down to the very end," the wife said, her deeply creased, sun-dried face twisting in a frown. She looked like the shrivelled bulb of a dead-man's ivy plant.

The couple were talking about the person who had kindly filled out Saya's immigration form on the ship only to blackmail her once they got ashore. She kept her face a blank as she listened to their exchange. The image of her dead brother shaking the branch of white spirit flowers back and forth in front of his lips replayed through her mind. It had eventually dawned on her what his gesture meant. He was signalling that she had to silence her.

In the drawstring bag were some seeds of the white spirit flower. She'd heard that in Japan a close relative, known as the mandala flower, was used to make healing potions, but among her own people, the seeds of this plant were considered dangerous: those who ate them became possessed by evil spirits; they began dancing wildly among the trees and seeing things you couldn't normally see. So at dinnertime the day before, after the returnees had exchanged their vouchers for cash, Saya got in line next to the woman at the serving station and whispered, "I give you money after eating, behind toilets." Looking pleased, the woman failed to notice Saya slipping one of the seeds into her soup. Although the food at the Intake Centre was better than what they'd been served on the ship, the portions remained meagre, and the meal that evening consisted of only steamed rice and miso soup: she could be quite certain the woman would eat every solid morsel she found in the warm broth.

Sure enough, when the woman came around the corner of the toilets, set a short distance apart from the dormitory building, her eyes were glazed and she seemed disoriented. It was an easy matter for Saya to sneak up behind her and draw the finger-hole knife across her throat. With a gurgling sort of groan, as if she were being crushed by a heavy object, the woman spewed blood in every direction and tumbled to the ground.

Giving a little shudder, Saya gently squeezed her son's curly head to her chest. Her sudden embrace startled the dozing boy, but he happily pressed himself harder against his mother. She stroked his hair.

"But don't you have to wonder if it was really suicide?" the man said after another long pause, and Saya stiffened. "From what I heard, they never found the blade she used."

"Oh, shush! If they started talking murder, who knows how long we'd have been stuck in that place?"

"Yeah, maybe that's what the bureau was thinking, too. Between our ship coming in and another one about to leave for Korea, they were all complaining about not having time to sleep."

Glancing out the window, the wife gave her husband a nudge and said, "Look," which brought the conversation about the dead woman to an end.

Saya turned her attention outside, too, and was shocked by what she saw. It was as if a vast herd of elephants had stampeded through a city and trampled everything flat. Charred trees and utility poles teetered precariously in a bleak landscape. Virtually no building worthy of the name remained standing – only a few jagged shells lit up by the soft morning sunshine. Rusty metal and broken timber poked up among the weeds that covered the ground everywhere but the roadways. Here and there on this desolate grassland stood crudely built houses and makeshift shanties. People could be seen hanging up laundry to dry or cooking breakfast over outdoor fire pits. Someone on a rickety bicycle wobbled along the street. A shirtless man rubbed sleep from his eyes as he stretched his neck. A bent old woman with a broom was carefully sweeping the ground in front of her hut – even in the midst of what looked like a giant garbage dump. Children were playing in nothing but their underpants.

"Wow," the man said gravely. "Hiroshima really did get hit."

"So it was all true – about this thing they call an atomic bomb," his wife said, leaning close to the window with her hand on the sill. Everybody in the car was craning to see. The weed-covered plain of rubble spread on and on into the distance, all the way to the smouldering brown hills in the distance. A grim silence replaced the buzz of conversation that had filled the car only moments before.

After proceeding through the desolated city for a time, the train approached a large structure still standing tall among the ruins.

"There's Hiroshima Station," said the man sitting across from Saya.

Both the main building and the platforms had lost their roofs, and a gaping hole was torn in the side of a nearby warehouse. The platforms were dotted with travellers waiting for their trains. A woman sat on her suitcase staring blankly into space. Two men stood talking and puffing on cigarettes. Another sat on his haunches, leaning against a pillar as if too tired to stand. People were chatting and laughing as they came and went. The place displayed the typical bustle Saya associated with train stations, but she sensed a deep emptiness lurking beneath the surface. It reminded her of the hollow trees she sometimes came across in the jungle. They spread their limbs, thick with leaves, but had yawning cavities in their trunks, filled with moist, dark air. Trees like that were never as healthy as they looked, and she knew they were destined to wither and die.

The train pulled in alongside one of the platforms and came to a halt, but almost immediately started up again in the opposite direction without letting anyone on or off. The wasteland they'd seen outside the window before reappeared, and the silence inside the car grew even heavier.

"They say even if you survived the bomb, you can get sick and die later on," came a voice from behind Saya. "Your wounds never heal and start smelling foul, or you suddenly start bleeding from your nose and gums, and you get fevers or you feel tired all the time, and just keep getting weaker and weaker. That's what I heard. Even the doctors who came to help have been dying, some of them. You didn't have to be here when the bomb went off, if you came into town right after, you're liable to get sick the same way and die. That's what one of the army doctors at the internment camp told our interpreter."

"That sounds pretty far-fetched to me, even if it is some revolutionary new thing," his companion said doubtfully. "You make it sound like the bomb puts some kind of curse on you."

Let them all be cursed, Saya thought, as she stared out across the ruins. Let every last one of these people be cursed. Like the sickened jungle, let the whole country shrivel up and die. The image of a Japanese soldier leering down at her in his filthy uniform flashed through her head, followed by the image of her brother lying dead in the mud with his limbs broken and his eyes hanging from their sockets.

Eventually, the train emerged from the ravaged city into the countryside, where green rice paddies rippled in the breeze. On the left-hand side rose a range of gently rounded mountains; on the right, a glistening blue ocean showed now and again. The train sped past the smaller stations along the way without stopping. Saya had no idea how long it would take to reach Toyama. She considered asking the couple sitting across from her, but she was afraid they might wonder about her origins as the other woman had done. So she sat without a word, hugging her son to her stomach, listening to the rhythmical clickety-clack of the wheels on the rails and breathing the smell of sweat and grime worked into the seats by previous passengers. When the boy said he had to pee, she lifted him to the sill so he could go out the window. With the mountains of luggage piled in the aisle making it so difficult to reach the toilets, others had been doing the same. A little bit of spray flew in from time to time, but nobody bothered to close their windows because they knew the air inside would quickly become unbearably stuffy from all the sweating bodies in the car. The passengers simply endured the discomforts of sweat and grime and flying urine as they sat longingly counting off the minutes to their arrival.

The train made lengthy stops at major stations like Okayama and Osaka. Continuing passengers descended onto the platform to fill their canteens and buy box lunches using the special meal coupons they'd received at the repatriation centre. Saya always remained behind on the train. If she got lost, she might never be able to find her way to Toyama. So she made do with the rice balls and hard tack they'd all been given before departure, and never left her place by the window.

At these larger stations, she saw multitudes of people shouldering tired old rucksacks or hugging large cloth-wrapped bundles, waiting for their trains to arrive. Not one of them appeared to be on just a pleasure outing. When the trains came in, everybody would rush to get on all at once in the hope of claiming a seat, climbing in not only at the doors but through the windows. The aisles and even the passages between cars would fill, and the trains would pull out again with passengers standing on the steps in the doorways, clinging to the handrails. Watching these people, Saya was reminded of ants flooded out of their home by heavy rains, crawling all over each other as they milled about, trying to decide where to build their new nest. But she was also amazed at how much energy these particular ants seemed to have, chattering and laughing like bright-eyed children at play.

Every now and then she would see a coach that was nearly empty, and she soon realized these were ones reserved for occupation personnel. White men in green uniforms sat reading newspapers with pipes in their mouths, or chatted with lipsticked young Japanese women sitting beside them. For the most part, the streams of travellers in tattered uniforms or shabby, patchwork clothing moved past without taking the slightest notice, as if they simply weren't there; only rarely did she see someone cast an angry glance through the window as he walked by. The apparent indifference surprised her. Could these really be the same people who'd threatened her own with brandished swords? They were the ones being occupied now: they ought to be angry. Instead, they seemed as passive as earthworms pulled out of the ground.

The view outside the window continually changed as the train clattered along the rails all day long, moving from large stations to small, from cities jammed tight with gray office buildings and private houses to hamlets surrounded by rice fields. In the morning the passengers had been animated with conversation, but as the day wore on they became more subdued. Voices fell low, and were mixed with frequent sighs. The initial excitement of being on the last leg of their journey home began to give way to worries over what would await them in the coming days and months once they got there. Saya, however, felt no such concern. Anxiety is something that comes when one thinks about tomorrow. But for Saya, tomorrow did not exist. In the jungle where she'd been born and raised, she had known only the present: now the sun was shining and she had plenty of food; now the rain came down and she had nothing to eat; now the rains had stopped and fruit hung from a tree outside her palm hut again.

So as the repatriation train continued its onward journey, Saya passed the time gazing at the ever-changing present revealed in the window. Evening came, and the landscapes beyond the glass slowly faded in the twilight. Inside, the car grew darker, and the sound of voices dropped even lower. Many of the passengers were now dozing. Saya took an areca nut from her drawstring bag and put it in her mouth. As she slowly ground the nut between her teeth, turning her tongue crimson, the clatter of the train rolling down the tracks became the lash of a storm blowing through the Malayan jungle, and the sweaty, sooty odour in the coach gave way to the smell of tropical rain and moisture. She stood in the darkness of the forest during a sudden squall, leaning against the trunk of a tree as she waited for the rain to pass. The leaves trembled beneath the drum of raindrops as the downpour continued without pause. She became as one with the plants and trees around her. The footsteps of time faded into the distance, and she found herself in a place that had no bearing in time or space.

7

The aging blue Volkswagen moved along the road atop the levee of the Senbashi River in the orange glow of the setting sun. The sharp blue peaks of the Tateyama Range stood tall against the summer sky and the collective flow of water from those mountains pushed quietly toward Toyama Bay in the river below. The elevation of the levee offered an unobstructed view of the countryside spreading out on either side. In the driver's seat, Asafumi marvelled at the big box supermarkets, new residential subdivisions, company dormitories, and gravelled lots that had sprung up among the fields of green rice.

"Man, things sure have changed around here," he exclaimed. "When I was a kid, this was nothing but farmland as far as you could see."

Shizuka twisted her face into a frown as she turned to look out her open window. "Development is like cancer," she said. "It proliferates without any regard for overall harmony, and ultimately brings death to its host, Mother Nature. They say deserts around the world are growing by a collective 11.3 million hectares every year. That's almost a third the size of Japan. Rising concentrations of carbon dioxide in the atmosphere will raise temperatures around the globe an average of two degrees centigrade by the year 2100, and in some places the increase could be as much as ten degrees. We're rushing headlong toward extinction at our own hands."

He could hear the irritation in her voice as she ran through the numbers. They were on their way to visit his folks, and it had put her in a bad mood. For a full week since arriving in Toyama, they'd managed to put off the inevitable with one excuse or another – they hadn't finished unpacking yet; they were still too exhausted from the move. But last night, Asafumi's mother had called to say that his father and brother were back from the sales trip they'd been on and it was time they came by, making it sound very much like an order. She refused to take no for an answer. Asafumi knew he needed to talk to them about getting started with the family business, and he was eager to show them the old notebook too, so he decided he'd had enough of his wife's foot-dragging and told his mother they would both come for dinner today. Not surprisingly, Shizuka had made a sour face.

"But for all we know, the whole planet could get blown to bits even before desertification gets us," Asafumi said. "There's no telling when countries in the Middle East or Asia might lose their cool and start trading neutron bombs, or some aliens from outer space might attack us."

"Yeah, right," Shizuka said, flashing a crooked smile his way as she sank back into her seat. Asafumi took heart at the apparent break in her sullen mood.

At the Product Development Lab too, Shizuka's bluntness had not gone down well with her male colleagues. She would state her opinions candidly, with none of the diffidence expected of young women, and it would make them bristle. They whispered behind her back that she was sexually frustrated, a hysteric.

But Asafumi had thought her plainspoken manner refreshing. He found it far more attractive than the endless flirting he got from women intent on catching a husband. Once they were living under the same roof though, he began to think that maybe his colleagues had a point. She was constantly getting up in arms over one thing or another – usually for reasons he simply couldn't fathom. Harsh words would come flying his way like a sudden barrage of stones. He had learned to simply wait for the onslaught to pass, telling himself philosophically that it was a burden he bore of his own choosing.

After glancing over his shoulder to make sure nobody was trying to pass, Asafumi steered onto a ramp descending the embankment. At the bottom they came to a broad paved road that stretched out across the paddies. The local politician had sponsored a bill to fund this twelve-meter-wide thoroughfare as the first step toward developing the area into a major new industrial zone. Their blue Volkswagen tooled along the industrial main street of the future as if it owned the place. It was an old beater with little to recommend it – lousy mileage, slow on the pickup, not much cargo room – but Asafumi was perversely fond of its dumpy styling.

At the point where it crossed some railroad tracks, the road through the paddies abruptly narrowed to a third of its former width. The cosy little streets of Senbashi spread before them, and an evening haze hung over the sea beyond.

Senbashi had started out as a none-too-prosperous fishing village a short distance away from Toyama Castle and the town that had risen in its immediate vicinity. When the lord of the domain began promoting itinerant medicine sales as a new local industry around the turn of the eighteenth century, quite a number of villagers had decided to take up the trade. The fishing port remained active, and the sections of town nearest the water were still made up mostly of fishermen's homes, but the central districts were dotted with drug wholesalers, pharmacies and small pharmaceutical factories, a clear testimony to the dominant industry in town. When you saw an imposing two-storey house surrounded by a stone wall or fence, you could be pretty sure it belonged to a family that had been in the business for many generations – or whose forebears once were. The thought of someday being able to put up their dream home back in Toyama was what kept the medicine peddlers going as they travelled about the country, bowing their heads to customers day in and day out. They had made thrift and hard work their motto, and dedicated themselves to building up their savings.

Asafumi swung the car onto Main Street and continued past a photo studio, a doctor's office, and a small grocery store. Seventeen years had gone by since he left for college, but the town had changed very little. He did notice that storefronts had been updated, homes had acquired replacement windows, and office buildings had new coats of paint, but the street was no wider and the rooflines were the same as ever. This was a town crisscrossed by waterways and canals, the numerous bridges over which had given it its name of "a thousand bridges". Any attempt to modernize would require razing everything to the ground and starting over, so unless a major earthquake came along to get things going, it wasn't likely to happen.

He turned onto a narrow side street running right next to a canal that had no guardrail. They came across some children playing, then a bent grandmother pushing a baby stroller. Veering too sharply to avoid a pedestrian could result in a wheel dropping over the edge, so he proceeded carefully. Before long they arrived at a two-storey Ferro concrete house surrounded by a stone fence standing in the evening twilight.

As with the homes of other families in the business, the house Asafumi grew up in had been an imposing wooden structure topped with a tiled roof fit for the main tower of a castle. But his older brother had begun preaching the virtues of cement construction shortly after he got married, and the house had been rebuilt. Ten years later, the once attractive home was beginning to look like a cheaply constructed kindergarten building, but no one in the family dared to mention the fact out loud. Every time he laid eyes on the structure, Asafumi promised himself that when he built his own house, it would be in the traditional style. He renewed this vow once again as he pulled between the gateposts into the front drive.

The crunch of tires on gravel brought his brother's two young children to the door – his seven-year-old niece Mutsumi and five-year-old nephew Takeshige. They quickly disappeared inside again and could be heard calling out, "Uncle Asa's here!" Seconds later, Asafumi's mother Takiko appeared. She wore a white apron over a light-brown dress with a small flower pattern, and the waves in her hair suggested that she had just come back from the beauty parlour.

"I was thinking you should be getting here any minute," she said, a broad smile parting her round cheeks. She crouched at Shizuka's window. "It's so nice to have you here, Shizuka. How are things coming along? Are you about moved in?"

"More or less, I guess," she said, sounding daunted already. As if seeking an escape, she quickly turned to reach for the gift she'd placed in the back seat. Asafumi cut the engine and climbed out.

"We're all ready for dinner," Takiko said as she cheerfully led the way into the house.

The traditional *tatami*-floored parlour just off the entrance foyer had been set up for the occasion. Platters of sashimi, fried prawns and sushi were spread out on the table. As a boy, Asafumi remembered the fancy meals they'd had whenever his father returned from one of his trips; today they were also celebrating his and Shizuka's move to Toyama, so his mother had pulled out all the stops.

His father Kikuo and brother Kōichirō were already ensconced in front of the decorative alcove, pouring beer for each other. With their heavy jowls, identical flat, broad noses, and sun-tanned skin from years of travel, they almost looked like twins.

"Ah, there you are. We were wondering when you'd get here," Kikuo said. His face was already glowing from the alcohol. Asafumi lowered himself onto the floor next to him.

Near the door, Shizuka was trying to hold up her end in the ongoing exchange of pleasantries by presenting Takiko with the gift she'd brought along. The two children immediately recognized it as a box of sweets and began clamouring for a treat. Their mother Miharu came in and told them to settle down. Asafumi sensed his wife's growing tension at the unfamiliar workings of her in-laws' household, but he chose not to step to her rescue. She was going to have to learn to get along with them all.

While the women went to get the hot dishes from the kitchen, Kikuo and Kōichirō poured some beer for Asafumi and asked him how his grandfather's house was working out.

"It needs a lot of work, but at least we have a roof over our heads to keep the rain off," he said with a touch of sarcasm.

"Yeah, those folks we had renting the place were pretty rough on it," Kōichirō grumbled.

The house had been occupied for fifteen years by the Yazakis, a family of six headed by the son of a man Kikuo knew through his work. With four growing children scribbling and taking gouges out of the already time-scarred walls and pillars, the place had been left considerably the worse for wear.

"Maybe so," Kikuo said, "but houses get even more run down when they're empty. Without the Yazakis living there, it'd be a complete ruin by now."

Talking about the house reminded Asafumi of what he'd brought along to show them. Pushing his beer glass to one side, he opened his bag and pulled out the dog-eared notebook.

"I found this the other day," he said. "In the shed."

"A sales register?" Kikuo exclaimed, as he put on his reading glasses and looked it over in surprise. "Good grief! You don't shove something like this in the shed and forget about it!" He sounded genuinely upset. Notebooks like this were the very lifeblood of their business.

He flipped it open to the first page. "Ōyama Village I know well enough, but where the hell is Magawa?" he wondered aloud. For his entire working life he'd been making his rounds based on books like this, handed down from one generation to the next, so he had no trouble reading the handwriting that Asafumi had been unable to decipher.

Asafumi couldn't recall a place called that, either. Nor, it seemed, could Kōichirō. Neither of them spoke up.

"Oh, here," Kikuo said as he continued to study the page. "It says 'Tateyama Line Awasuno Station.' They shut that station down, as I recall. Quite a while ago."

"What about you, Miharu?" Kōichirō called to his wife, who was busily setting out small plates at each place around the table. "You grew up in Ashikuraji. Ever hear of a place called Magawa out that way?"

She tilted her head in contemplation, her big round eyes drifting up toward the ceiling.

"It looks like he went through Magawa on his way to places called Hachisoko and Senninhara," Kikuo added as he flipped ahead through the pages. "And a bunch of others. They all seem to be along a route called Mandala Road."

"What about that?" Kōichirō said. "Ever hear of Mandala Road?"
Miharu shook her head.

"This is really strange," Kikuo mumbled to himself. "Every one of
them is dated April 1947 and just says 'Placed.' That's all. There's no
sign he ever went back to collect."

"Placed" meant Rentarō had acquired the family as a new
customer and left a medicine kit with them. But the way these sales
worked, the peddler didn't actually start making money from the
customer until he went back a second time. For Rentarō to leave
kits with these families and then never visit them again was definitely
odd. Asafumi understood that much, even though he'd never actually
worked in the business himself.

"Do you suppose he got too busy making the rounds of other
customers?" he said.

Kikuo let out a long gravelly grunt as he thought about this,
dropping the corners of his mouth so his teeth peeked through. It
made him look like a growling bulldog.

"1947 wasn't very long after the war," he then said. "From what I
heard, everybody'd run out of medicines during the war, so around
that time the salesmen were dashing here, there and everywhere trying
to meet the demand. Like a bunch of baby chickens, I remember
somebody once saying. It seems like my dad and brother were away
an awful lot, too, so I suppose this route could have gotten lost in
the shuffle."

"But no peddler's going to forget about new customers he's
found," Kōichirō countered. "Especially so close by. Ōyama's only a
stone's throw away."

Kikuo folded his arms and grunted again.

Asafumi finished the beer in his glass. He'd started wondering if
something bad had happened farther along the route that prevented
his grandfather from ever going back that way, when Kōichirō turned
to him.

"You know, Asafumi, since you're joining the business, maybe
you should start by checking out these places on Mandala Road.
See what you find. If you're lucky, maybe you can even get them to
let you leave some new kits. You can't very well ask them to pay for
what Grandpa left with them more than half a century ago, but you

41

might be able to use the prior connection as a way of getting your foot in the door again. At least it ought to be easier than finding new customers from scratch."

"I like it," said Kikuo. "Go on out there and see what you can cook up on your own. It'll show you exactly what we're up against in this business." He actually seemed amused by the idea.

Asafumi was taken aback. This was not at all what he'd expected. He thought he'd be learning the ropes by accompanying his father or brother on some trips as an assistant first.

While he was still trying to decide how to respond, Kikuo spoke up again. "I always assumed my dad had given me all his books before he died. But now this shows up. You didn't happen to see any more of them, did you?"

"No, just the one. It was in a tin box that I suppose must have belonged to Saya."

The name brought a scowl to Kikuo's face. "That woman," he said in disgust. "For all we know, she could easily have tossed a whole bunch of these out without the first idea what they were."

Asafumi could plainly see the deep animosity his father felt toward Saya.

8

"Fukui! Next stop, Fukui!"

A faraway voice drew Saya from her sleep and she opened her eyes. A conductor was making his way through the car, announcing another station. Outside the window, the pale light of morning was creeping across the eastern sky. Passengers getting off began to gather their things together. Not Toyama yet, Saya thought, and closed her eyes again.

She drifted in and out as Kanazawa was announced, and then after another indeterminate length of time the voice called Toyama. Saya was instantly alert, like a mother hen whose nest is under attack.

By this time, day had fully broken. After being on the right-hand side all day yesterday, the sea was now on the left. Most of the people around her began tidying themselves up and getting their luggage ready. They'd been assigned to coaches roughly according to destination, and nearly everyone left appeared to be getting out here.

The train slid into the station. Saya woke her boy, and they joined the stream of passengers descending onto the platform. The press of the crowd carried them toward the main building against an oncoming flow of travellers laden with bulging bundles, hurrying toward departing trains.

"Welcome home!" came a shrill voice over the general commotion. "Welcome to all our brothers and sisters returning from overseas! We know you've had a long and exhausting journey, so we've prepared some hot tea for you. Please stop by for some refreshment."

Saya looked to see a young station attendant with an arm band shouting into a bullhorn. Nearby, a group of schoolgirls was passing out tea and offering to help passengers with their luggage.

People were pushing and shoving every which way, like the crowds she'd observed from the train window in stations en route – except this time she and her boy were right in the middle of the throng. It was as if everybody in the world had decided to move house all at once. Gaunt, hollow-eyed people in shabby clothes dragging duffel bags behind them. A man hobbling on crutches. A man with ugly burn-scars on his face. A man missing an arm. A rugged-looking ex-soldier with gaiters around his legs and a tired old army cap on his head. A slick-haired man in coat and tie on his way somewhere in an obviously good mood. A woman dressed oddly in kimono and trousers with a name tag sewn to her chest, making her way in mincing steps. People clutching large bundles in their arms waiting their turn in front of the ticket windows. But they weren't really there for train tickets, Saya thought. Their sights were set on something beyond. They faced forward in line with an eager look in their eyes, as if whatever it was they were seeking dangled only a few steps away. All that these people could see was what lay ahead.

Beneath a sign saying "US ARMY RTO" stood several Americans with rifles in their hands, looking bored. Their eyes swept blankly over the passing throng. The travellers walked by without taking the slightest notice, carrying on with their chatter as if the foreign soldiers weren't even there.

Saya felt the same odd sense of disconnection she'd felt when she saw the coaches reserved for occupation personnel. Two utterly different worlds existed side by side: the world of the white man's army, making a quiet show of force; and the world of the hungry, impoverished Japanese, scurrying one way and another with great clamour. As at the confluence of muddy and clear streams, the two worlds remained apart, forming separate currents within a single river. For both of these worlds, it was as if the other existed only in its dreams.

She must make sure not to get dragged into either of those dreams, Saya thought. People were always trying to drag you into their dreams. But once you let them do that, you became lost. Everything you said and did would become part of the dreamer's dream.

Holding the boy's hand, Saya proceeded straight on out of the building. In front of the station stood a jumble of small shanties, patched together from boards and tin sheeting, with all manner of food and sundries offered for sale. It reminded her of small town markets in Malaya. Beyond this collection of crude sales stalls was a cluster of larger buildings, their walls scorched black. So the ravages of war had reached this city, too. Above these blistered buildings, a range of blue-green mountains rose high against the distant sky. Her mouth fell open as she gazed up at their massive forms: never before had she seen such towering peaks. The ridges were shrouded in a haze that melted into the blue sky. The mountains looked transparent and cold.

The smell of cooking wafted their way from the market. Her boy tugged at her hand and said he was hungry. They started in among the stalls.

Torn leather shoes, army helmets converted into cooking pots, used clothing and cotton work gloves, vegetables and fish, soap and nails, bean-jam cakes and sweets – everything you could possibly want was spread out for sale. Women kept a tight grip on their purses as they dickered over prices. Barefooted kids with dirty faces ran in and out among the shoppers. A bright, bustling atmosphere filled the air. Behind the merchandise on display stood men in worn-out army fatigues held together with patches.

Some were touting their wares at the top of their lungs.

"What a bargain! What a steal! A whole heap of potatoes, only thirty yen!"

"Step right up, ladies! Get your laundry soap here! Just came in! Buy today, or weep tomorrow!"

Others monotonously intoned what they had to offer.

"Umbrellas, matches, charcoal... Umbrellas, matches, charcoal."

There were also men standing idly off to one side, puffing on stubby cigarettes and joking among themselves, paying no attention to the shoppers drifting by.

The ubiquitous army fatigues as well as the sellers' ages told her that the majority of them were soldiers back from the war. Looking at their sun darkened faces gave her a bitter taste in the mouth. One of them met her eyes.

Don't you look at me!

She stiffened, expecting a sharp rebuke or a flying fist. Instead, the man addressed her in a friendly manner.

"Care for some roast corn, ma'am? It's mighty tasty."

Forcing a smile, Saya started to move on by, but her boy gripped her hand tightly and dug in his heels. The savoury smell of the corn was too tempting.

"How much?" Saya asked reluctantly.

"Five yen."

As she got the money out, the man wrapped an ear of corn in a square of newspaper and handed it to the boy.

"Here you go, sonny. Eat lots so you grow big and strong."

A warm, utterly unaffected smile stretched across his face.

The hostility she'd felt lost its object and quickly shrank away. The next thing she knew, her son was dragging her up and down the narrow alleys to buy hot sweet potatoes and fritters and watermelon, until all of a sudden she realized how quickly the cash she'd received at the Repatriation Relief Bureau was disappearing. She had expected a thousand yen to go a long way. It frightened her to see that just a few things to eat had already taken such a big chunk out of the money her brother had worked so hard to save for her.

The boy was still pleading for more, but she told him to be quiet, and led him back to the station entrance. There Saya opened her suitcase and took out the scrap of paper bearing Rentarō's address, heavily creased from being folded and unfolded so many times. Looking around her, she saw a young woman standing by the entrance searching every passing face.

"Excuse me," she said, going up to her.

When Saya realized she'd instinctively bent nearly double in front of the woman, a deep sense of humiliation surged through her.

Under the Japanese occupation, the local population in Malaya had been subject to immediate arrest if they failed to bow to an occupying soldier. Those detained were beaten until their legs would no longer hold them up, or were forced to remain standing for hours on end, holding heavy weights over their heads. Like the sensitive-plant that droops its leaves at the slightest touch, it soon became second nature for everybody, including Saya, to lower her head at the first sight of khaki. The ingrained habit had now surfaced automatically when she went to ask this person for help. Though furious with herself, she suppressed the feeling as she raised her head to see the plump-faced young woman looking inquiringly at her. Telling herself this was neither a soldier nor anyone else she needed to be afraid of, Saya held out the paper with the address.

"I want to go here," she said.

The woman glanced at the address. "Oh yes, Senbashi," she nodded. "There's a bus, so that'll be easiest. The bus stops are over there," she said, pointing off to one side of the free market. "That's where you need to go."

Saya had difficulty understanding the woman's dialect, but she recognized the word "bus" and assumed that's what the woman was pointing to. She thanked her and started to turn away, but the woman quickly asked if she was one of the returnees. When Saya said she was, she grabbed her arm.

"You didn't happen to see a man named Mamoru Taniguchi, did you?" she said. "He was supposed to be on today's train. A tall man, with a mole on his cheek."

Saya shook her head. The woman gave her a disappointed smile and let go of her arm. The next minute she was intently scanning the passing crowd again.

It took several more inquiries before Saya actually found the bus to Senbashi. She helped her son aboard, and the bus pulled out almost right away, wending its way through the war-scarred city. Shabby little houses stood surrounded by scorched earth. Here and there among the ruins she noticed vegetables being cultivated. A few new buildings had already gone up, but for the most part, the rubble had yet to be cleared away.

Green army jeeps without tops drove about the battered city. Children chased after the speeding vehicles shouting "Haro! Haro!" and the American soldiers tossed them gum and chocolate bars.

Eventually the blackened scenery gave way to open countryside rippling with budding rice. The bus bumped slowly along the unpaved road. In the distance beyond the green paddies she could see the ocean glinting in the sunlight.

Saya thought of the first time she had laid eyes on the ocean, when her brother had let her come along on a trip to Kota Bharu. Beneath a spectacularly clear blue sky, they floated down the mud-coloured river on a raft loaded with aromatic woods and medicinal plants.

It had been soon after the red flower of womanhood first blossomed between her legs. Feeling a sudden desire to see the world outside the jungle, she decided to try asking Kekah, her third oldest brother the one she was closest to. He took loads of jungle produce into town from time to time, and brought back clothing, cooking pots, knives, and other necessities. When she asked him, he looked surprised and wanted to know why: none of the other girls had ever asked anything like that before. She didn't really have an answer. It was just a vague itch, something restless inside her that made her want to do this unheard-of thing. She couldn't explain it to herself either. But as she stood there, not knowing what to say, staring at a spot over his head with her lips in a pout, he smiled and said, "Sure, you can come." It turned out he was already getting ready to make a trip. And although he often only went as far as Kelintasan, where he transferred his load to a Chinese merchant's boat going on to Kota Bharu, this time he would be taking his raft down the Derak River, all the way to the big city on the coast.

"I found this great new buyer," he said with a shrewd glint in his eyes.

It became an unforgettable journey for Saya. The brown river gradually grew wider, and Malay villages began to appear on either side. Through gaps in the trees lining the riverbanks she could see wooden structures with raised floors and thatched roofs. They passed through stands of what she'd always known as "skynut" and "white tear" trees, and learned they were called "coconut" and "rubber" trees outside her tribe. Large swaths of virgin jungle had been cut down and replaced with vast plantations. Trees of exactly the same height and shape stood in neat rows as far as the eye could see in every direction. Seeing these plantations made Saya feel as though she couldn't breathe. In her world, the land was covered with endless varieties of trees and plants, most of which she didn't know. When she walked among them, the few she did recognize served as landmarks for finding her way about. But here, every tree was identical. It was frightening to think that if you wandered into of one of these forests with only one kind of tree, you might never find your way out.

And the tree plantations were not the only thing she found frightening. When the river had grown so wide she thought surely the earth would pull apart, they came to a place where there were virtually no trees at all, only houses. This was Kota Bharu. The town of Kelintasan had not particularly surprised her. She had seen it from afar a number of times before, and it was much like the Malay villages in the jungle, except with wider streets and quite a few more of those same thatched houses on stilts. But here, the houses went on forever no matter which way she turned, and they weren't all the familiar wooden houses with thatched roofs. Many of them had hard, shiny roofs, and some of them were shaped like square boxes, with roofs as flat as their walls.

Then, when they'd floated on past Kota Bharu, the earth suddenly came to an end. It broke away to the right and left, leaving nothing but water ahead. Far in the distance, the water rose up to touch the sky. And from that place where water and sky touched, an endless parade of undulating waves rolled gently toward the shore.

Thinking they might be pulled into the seam between sea and sky, she turned to Kekah in alarm. Her brother sat calmly at the front of the raft talking to his Malay chum. He laughed her off.

"This is the ocean, Saya."

Once reassured, she became mesmerized by the gentle rise and fall of the waves. The smooth expanse of the sea began to look like a cushiony blue bed on which she could fall asleep. It made her think of the cloth slings the mothers in her tribe used to rock their babies to sleep.

That was exactly it, she now thought. That was exactly what the sea had been – a giant baby sling. She had been brought to this alien place sleeping like a child in a vast blue baby sling.

The blue of the ocean was blocked from sight again as the bus came to the edge of another town. Soon they were driving along a street lined on both sides by low, two-storey buildings with latticed windows and gray tiled roofs. They must be from older times, she thought. The bus came to a halt near a bridge that spanned a large river running through the centre of town.

When she saw that everybody else was getting off, Saya woke the boy sleeping at her side and followed suit. Before going down the steps, she showed the driver the scrap of paper with the address. He took it and held it outside his window for better light.

"Tamaishi 3-chōme would be over closer to the ocean," he said, and pointed to a street running beside the river. Reeds grew along both banks, and green water weeds could be seen swaying in the water. As she gazed down at the clear-flowing stream, she felt the fatigue of her long journey melting away.

An old man walking with a cane came toward them from the other direction. Saya thrust out her scrap of paper again.

"Oh, yes, the Nonezawas," the man said. "Go straight on down here to the third street and turn left, then ask again."

When she turned the corner she found herself on a narrow lane alongside a canal with houses standing eave-to-eave on both sides. She saw someone sweeping the area in front of one of the houses with a bamboo broom and showed her the address. The woman pointed a few doors down to an imposing wall with a tiled ridge. Through the pine trees rising over this wall, Saya could see a two-storey house with the corners of its tiled roof curling upward. It reminded her of the houses rich Chinese merchants built in Kota Bharu, and she took it as a good sign. The owner of a house like this surely had to be very well off.

Saya stood in front of the gray stone gate and compared the writing on her piece of paper with the wooden nameplate attached to the gatepost. The shape of the characters looked the same. As she peered in through the gate, a woman emerged from the front door with a shopping basket over her arm. Her deeply wrinkled face reminded Saya of an alligator.

The woman noticed her right away and came toward her with a questioning look. "Can I help you?" she said.

"I want to see Mr. Rentarō," Saya replied.

The woman eyed the two of them warily. "Can you tell me what it's about?" Her voice was a mixture of curiosity and caution.

Saya simply repeated what she had said before. "I want to see Mr. Rentarō."

"What about?" the woman said, her tone now more insistent.

Just as Saya finished saying for the third time, "I want to see Mr. Rentarō," she heard a familiar voice calling from inside the house.

"Hey, if you're going shopping, could you find out when the next distribution of cigarettes will be?"

"Mr. Ren!" Saya said, pushing her way past the woman through the gate.

Rentarō appeared in the doorway. The square, forceful jaw; the thick brow; the quick, flashing eyes. His head was large for the size of his body, and it had made her think of the dolls the healer used when putting curses on people. All that was exactly as she remembered. But he also looked different. His complexion, once as dark as a Malay's, was now much paler, and gray had come into his hair. The eyes that had had such a sharp glint in them when talking to Chinese merchants now looked wearier. Was this really the man she had crossed that huge ocean to see? Could this really be the Rentarō she'd known before? She wavered. But just then the boy squeezed her hand, and it brought her back to earth.

"Mr. Ren, it's me. I came."

The words burst from her mouth, propelled by everything she had been holding pent up inside her – from all that she had gone through in Kota Bharu after Rentarō's departure; from her tense days at the internment camp and aboard the repatriation boat, fearing exposure at every turn; from the frustrations and despair and hope and vexations that had been weighing on her. She felt as though she might explode as memory after memory welled up inside her all at once.

Rentarō simply stood there like a pillar, giving no sign that he had even heard her. Saya pushed her boy forward.

"Look, Mr. Ren. It's Isamu. Your son."

She thought she heard the cry of a barking deer and instinctively turned to look. The woman with the alligator face had come up beside her. Her lips were pressed together in a straight line, and yet from somewhere inside her thin little body came a sound like the cry of the barking deer in the quiet of the jungle night.

9

Shizuka's hackles rose as she helped in the kitchen after dinner. In a roundabout sort of way, Takiko was laying down the law for what was expected of her as the wife of a man in the family business.

"I'm so pleased that Kikuo will have both his boys working with him now," she said. "But it's going to be a big adjustment for you, Shizuka, so you'll need to keep your chin up."

Picking up the apron she'd removed during the meal, she tied it once again around her ample belly and started briskly on the dishes.

"Sure," Shizuka said meekly as she dried a plate.

The smile that was spread across her mother-in-law's plump cheeks gave her the beatific look of the goddess Kannon on mail-order picture scrolls. The woman's freshly permed black hair stood in for the halo.

"Naturally enough, a salesman has to spend most of his time out on the road, so Asafumi's likely to be travelling eight months of the year. In the meantime, you've got plenty to worry about here at home. You be sure to watch your step anytime he's away. In a place like this, every woman in town thinks she's your mother-in-law. Do the slightest thing out of the ordinary and tongues start wagging."

"Such as?"

Standing with her stomach pressed to the sink like a suckerfish, she threw Shizuka a sidewise glance. The ¥2,000,000 kitchen had been custom made from a line of integrated components produced in Germany.

"Such as going off on a trip without saying anything to your neighbours, or letting a man into the house while your husband's away. Somebody's always going to notice, no matter how trivial a thing it might seem, and the next you know everybody's talking. Isn't that right, Miharu?"

Miharu was busy covering leftovers with cling wrap. "Exactly," she said. "Like when I started driving a cab. You know what people said? That I'd dumped my kids and run away. I guess because I was never home during the day. I didn't get wind of it until I was out doing some shopping on my day off and somebody asked me how long I'd been back."

Her thick eyebrows shot up and her eyes popped wide as she burst out laughing.

Miharu drove a taxi from six until three every day, a job in which her cheerfulness and easy way with people served her well. These same qualities were the key to her being able to live under the same roof as Takiko, who tended to be moody from keeping her personal feelings shut tightly inside her.

"But when I told her I was driving a cab to make a little extra money, she changed her tune in a snap. She suddenly starts gushing about how industrious I am for being so young, and how other young salesmen's wives should learn from me, too – like I'm some kind of shining example." Jokingly, she gave her chest an exaggerated thump.

Her daughter looked up from the TV in the next room. "Mom's a shining example, yaaay!" she whooped.

"I don't see her shining," her boy joined in loudly.

"Simmer down," Miharu scolded, and the children went back to their show, still snickering. As she put the leftovers in the refrigerator, she addressed her sister-in-law again. "You know, Shizuka, you were working when you lived in Yokohama, at least until recently, so maybe you should look for a job here, too. You did research for new snack foods, right? After going through college and everything, there's no sense in letting your degrees go to waste just sitting around at home."

"That's right," said Takiko. "Back in my day, none of us wives had much schooling, so about all we could do to help was paste up envelopes for medicine packets or the paper balloons they gave out to kids, but you've been all the way through graduate school. You've got a master's degree."

The two of them seemed bent on making her into another shining example for young salesmen's wives to follow.

"Having a master's doesn't do me one bit of good when the economy's in the toilet," she scoffed.

"Some of the bigger drug companies have research centres in Toyama and they advertise openings now and then. You should definitely apply," Miharu pressed, as if she were talking about a golden job opportunity for herself.

Shizuka gave her a crooked smile. "Drugs are a whole different field from foodstuffs. I wouldn't have much of a chance without a pharmacy degree."

"You don't think so?" Takiko said. "My side of the family was in the business too, going back for generations, and until the 1950s or so we were still making our own medicines. But then they passed a law that said you had to be a pharmacist or doctor to put medicines together. I remember my dad grousing about it. He said things were so much easier when they used to be able to mix their own at home."

"The Nonezawa side always prepared their own medicines, too," Miharu said. "These days the medicines come through the co-op the salesmen formed, but everything used to be homemade. We actually still have a lot of the herbs and stuff that went into them upstairs – don't we, Mother?"

"We certainly do," she said, and then noticed the expression on Shizuka's face. "You look interested. Would you like to see them?"

"Oh, yes," Shizuka said eagerly. Scientific experiments had fascinated her ever since she was a little girl in elementary school. She had been completely enthralled then by the magic of electrolyzing water and synthesizing oxygen, and this talk about mixing things to make medicines was having a similar effect.

Takiko removed her apron. Asking Miharu to finish up in the kitchen, she led Shizuka back down the hall to the front parlour and slid the door open. With the food cleared from the table, the three men were sipping glasses of whiskey as they pored over a road atlas, trying to locate the places listed in Rentarō's sales register.

"Dear?" she said, dropping to her knees in front of the door. Kikuo looked up from the map. "Do you mind if I show Shizuka the things you have upstairs in the medicine room?"

"Sure, sure, go right ahead," he said with the magnanimous air of someone who is the complete master of his domain.

Takiko bowed low and closed the door.

It exasperated Shizuka to see her mother-in-law behaving so subserviently all the time, as if she were merely a servant in the house. Had she never stood up to him? Was she always the servile dog, even in the bedroom?

Rising to her feet, Takiko led her up an imposing staircase with a chandelier hanging overhead and ushered her into a room outfitted in the Western style. Built-in shelves lining two of the walls were jammed with books and papers on pharmacology. Under a window on the outside wall was a desk with a computer monitor and keyboard sitting on it. This was Kikuo and Kōichirō's workroom, Takiko explained, where they hashed out schedules for their customer rounds and packed their baskets before departure. Kōichirō had recently decided they should computerize their customer lists and was entering data as time permitted, she added, her voice filled with pride at her son's entrepreneurial spirit.

She turned to face another set of shelves in the corner, which seemed to have been left untouched by any encroaching modernity. These shelves were filled with a smaller version of the glass jars country grocers used to use for bulk sales of rice crackers, chocolate and such, their aluminium lids blackened with age. The old-fashioned jars were filled with dried plants and animal parts, reminding Shizuka of the herbalists' shops she'd seen in Yokohama's Chinatown. Labelled with names like amomam, areca, strychnine, camphor, and cloves, their contents were so old that they had all faded to pale shades of yellow or brown.

"We moved these here from Grandpa's house after he died – the house you're living in now. Dad insists they're valuable, they should ultimately go to a museum, but they're such a chore to keep clean," Takiko said, as if to make excuses as she brushed a finger through the thin coating of dust on one of the jars. The object inside the jar caught Shizuka's eye because it looked a little different from the others: a slightly twisted cylindrical object with deep wrinkles all over its surface. She saw that the label bore the characters for "tiger" and "phallus."

"Oh, dear," said Takiko with a wry smile. "It's a tiger's wee-wee."

Shizuka peered through the glass at the shrivelled organ that once belonged to a ferocious beast. Faded to a light brown colour, it was angled across the jar to fit, and it wasn't difficult to imagine its original size.

"It must have been really big," she said.

Takiko moved in closer, too. "But it looks pretty pathetic when it gets to be like this."

As they both studied the tiger's penis with their heads nearly touching, Shizuka was reminded of the events of three years earlier, when she'd met Asafumi's mother for the first time. She had recently all but moved in with Asafumi at his cramped two-room apartment consisting of a single bedroom and an all-in-one kitchen-dining-living room. They were in bed on a Sunday afternoon, making love, when the doorbell rang. With long hours at work leaving them too worn out for sex on weeknights, they treasured their weekends when they finally had the time to get in the mood, so they ignored the door and went on with their lovemaking. But the doorbell kept ringing, over and over. It was like trying to move your bowels with someone pounding on the bathroom door, and it distracted them both. Soon Asafumi's erection began to wilt.

"I'll go see who it is," Shizuka said, pushing herself away. She threw on one of Asafumi's sweatshirts, pulled on a pair of stretch trousers, and quickly ran her fingers through her hair as she started for the door.

When she opened it, a woman stood there with a bundle in each arm. Alarm bells began to go off somewhere at the back of her mind, but unable to identify immediately what might be triggering them, she simply said, "Yes? What is it?"

For several moments, the woman merely stared at the three ducks doing a line dance across the chest of Asafumi's sweatshirt. Then she glanced through the narrow entryway into the apartment before looking Shizuka in the eye and saying, "I'm Asafumi's mother."

Oh! thought Shizuka, and in the same instant, *Of course!* But before she could so much as open her mouth, the woman had already kicked off her shoes with an "If I may", and barged on inside, making a beeline across the living room toward the bedroom. She moved with the speed of an alley cat released from a cage. Shizuka spun around in dismay. The sliding door between the two rooms stood wide open. Asafumi was frantically pulling the quilt over himself as his mother stood stiffly in the doorway.

"What're you doing here, Mom?" he said, trying to sound as nonchalant as possible – no easy feat when he was lying there stark naked except for the edge of a quilt covering his loins. To make matters worse, he hadn't pulled the quilt quite far enough and his drooping cock peeked out, still semi-engorged and glistening with fluid. Takiko stood frozen to the spot for several seconds, as if stunned to realize for the first time since giving birth to him twenty-seven years before, that her son had been endowed with a penis also for purposes of sexual intercourse, but she soon collected herself.

"Glory me, even if this *is* your day off, what kind of person is still lolling about in bed past noon? Hurry up and get something on, dear. In the meantime, I'll just avail myself of your facilities, if you don't mind," she said, and scurried off to the bathroom. In the brief time she gave them, Asafumi threw on some clothes and Shizuka tried to make herself a little more presentable.

When his mother returned, Asafumi introduced Shizuka to her as "Miss Okamoto, a colleague from work", and they sat down for a cup of coffee as if nothing the least bit untoward had taken place, exchanging small talk about how it was finally starting to look like spring, the plum trees were in full bloom in the Sankeien Garden, and so on, trying to dispel the awkwardness they all felt by discussing the weather. After spending a half-hour or so with them in this stiff conversation, Takiko explained that she was in fact on her way to Hakone with an old friend from junior high, and got up to leave. Only later did Shizuka learn that Asafumi's sweatshirt with the three ducks had been a gift from her.

As she recalled this incident, the shrivelled penis she and Takiko were staring at together started to seem like the other one – the one that had wilted so rapidly beneath the two women's gaze that day. Embarrassed, she shifted her eyes away, and noticed beneath the bottom row of jars an entire shelf full of notebooks that looked just like the one she'd found in the shed.

"Are these all sales registers, too?" she asked.

"Pardon?" Takiko said, as if awakening from a trance, and turned to look. "Oh, yes, yes. Some of them go all the way back to the Edo period."

Shizuka pulled out one that was a little taller but not quite as thick as the others. The label on this one did not say "Medicine Kit Register." She had a hard time with the ink brush style, but she thought she could make out the characters for "Formulary."

"That one contains the recipes for the medicines they made," Takiko said. "In the olden days, every house had their own formulas, and they handed them down in books like that."

Shizuka flipped through page after page headed by names like Yōjōtan, Shikintan, and Kikontan. "There were a lot of them, weren't there?" she said.

"Uh-huh. But out of all the formulas in there, the one they made the most of by far was Hangontan. It was based on a famous Chinese cure-all that was supposed to raise even the dead, but the versions sold in Japan were all homemade. I remember being told that during the Edo period there were at least a dozen different formulas by that name in circulation. This house had its own recipe, too, which they claimed was identical to the original Chinese version that could bring back the dead. The story they told was that they'd rescued and nursed some shipwrecked Chinese sailors who'd washed ashore near Senbashi, and the sailors had given them the formula as a way of thanking them."

Shizuka found the recipe for Hangontan in the first section of the notebook. She saw ingredients such as turmeric, cattle yellow, realgar, and poultry breath listed in a delicate hand, together with amounts and mixing instructions. While she was trying to decipher what it said, Takiko yanked the notebook from her hands.

"Now, now, we can't have you getting too caught up in this sort of thing," she said teasingly. "What you need to be concentrating on right now is making babies, not making medicines."

As she watched Takiko put the book back on the shelf, all Shizuka could manage was a spiritless, "Uh-huh."

Her mother-in-law's eager inquiries about whether she was pregnant yet – in some cases delivered to her face, but more often by way of Asafumi – had predictably commenced shortly after the wedding. To Takiko, children were what marriage was all about, and the fact that Shizuka was already thirty-two had her worried. Shizuka did a slow burn whenever the subject came up, but, ignoring her obvious annoyance, Takiko pushed ahead.

"It seems to be some kind of fashion these days to marry late and even then to hold off on starting a family, but the simple fact is, it's best to have your kids while you're still young and strong. And that's not all. Once Asafumi starts travelling, you're going to have a lot less chances for you-know-what, so if you don't make up your mind and get things going now, you could wind up waiting a long, long time."

"Well, this is one of those things where even making up your mind isn't enough if the gods don't smile on you," Shizuka noted, hoping to put an end to the topic.

"Shall I let you in on the secret?" Takiko said, her plump face beaming with parental solicitude. Shizuka had no choice but to nod, and Takiko leaned close to her ear to whisper, as if it were indeed a great secret that no one else must hear, "Always keep your bathroom spick-and-span."

Shizuka stared at her. Did this woman really believe something like that could make a difference? Or was she just uncomfortable talking too openly about sex with her? Between the dead serious look on her face and the suggestive wink she gave, it was impossible to know for sure.

Shizuka was finding her mother-in-law difficult to read. She seemed easy and relaxed, and she had an ample supply of platitudes to offer no matter whom she was speaking to, but that definitely did not mean she was a pushover. According to Asafumi, when this house was being rebuilt, she had handled all the work with contractors herself while her husband and son were away, managing the budget out of savings she had set aside over many long years and keeping the project rolling forward without a single hitch. There was clearly more to the woman than met the eye.

Takiko lowered herself onto the chair in front of the computer desk before going on with the motherly advice she so obviously enjoyed giving. "And best of all, when you have a child, you've got something to occupy you while your husband is away. When you're married to a salesman, you spend two-thirds of the year sleeping by yourself, and any warm-blooded woman's going to get lonely after a while. Times like that, you'll be glad you have something worthwhile to do."

"These days, there're lots of worthwhile things a woman can do besides raising kids," Shizuka said, getting fed up with this endless harping on children. "If I go back to work, I'm sure I'll get the same satisfaction from my job."

With them both unemployed, Asafumi had decided to try his hand at the family business, but until he actually got started there was no telling how long he might last at it. She had too many other worries right now to be thinking about having children.

"You can't have relations with a job, you know," Takiko retorted, and Shizuka inwardly rolled her eyes at the old-fashioned turn of phrase as her mother-in-law went on. "It's hard sleeping alone when you're young. But if you have a baby, you nurse it, you rock it in your arms, you tend to it when it wakes up crying, and the days just fly right by. By the time the child gets a little older, the urges you once had go away, and after that it's not so hard sleeping alone anymore."

Takiko folded her fleshy arms together like two fat snakes. The bright fluorescent tubes overhead cast a harsh blue light on her pale skin.

"So the object is to distract yourself from loneliness while you bide your time until menopause? How unimaginably dull," Shizuka said, making no effort to soften her words.

Takiko was unfazed. "You're right. It *is* dull," she said. "You hold down the fort, you raise the children, and you live in gratitude for all the sacrifices your husband is making. That's what it means to be married to a travelling salesman. While you and the children live in a fine house and sleep on plush futons, he has to bed down on a thin, hard mattress in some cheap traveller's inn. Then he gets up every day and walks his legs off on customer rounds. And since that's what makes your comfortable life possible, you can only feel grateful. I suppose this all sounds very old-fashioned to you, but it's important to appreciate what you have. Because no matter what a person does, no matter how a person lives, nobody ever thinks it's enough."

"And what about the stories I've heard about the men taking up with other women on the road?" Shizuka asked, thinking of Rentarō. Takiko's view of a woman's place reeked of hidebound Confucian values, and she was losing patience with it. But as Shizuka stood there, bristling like an antenna in a thunderstorm, Takiko merely pressed her well-rounded shoulders against the back of her chair and smiled.

"Well, men will be men," she said. "It's best not to ask too many questions about that."

"That's hardly fair. The wife's supposed to avoid raising eyebrows and just count her blessings, while her husband's out on the road sowing his oats?"

"Let me tell you something, Shizuka. You seem to think men and women belong to the same species, but they don't."

This was a statement that flew in the face of everything she'd ever been taught. Men and women were equal. Biologically speaking, some female X chromosomes mutated over time to produce Y chromosomes, and that led to the emergence of males, who had both X and Y chromosomes. Along the way, the woman's clitoris grew into the man's penis. In other words, a man was merely a variation of a woman.

"Oh?" Shizuka said combatively. "What exactly do you mean?"

"Men are monsters," Takiko declared bluntly.

"Monsters?" she repeated.

"That's right. Most men are little boy monsters who never grow up. It's perfectly normal for boys to be selfish little horrors who think only of themselves, of course, so basically what a woman needs to do is learn to indulge her man, let him go on being a little boy. That's where a woman's happiness lies. If as occasionally happens he actually manages to grow up, then he becomes a real monster. He starts thinking the whole world belongs to him and he can do whatever he wants. Women and children are just playthings to him, meant to be banged around like any other toy. He quickly gets bored with them and goes running off somewhere else to play."

Seeing the obvious scepticism on Shizuka's face, Takiko propped her hands on her knees and leaned into her point as she went on.

"Suppose I tried to tell Kikuo he can't do this, he can't do that. He's liable to get bent out of shape and start womanizing and carousing all the more. But if I turn a blind eye to his little lapses and just keep telling him how much I owe him, then I know I can at least count on him not to go off the deep end. So the trick is to keep thanking him and building him up, come what may. Don't let the little horror turn into a monster – let him stay a kid. That's what a smart woman does."

"So you're basically saying that we have to pull the wool over their eyes?"

Takiko bobbed her head gently up and down like a willow branch. "That's right, dear," she said. "Men and women get along by pulling the wool over each other's eyes."

A storm of protest was brewing inside Shizuka as she listened, but she held it in check. Deep down, she knew all too well that her mother-in-law was right.

10

Once she had learned that Asafumi and Shizuka were on intimate terms, it didn't take long for Takiko to begin nagging them about wedding plans.

"My parents are saying it's time we got married," Asafumi said one day as if relaying a directive from above, and it put Shizuka in a huff.

"Your parents are saying?" she snapped in her aggressive way. "And how exactly do *you* feel about it?"

"Oh, I've been thinking the same thing," he replied quickly, as if cowed by her fierceness. Then he rephrased it: "Will you marry me?"

Shizuka shrank inwardly at the seriousness she detected beneath his diffident proposal. She was in fact seeing another man.

His name was Hiroyuki. She'd met him in her fourth year out of college, about the time she had finally begun to feel fully adjusted to her job. But at the same time, she also felt as though she'd run into a wall. If she reached out to touch the wall, her hand sank in up to the wrist, and if she bumped it with her body, it gently absorbed the shock, but if she then kept pushing on it, she started to feel suffocated. That was the sort of wall it was. The wall of society around her, hemming her in.

· When she first graduated from college and joined the working world, she'd expected a whole new life to open up. She would be earning her own money, and could become a truly independent woman. But once she started to settle into the job, she quickly realized that what little independence she gained had come at the cost of tying herself indefinitely to the company she agreed to work for.

When the wall began to put thoughts of quitting in her mind, she decided to use some of her vacation time and get away by herself for a few days. Azumino seemed as good a place as any. She checked into a room at an inn in the valley popular with skiers in the winter, and set out on a walk to fill the time until dinner. A road that ran between rice paddies on either side soon led into wooded hills ablaze with autumn colours. The road's winding progress toward some unknown destination seemed a perfect reflection of her state of mind.

Did she want to stay put in her present job, or should she leave? If she did leave, then what? She was having trouble knowing her own mind.

As she walked along the sloping road, with the autumn air like thin sheets of ice in her lungs, she noticed someone crouched amid some pampas grass at the side of the road a short distance ahead. Dressed in a business suit, the short, thickset man was trying to fix an advertising banner to the guardrail. "Lots for Sale: Hōraisan Subdivision", it said. A dust-covered car parked nearby had several more banners bearing the same message poking out of its trunk. The man seemed to be having difficulty getting the pole that held the banner to stand up straight. His suit jacket was wrinkled, and flecks of brown grass and white pampas plume dotted his short, frizzy hair.

The sight of someone in full coat and tie struggling with a flagpole on a deserted mountain road seemed oddly comical, and Shizuka had to stifle a laugh. He heard her steps as she approached and turned around. His large eyes and wide mouth made him look a bit like a hippopotamus.

Seeing the expression on her face, he pouted his wide lips and said, "Instead of standing there laughing at me, maybe you could give me a hand."

It came out as if he were speaking to someone he'd known for ages. And there was such a hapless tone in his voice that, very much to her own surprise, she found herself answering in kind.

"Sure," she said.

That was how she'd met Hiroyuki. While she held the flag for him, she learned that he was working for a real estate developer based in Yokohama. Since that was where she lived too, she gave him her phone number, and almost as soon as she was back at work, she got a call from him at her apartment. They were soon seeing each other regularly.

As it turned out, he wasn't actually an employee of the developer he'd mentioned, but a free-lancer who signed on by the job. He would get a call whenever the company needed to supplement its in-house staff in order to market a particularly large new subdivision. Since the projects were large, he also stood to make out very nicely: he grumbled that the economic downturn had taken a bite out of his income, but even so, a single job could earn him half of what the typical salaried worker made in a year.

"But I'm always broke. My ex is still squeezing bucket loads of money out of me from our divorce settlement."

He griped a good deal about his former wife, yet Shizuka also got the impression that he wasn't entirely over her. "I call her sometimes to give her grief about it," he said, as if they were a couple of kids who couldn't stop squabbling about something.

He was what you could call smooth. Smooth, yet definitely not much to look at. Even after they started sleeping together, she couldn't stop asking herself why she was going out with a guy like him.

Not only that, he talked as if all sorts of women were falling over each other for his attention. He would rattle on about the eighteen-year-old he'd taken on a date, or the co-ed he'd let persuade him to buy her a blouse.

"I don't believe you. You couldn't possibly be that popular," Shizuka snorted, but she wasn't actually so sure. After all, if *she* was going out with the guy, there was good reason to think that other women might be interested in doing the same.

It was in fact precisely because Hiroyuki talked about dating other women so much that Shizuka had started seeing Asafumi. If Hiroyuki was a man of the world, impossible to pin down, Asafumi was a simple child at heart, as transparent as day.

Hiroyuki caught on in practically no time at all. "Well, well, so you're having a good time for yourself, too," he teased, but he made no effort to probe.

For his part, Asafumi never suspected a thing. Shizuka saw him on the weekend and Hiroyuki during the week. Since Hiroyuki's real estate work generally kept him busiest on Saturday and Sunday, it all worked out quite well. With an active and stimulating sex life, the dissatisfaction she'd been feeling in her work dissipated. She was in fact feeling very comfortable with her circumstances when this sudden talk of marriage threatened to upset everything.

"I'm perfectly happy with the way things are," she said evasively, and she could immediately see the hurt on Asafumi's face.

Unfortunately, they lived in a world that did not approve of merely keeping things the way they were. A capitalist society is built on the premise of unceasing progress. The state, the corporation, and the individual are all regarded as healthy only to the extent that they remain constantly in motion, driving ever forward. Employees must gain advancement, singles must wed, and the married must start a family.

In what seemed like no time at all, Asafumi's parents were talking about coming to Yokohama to meet Shizuka's parents. Saying no would effectively be to reject Asafumi's proposal: she would lose him. If she wished to keep things as they were, she had no choice but to acquiesce.

Her own parents were divorced, and her mother still lived in Yokohama, alone, while her father lived in Tokyo with his new wife. So Shizuka explained the situation to her mother, emphasizing that she had no intention of getting married, she just needed her to meet Asafumi's parents in order to smooth things over. "You're only delaying the inevitable, you know," her mother observed dryly, before somewhat reluctantly agreeing to the meeting.

So it was that Shizuka and Asafumi, her mother Tamae, and Asafumi's parents Kikuo and Takiko met for dinner at a Chinese restaurant on the forty-third floor of the Landmark Tower in Yokohama's Minato Mirai 21 development. On one side they looked out over the hills surrounding the port city, covered with homes and buildings of every kind; on the other they had a grand view of the Rainbow Bridge stretching across Tokyo Bay and the tracts of empty reclaimed land waiting to become part of the stalled Tokyo Waterfront Subcentre. Shizuka had chosen the venue in the hope that the Nonezawas would be so dazzled by the futuristic buildings and spectacular scenery that the entire question of marriage might simply fade into the background. And sure enough, the couple raved about the ultramodern urban development on their way up and leaned close to the glass for a better view when they were shown to a table by the window. But that was as far as her scheme had panned out. The topics Kikuo and Takiko raised during dinner were clearly intended to elicit information about Shizuka's family and upbringing, and when the meal was over, Kikuo lost no time in getting to the point.

"I must say, you've raised a fine daughter," he said, addressing Tamae. "I'm delighted to know that she's agreed to marry our son."

Asafumi, who had been staring absently out the window, jerked his head back to the table in alarm, even as Tamae was turning to Shizuka with a look of sudden bewilderment.

"I didn't realize you'd made up your mind, dear," she said.

Shizuka avoided Asafumi's eyes as she answered. "We haven't gotten that far yet."

"That's right," he said. "I only said we were considering it."

Kikuo and Takiko's faces froze, like on a pair of wooden dolls.

"But you already seem to be living together like you're married anyway, and I think this is really one of those things that ought to be put on a proper footing. Otherwise—"

"I was married twice," Tamae broke in abruptly. Kikuo was obviously taken aback at being interrupted, but she ignored him and went on. "Shizuka is the child of my first husband. He was only playing at being a proper husband while running around with other women behind my back, so I divorced him. And my second marriage was basically a train wreck. So I've always told my daughter: forget about getting married. You'll just wake up one day with your tits sucked dry, the best of your youth gone, and nothing more to look forward to in the future."

She was looking Takiko straight in the eye as she finished. Shizuka could see right then that the latter had taken a deep dislike to her mother. She learned later that the Nonezawas had in fact tried to persuade Asafumi to break up with her after this meeting.

But Shizuka had married him anyway. Once their relationship became known at work, their bosses and colleagues had started pestering them about when the happy day was going to be, and as if prompted by each such inquiry, Asafumi kept repeating his proposal. She simply got tired of saying no.

She thought that taking two lovers had let her break through the wall she'd come up against in her fourth year out of college. But the wall of society had caught up with her and penned her in again.

Her mother poked fun at her when she told her of her decision.

"I guess you just have to get burned for yourself before you can really understand," she said.

Shortly before the wedding, Shizuka received a call from Hiroyuki.

"I don't figure this has to change anything between us," he told her.

"Who're you kidding?" she said, turning him down point-blank. But before six months were out, they were secretly meeting in hotel rooms again.

"Maybe we should invite your husband to join us sometime," he casually suggested more than once, and it sent a chill through her each time. After marrying Asafumi, her assignations with Hiroyuki brought increasing pangs of guilt.

So there had been relief in knowing that their move to Toyama would put an end to her relationship with Hiroyuki once and for all. Yet, in all honesty, it wasn't necessarily clear that it was really over for good. Deep inside, she still clung to the possibility of calling him again someday.

Her mother-in-law was right. Men and women got along by pulling the wool over each other's eyes. That was exactly what she was doing to Asafumi by keeping this secret from him.

11

The atmosphere was thick at the Nonezawa house. It reminded Saya of the miasma over a bottomless swamp, and to shield her son from its unhealthy vapours, she'd told Isamu to sit behind her as they knelt facing the family on the *tatami*. The boy was seeing his father for the first time since becoming old enough to really remember, and he looked bewildered by it all.

Rentarō sat with his back to an alcove decorated with a knobby round-timber post, his kimono open in front to expose both knees. He was taking short puffs on a cigarette, pretending to be absorbed in the swirls of smoke rising from its tip, but his mind was on the two women glaring icily at him from the side. One sat with the sternness of a soldier in uniform, her back straight as a rod and every fold of her kimono precisely in place. From both her age and her matriarchal manner, Saya assumed she was Rentarō's mother. The other was the alligator-faced woman she'd met at the gate. This woman had identified herself as Rentarō's Japanese wife even before they entered the house. With the cry of a barking deer still lingering about her, she had calmly declared, "I'm Rentaro's wife. Perhaps we can go inside to hear what you have to say." Now the the two women were pressed shoulder to shoulder, like the first two leaves of a new seedling, projecting dark, bitter rancour toward Rentarō while making disgusted faces in Saya and Isamu's direction, as if looking at two giant turds he had produced.

On the other side of Rentarō sat a round-faced man with bulging lips. The way he addressed Rentarō told Saya this was his younger brother.

Saya had been stunned when Rentarō described her to his family merely as someone he'd known in Malaya. To hear all that they had been to each other and done together reduced to such a cold, nondescript phrase was both shocking and infuriating.

She remembered well the day they'd first met. He was drinking tea at an herbalist's shop in Kota Bharu's Chinatown, with a huge cloth-wrapped bundle sitting on the floor beside him, repeatedly wiping sweat from his forehead. He wore a moustache and his clothes looked freshly cleaned. This was years before the Japanese army landed at Kota Bharu and began advancing toward Singapore on thousands of bicycles.

She had just arrived with her brother Kekah on her first trip to Kota Bharu. Everything she saw and heard in the city was new to her, and she felt as if her whole world had been turned upside down. An Englishman in earth-tone clothes stood so tall and straight she'd thought for a moment he was a tree; her brother laughed at her when she commented on how pale his skin was and asked if he was sick. Kekah made fun of her again when she screamed at the sight of a shiny box on four wheels passing by, rumbling like when the earth shook. She'd had no idea there could be so many Chinese in one place before, and she'd never even heard of Japanese. So when she first saw Rentarō, she assumed he was from China. Only when her brother leaned over to whisper, "My new Japanese buyer," did she learn that he was the "great new buyer" her brother had talked about before the trip, and that he wasn't Chinese.

Rentarō was speaking to Kekah in Malay, which was similar enough to the language of her tribe for her to pick up the gist of the conversation. He needed ingredients found in the jungle for making his medicines, and wanted to establish a source he could deal with directly instead of having to go through a middleman. Her brother was nodding enthusiastically. Saya couldn't understand why he should want to get involved in something so bothersome. If he agreed to the deal, he'd have to make lots of trips down the river by raft, like this time, which would mean having to spend long periods away from their tribe.

When they finished arranging a deal, Rentarō turned to Saya and asked, "And who is this young lady you brought with you today?"

"My little sister," Kekah said.

"Is she all right?" he asked.

"She's just feeling a little overwhelmed because it's her first time in the city."

With the attention suddenly focused on her, Saya blushed. Rentarō gave her a smile before reaching into his bag to take out something flat and shaped like a leaf. It was made of paper in red, yellow, green, and other colours. When he brought it to his lips and blew, it began to puff up, and as he continued blowing into it, it grew into a perfect sphere.

"Paper balloon," he said in Japanese, batting it lightly into the air with the palm of his hand. Saya's eyes grew wide with wonder. She'd never seen anything like it before. It was as if a rainbow rolled into a ball was dancing up and down in the air.

Rentarō lobbed the rainbow ball in her direction. It floated toward her in an arc and made a puffy sound as it hit her chest. The sphere felt crinkly in her hands, like the sloughed-off skin of a snake. It seemed terribly fragile, and she was afraid she might crush it. She cupped her hands under it as gently as she could, as if holding something precious, and whispered the words Rentarō had said, "Paper balloon."

He chuckled, and smile lines formed on either side of his moustache. He seemed like a very nice man.

"So what you're telling us is that you shacked up with this woman when you were in Malaya, and that little boy there is your son. Is that right?"

The voice of Rentarō's wife sliced sharply through the toxic air hanging in the room.

Rentarō nodded heavily, his cigarette now barely more than a stub between his fingers. "After all, five years is a hell of a long time to be living overseas. I hired her as an assistant because she knew so much about the plants I needed for my medicines, you know, and then one thing just sort of led to another…"

Much of the dialect they spoke in this part of Japan slid incomprehensibly past Saya's ears, but she could still make out enough to know they were talking about her.

Exactly, she thought. Rentarō was after the knowledge she'd picked up from following the medicine man around. After getting to know Rentarō in Kota Bharu, Kekah began bringing him along to the jungle once each year. When they came, Kekah would ask Saya to help them find the plants Rentarō needed. The healer himself had refused to offer any such help, saying he couldn't share his secrets with strangers from outside the jungle, and he forbade Saya from taking Rentarō into the forest with her brother, too. There was a cutting edge to his voice – he sounded sterner even than when he rebuked her for breaking the branches of trees where this or that spirit lived, or for treading on precious healing plants.

People who come from outside never really see the forest. Everything they touch shrivels and dies, turning into a seed of misfortune. You mustn't have anything to do with them. If you help them, you become one of them.

Saya was shaken. She understood that being called "one of them" – an outsider – meant to be cut off. But the healer's warning also provoked a rebelliousness in her. So in the end, she had turned her back on him – which was the same as turning her back on the tribe. She chose to go with Rentarō, and ran headlong out of the jungle.

It all came back to the rainbow ball. The ball had been her most prized possession from the moment she first returned with it to the jungle until its paper skin tore to shreds. Even after it was gone, she kept it forever in her heart. It symbolized her every dream.

All of the dazzling new things she had seen and experienced in Kota Bharu were condensed in that ball: the bright, colourful clothes; the tasty, tender foods; the furniture polished to a fine sheen; the transparent walls that shut out the wind but let in the light; the machines that raced at high speeds without ever running short of breath. On and on – an endless parade of novelties that had her in an almost constant state of amazement. Somehow, in Saya's mind, they were all inextricably linked with Rentarō. Going with him meant going back to that place of wonder.

"In all fairness, peddlers getting the itch when they're on the road kind of goes with the territory…"

The younger brother's mumbled defence broke through Saya's thoughts and brought her back to the present.

"That may be so," the older woman replied, "but part of the bargain is that they don't bring those dalliances home with them." She gave Rentarō a hard look. "If your dead father knew about this, he'd call you a disgrace."

Avoiding Saya's eyes, he said, "That's exactly why I made sure she was provided for before I left."

Both women looked at Saya with daggers in their eyes. The younger one opened her mouth to speak, but the other beat her to the punch.

"So tell me this," she said, shifting on the *tatami* to face Saya. "What exactly did you come here for?"

Saya gestured toward Isamu behind her. "For boy to see father."

"All right. In that case, now that he's seen him, I guess you can go home."

She shook her head. "I will live here."

Their faces froze. Saya's eyes moved around the room, calmly taking in each face as she continued.

"I am wife to Mr. Ren. I will live where he live."

"*I'm* his wife!"

The outburst from the woman with the alligator face was mixed with the cry of the barking deer.

When you begin to hear voices inaudible to your ear, that is when dreams turn to reality. The dreams of those you hear will come forward to swallow you up. You must be very careful. Saya remembered the healer telling her this.

She looked at Rentarō. "I understand it," she said. "So, I am wife number two."

Life began returning to the woman's shrunken eyes. Saya imagined the shrivelled, dried-up skin reviving as well, and before she knew it a real live alligator might be snapping its jaws at her. She needed to head off the attack.

"You say so, Mr. Ren," she said. "You say I am wife number two."

The woman turned to glare at her husband again. Rentarō fumbled for words.

"That's... I mean... you have to understand, the Malays are Muslims. Their religion says they can have more than one wife. Up to four, I think it was."

"This family is not Muslim," his mother said bluntly.

"But when you're in Malaya, those are the terms they understand, so..."

He trailed off, gazing awkwardly up at the ceiling to avoid looking at either of them.

Saya couldn't understand why proposing to be Rentarō's second wife had created such a stir. The people in her tribe were not Muslims like most Malays, but it was nevertheless common for the stronger men to have two or three wives. To have more than one was a sign of stature. So when Saya said goodbye to her tribe, she proudly declared that she was leaving to become Rentarō's second wife, and she wore that label throughout her time in Kota Bharu. Far from finding it objectionable, people thought more highly of Rentarō for it – as they did with anyone who had extra wives. So she couldn't see what the problem might be here. To judge from the size of their home, the family was obviously well-to-do, and Rentarō was its head. As a man of means, he should be able to have as many wives as he wanted.

"This is Japan, and nobody has two wives here," Rentarō's mother snapped. "The very idea!"

The woman beside her nodded indignantly.

"That's right," the brother spoke up again. "And especially when we're still struggling to get back on our feet after the war, you can't go bringing some strange woman into the house along with her extra baggage."

For a long, uncomfortable moment, a silence that grated like branches creaking in the wind filled the room. Then Rentarō stubbed out the cigarette he'd managed to smoke down almost to the very end.

"I think maybe I need to have a little talk with Saya in private," he said.

Nobody said a word. Signalling Saya with his eyes as he got to his feet, he stepped to the paper panel that separated the room from the hallway and slid it open. Saya rose with Isamu to follow.

He turned down the passage toward the rear of the house. The faces of three children peeked out from one of the rooms. He barked at them to close the door and they disappeared from sight. As they passed, Saya heard the muffled voice of a woman inside. There were apparently others in the house.

Rentarō led her through one of several wooden doors opening off the hallway. The moment she stepped inside, she recognized it as a place where medicines were prepared. The built-in shelves were lined with jars and boxes of all shapes and sizes as well as assorted chemist's mortars. A strong medicinal odour hung in the air. On the wooden floor sat a young man with close-cropped hair, packing envelopes filled with medicines into a container woven from strips of bark.

"Make yourself scarce for a while, will you, Asatsugu," Rentarō said.

The fellow eyed Saya curiously, but got to his feet without a word.

"And just so you know, the trip we planned starting tomorrow is going to have to wait a bit," Rentarō added.

"But everything's all set," Asatsugu protested.

"Don't worry. It'll only be for a few days."

Rentarō's tone made it clear there was no point in arguing. The boy looked obviously disgruntled as he headed for the door.

Saya took a deep breath. The familiar smell awoke fond memories of the house they'd lived in back Kota Bharu. It was a fine house, raised on stilts, with a pine-tarred shingle roof. The front steps led up to a broad porch furnished with rattan chairs and tables for entertaining guests. The interior was partitioned into four rooms, but the dividers between them could be removed to make it a single space, with louvered shutters all around the outer walls opening it to the outside.

Rentarō used one of the four rooms to store his raw materials and prepare medicines to be sent to Japan. There, steeping in the smell of musk and aromatic woods that filled the air, Saya had helped him organize his many different curatives and pack them into boxes for shipping. Sometimes she helped him with the mixing of this or that concoction, too. One of them was a skin ointment they made from sulphur, wood tar, borneol and rabdosia to give out for free. Since skin problems were very common among the Malays, people were tremendously grateful. They also had a malaria-and-flu powder they frequently gave away, as well as a preparation that relieved pain and cleared the bowels. Saya had been amazed how generous Rentarō was.

They'd received a wide variety of visitors at that house – Japanese businessmen on overseas assignments as well as Malays, Indians, and Chinese. Once the Japanese army arrived in Kota Bharu, officers of the occupying forces joined the crowd. Whenever Japanese guests came, Rentarō would take them inside to talk quietly for a time before asking Saya to bring food to the front porch for a hearty meal. She loved to watch him drinking and laughing with his countrymen. Those were the days when she still believed that the Japanese had come to help Malaya win its independence, as Rentarō had told her. She was proud to see her man rubbing elbows with people who were working for the betterment of her country.

MASAKO BANDŌ

When Asatsugu went out, Rentarō shut the door firmly behind him and turned to look at her.

"Saya, Saya, Saya," he sighed, reminding her immediately of the time he'd given her that name.

One day, when she was guiding him through the jungle to gather the plants he needed, he had asked her her name. Embarrassed, she had repeated the Malay phrase for "My name is..." several times without being able to finish the sentence: *Nama saya... Nama saya...* Her name was in fact Kesumba. She'd been named after a tree that produced a bright red fruit, which the men of her tribe had once used for war paint. But by custom, an unmarried woman spoke her name only to the man who was to become her husband. Everyone else referred to her only as her father's first or second or third daughter, and then once she was married, as so-and-so's wife. In effect, a woman had no personal name to anyone but her parents and her spouse.

The day Rentarō wanted to know what she was called, he was still a virtual stranger. So custom said she couldn't tell him. In fact, she had never even been asked that question before. That was why she kept getting stuck on *Nama saya...*

Rentarō laughed and held both hands up for her to stop. "All right, all right," he said. "I'll just call you Saya."

And so Kesumba had become Saya.

"Mr. Ren," she now said, stepping toward him. But before she could take a second step, Rentarō fired a question at her in the tone of a cross-examiner.

"Why didn't you stay in Kota Bharu?" he demanded. "The landlord said you could stay in the house as long as you wanted, and I left you plenty of money."

Saya couldn't help noticing that even here, out of his family's sight, he made no show of affection for them, by taking his son in his arms or telling her how much he'd missed her. His expression remained stiff and remote, and there was no trace of the man who had so lovingly run his hands over her smooth skin, who had taken such delight in draping her with pretty clothes or watching her enjoy something to eat. But she was no stranger to the abrupt changes in character the outcome of the war had triggered among both victors and losers. She looked at him coolly.

74

"The money you give me is scrip, so it become no value when war is over."

Creasing his salt-and-pepper eyebrows, he gave her a strained look. He must have known perfectly well that Japan's defeat had made the occupation's military scrip worthless.

"Then you should have gone back to the jungle to wait for me. I told you I would come and get you someday."

She pulled Isamu in front of her and looked him straight in the eye.

"But we wanted to see you."

"Right," he said weakly. "I can understand that."

No, you can't, she said to herself. *You can't possibly understand why I wanted to see you. Why I even became a different person in order to come here.* But she remained silent. A woman didn't want to reveal too much to her man; it was best to hold something back – to keep her true feelings hidden. Like a finger-hole knife slipped into her hair.

"Look, Saya," he said. "I'd like you to reconsider. It's going to be really tough for you, living in Japan. And even apart from that, you can see our situation here. We already have a full house. It's not just my own wife and kids, but my brother's family too – ever since they lost their place in an air raid. We simply don't have any room for you."

Saya shook her head. She'd prepared herself to endure whatever she might encounter.

"I will live here," she declared.

12

Shizuka had gone to shop for dinner and Asafumi was dozing in front of the stereo when the phone rang.

"Guess what? I found your answer," Miharu's chirpy voice rang out on the other end of the line. "There really was a Mandala Road out Tateyama way."

"Oh?" he said vaguely, as he tried to recall through his grogginess where he'd heard that name before.

"I asked my grandpa," his sister-in-law explained, "and he recognized it right away."

The mention of "grandpa" finally made the name click: it was the road referred to in Rentarō's sales register. The evening he and Shizuka went to his folks' for dinner, he'd searched the pages of the road atlas with his father and brother, but having found no trace there of either Mandala Road or the villages that were supposed to be along the way, he'd totally forgotten about it since.

"Do you think it's still there?" he asked, as he lowered himself back onto their brand-new beige carpet in front of the wide-open doors to the veranda. An autumnal sun cast its light on the garden, where the lush green of summer was beginning to fade.

"I don't really know, but he knew the names Hachisoko and Senninhara, too, so I think it probably is," she said. "Were you still planning to try and find those old customers?"

During the month of August, Asafumi had spent three solid weeks attending classes at the prefectural training centre from nine in the morning to four in the afternoon every day, immersing himself in the how-tos of the business, and in all that time the idea proposed by his father had never really re-entered his mind. But he answered without even thinking, "Yep, that's the plan."

The moment he said it, the sense of being pulled into the past that he'd experienced when he first laid eyes on his grandfather's sales register came over him again, as if Rentarō were standing there and reaching out his hand.

"My training's finished now, so it's perfect timing," he said, feeling fired up for action. "I can get going right away."

"Then you should stop by our place in Ashikuraji to talk to Grandpa and get directions. In fact, if you'd like, I could go with you."

Kikuo and Kōichirō had just left on a sales trip. Miharu apparently felt at liberty to spread her wings when they were away.

"That'd be great," he said.

Asafumi wanted to explore by car, so if he swung by to pick her up, they could drive out as far as Ashikuraji together. After learning whatever he could from the Yasudas, he would go on from there to check out Mandala Road. Miharu could spend the rest of the day with her folks before returning to Senbashi by train.

"And while we're at it, I can show you the sights!" she said in a burst of excitement. "You can stay for lunch, and continue on your way in the afternoon."

"It's sounding better all the time," he responded, catching her enthusiasm. This would be his first outing with any woman besides his wife in a very long while. It felt almost like making a date. "I'll see you first thing the day after tomorrow, then," he said, and hung up the phone.

"Who was that?"

He nearly jumped out of his skin at the sound of Shizuka's voice. Turning, he found her standing in front of the veranda with a shopping bag clutched in each hand.

"Miharu," he said, then shifted around to face her. He felt as if he'd been caught doing something naughty; somewhere inside, tiny pangs of conscience for planning a date behind his wife's back began gnawing at him. In an effort to quell the feeling, he quickly went on, "She said her grandfather knows about Mandala Road. Remember? From that notebook you found. She's gonna take me to talk to him the day after tomorrow, and then I'll head on out to see what I can find."

"Ooh, can I come, too?"

She set the groceries on the veranda and stepped up into the house.

"No," he blurted.

"Why not?" she asked, her thin lips in a pout.

The word had popped out before he could even think. He scrambled to come up with a plausible reason. "I'm driving straight on from the Yasudas to find Mandala Road, and once I do, I'll be stopping at the villages along the way to see if any of the houses listed in the register are still there. If I find any, I'll want to see if I can sign them up again, so it could easily turn into real work. I can't have it looking like we're just some young couple out for a drive."

"I suppose that's true," she said grudgingly, then picked up the groceries again to take them into the kitchen. A month after their move, the house was finally starting to feel settled. Thanks to the furnishings they'd brought with them from Yokohama – a table and two chairs in the kitchen; the low-slung sofa, sound system, and TV in the sitting room – even this old country house had acquired some of the atmosphere of the modern city apartment they'd left behind.

"But actually..." Asafumi started, and then hesitated.

"Actually what?" Shizuka asked from the kitchen.

Asafumi battled with his conscience for several more moments before finally yielding. "Well, you *could* come with me as far as Ashikuraji. Miharu mentioned showing me the sights around town, and there's no reason you couldn't tag along for that. Then you can just catch the train back with her."

"Oh, goody!" she exclaimed. "I was reading about Ashikuraji in a travel book, and it sounded like the place has a really interesting history. I guess it got its start when mountain ascetics and monks from Tateyama set up a religious community there back in the fourteenth or fifteenth century..."

Asafumi pretended to listen as Shizuka bubbled on about what she'd read, but he was nursing a feeling of letdown. Not that he was particularly attracted to Miharu, or that he'd actually thought of fooling around; he was simply disappointed with himself for having let his conscience push him into suggesting such a lame compromise.

He stretched out on the floor in front of the stereo set, and turned the volume back up. He'd been listening to a classical FM station when the phone rang. A piano work by Eric Satie was now playing. As he closed his eyes and let the clear, crisp notes being picked out on the keyboard wash over him, childhood images of Rentarō and Saya living in this house began flickering through his mind.

During his primary school years, he often used to ride out here on his bicycle after class. When he'd pedalled for fifteen minutes or so along a road through the rice paddies, a grove of trees like the ones around a shrine came into view. In front of the grove stood a small single-storey house. By the time Asafumi was old enough to remember, Isamu had long since grown up and left the nest, so Rentarō and Saya were living here by themselves. He would ride through the gate and around the corner of the house, right up to the veranda. At the squeak of his brakes, Saya's round, always placid face would peek from inside. She must have been around sixty then. The years had brought wrinkles to her dark skin, but the brightness in her eyes and the full, red lips that suggested a camellia in bloom still told of how attractive she must have been in her youth.

She would simply smile, offering no words of greeting before turning to look back into the house. "It's Asafumi, dear."

Rentarō was usually sitting right here, in this room next to the veranda where Asafumi now lay on the floor. He'd be ensconced in his *tatami* chair watching TV. As young Asafumi stepped up onto the veranda and came inside, he would look up from whatever he was watching and break into a broad smile, his false teeth flashing brightly while his eyes almost disappeared amid his well-worn creases.

"Hey there," he said. "Good to see you."

But Asafumi was never entirely sure his grandfather recognized him as Kikuo's son rather than one of Uncle Asatsugu's or Aunt Tano's kids.

Asafumi would sit down beside him and say, "Tell me about Malaya."

"All right, sure," he would nod, always delighted to be asked. Saya would quietly switch off the TV, and he'd launch into one of his usual tales. "They have this tree in Malaya with flowers that look like golden rain is falling."

Listening to Rentarō was a little like listening to a tape on auto-rewind. Soon Saya would bring Asafumi a snack and some juice. The food was often something unusual, like sugar-glazed bananas or green jelly-cakes made with rice flour. The novelty of these snacks was in fact one of the reasons why he was so fond of visiting.

Saya almost never joined in the conversation. She always seemed to have some cooking or cleaning or garden work that needed attention. Unlike the restless, flurried manner in which he'd seen his own mother and women from the neighbourhood go about such tasks, she moved with the easy grace of flowing water. And as she chopped some vegetables, or dusted the top of the tea cupboard, or swept the yard in front of the veranda with a bamboo broom, he could hear her humming in a way he'd never heard anywhere else. *Whoooon whooooon...* This was the theme music that played quietly in the background of Rentarō's many tales. Asafumi travelled through the Malaya of Rentarō's memory to the sound of Saya's gentle voice.

He came to know the *arf! arf!* of the barking deer that rang through the forest night. The startled wild boar charging through the underbrush like a sudden gust of wind. Downpours that lasted a week without pause during the rainy season. People who lived by roving about the jungle from place to place, and people who lived in boats on the water. The hustle and bustle of Singapore. Depending on his mood, Rentarō might start in the jungle, or on the boats, or in the tumult of the city, but his rambling recollections eventually wound up at the same place every time.

"The women of Malaya, they're really something else. So passionate, so frisky." Asafumi could never resist stealing a glance at Saya when Rentarō got going on this familiar refrain. "Go to bed with them and it's like dipping your pecker in warm kudzu sauce. Pure heaven." Young as he was, Asafumi could sense that such talk might be embarrassing. But Saya just smiled and let Rentarō repeat his bedroom tales without a word. She went on doing her chores with that humming deep in her throat, until Rentarō's voice gradually dropped to an inaudible mumble and he sank into a sea of private memories. Like the notes she hummed, she was simply part of the background. She saw to Rentarō's needs with the unobtrusiveness of a black-suited stagehand. Not once did she direct a scolding word toward Asafumi, or even raise her voice. She was an invariably quiet presence, as serene as the grove of trees rustling in the breeze beyond the garden. It was hard for him to understand why his mother and father kept calling her an awful woman and discouraged him from coming.

This place he visited to see Rentarō and Saya felt different from anywhere else he knew. It wasn't like school, where the constant din and movement kept his head spinning; nor like his own house, where his mother exercised strict control; nor again like the streets around town, where he and his friends played hide-and-seek or war. It was a place where the sound of swaying trees, the burble of Rentarō telling his stories, and Saya's muffled singing all flowed together; where time seemed to go round in circles, much like his grandfather's stories. It felt to him like taking a stroll down a familiar path with nothing to worry about, just picking out small seasonal changes along the way. He found it a very comfortable place to be.

His parents made no effort to conceal their contempt for Rentarō. "Look at him," they said. "The minute your grandma's gone, he shacks up for good with that hussy of his."

But Asafumi had never quite been able to accept their view of his grandfather and Saya. He saw something different in the two of them that conventional phrases of social disapproval couldn't touch. He could never quite put his finger on what it was, but they were neither like his own parents, who had basically learned to ignore each other's shortcomings so they could put up with each other, nor like Aunt Tano and her husband, who were both on their second marriages and acted as if they'd found true love.

He never saw them engage in an extended conversation with each other. Rentarō was immersed in a world of long ago, while Saya seemed to live in a realm all her own. But their two worlds were not entirely separate, either. Even though they both kept to their own boundaries, there was a certain fuzzy area out on the fringes where their two worlds came together.

In retrospect, Asafumi thought the comfortableness of their home lay in this borderland where their two worlds intermingled. Rentarō told his stories as much for himself as for Asafumi, and a snack and drink were the extent of Saya's attentions. Neither of them made any kind of fuss over him, and that was precisely what put him so at ease. He ate the treat he was given, and then, when he grew tired of listening, he said, "I think I'll go," and got to his feet. Saya smiled and Rentarō's eyes lit up. By the time he stepped down into the yard, straddled his bike, and looked back into the house, Saya would be clearing away the glass and dish he had used. Rentarō would be leaning back in his tatami chair, gazing blankly at the ceiling. The atmosphere of the house before he came and after he left was always the same. Perhaps those were moments when he brushed against eternity.

The two of them rarely left the house. With it increasingly difficult for him to get around, Rentarō preferred not to go out, and Saya's excursions went no farther than the shopping district in Senbashi, or at most the city of Toyama. Still, every so often Rentarō would respond to an invitation from Asafumi's father or his siblings to visit their houses, or go out to eat, or make a trip to a hot spring somewhere. Even on these occasions, Saya stayed at home.

So far as Asafumi could recall, she never once visited the house in Senbashi. She always remained behind when Kikuo drove out to fetch Rentarō to the main house.

"Don't you ever go anywhere?" he remembered asking her one day when she was sweeping the open patch in front of the veranda. She stopped in surprise.

After a long pause, she finally said, "I go many different places."

"But you're always at home when I come," he said, and immediately saw a flash of scorn in her eyes.

Every so often, something fierce would skim like a bird of prey across Saya's placid face. It could be an icy stare, or a flare of anger, or a look of contempt. She'd been living in Japan for over thirty years by this time, and both her dress and her mannerisms were no different from any other woman her age around town. But these occasions reminded him that she did in fact come from another country. The Japanese mask she had donned would split open, and an alien fierceness would show through. It made him want to take a step back and cover his eyes, but the impulse never lasted more than a moment. And for her part, Saya would give him an awkward look and then snap the crack in her mask back together again.

In this instance, as always, her next words were gentle. "Even when I stay home, I can go anywhere I want," she said.

"What do you mean?" he asked.

She just smiled and laid her hand on his shoulder for a moment before turning back to her broom and resuming that distinctive, deep-throated humming of hers.

Whooo oo-oong, whoooo oo-oo-oo-oo-oong nnnng nnnnnng.

The strange sounds always seemed to carry him somewhere far away.

Whoooo oo-oong nnnnng. Saya's voice began to insert itself among Satie's piano notes. The two sounds were utterly different, yet in their depths they held a stillness that let them blend together.

As he lay there on the carpet, Asafumi wondered what had been behind the mask that Saya wore.

Feeling a sudden warmth at his elbow, he opened his eyes to find Shizuka stretched out on the floor beside him. He put his arm around her and pulled her close.

"What're you thinking about?" she asked, tilting her head against his shoulder. Her hair was moist with sweat.

"About Saya," he said.

Her eyes roved about the room from where she lay. "Did she go on living here by herself after your grandfather died?"

"Uh-uh," he said as he felt for her nipple through her clothes. Shizuka let out a hum of pleasure as she wrapped a leg around his.

"What'd she do?" she breathed in his ear.

As the first sweet waves of arousal passed through him, Asafumi tugged on a thread in his memory and managed to pull out an answer. "She just disappeared."

Rentaro's funeral service had been held at the house in Senbashi. It was in the coldest part of the winter. On this occasion, too, Saya stayed away. Nobody in the family even mentioned her. Her son Isamu, who had supposedly been living in Osaka ever since first striking out on his own as an adult, did not appear either – though it may have been because word failed to reach him. Not until sometime in the spring did Asafumi get to wondering about Saya and pedal out to see how she was doing. He found the house empty. The furniture and Saya's things were mostly gone, except for the table and tatami chair in the sitting room where he'd always found his grandfather. He remembered asking his parents and being told that she'd gone to live with Isamu.

"So that's where she is now?" Shizuka asked, pressing her hips against him. He could feel himself growing erect.

"I imagine so. But we've lost touch, and I don't think anybody knows where Isamu is anymore."

Asafumi slipped his fingers under her waistband. She took this as her cue and began removing her trousers.

The doors to the veranda stood wide open, but neither of them had friends or acquaintances in the area, so they didn't need to worry about anybody dropping in. Asafumi slipped out of his trousers, too. It would have been little bother to move into the bedroom, but he'd noticed since coming here that Shizuka liked making love in the sitting room with the doors open to the garden. She finished kicking off her panties and lay on her back with her legs apart and the garden filling a large corner of her vision.

The nakedness of her pale bikini area, highlighted by its dark tufts of pubic hair, stood out in sharp contrast to her upper body, still covered up in sweatshirt and bra. Asafumi lowered himself between her open thighs.

All her signals seemed to say she was more than ready, but he found her threshold dry, and he couldn't penetrate. She pulled at his hips with both hands, obviously eager to have him inside her, yet that very part of her refused him admittance. In growing frustration, she lifted her hips toward him. When he finally felt the tip of his penis catch hold, he quickly thrust inward, ignoring the squeaks of resistance, edging deeper with each push. As he entered, he could feel the fluids beginning to flow, but his progress remained anything but smooth.

This was not something new. It had been happening every third time or so since right after they were married, and it always made him mad. Cursing to himself with increasing aggravation, he gave an extra hard thrust.

"Ouch!" she cried, and pushed him away.

"Sorry," he said reflexively, and immediately regretted it. Why should he be apologizing? It was her damn dryness that was to blame. But to point that out would only get him into trouble, so he held his tongue. His dissatisfaction spread down to his loins, and his erection began to wilt.

He let out an exasperated sigh as he rolled off onto the floor. Shizuka frowned and covered her crotch with the trousers she'd dropped at arm's length. Depressed at the sight of his limp penis, Asafumi turned on his side and raised his thigh to hide it.

They lay like that for quite some time, unmoving, still naked from the waist down. The pure, clear sound of Satie flowed from the speakers into the air of discontent hanging in the room.

Shizuka mumbled something as she sat up to put on her panties, but Asafumi was still commiserating with himself and failed to catch what she said.

"Huh?"

She lay down beside him again. "I was just wondering about Saya – if she was still with us," she said mildly, as if neither coition nor interruption had taken place.

How was it that women could jump so easily out of one moment and right into another? They seemed to be able to turn themselves into a completely different person in no time flat. Was it only a delusion, or did they actually know how to remake themselves in the briefest of instants?

"I have no idea," he answered brusquely as a vague sense of gloom continued to spread inside him.

13

At the Nonezawa house, Saya and Isamu were accommodated in a storeroom with wood-panelled futon closets built into one wall and large wardrobes and chests of drawers lining most of the other three. It was a dim, cramped space with only one small window letting in light from the outside, but Saya did not mind. It reminded her of a cave in the jungle. The gray walls and the dark lacquer of the furniture were the glistening face of the rock. The moist coolness of the air was like being deep inside a cavern. She sat on the wooden floor with her arms around her son and took in the sounds of the house as if listening to the drip of water on the cave floor or the moaning of the wind at the entrance. *What're we supposed to tell the neighbours? It's so embarrassing. I can't show my face in public... My life is over. I can never trust you again... Good grief, Rentarō, you've really gotten us into a mess this time... Now don't you go talking to that kooky woman, dear. She's a monster... You make me sick, Dad! What'd you have to bring somebody like that into the house for?... This place has turned into a living hell. I wish I could just forget any of it ever happened...*

Some of what she heard was just light chatter, some of it, deeply felt emotions bubbling to the surface. Saya tuned her ear to it all, trying to understand what sort of jungle this big house was.

In addition to Rentarō, the place was occupied by his mother, wife, and three children. And ever since their house burned to the ground in an air raid, his brother and wife and their two children had moved in as well.

From Saya's point of view, they were all her enemies – except for Rentarō. And even he could hardly be called a friend, for he was no less eager than the others to send her and her boy back to Malaya. It was like being surrounded by scorpions in the jungle. You had to be careful not to provoke them, or they might come at you with their poison-tipped tails held high. Saya's first concern was to avoid stirring them up.

When she and Isamu awoke each morning, they waited patiently in their room while the family had their breakfast. Only after everybody was done and the dining room was silent again did they emerge to find two places set at the now deserted table. They sat down together to eat the steamed rice and vegetables that had been left for them, sometimes with a bite or two of dried fish.

As they ate, they could hear Rentarō's mother and sister-in-law doing the dishes in the kitchen next door. Between their chatter about what to make for lunch and what time they should go shopping for dinner that day, Saya managed to pick up a good deal of information about the Nonezawa household and her situation in it.

Rentarō went off each morning to help mix medicines at the guild, taking his oldest son Asatsugu with him. Although he pretended it was to make sure nothing was overlooked in their preparations for the next sales trip, he continued to put off their departure from one day to the next. His brother Tomijirō had a job in Toyama. The long back-and-forth from Senbashi was wearing him down, so he was on the lookout for a rental in the city, but there were so many other families in the same situation that he'd been out of luck. The children's school suffered from a shortage of books, which made it hard for the students to learn. Rentarō's wife complained of headaches and had taken mostly to her bed. "Who can blame her?" her mother-in-law said, lowering her voice as if to keep Saya from hearing.

Saya again waited until they were gone before entering the kitchen to wash up the dishes she and her son had used. Then they returned to their room together.

During the daytime hours, the house became an all-women's realm. And the women of that realm went about their business as if Saya and Isamu weren't even there.

Saya was like an invisible spirit living in the jungle of the Nonezawa household – unseen but ever-present, and by no means benign. To the other women there, she was a decidedly malignant presence, who brought nothing but grief with her. For she was still young, and she could turn men's heads.

Had Saya been as old and dried up as Rentarō's wife, the latter's hatred might have been tempered a little. She might even have found it possible to open her arms to her as a fellow victim of Rentarō's unfaithfulness. If she knew Saya had no claws left to sink into a man, she could have reached out to her without worry.

But it isn't until a woman is no longer a woman that she ceases to be a rival. Saya was not yet thirty, her body still youthful and full. She was neither withered and wrinkled like Rentarō's wife, nor flat and figureless like Tomijirō's. The long sea journey had taken a certain toll, but she had not lost her strong, ripe femininity. And so she was damned in the Nonezawa women's eyes.

At some deep level, human events invariably flow in the direction of human desires. Saya soon began to act as the women feared – as they feared, yet also wished. She sowed discord in the Nonezawa jungle, provoking storms of jealousy and resentment that shook every leaf.

First to be affected was sixteen-year-old Asatsugu. Saya had noticed the boy staring at her. *I can't believe my old man actually slept with this woman*, his eyes seemed to say. *He buried himself in her body.* She heard both disgust and envy in his silent voice, and between them, she found her opening.

"Master Asatsugu," she called out one day as he emerged from the medicine room into the dim hallway. Stopping short, he eyed her warily. She padded up to him as quietly as a panther. "Tell me please where broom is kept," she said to the boy, who had recently begun to have wet dreams at night. "I want to sweep room."

With loathing and desire reeling inside him, he led her to a closet at the end of the passage and took out a broom. Saya pressed the handle between her breasts as she thanked him, stretching the fabric of her top to reveal the fullness of her bosom. She saw him noticing, and something warm stirred deep within her.

"So many things I not know," she said, her words calculated to make the boy see her as a victim – as a hapless woman trapped in a foreign land by his father's deceit. Saya gave him a sunny smile to encourage the sympathy she sensed was gathering. "You are very kind boy," she murmured.

Unsettled by his conflicting feelings for her, Asatsugu's anger toward his father intensified.

Saya next reached out to Tomijirō. As he sat on the veranda smoking a cigarette, gazing at the autumn colours of the garden shrubs, she slithered up to him like a poisonous snake.

"I have question about Mr. Ren," she said.

Tomijirō, for his part, was eager to know how his brother had managed to find himself a girl like Saya in Malaya. She opened up without hesitation, describing how kind Rentarō had been to her in Kota Bharu, and how happy they'd been in their fine house and garden. She told him of the endless variety of sweet fruits they'd enjoyed, of the beautiful flowers in their rooms, of how their neighbours had called them the perfect couple. She mentioned only the good things, and kept quiet about the abuses committed by Japanese soldiers, the oppressive fear that hung over the town, the relentless stress Rentarō had lived under.

Tomijirō, she knew, was hearing it all as if she were speaking about herself. She was the sweet fruit his brother had eaten, the pretty flower his brother had enjoyed. The more idyllic her description of their life in Malaya, the more cheated he would feel. The war had brought him misery and danger, while his brother was living it up with the exotic young woman now sitting before him. Why should Rentarō have been so lucky, and not him? Saya sensed the resentment growing in his mind. His jealousy sent a wave of satisfaction rippling through her.

"But when I come to Japan, Mr. Ren, he change. He become cold to me. Why is this?"

"I don't think he's being deliberately cold," Tomijirō said grudgingly. "It's just that he has his wife to think about, and he doesn't know what to do."

"I not know what to do also," Saya murmured in a way intended to provoke his sympathy and heighten his ill-feeling toward his brother.

An increasingly dark mood settled over the house. Asatsugu and Tomijirō moralized to mask their jealousy, taking every opportunity to snipe at Rentarō. It was outrageous – keeping a mistress right here at home! The women lost little time adding their voices to these complaints. For Rentarō there was no peace in his own house anymore. But he could hardly just shrug it all off and leave on a sales trip. Who knew what might happen in his absence? He was trapped in a tangle of thorns, unable to move.

Saya looked on with satisfaction. She was glad that the man who had hurt her so much was now getting hurt himself.

Rentarō still had no idea what she'd been through in Kota Bharu. She had kept silent about that. She wanted to hold it in reserve. It was her finger-hole knife, to be used at just the right moment. She was biding her time.

The children of the household lived in a separate world. They were jungle sprites. Isamu played with them in the autumn sunshine.

Saya liked to watch from the small window of the wardrobe room as her son raced about the yard with Rentarō's younger boy, Kikuo, and Tomijirō's two boys. As the smallest of the bunch, Isamu worked hard to keep up, dashing here and there, jumping up and down, kicking fallen leaves into the air, stopping to catch his breath. He was picking up the language at an amazing pace.

The boy was Saya's piece of Japan. The more fully he could blend in with this land, the more firmly this land would become rooted in her.

From that same small window, Saya could see the privy shed, linked to the main house by means of a covered walkway. One day, as autumn drew on, she saw Rentarō crossing this walkway, and her eyes lit up. She knew he had been gone in the morning, so he must have come home early. It was unusual for him to be around the house in the afternoon. The padded robe he'd changed into showed he was done with work for the day. This was her chance.

She slipped out of the room to meet him in the hallway and grabbed hold of his sleeve. "Mr. Ren," she said in a low voice. "I must talk to you."

He glanced nervously up and down the corridor, but this was the hour of the day when time came to a standstill in the Nonezawa house. The women had gone shopping for dinner or were visiting neighbours, and only the spirits were present. Having realized this, he turned back to Saya.

"What is it?" he asked.

Saya smiled and led him back to her small room. After closing the door, she stood in front of it to block the only exit and, before he had a chance to stop her, swiftly removed her clothes.

The dim light in the room fell on her full-figured nakedness. She pointed to a round, wrinkly scar marring the light brown skin beneath her stomach, and to another on the inside of her thigh. Then she parted her pubic hair to reveal a third just above her crack. Scars from burning cigarettes. Rentarō's face filled with horror.

"Japanese soldiers do this," she said.

"But... why?" he asked hoarsely.

"After you go back Japan, Kempeitai come to take Mr. Xu away," Saya said, fixing her eyes firmly on his as she began her tale.

Rentarō had left Kota Bharu a little over two years before the end of the war. Disturbing news was pouring in from the front lines: Japanese troops had evacuated Guadalcanal and fought to their deaths on Attu; Allied forces had landed in New Guinea. With such reports starting to pile up, he left for Singapore to discuss the situation with the owner of the main store there. Soon afterwards, Saya received a brief letter in which Rentarō wrote in Malay that he needed to go back to Japan for a while and would return when the war situation stabilized. It turned out to be the last she heard from him.

Then began her nightmare. Someone informed the Kempeitai that Mr. Xu, their Chinese landlord, was a member of the anti-Japanese resistance, and they came to arrest him. The Chinese community had been singled out for harsh treatment ever since Japanese troops first arrived in Kota Bharu. Anyone suspected of offering support to the Nationalist Chinese in their fight against Japan was detained for questioning, in most cases never to return. According to some accounts, suspected collaborators had been massacred by the thousands immediately after the Japanese rolled into Singapore. They'd been herded onto the beach, forced to dig their own graves, then stabbed in the back with bayonets. The beach was soon piled high with corpses, many of them left to be washed away by the surf. With such stories making the rounds, Xu's wife was understandably distraught. The entire neighbourhood feared for her husband's safety.

Several days later, Kempeitai officers forced their way into Saya's house with their swords drawn. They ransacked every room, shredding clothing, smashing dishes, and breaking furniture, before leading her away to headquarters. There she was tortured. They wanted her to admit that she'd conspired with Xu to get close to Rentarō and steal Japanese secrets. They beat her savagely, then stripped her naked and pushed a burning cigarette into her crotch. The fists and boots that struck her were the least of it. They wrung her arms to the breaking point. They forced water down her throat until her stomach swelled up, then kicked her in the belly until it spewed back out of her mouth and nose, eyes and ears. They held a sword to her throat and screamed at her to confess. But confess what? She had no idea what they wanted to hear. "You were there. You listened in, and then you leaked what you heard to Xu," the officers kept repeating. But no matter how much they hurt her, she had nothing to tell. The men had always done their talking inside the house, telling her to stay outside until they were finished. She'd never been close enough to hear anything they discussed. But trying to explain this only fell on deaf ears. "You expect us to believe that, you fucking shit? Wipe that fucking grin off your face or we'll slit your fucking throat. You heard plenty, and you passed it all on. We know everything. So cough it up, you stubborn fucking shit, or we'll show you what real pain is." Cursing, baring their teeth, they kept finding new ways to make her suffer. But no amount of torture could squeeze anything out of her, for she'd genuinely been kept in the dark.

As she lay battered and limp on the cold, hard floor, she heard them talking above her. *She was just the guy's whore anyway, so I say we dump her at the P-house. They're always asking for more local talent. Yeah, good idea. Can't ever have too many bitches. Even savages are better than nothing, right?* There was laughter.

The events that followed left even deeper marks on Saya, body and soul. Most of the scars her skin now bore were in fact from after the torture. But she was not yet ready to reveal those humiliations. There are some things a woman will keep to herself until the last of the last possible moments.

Instead, Saya burst out, "You leave me! You not help me! I wait and wait, but you not come to help me!"

Bitterness seemed to erupt from her every pore. He stood staring at her naked figure, unable to speak.

It was because of him that she'd had to go through it all. It was because he'd abandoned her and gone away that the Kempeitai came for her. That was when her trip through hell began.

The grievances she felt were like a fever rising inside her. She glanced toward the wooden crate in the corner of the room. It held the things she'd taken from her small travel case – all her worldly possessions. Buried among the seeds in the drawstring pouch was her brother's finger-hole knife.

She saw herself lunging at Rentarō with the blade in her hand, drawing it across his thick neck as she'd done with the blackmailer in Ujina. A spray of blood splattered across her eyelids.

"I had no idea..."

Rentarō's voice broke through her crimson rage.

"I really had no idea," he repeated as he fell to his knees before her and touched the burns on her skin. "Please forgive me... I was worried for you, but..."

There was genuine tenderness in his voice. This was the Rentarō she remembered. The man who'd feasted his eyes on her in her brightly coloured sarong, or ran his hands over her body telling her how beautiful she was, what smooth skin she had, what a perfect treasure she was. The man who'd delighted in taking her to the Chinese restaurant and watching her eat for two when she was pregnant. The man who'd held her newborn baby in his arms with a smile that stretched from ear to ear. The man she'd led through the jungle in search of herbs and roots. The man she'd gone shopping with in Kota Bharu. The man she'd made love to all those countless times – in the dim daylight filtering through the louvered shutters, or in the steamy darkness of the summer nights... Memories of those days flooded back through her mind.

"You poor thing... I can't begin to imagine how you must have suffered."

Rentarō pressed his face to her stomach and wrapped his arms around her waist, sliding his hands over her body as over a priceless sculpture. Saya felt something stir in her loins. The pull of gravity between bodies that have once been intimate took hold, and the desire she was so sure had died pulsed back to life.

She touched his cheek, then slowly ran her fingers down his neck before she, too, sank to her knees. Facing him, she laid her hand on his thigh, bare beneath the open skirt of his kimono. The touch of his hairy, masculine skin sent a charge through her, and she could not remove her hand. Sliding her fingers under the folds of his kimono, she stroked the inside of his thigh for a moment before reaching toward his groin. She lifted the edge of his loincloth and wrapped her hand around his soft penis. He dropped his hips to the floor. Leaning over him, she took his cock in both hands and began stroking it firmly up and down. It slowly raised its head.

The pale light from the window barely lit up the room. They were in a world of semi-darkness, a time that was neither night nor day. His penis grew stiffer as she continued her massage. He splayed his legs like a frog, and his eyes drifted dreamily up toward the ceiling. As she prepared to straddle him, he seemed abruptly to recoil at what he was about to do and gasped, "No!" But there was no strength in his protest.

The feebleness of his resistance spurred her on. She thrust her breasts forward, hard against his chest. As if yielding to their pressure, he slowly fell back onto the floor. A sultry wetness dripped from the walls of Saya's cave. She lowered herself onto his erect penis.

The centre of her being exulted in pleasure. His penis felt the tremor and flexed its strength. It began to move within her, lifting her into the air as Rentarō held her by the hips.

From outside the window came the ring of children's voices, but the two lovers no longer heard. Moans escaped Rentarō's lips as he continued to thrust. The cave resonated with deep moisture. Saya arched her back, straining to capture every vital quiver inside her. They were like two beasts in the jungle, male and female, driven by nature to mate.

Rentarō stifled another moan as he came to a climax. Saya felt the flood inside her. A fountain of warmth filled the cave. It was a spring that would never run dry.

In the days that followed, Rentarō visited her room in secret to enter that cave again. It was a place he could not find in his wife, whose body had long since dried up. He yearned to take the waters freely, away from disapproving eyes. Once his desire had been rekindled, it could only grow.

Saya's feelings for Rentarō swung violently back and forth. One moment she hated him with all her heart, vowing to kill him; the next she ached to be in his arms, her love revived. She didn't know what she wanted anymore.

As autumn deepened, Rentarō came to a decision. "I'm going to find a house for Saya," he announced.

The women cried out in disbelief. The men said he must be crazy. Where did he think he was going to find such a place? And in any case, there was no money for rent. One after another, his family raised objections. But he had made up his mind. He would do whatever it took to be able to go on drinking the water that flowed from Saya's fountain.

Saya now knew Rentarō belonged to her. She had found a way out of her dark wilderness.

14

The peaks of the Tateyama Range rose breathtakingly against the sky. In the back seat of the Volkswagen, Shizuka craned her neck for a better view. Rice fields stretched out on both sides of the road as far as the mountains. Everything in the landscape appeared soft in the morning sunlight, as if seen through a layer of transparent film.

"The pointy peak in the middle is called Tsurugidake, and from there we have Bessan, Oyama, and Jōdosan, and then the taller one on the far right is Yakushidake. It's the water from all those mountains that drains into the Jōganji River and flows down through Toyama to the sea."

Miharu was offering a well-rehearsed commentary from the front passenger seat. She'd no doubt given this little speech countless times before while ferrying sightseers around the area in her taxi. But to Shizuka, mountains were just mountains, and it made no difference to her what the pointy one's name might be.

"Uh-huh," she nodded mechanically, feigning interest as she stole a glance at Asafumi. As always when at the wheel, he wore his glasses and had the radio going. Pursed lips betrayed his bad mood. She could tell he was still stewing over the tiff they'd had earlier.

It had all begun when he remarked over breakfast that his drive out to Mandala Road might end up being an overnight trip.

"In that case," she'd responded lightly through a mouthful of toast, "maybe you could scout out a hot spring in the area so we can go back together sometime."

He scowled. "This isn't a pleasure trip, you know."

His tone made her bristle. "But you're not exactly working, either," she said, "so it sort of halfway is."

He sat with a sullen look on his face and said nothing more. She understood that her reply had hurt his pride, but she didn't think she'd said anything wrong, or that she needed to apologize, so she fell silent, too, and that meant the thorns that had cropped up between them remained in place. Their discord was papered over by the rush to go and pick up Miharu, but it hadn't actually gone away. Even as they made their way toward Ashikuraji, she could see Asafumi's lingering irritation peeking through from time to time like the moon on a cloudy night.

Friction like this had become a frequent occurrence since their move to Toyama. Whether as colleagues at work or companions in unemployment, they had always been equal partners in Yokohama, but that was no longer the case here. Asafumi had now taken on the role of the traditional husband, with the full weight of his family behind him, and Shizuka was reduced to being his wife. While he went off to classes at the prefectural training centre, her job was now that of a housebound homemaker. She split her time between sprucing things up around the house after the initial clutter of their move, and working to get the overgrown garden under control. These tasks had in fact given her both satisfaction and pleasure – yet she couldn't help feeling a little uneasy about how their relationship had changed. Was she now destined to be stranded forever in this distant prefecture as the wife of a travelling salesman? It made her feel short of breath just to think of it.

That can't be my life! she wanted to shout. But then what exactly did she want her life to be? She really had no idea.

"Go right at the next light," Miharu said.

Asafumi turned onto a wide road with fresh white lane-stripes.

"This must be new," he said.

"They just opened it this year. It makes it a whole lot more convenient to get from Senbashi to Kamidaki."

"Didn't you used to have to take that narrow road along the Itachi River that wasn't much more than a farm lane?"

"That's right. I even got stuck in the ditch once, thanks to it having no guardrails."

The two in front chattered away together in the local dialect. Shizuka eyed her chirpy sister-in-law. She seemed even more animated than usual, presumably because she was going home to see her folks. With lipstick on and a gold chain around her neck, she'd dressed up for the occasion; she looked the very image of the young married woman of respectable means. What a difference from Shizuka herself, who'd come in her usual jeans and jacket.

How can this woman be so upbeat all the time? Shizuka wondered. Unlike their mother-in-law, who practically made a mantra of saying how happy she was yet always seemed to have a vague aura of gloom about her, Miharu was, to all appearances, utterly content with her life. But was that actually the case, or merely a pretty facade she put on? That was the question.

Maybe she just acts cheery to try to convince herself she's happy, Shizuka thought cynically. She'd always taken a dim view of people who bubbled and gushed over everything. She realized that it served as a kind of social lubricant, to keep things flowing smoothly between people, but it still seemed phony to her, like an act. This sense she had of a gaping divide between herself and other people made her wonder sometimes if she wasn't partly made of stone – of some crystalline rock whose structure can be described with a precise chemical formula, and whose slippery surface is embedded unchanging in the folds of eternity.

"This is the town of Iwakuraji we're coming into now," said Miharu, glancing toward Shizuka in the back seat. "And that's Oyama Shrine."

Shizuka smiled automatically and peered in the direction she was pointing. A dark stand of cedars rose alongside the wide, rock-strewn bed of the Jōganji River. Across a large parking lot, she could see a tall gray *torii* made of stone at the entrance to the wooded grounds, straddling the approach to the shrine.

"Oyama Shrine is actually split into three separate parts, with the front altar located here, the prayer hall at Ashikuraji farther upriver, and the main shrine on the summit of Mount Tateyama. The three places together are considered one shrine. Since the summit's blocked off with snow more than six months out of the year, worshippers who arrived during those months could pray at the two more accessible spots closer to town. This was also one of the main places where people who did make the climb started from, so at one point during the Edo Period the community grew to have twenty-four lodges for the pilgrims and was quite a lively place. Though if you go by lodge count, there were thirty-three in Ashikuraji, so I guess that was even more popular among the climbers."

As a born-and-raised native of Ashikuraji, there was a distinct note of pride in Miharu's voice as she said this.

Past the shrine, the car skirted the edge of Iwakuraji and emerged onto an open road that followed the course of the river up the valley. Because it ultimately connected with the Tateyama-Kurobe Alpine Route popular among tourists, the road had been improved, but the only sights along this section of the highway were the rice fields being cultivated between mountains pressing closer and closer on both sides of the river, clusters of farmhouses here and there, and the occasional roadside restaurant. Before long they came to Ashikuraji, perched on a shelf of land set back a short distance from the river.

The village that had sprung up to serve the faithful on their pilgrimages to Tateyama during the Edo Period still retained its rustic character. The Yasudas lived along a narrow lane that sloped down toward the river. Their wood-frame stucco house stood in the midst of rice paddies on a terraced lot with a stone retaining wall but no surrounding fence.

Asafumi pulled off into what was essentially their side yard and cut the engine. As he removed his glasses, Miharu opened her door and hopped out. "Mommy! Daddy!" she called out like a small child, and quickly disappeared around the corner of the house. Shizuka and Asafumi followed.

The home faced south, looking out over the river beyond the trees and shrubs in the landscaped garden. Except for the front entrance, a veranda stretched its entire length. The sliding glass doors along the veranda had been opened to let air into the shaded interior.

"I was just thinking it must be about time," came a woman's voice from inside.

Miharu poked her head through the front door and beckoned for them to enter. Shizuka held back, letting Asafumi go first.

Inside, Satoko Yasuda was kneeling in the foyer. She bade them welcome as they entered, bending deeply at the waist until her forehead nearly touched the floor.

Caught off guard by the formality of her greeting, they both hastily returned the bow. Asafumi presented the box of cakes they'd brought along, which prompted a profuse expression of thanks and another round of courtesies before they could finally remove their shoes to be shown into a formal tatami parlour right next to the entrance hall. In the centre of the spotlessly clean room was an imposing low table that had obviously been made from a single piece of wood, polished to a fine sheen.

"Here, sit over here," Miharu said loudly, urging them toward floor cushions placed next to the table.

Satoko knelt nearby. "It's such a pleasure to have you come," she said again in welcome. "I'm afraid the house is always a mess, but please just ignore it. My husband should be back any minute. He had some business to take care of up at the farmers' co-op. So, how are the folks in Senbashi? Are they well? Between our grandson getting married and the harvest, I'm afraid we've just been too busy to pay them a visit."

As she listened to the words pouring out in a single uninterrupted stream, Shizuka decided Miharu must have inherited her talkativeness from her mother. When Miharu left for the kitchen saying she would make some tea, Satoko began asking Asafumi about recent goings-on at the Nonezawa household.

Shizuka sat as quietly as a doll, gazing blankly out the open veranda doors. Beyond the camellias and azaleas and plum trees in the garden rose a bank of blue mountains. She noticed some deflected light between the trees – arced like a small rainbow and disappearing among the leaves. She watched the light flicker for several moments, until her heart skipped a beat when branches suddenly began to shake and an old man stepped out from behind. He walked toward the house, adjusting the front of his trousers as he came. Bare scalp showed through his thinning gray hair and he had a bit of a stoop, but he was a broad-shouldered man of sturdy build, with a square jaw and flat face that positively glowed with health. His eyes looked as though they were glued permanently in a smiling expression.

Just as Shizuka realized that the little rainbow had been this man peeing in the bushes, Satoko's voice rang out. "There you are, Grandpa! Kōichirō's brother is here. He has something he wants to ask you. Come join us."

His walk was bowlegged as he approached. There was white stubble on his chin.

"Oh, is that right, is that right, you're Kōichirō's brother, are you? It's good of you to visit us way out here in the sticks," he said, his broad grin revealing several missing teeth.

With a polite bow, Asafumi introduced himself and Shizuka. Once they'd gone through the usual exchanges involved in such meetings, he got straight to the point. "I came by today because Miharu said you might be able to tell me something about Mandala Road."

Grandpa Mitsuharu sat down on the edge of the veranda. "Mandala Road, eh?" he said, rubbing his stubbly chin. All eyes were focused on him. He looked off into the distance and thrust out his lower lip as if pondering something. The geniality he'd shown a moment before seemed to have vanished.

He sat for so long without saying anything that Satoko spoke up again. "I thought you knew all the roads around here from when you used to work as a guide."

Mitsuharu finally twisted his head around to look at Asafumi. "What makes you so interested in Mandala Road?" he asked.

Asafumi explained about the old notebook they'd found.

"So you're thinking of trying to sell medicine kits? I'm pretty sure most of the villages out that way have been abandoned. Wouldn't surprise me if there weren't any left at all."

99

"That's what I'd like to find out. The register mentions places like Magawa, and Senninhara, and Dobō."

Old Mitsuharu stroked his chin with a blue-veined hand as he nodded at each name Asafumi mentioned.

"Uh-huh, uh-huh," he said. "Those names used to come up quite a bit, I remember. The village in front of Awasuno Station was called Magawa. It's all gone now, the station and everything, but that used to be where Mandala Road started."

"So where exactly do I need to go to find the road now?" Asafumi asked, his voice rising with enthusiasm.

Mitsuharu looked away and fell silent again, gazing out at the garden. He seemed reluctant to answer, and Shizuka found herself wondering why. Then suddenly he turned to her.

"Are you going, too?"

She quickly shook her head, and he nodded.

"That's good to hear," he said. "Tateyama's always been no women allowed."

As Shizuka was puzzling over what to make of this antiquated notion, Miharu entered with the tea things on a tray, laughing.

"Don't be silly, Grandpa," she said. "Your head must still be in the Edo Period. These days lots of women go all the way to the summit shrine."

Mitsuharu gave Asafumi a look of exaggerated dismay. "I guess it's just like they say: all that's got stronger since the war is socks and women."

Asafumi shifted in his seat, not knowing how to respond.

"In any case, Grandpa, he needs you to show him where he can find Mandala Road," Satoko said, setting some paper and a felt-tipped pen on the veranda in front of him. "Here, you can draw him a map."

He still seemed to hesitate for a moment, but then picked up the pen and started sketching.

"This is Awasuno, which is a little ways up the river from here, over on the other side. When you get there, you need to take this road, and then when you get to about here, I think, you should find a turnoff that heads deeper into the mountains."

It was such a crude map that Shizuka had her doubts about its usefulness. The old man was apparently drawing only the old logging roads. If Miharu hadn't elbowed in to show where the paved roads were, Asafumi probably wouldn't have been able to make head or tail of the diagram.

Running out of space, Mitsuharu reached for another piece of paper. He extended the winding road onto this second sheet, and at the end wrote "YAKUSHIDAKE".

"You're kidding," Miharu said in surprise. "Mandala Road ends up on top of Yakushidake?"

Her grandfather tossed the pen aside and said, "That's right," then turned to Asafumi. "Have you ever been up Yakushi?"

"No."

"Out around Arimine, which is underwater now because of the dam, they used to say you're not a man until you've climbed Yakushi. I suggest you forget about Mandala Road and just go climb the mountain instead. Take the normal route, starting from Murodō and following the ridgeline through Goshikigahara to Yakushi. There's nothing quite like the view you get from there – you see all these mountaintops poking through the clouds like islands in the ocean. I could show you the way if you like."

Miharu gave him a playful slap on the shoulder. "There you go again, Grandpa. You know you don't take people up the mountains anymore."

"What're you talking about? There's still plenty of spring left in these here legs."

"Have you forgotten about that tumble you took from a rock when you went fishing not so long ago?" she fired back.

"With a granddaughter like you, who needs enemies?" he groused, and everybody burst out laughing.

But even as light-heartedness spread all around her, Shizuka couldn't help wondering why he had seemed so intent on discouraging Asafumi from exploring Mandala Road.

15

Rentarō found a house for Saya. It was a small farmhouse in a rice-growing area not far from town. He had a business connection to thank for being able to find a place at a time when so many others made homeless by the Toyama air raids were in the hunt as well. A war widow had been living there with her children. But raising two young ones as a single mother was proving to be too much of a struggle, especially with the constant shortages, so she'd decided to move back in with her parents and put the place up for rent. Rentarō's brother was a little peeved when he first learned of the find, since he'd been searching for a place much longer than him. But then he discovered that it was a thirty-minute walk from town, making it inconvenient even for getting to Senbashi, let alone to downtown Toyama where he worked, and his envy quickly ebbed.

The news that Saya would be leaving eased some of the tensions that had built in the Nonezawa household. Rentarō's mother was suddenly seized with generosity toward the woman who now faced the task of setting up house for herself and a small child in an alien land: she quickly put together an odd assortment of dishes, cooking utensils and bedding they no longer needed and gave them to Saya to use. On a sunny, late-autumn day, the items were loaded onto a cart and Saya left Senbashi behind.

Rentarō pulled the cart as Saya walked along beside him, holding her suitcase in one hand and Isamu's hand in the other – just as she'd done when they first arrived in Japan. After trudging past a seemingly endless succession of old wood-frame houses crouched shoulder to shoulder along narrow streets, they finally emerged into open countryside. Even at this early hour, farmers were already hard at work in the fields; hanging freshly cut rice to dry here, threshing already dried sheaves there.

Saya had remained holed up inside the house almost the entire time she'd been in Senbashi, and this was her first trip outside the town. Her pace slackened as she looked around curiously at everything she saw.

The harvested rice paddies gave way in the distance to dark forests, which rose up the sides of the mountains beyond. The steep peaks visible even farther off were white on top. She asked Rentarō what the white was.

"Snow," he said.

She had never seen snow before, but she did know the word. It was supposed to be fluffy, like cotton, but icy cold, and when the sun shone on it, it would turn into water. Now she gazed up at the white-topped summits in the distance and wondered exactly what all that meant.

Rentarō noticed her staring at the mountains and laughed. "It won't be long now, you'll get to see all the snow you want, and more," he said. "Winter's right around the corner."

This was another word Saya didn't really comprehend. Winter, she'd heard, was when the days got really cold. But to her, days were either rainy or sunny, and the notion of a time of year that was cold and snowy didn't quite register. As a matter of fact, she'd been shivering from the cold already. She understood that this was only autumn, and winter was supposed to be even worse, but she had a hard time imagining what it meant to be worse than this.

"The climate here is different from Malaya. It affects the way we live and the kind of people we are." With the cart rumbling behind him, Rentarō spoke as if explaining things to a child. "Are you sure you'll be okay by yourself with the boy? You have to realize I won't be able to come see you all that often."

"I be okay," she said. She'd been finding her way through the jungle all her life. She was confident she could find her way here, too.

A house came into view. Beyond it stood a grove of trees, protecting it from the wind, and the other three sides of the property were surrounded by a hedge. As they passed between decaying gateposts into the front yard, she saw that the place was really quite small – perhaps half the size of the house she and Rentarō had had in Kota Bharu. It was an old building, with a thatched roof, its siding weathered completely black. But it was obviously much sturdier than the makeshift huts she'd been used to in the jungle. Plus there was land all around it for growing vegetables.

With Isamu's hand still in hers, Saya walked solemnly toward the house.

"It may not look like much, but there're lots of people who'd jump at the chance to live here. We're lucky we found anything at all," Rentarō said as if making excuses. He seemed to think she was put off by how run-down the place looked.

"I like this house, Mr. Ren," she called to him from behind as he pulled the cart around the corner and up to the veranda.

He returned to unlock the front door. Saya peered over his shoulder into a dirt-floored room. She could see in the dim light that there was a small kitchen area at the back. Rentarō took off his shoes and stepped up onto the tatami in the next room to slide open the rain shutters enclosing the veranda. The house had one more tatami room behind the first and that was all.

Rentarō began pulling things off of the cart by the veranda and hauling them into the house – a set of futons, a saucepan, a few dishes and other household items tied up in a cloth bundle, plus enough food to last perhaps two or three days. In almost no time at all she was moved in.

While Isamu amused himself pushing the empty cart around the yard, Rentarō sat down on the veranda and fished a cigarette from the pocket of his rumpled suit jacket.

"Well," he said after lighting up, "I think we've got you pretty well covered for basic necessities, but the real question is going to be food."

Saya knelt down beside him. He was certainly right about that: food was her first and foremost worry. She'd heard about all the shortages since the war. Back at the Senbashi house, Tomijirō's wife and a neighbour woman were talking outside the fence one day about what a big help U.S. relief supplies had been, jokingly saying *Thank you, O beneficent ones!* She was shocked to hear them sounding as though they'd kiss their American masters' feet just for getting a few bites to eat from them. Sure, food was important. But you didn't give up your soul for it. Food from your enemy was like bait in the traps her people set to catch animals in the forest. No one in her tribe back home would be so quick to accept food from anybody they'd once fought. Anything like that would be looked at with a very suspicious eye. If these people really felt so grateful for the aid of those who defeated them in the war, it meant they'd sold their souls for food.

"Do you have any money?" Rentarō asked a little hesitantly, broaching an awkward subject.

"Only a little," Saya said in a low voice. She'd been spared having to spend very much during the time she was in Senbashi, but the better part of what she'd received in Ujina was already gone.

Frowning as if he'd expected as much, he took a drag on his cigarette.

"For the time being, until you get settled, I'll plan to bring you what I can from the house, but eventually you'll have to get a garden going and grow your own food."

He was looking past the small area in front of the veranda to what had obviously been a large vegetable patch. The owner of the property had stripped it clean before moving away, and all that was left now was the furrowed brown earth.

"Yes," Saya said. Her family had always had vegetable plots next to their huts in the jungle. Growing food had been part of her life since she was a little girl.

"And if you've got any kind of document that says who you are, you need to give it to me. I'll take it down to the Rationing Department and see if I can get some coupons for you. Though there's no telling whether they'll give somebody from Malaya the same treatment as regular citizens."

"It's no problem. I have this," Saya said, opening her suitcase to take out her Repatriation Certificate. She handed it to him. "Now I am this person."

Rentarō studied it for several moments. "Who's Kim Suk-hwa?" he finally asked.

"A person I meet in Kota Bharu," she said simply, and seeing that he was about to ask for further elaboration, she headed him off by adding, "She is dead person, so no worries."

It was clear that Saya did not want to talk about it, so somewhat grudgingly he let the matter drop. "Well," he said as he slipped her certificate into his jacket pocket, "even if she was Korean, she was born in Japan, so if this is who you are now, I'd think there's a good chance I can get you the coupons. I'll take this in and do the paperwork for you."

He tossed the stub of his cigarette into the yard and stood up. Realizing he was about to leave, Saya grabbed the edge of his jacket. He folded his hand over hers and said, "I have to go. I'll never hear the end of it if I'm away too long." He gently stroked her cheek as she made a sad face. "I'll be back tomorrow, okay?" he added.

She nodded forlornly like a child, and he started for home, pulling the empty cart behind him.

Once he was gone, the sadness slowly ebbed from Saya's face. Stretching as she rose to her feet, she surveyed her new domain in the bright, late-morning sun. Isamu had already gone to explore the grove of trees beyond the garden. The furrowed ground extended around the other sides of the house, too. With this much land, she could definitely make a new life for herself and her little boy.

Exactly what kind of life it might be, she had no way of knowing. For the moment, she remained torn between her conflicting feelings for Rentarō. But now that she had at least left that gloomy house behind, she thought she saw a glimmer of light coming into view.

Might she actually be able to make a fresh start with Rentarō in this place?

Feeling as reinvigorated as spring leaves after a rain, she set about putting her new home in order.

16

Asafumi started the engine as Shizuka dropped into the passenger seat beside him. Miharu had agreed to take the Yasudas' SUV and lead the way to where Mandala Road started. Once they got to the turnoff, Shizuka would switch cars and double back with Miharu. Asafumi had his window down and was in the middle of thanking Miharu's parents for a delicious lunch when the SUV pulled out, and he was grateful to be freed from a lengthy round of farewell courtesies.

As he set off in pursuit, Shizuka said, "A bit heavy on the salt, don't you think?"

It took him a moment to realize she was talking about the food Satoko had served them for lunch. At times like this, Asafumi could see the woman in his wife showing through. She was incapable of visiting another woman's house without making some comment about her performance as mistress of the household. Whether she approved or disapproved of what she'd observed wasn't the point. She invariably saw herself in competition with her.

"You think so? I thought it was all pretty good," he said, with perhaps a little more emphasis than was strictly necessary if he hadn't had an urge to tweak his wife's competitive streak.

"Oh, I didn't mean it wasn't good. I just thought it was a tiny bit on the salty side."

It wasn't like Shizuka to backpedal. She'd always been one to speak her mind without mincing words. But it seemed to him that she had withdrawn into herself and was holding back more since their move to Toyama. This morning was a good example – the way she'd clammed up when he objected to her suggestion that he check out the hot spring situation. Before this, he'd have expected her to push right back with a quick retort, like *What's so wrong with mixing business and pleasure?* But somewhere inside her, the gears weren't engaging the way they used to, and their discordant grinding was beginning to grate on him.

He pulled a cassette from the stack of tapes he'd thrown into the car and pushed it into the player without even looking at what it was. A lilting Elton John tune began playing through the speakers and it had an immediate calming effect on him.

Miharu led them out of the cosy village along the edge of a bluff overlooking the river, driving straight toward the heart of the Tateyama Range. The higher elevations on both sides were beginning to show some autumn colours. Several ski lifts climbed the side of the mountain across the river as if attached there by giant staples. The slopes of Awasuno awaited the arrival of winter.

"You regret that we ever came to Toyama, don't you?" Asafumi said, deciding to broach a subject that had been weighing on his mind recently.

Shizuka paused only the briefest moment before answering. "I suppose so."

"But you were originally in favour of coming, you know."

"I know." There was irritation in her voice. "Have I complained?"

Yes, you have, he thought. Maybe not verbally, but with your whole being.

"How about you? Now that you've finished that course, are you all fired up about becoming a drug salesman?"

He wasn't quite sure how to respond to this return jab. The course was just a bunch of classroom lectures. He hadn't actually gone out on the road to approach prospective customers yet. It was probably like boning up for the written test to get a driver's license – which is to say, a far cry from the real thing.

"I really couldn't say yet," he answered.

She grunted ambiguously and sank back into her seat with a frown.

Their conversation came to a halt, and Asafumi reached over to turn up the music. The mellow strains of the Elton John love song made him feel sentimental. He and Shizuka had never run out of things to talk about before, from new developments in their research to the latest gossip about their colleagues. Even after losing their jobs, they'd shared their uncertainties about the future and discussed what they needed to do. Now, since coming to Toyama, they'd lost their sense of common footing. By returning to the town where he grew up and taking the first steps toward joining the family business, Asafumi had found a new foothold for himself, but the ground under Shizuka's feet had simply caved in and vanished. He remembered hearing somewhere or other that one of the most important things for couples in their old age was to find a hobby they could enjoy together. Maybe that was what the two of them needed now, he thought wryly – a shared hobby.

He'd really been looking forward to this trip. It wasn't actually going to take him so far away that he couldn't make it back the same day, but he knew the idea of staying overnight somewhere was prompted by the desire for a break from the awkwardness he felt in their new life together. In fact, even before Shizuka opened her mouth, he had secretly been thinking he might take the opportunity to soak his tired bones in a hot spring somewhere. So when she suggested precisely the same idea, it felt as though she'd caught him red-handed, and he'd snapped back at her out of guilt.

Up ahead on the right, a brand-new bridge painted bright red came into view, and Miharu's turn signal began flashing. Asafumi hit his signal too. Then, just as he was making the turn onto the bridge, Shizuka said something he couldn't catch.

"What'd you say?" he asked, quickly lowering the music.

"Nothing," she said. With the car suddenly much quieter, she seemed hesitant to speak up again.

"Come on," he said impatiently. "What?"

"It's really nothing."

In that case you shouldn't have said anything to begin with, he thought. She was holding back again, and it was getting on his nerves.

The two vehicles started across the bridge. They could see the Jōganji River flowing down the middle of the broad, rock-strewn bed far below. After staring at the clear blue surface of the water for several moments, Shizuka seemed to change her mind.

"Every time we see your mother, she's on my back about having a baby."

"That's nothing new. It's been her constant refrain since we first got married." Shizuka's own refrain had been that there was no way she could consider having a child yet, and Asafumi knew she felt badgered, but he tried to brush it off. "You know how old women are. They always have to be grumbling about something. Just let it go."

Shizuka continued without smiling. "Maybe you could find a convenient time to let it slip that I might not be able to have children at all."

"Are you serious?" He turned to look at her in surprise. She was staring straight ahead, her face like stone.

"Think about it. We haven't been using any precautions since we got married, and even after all this time I'm still not pregnant."

He realized for the first time that Shizuka was having genuine doubts about her fertility.

"I read that people today aren't as fertile as before, so it's not just us," he said. "It used to be common for men to have sperm counts over a hundred million per millilitre, but nowadays I guess the average is only between twenty and fifty."

He was repeating what he'd picked up recently in a magazine article. He'd also learned that the World Health Organization defined less than twenty million as "oligozoospermia", meaning low sperm count, and wondered with a shudder if he might be included in that group, but he chose not to mention this.

"Tell your mother that, too," she said.

Shizuka always referred to Takiko as "your mother." She never said "Mother", and avoided addressing her that way even when they were with her. Her stubbornness about this was something else that had been bugging Asafumi lately.

"All right. After I get back," he said. It was easiest at this point just to agree.

Why couldn't she be a little more like the cheerful, easygoing person in that car up ahead? he thought to himself. He'd really enjoyed his chat with Miharu this morning, when she was sitting where Shizuka sat now. The girl he'd dated for two years in college had had a bright and sunny personality, too. Cheerful as ever, she'd come to him one day and told him she'd found someone else.

His attraction to Shizuka was, in a way, a reaction to that experience. Having been let down by a cheerful, easygoing girl, he'd swung to the opposite extreme and chosen someone serious and high-strung. Now he found himself being drawn again to the other type. It was pathetic.

The road climbed into wooded mountain terrain. They entered a reforested stand of cypress, and soon after that a smaller road forked off to one side. Miharu took the turn. She drove on through the dim light under the forest canopy for a short distance and then came to a stop. Asafumi pulled up behind her. As he and Shizuka got out, Miharu emerged from the SUV, and they all gathered in the middle of the road.

"If Grandpa's map is right, this should be Mandala Road," Miharu said, pointing downward.

Asafumi peered through the shade at the road leading on into the mountains. It was narrow, but at least it was paved, and he'd seen no signs posted saying the road was closed farther on, so he could assume the way was clear. If he drove for a while and failed to find anything, all he had to do was turn around. He thanked Miharu for showing him this far.

"If you're late getting back, my folks said you're welcome to spend the night in Ashikuraji," she said. She looked at Shizuka. "Shall we be going then?" She moved toward her car.

"Drive carefully on these mountain roads," Shizuka said before turning to follow.

As he watched her go, in her jeans and jacket, she looked like a tiny wire figure beneath the cypress trees towering overhead.

He got back behind the wheel of the Volkswagen and switched on the ignition. The SUV pulled up to a bend in the road a short distance ahead and stopped to turn around. Miharu waved for him to pass, so he slipped on by, glancing in the rear-view mirror and giving his horn a single short toot as he set off on his way through the semi-darkness of the forest.

17

Shizuka was in a glum mood as she watched the blue car pulling away. She knew there was a gap between what she had said to Asafumi and how she really felt, and it left a sour taste in her mouth. The problem was that she hadn't been able to figure out even for herself what her true feelings were.

Miharu finished turning the car around and headed back the way they had come. After leaving the cypress forest behind, they drove on between a dense growth of trees beginning to change colour. Miharu deftly steered the SUV around curves hemmed in on both sides by thick foliage.

"Wow," Shizuka said. "I guess I shouldn't be surprised since you drive a cab, but you sure know how to handle a vehicle."

Miharu gave a little chuckle. "I've always loved driving. Being able to take myself anywhere I want," she said, keeping her eyes on the road. "But you should have seen the reaction I got when I announced I wanted to drive a cab. Kōichirō and Dad both thought it was ridiculous. 'Cause they have this preconceived notion about women being lousy drivers."

"I hate to say it, but that notion does actually fit in my case. I could be the poster model."

Shizuka thought back to when she first obtained her license and began driving on her own. It seemed to her like an endless string of close calls. The stress just wasn't worth it, she decided, and she gave it up.

"It's a matter of confidence," Miharu said. "That's what I figure when I see some woman driving erratically around town. It's like they think all the other drivers and pedestrians are watching their every move, you know, so they're driving on eggshells, trying not to make a mistake, but that's exactly what makes them do such stupid things. I figure they're probably the same way at home, worrying what their husbands or in-laws think of everything they do."

"And you don't?" The question popped out before Shizuka could even think.

Miharu burst out laughing. "Oh, sure, I'm that way too," she said. The car emerged from the forest and the view opened up as they arrived back at the Awasuno ski area. She stepped on the accelerator. "The difference with me is knowing I don't need to worry about that when I'm driving. I know nobody's looking over my shoulder. With these other Nervous Nellies, it's like they've got their husbands or in-laws right there in the car with them all the time."

Shizuka wondered if that was how she used to drive, too – as if someone was constantly looking over her shoulder. It was before she got married, so she wasn't worried yet about what her husband thought. But she'd certainly been on pins and needles. She'd always assumed it was from not knowing when or where someone might jump out in front of her – fear of the genuine dangers involved in operating a car. But maybe it came from a more generalized sense that the whole world was watching over her shoulder.

"So how exactly do you keep from taking your husband and in-laws along with you?" she asked.

Miharu remained silent as she reached the end of the bridge across the Jōganji River and turned onto the main road leading back to Ashikuraji. There was almost no oncoming traffic.

"Maybe it's my family background," she finally said when she finished shifting up again. "I imagine you noticed. We're female dominant. I guess Grandpa could hold his own as a mountain guide, but at home he's always been pretty quiet, never throws his weight around the slightest bit, and since my dad married into my mom's family, she always kept him under her thumb, too."

"You were lucky." There was a note of genuine envy in her voice.

"My grandma told me once before she died that Grandpa had a hot temper and got into lots of fights when he was younger. But somewhere along the way he settled down, so it worked out all right."

"Sometimes people can be really different on the inside from the way they seem on the outside," Shizuka said thoughtfully. She was remembering how her own father had lorded it over her mother. And to all appearances, her mother had always been the submissive wife. It wasn't until she sued her father for divorce on grounds of adultery, when Shizuka was in college, that it became clear just how much resentment had been building up under the surface all those years. She demanded a huge settlement, and since he knew he was at fault, he paid what she asked. When she turned around and opened a second-hand shop with the money, it became equally clear that her plans had been several years in the making. Shizuka recalled the shock she'd felt when she realized what a calculating woman her mother was – secretly planning her life after divorce while still playing her half of the harmonious couple who never went through the slightest rough patch in their marriage. No doubt her own attitude toward male-female relationships had been shaped very much by her parents' breakup. The sense of togetherness she'd observed in Miharu's family was exactly what she'd once believed she had in her own, only to have that faith betrayed.

"But marrying into the Nonezawa family was like returning to the Middle Ages," Miharu said as she rounded a bend with a practiced touch. "When your mother-in-law's the type who kowtows to her husband with both hands to the tatami, you really have to find a way to get out of the house and breathe some fresh air – like driving a cab."

"I had a feeling it was something like that. That's exactly why I hate having to visit," Shizuka said.

Miharu rolled her eyes. "I hear you," she said, and they exchanged conspiratorial smiles.

They arrived in Ashikuraji. Souvenir shops dotted both sides of the road as it made its way through the village. With the Tateyama Museum located here in addition to the Oyama Shrine, quite a few tourists could be seen walking about even on a weekday. Slowing the car, Miharu suggested they stop for some sightseeing before going back to the house. With no objections from Shizuka, she pulled into a parking lot a short way back from the main street. As they headed for the cedar-shaded grounds, Miharu reminded Shizuka that this was part of the same shrine they'd driven past in Iwakuraji.

"According to Grandpa, during the Edo Period, missionaries went out from here all over the country to promote pilgrimages to Tateyama. Between keeping up with farm work and taking care of the pilgrims who came to climb the mountain, summers were pretty busy, so they'd go during the winter, taking with them mandala paintings of Tateyama to illustrate their talks, as well as a supply of talismans to sell. They also took orders for burial shrouds and brought along medicines as gifts for their hosts along the way. They didn't actually collect payment for the shrouds until they came back with the goods the following year, and apparently it was this whole mix of things that, in the end, led to Toyama's medicine peddlers and the way they operate. So actually, my family has some longstanding connections with the business, too."

Miharu offered a crisp summary of the history as they walked through the humid grounds.

"When there're plenty of other mountains to climb all over the country, what makes Tateyama so special that people would want to come here?" Shizuka asked.

"Oh, that's easy," Miharu said, stopping to lean close to her. "It's because this is where hell is."

Shizuka's eyes widened in surprise, and Miharu burst out laughing.

"According to legend, of course," she said. "But even now, if you look at copies of the Tateyama Mandala being sold at the pilgrims' lodges here, you'll see scenes from hell painted in at the foot of the mountain. There're children stacking pebbles in the Riverbed of Sai, women falling into a pool of blood, sinners being burned alive or forced by devils to swallow molten metal – a whole bunch of different scenes of torture. I guess those were the images of hell people had way back when, and they believed that if they visited Tateyama's Hell Valley and then climbed Mount Oyama to worship at the summit shrine, they could go home knowing they would be reborn in the Pure Land Paradise when they died."

By this time the two women had emerged from the shrine grounds and come to a small river spanned by an arched bridge with vermilion railings. Miharu stopped at its foot.

"Look, you can see the whole range from here," she said, lifting her hand toward the string of peaks stretching across the clear autumn sky. Patches of colour were beginning to show here and there.

Shizuka raised her eyes in the direction she was pointing. Asafumi was somewhere in those mountains now, she thought to herself.

"This is known as the Cloth Bridge," Miharu said as she wrapped her hand around the little *stupa*-like ornamentation on top of the railing post. "It was traditionally supposed to be the bridge to salvation for women. Otherwise, according to the old beliefs, women fell into Hell's Pool of Blood when they died. But since they weren't allowed in the mountains, they couldn't climb through Hell Valley to the top of Oyama to pray for salvation the way men could. So instead they were offered a path to salvation through a ceremony held here called the Cloth Bridge Rite. On the autumn equinox each year, thousands of women got dressed in white kimonos and crossed from the Lord of Hell Hall on one side to the Granny Uba Hall on the other. They walked on rolls of white cloth spread on the ground and over the bridge all the way between the two halls, and I guess it was a pretty impressive sight. Participants apparently got some kind of certificate that promised they'd be reborn in paradise. Of course, anybody who wanted in had to pay a pile of money for the privilege. As they say, money talks even at the gates of hell."

Standing on the bridge, Shizuka thought about the women who'd walked across it praying for a place in heaven, believing that the very expensive rite was the only way they could be saved from the Pool of Blood. They'd been duped. They let themselves be taken in by a religion concocted by men, and all they'd really done was help fill the temple coffers.

"So you were condemned to the Pool of Blood just for being born a woman? That doesn't seem very fair, does it?" she said dryly, while thinking how absolutely infuriating it was.

"You can say that again," Miharu burst out as she came up beside her. Together they gazed down over the railing at the water.

They heard a voice behind them. "Here it is! Here it is! The bridge!"

A rotund, oily-faced man getting on past middle age had come up behind them accompanied by a group of three men and two women, all probably in their twenties. The older man was obviously the boss. The two women were tripping along on either side of him in matching leopard-print miniskirts and platform boots; their hairstyles and makeup matched as well, but their features were far too different for them to be twins, or even sisters. They were clamouring that they wanted to go for ice cream.

"Wow! You get a really great view of Tateyama from here."

The boss's remark prompted the three young men to turn toward the mountains, but their eyes said they couldn't have cared less, and the two girls just went on chattering without the slightest awareness of their surroundings. They all trooped on across the bridge without even pausing.

They could have been sex-shop workers on a company holiday. After the group was out of earshot, Miharu said with disgust, "No matter how old they get, men are such suckers for the hot young things. Maybe they came up with that story about the Pool of Blood because they're actually afraid of the effect we women have on them."

"How do you mean?" Shizuka asked with interest. She had been leaning over the railing, watching the water flow by below.

"With us around, they're always too horny to get into paradise. But if they send us off to hell, they can all be saved."

Bringing her palms down with an emphatic slap, she pushed herself away from the railing. Shizuka fell in step beside her, and they proceeded across the bridge. They came to a small structure on the other side.

"This is the Granny Uba Hall," Miharu said. "It's Granny Uba's miraculous powers that supposedly make it possible for women to get into paradise, too."

Inside the building was a timeworn wooden statue dressed in a white robe – a gnarled old woman sitting with one knee raised. There were deep creases in her forehead, and she stared back at you with big, sunken eyes in a face painted dark red. Shizuka thought she looked more like someone trying to scare people off, not usher them into paradise.

"According to legend, Granny Uba came down here to earth bringing seeds with her for different kinds of grain and hemp. Then, after she died, she became the god in charge of our passage from life to death."

"So a woman can't get into heaven, but she can become a god?"

"Wow, I never thought of that before," Miharu said, her eyes going wide. "And if you're a god, falling into a pool of blood should be no big deal."

"That's right."

Standing there in front of the small worship hall, Miharu folded her hands as if in prayer and called out playfully, "O dear Granny Uba, won't you please turn *me* into a god, too?"

18

The morning of the first snow, Saya thought she must have died. The whole world had turned a glistening white – from the ground in front of the veranda to the bamboo in the corner of the garden, the rice fields beyond the hedge, and the mountains in the distance. Where could this be but the world of the dead? A deep hush was in the air. Drawn by the stillness, she started to step down into the yard. An icy chill stung her bare foot like a burn, and she quickly drew it back. She must still be alive after all, she thought. She noticed that a small, fluffy white drift had formed at the end of the veranda, so she took a pinch of it and put it on her tongue. When it quickly melted into water she knew this had to be what they called snow. She took a deep breath, inhaling the air of the miraculous event she could never have experienced in Malaya. A smell like burying her face in a clump of sigh grass filled her lungs.

People don't actually die so easily, she thought.

She had died a thousand deaths at the P-house in Kota Bharu. But she had also come away from each of those deaths knowing that she was still alive.

The house had been set up by the Japanese army to serve the troops occupying the area. It was located in the jungle just outside of town, in a compound surrounded by a chain-link fence. There, in a long row of tiny, cell-like rooms constructed crudely of *nipa* palm and banana leaves, Saya was forced to let Japanese soldiers have their way with her day after day.

They were hellish days. The parade of soldiers went on endlessly from morning to night. One after another they came, thrusting their swollen organs into her the moment they arrived. She was convinced it would kill her – that she would die by the penis.

Constant surveillance ruled out any chance of flight. The boss was Japanese – a civilian. Seven of the girls were Korean, and there was just one other Malayan besides herself. She'd been offered a job working for the occupying forces, and it had turned out to be this.

Even on a slow day, Saya had to service at least ten men, and the number could easily jump to twenty. The army required the men to use condoms, but most of them insisted on going unsheathed. Never mind if she was still dripping with semen from her last customer, they rammed themselves into her without the slightest care. If she made any fuss, they would jab her with their swords, or burn her with cigarettes inside her thighs or on her neck. Crying out in pain only made them laugh.

They must be evil spirits, thought Saya. The evil spirits that haunted the forest, coming to torment her here as unshaven men with military haircuts in grimy uniforms.

She felt as if she'd wandered into the forest of no return. It was a place filled with horrible demons, and once you set foot in it, you could never find your way out. You would just walk on and on until your strength gave out and you fell down dead. That's what her people said.

She wanted nothing so much as to rip the men's cocks off at the root. If only she had some blades between her legs, she thought. But all she had was a soft hole, toothless as a baby's mouth. When the men pushed her knees apart and forced their way into her, she could only wail in distress, helpless as a newborn.

"We're nothing but toilet holes to them."

That's what Kim Suk-hwa had said. She was Korean, but she'd been assigned the Japanese name Ayako, and she spoke fluent Japanese. Once she discovered that Saya had picked up quite a bit of the language, too, she began sharing her woes with her whenever they were given a break to take a bath or do their wash.

"Just for helping with wounded soldiers and their laundry, I'd get a regular salary, room and board, and even nice clothes to wear – that's what the sweet-talking cop told me when he got me to come. The lying bastard. Instead they locked me up in a place no bigger than a prison cell so twenty and thirty guys could do their business on me every day.

"And believe it or not, we've actually got it easy here. Just be glad you're not on the front lines somewhere. This is happy tunes by comparison. You should've seen what I had to go through in China. The room and board they promised turned out to be a tiny cubicle with a filthy straw mat and a couple of lousy rice balls I had to gulp down while guys were coming on top of me, and all I got to wear was the sweat and grime that rubbed off their skin. By the time the boss took his cut, the pay was next to nothing, too. I could be passing out, with my twat swollen up like a balloon from being poked all day long, and the men wouldn't give a damn. They'd just climb right on and let it squirt. That's why I say we're nothing but toilets to them. Living, breathing toilet holes. Hey, suck my dick, bitch; hey, open up and show me your twat, bitch; hey, let me feel inside, bitch – there was nothing they didn't want. And the officers, they were the worst, acting so high and mighty. Fucking me with their sword, or making me do it with their dog while they sat there watching, thinking it was funny. No human heart beat in those chests, that's for sure. And if their precious toilet didn't act just the way they wanted, then the shit would really hit the fan. They'd come at you with their swords actually bared or beat you till your bones broke – worse than they'd ever treat a dog. A lot of the girls brought in with me got sick and died, and some decided to end their misery themselves. Once in a blue moon you'd get a guy making excuses, trying to be nice. *It's the war, the war's made us all go a bit wild, all we're looking for is some comfort.* But if you ask me, anybody who loses it that easy isn't much of a man to begin with. Oh, yeah, I had some young kids who put their hands together to thank me afterwards, saying now they could die without regrets. But even guys like that, they didn't really see me as a person. I was still just a shithole. They were thanking the god of privies for letting them take a good dump and feel all refreshed inside before they went off to die."

Though Korean by blood, she'd been born and raised in Japan, speaking more Japanese than Korean, so when given a chance to unload in her more familiar tongue, all the bitterness pent up inside came pouring out with the force of rainforest rivers during the monsoon and buried Saya up to her knees, her waist, her chest in torrents of rancorous mud.

"You're lucky because at least you're in your own country," Suk-hwa said. "The rest of us are so far away from home, where could we possibly run? Those Japanese bastards. I've never hated anybody like I hate them. They're all devils!"

"But not everybody from Japan is same," Saya objected, thinking of Rentarō.

Suk-hwa snorted. "Sure they are."

"Some men not soldiers are nice. I know one man, he is very kind to me."

"So what happened to him? Where's he now?" Suk-hwa mocked.

"He go to Japan. He will come back soon to get me and my son."

Suk-hwa opened her mouth wide and laughed. With several chipped teeth in front, she somehow managed to look both creepy and sexy at the same time.

"Once a man's gone home to Japan, there's no way he's coming back to get you," she said.

"Maybe he not come now, but he come when war is little bit quiet down," Saya insisted.

"Don't kid yourself. I know what Japanese men are like. I'm a P-girl. I'm the hole they polish their poles in. I've rubbed hundreds and thousands of their poles with my insides. I know them through and through – literally."

She briefly seemed to turn her scorn on herself before continuing as before.

"I don't care how nice the guy is – put him in a uniform and send him to the front, and he'll be the same as the rest. Do you have any idea what the bastards did in China? I overheard some officers talking about it once. They went on a rampage and massacred tens of thousands of civilians, maybe hundreds of thousands – even babies and old people. And the officers were boasting about it. Proud of themselves. That's what they do – they kill people. With their swords in the countries they invade, with their pricks in these fucking P-houses. If they have any hearts at all, they're made of razor steel. And they can't get enough of how it feels to jab that steel into human flesh."

It was true. Every time a soldier stuck his penis in her, it was like being split open with a sword. And each time was like a separate death. At some point, there'd be one too many, and she wouldn't be able to drag herself back to life. Two of the P-girls died while Saya was at the compound – one from a miscarriage, the other simply from the endless, brutal sex. If her brother hadn't rescued her when the third full moon came around, she would almost certainly have followed in their footsteps. By agreeing to spy for the Japanese, Kekah had managed to find out where she was being held. Then he played up to one of the guards and got him to let her escape under the cover of darkness. Still, all that she'd been forced to endure in that compound remained branded deeply in her skin; she knew it would never be worn completely away...

"Mommy?"

She heard Isamu calling to her through the open veranda doors. Rising to go back inside, she crawled under the covers again in their shared futon.

"Look, Isamu. Snow. This is what's called snow," she said, gazing out at their white surroundings.

Isamu's eyes popped wide as he turned to look outside, and suddenly he was clinging to her in fright.

In the coming weeks, Saya began to think that, even without knowing what snow was, the boy had instinctively sensed what its arrival meant, for the season that followed was one of many hardships. Much of the time they spent shivering from the cold. They made trips to the river to gather firewood for the hearth in their dirt-floored kitchen. The neighbours got theirs from a communal woodland nearby, but as an outsider, Saya didn't have the courage to join them. Even little Isamu carried his share as together they made their way home, weighed down by the driftwood they tied with straw rope to their backs. But others came to the river as well, mainly wartime evacuees from the cities, and there wasn't nearly enough to go around. When they could find no sticks to burn, Saya and Isamu huddled together under the bedclothes to keep each other warm.

Winter also brought a drop in the supply of food. Rentarō had registered them for coupons entitling them to inexpensive rations, but the amounts were still far too little. They could never have survived without the food and supplies he brought them every four or five days. When they went to pick up firewood, Saya also searched the riverbanks for plants that might be edible. She was willing to try anything that didn't look too tough. The practices she'd learned from the medicine man came in handy. "You start by eating just a tiny bit," he had told her, "then see how it affects you. You have to pay attention to how every part of your body looks and feels. That's the only way to find out if a plant is poisonous. Test it on yourself." Following his instructions, if a plant upset her stomach, or gave her a rash or a sick feeling in the chest, she wouldn't eat another bite no matter how good it tasted. Even so, she found herself doubled over in pain a number of times. Because she sometimes waded into the icy river after plants she thought might be edible, her toes, her fingers, and her heels became as cracked as dried mud.

Now and then she would go into Senbashi to buy black market coal or something more to wear, but these were typically five to twenty times as expensive as the things they could get with the ration coupons. What remained of the money she'd received at the Repatriation Relief Bureau quickly ran out. When the last of it was gone, Saya groped the bottom of her purse in disbelief. She'd gone to the length of killing a woman for what turned out to be a pittance.

When she told Rentarō that she was broke, he began giving her small amounts himself. There was a world of difference between making do with her own dwindling resources and living off what someone else provided, even if it was only a small sum. Now she actually looked forward to going into town with her purse in hand. To Saya, money was a kind of magic. It had never been part of life in the jungle, so she had grown up ignorant of how it could be used. Not until she travelled to Kota Bharu with her brother did she discover its special powers. Her pulse quickened whenever she saw Kekah exchanging small pieces of paper for a shirt or something sweet to eat. To recall those days now invariably made her think of

Rentarō's paper balloon. Watching the small, folded piece of paper expand into a spherical rainbow and float through the air had had the same effect on her as seeing bits of paper transformed into sweets or colourful pieces of cloth.

Even when she had nothing to buy, walking about town with money in her purse and Isamu's hand in hers was enough to set her heart racing the way it had when she first saw that paper balloon. Once she'd explained that she was a returnee, nobody seemed bothered by her broken Japanese. The town was full of people who'd come back from Manchuria or the South Seas. Some of them had been born there, or had lived there so long that their Japanese was almost as shaky as Saya's. "So you're back from Malaya, are you? Must have been pretty rough down there. It's where General Yamashita put the screws on that Percival guy, right?" Friendly shopkeepers would try to strike up conversations with her, but when she smiled stiffly and responded only with yeses and nos, they quickly took the hint and stopped. She always gave her name as Saya, and people started calling her "Saya from down south." They seemed to think it was a good nickname for someone with her dark skin.

By the time six months had passed, the whole town knew she was Rentarō's mistress. But everybody turned a blind eye in the same way they did when special trains carrying occupation troops clattered by. It was a time when war widows turned to prostitution, orphaned children slept on the streets, students worked as shoeblacks, and young women sold their blood so they wouldn't have to sell their bodies. A returnee woman and child getting by *without* a man's help would have given people more to talk about.

Whenever Rentarō came to visit, Saya quickly shooed Isamu outside to play. The time they then spent making love under the bedclothes brought her the only real warmth she experience all winter long. She pulled him to her, pressed her eager loins to his, and savoured the intense pleasure. He, too, drank greedily from the fountain of her flesh.

After he was done, she would toy with his wilted cock and wonder how she could have been so crazy for it only moments before. It was no different from the ones at the P-house: the same sword by which she'd died a thousand deaths. The memory would make her fingers jerk harder. His penis would begin to stiffen again.

No, she thought. It was no different. No different at all. What she held was a sword. A penis that had become a sword.

With an urge to snap that sword in two, she would climb astride Rentarō and ride his cock hard until he came again. The more spent he looked when he left the house, the happier it made her feel.

The rapid swing from pleasure to resentment took away the animal abandon of their lovemaking in the storeroom. As he thrust himself in and out, Rentarō would turn into one of the soldiers in that compound outside Kota Bharu. The bitterness and hatred would return, and she'd wish she could tear his penis off with her hole. But then, as soon as he was gone, desire would come flooding back, and she would long to be in his arms, to be transported once again. The more she hungered for those moments, the further they seemed to recede, and the further they receded, the more desperately she hungered for them.

So it was, as one year gave way to the next, that Saya found herself surging first to this extreme, then to that, while Rentarō, caught in the roll of those waves, went back and forth between his own home and hers all winter long, leaving the sales trips to Asatsugu.

In due course, spring came round, and the black earth emerged from beneath the snow in the warming sun. About the time Isamu started to school at the beginning of April, Saya realized that her monthly red flower no longer bloomed. When she told Rentarō, he fell abruptly silent; then she didn't see him again for the next ten days. As she worked in the garden, turning the soil that had hardened over the winter, she was nagged by the fear that he might have abandoned her again.

He finally appeared at the door one morning after her boy had left for school. He was dressed in what Saya had learned to recognize as the civilian uniform Japanese men wore during the war, his ankles wrapped in gaiters over sturdy leather shoes. On his back was a large bundle, with the two tightly tied corners of its wrapping cloth digging into his chest. He stood at the threshold without coming inside and announced that he was going on a sales trip. One alarming thought after another began rushing through her head, but without taking the time to sort through them, she put down the dish she was washing and threw her arms around him.

"You will come back, yes?" she said, with pleading in her voice.

"I'm not going far. I won't be away long," he said, trying to reassure her. He pushed some money into her hand.

This was how he had left her in Kota Bharu, promising to return, yet never coming back. Afraid that he might be planning the same thing this time, she fixed her eyes on him and said, "I will come find you, no matter where you go."

He appeared startled by her words, but all he did was nod his head.

19

Hooking the fingers of both hands over the ties stretched across his chest, Rentarō turned and slowly walked out to the road. He could feel Saya's eyes drilling into him from behind, but he didn't look back.

The spring ploughing had begun, and many of the nearby paddies looked as if a giant catfish had rampaged through them. Along the dikes between them, horsetails poked their heads from the ground and clover flowers were beginning to loosen their tight buds. The steady burble of the irrigation ditches drawn from the Jōganji River told of rapidly melting snow throughout the Tateyama Basin.

The walk to Terada Station on the Tateyama Line would take him about an hour. He leaned forward against the weight of his five-tiered medicine baskets as he plodded steadily along the bumpy farm lanes. The ties dug into his upper arms, but he was quite accustomed to the heft of his merchandise after nearly thirty years of peddling. The greater burden for him now was what was weighing on his mind.

When Saya had turned up with Isamu on his doorstep, it had been like an atomic bomb dropping on his house. The blast had mowed down every member of his extended family and left permanent damage behind. He had tried to stave off a total breakdown of the household by exercising his authority as head of the family, but with everyone turning their backs on him, he had found himself left out in the cold. Of course, no one challenged him openly, to his face, but his mother never missed a chance to drop some snide remark or other, and his wife had withdrawn into silence. The two younger children sided with their mother and grandmother, and had taken to avoiding him. It was hardly surprising, since he'd never had a very close relationship with them anyway. His constant travelling meant he was absent a great deal, and during the five years he lived in Malaya he'd only made it back to Japan about twice a year. As for his eldest, the relationship had turned downright hostile. Concerned that Saya might come back and cause trouble at the main house if he were to go away, he'd been leaving the travelling to Asatsugu in recent months. "You make me do all the work, while you're off womanizing," the boy raged every time he got back. Tomijirō and his wife treated him coldly as well, taking the view that he was only getting what he deserved. He had become an outsider in his own home.

Everything that had happened in Malaya had belonged to another world. This was exactly what had made it possible for him to take a wife there, and to love her.

When he first met Saya, she was nothing more to him than a dark-skinned girl with big, round eyes. But in the course of his annual visits to the jungle near Kelintasan with her brother to replenish his stock of ingredients, he had seen her grow into a woman. Her knowledge of medicinal herbs and roots, the way she moved so nimbly through the forest, the bursts of strong emotion she displayed from time to time – not to mention the unabashed sexuality that came out in those moments – had all helped attract him to her.

His wife Yōko might as well have been made of straw. When they slept together, she lay there limply making dry, rustling sounds. She had always regarded the marital act as just a bedtime chore. The girls he sometimes picked up on the road weren't like that, but their come-ons were always so phony. Saya had something neither his wife nor the professional girls could offer. She was a genuine example of the unspoiled woman.

He dressed her up in nice new outfits, and gave her a taste for luxury. Soon the girl of the jungle he'd found dressed in shabby clothes turned into an attractive young woman. Then he fell in love with his creation. When the war began to go badly and he sought the safety of Singapore – the stronghold of the Japanese command in Malaya – he thought about her often, always picturing her living happily by herself in the well-appointed Malayan house they had shared in Kota Bharu. He was pleased with himself for having given her that good life.

The war soon took care of any potential fallout from what he had created. As talk in Japan turned to defending the homeland to the bitter end, his family in Toyama begged him to return, and eventually he decided it was time. He had always known that his life with Saya in Malaya couldn't last, and he felt a sense of relief that leaving for home would put a natural end to his time in that other world. In fact, he had no idea how he would ever have broken it off with Saya if the deteriorating state of the war had not given him the excuse.

Even so, as he set sail from Singapore, he saw himself going back to see Saya and Isamu once the war situation stabilized. This quickly changed after he was back in Japan, where conditions were far worse than he had ever imagined. Allied bombing had all but levelled the city of Toyama, burning most of the pharmaceutical companies to the ground. With the supply of medicines severely depleted, keeping food on the family table was a growing challenge, and as if that weren't enough, his brother and his family had lost their home and needed a roof over their heads.

The hardships continued even after the war was over. With such extreme shortages of goods and food everywhere, he spent all his time worrying about providing for his family from one day to the next. There was no room for Malaya or Saya or Isamu in his thoughts. The life he'd shared with them became more like something he'd merely dreamed of in that other world.

But then one day Saya and the boy had emerged from that dream to stand before him right here in Japan. He couldn't use the war as an excuse anymore, and there was no place for him to hide. To make matters worse, the woman he'd so lovingly shaped with his own hands seemed to have turned into a regular terror. From the moment she appeared on his doorstep with her fierce black eyes ablaze, he began to feel like a cornered animal – cornered by his own creation. He finally managed to find a house for her, to separate her from his family, only to have her drop the bombshell that she was pregnant again. It felt as if a bad dream had turned real and threatened to take over his life.

Terada Station was a small, wood-frame structure with a tiled roof standing by itself in the middle of the countryside. Rentarō walked into the waiting room and approached the ticket window.

"One to Awasuno," he said to the white-haired attendant.

"The train'll be here in about five minutes," the man said as he held out the ticket. There was dirt under his fingernails, suggesting he also worked in the fields.

Rentarō paid the fare and took the ticket. The station had two platforms – one for the line to Kurobe, the other heading out to Tateyama. He lowered his bundle onto the platform in front of a bench on the Tateyama platform and sat down. Pulling out a hand towel, he wiped the sweat from his face.

With grass encroaching on both sides, the rails stretched straight out in the direction of the Tateyama Range. Rentarō gazed blankly up at the snow-topped peaks, lined up like a mirage hovering in the middle of the sky.

In Toyama, it was once common for fifteen-year-old boys to climb Tateyama as a rite of passage into manhood. Rentarō had made the climb too, with a group of classmates led by their teacher. The gruelling trek, spanning three days and two nights, took them from the Midagahara Plateau to Hell Valley, Mikurigaike Pond, Jōdosan, and finally Tateyama. He still remembered the exhilaration he felt when he stood on the summit and gazed out across a row of pale peaks floating like islands in a sea of clouds. On their way back they had stopped for another night at the Tateyama Hot Spring, and he returned home the next day overflowing with pride that he'd made the grade.

Having now reached the age of forty-seven, Rentarō knew that an ascent of Tateyama could neither make you a man nor give you a new life. But his decision to set out for that same mountain and try to cultivate some new clients among the hamlets at its foot had probably come more than anything else from the subconscious hope that it might somehow break him free of the predicament he found himself in.

A heavy thud shook him from his thoughts, and he turned to see that a woman with a rucksack on her back and a canteen slung over her shoulder had lowered herself onto the bench beside him. She appeared to be around thirty. Beads of sweat stood out on her forehead, and damp, unkempt hair stuck to her pale, sunken cheeks. She was wearing a half-kimono and *monpe* work trousers – the way women had dressed during the war. The *monpe* were scuffed with dirt and looked pretty thin in the knees. She sat there struggling to keep her eyes open for several moments, then suddenly rolled her eyes up, showing only the whites, as if she were about to pass out.

"Are you all right, miss?" he asked.

With a jerk, she stretched her neck like a bird after a bath and looked at Rentarō. With a weak smile, she nodded and said, "I'm fine," but she sounded none too sure of herself.

A train painted dark brown came down the tracks from the direction of Toyama. He picked up the bundle sitting on the platform in front of him and hefted it onto his back. The woman wobbled to her feet, struggling not to tip backwards from the weight of her rucksack.

Rentarō moved toward the train as it pulled in. The doors opened and passengers began to get off. As he was about to step inside, he thought of the woman and turned to see how she was doing. He found her standing with one hand propped against the side of the car, breathing hard.

"Here, miss, let me help you," he said, taking her arm and helping her aboard.

"Thank you." The soft voice was pleasant in his ears.

It was a car with benches set along each side under the windows. He led the woman to a spot wide enough for both of them and helped her remove the rucksack from her back before she sat down. Then he lowered his own bundle onto the floor and took a seat on her left.

"Are you feeling okay?" he said after the train lurched into motion and began rolling across the open countryside.

"I seem to have caught a bit of a cold," she answered self-consciously.

Noticing her accent, Rentarō asked, "You sound like you're from Tokyo."

She nodded.

"You came all this way on a food run?"

After saying it, he realized she was going the wrong way if she was carrying food back to Tokyo.

The woman seemed to have noticed the incongruity, too, and a smile came into her eyes.

"Actually, we live here, now," she said. "After losing our house and everything in one of the air raids."

"They say the bombings in Tokyo were like hell on earth," said a voice on the other side of Rentarō. It came from a mousy-looking man wearing dark glasses, with a round face and high cheekbones.

The woman eyed the man's glasses uneasily as she gave a half-hearted nod, then weakly leaned her head back against the window. Rentarō undid the cloth around his bundle and took out a small paper packet from the fourth basket.

"Try this," he said, holding it out to her. "It's a fever powder. You should take it right away."

She looked unsure and shook her head, but reconsidered when the fellow in the dark glasses said, "It's your lucky day, miss – running into a medicine man." She unfolded the little packet and made a scoop of the paper to pour the powder into her mouth, then washed it down with water from her canteen. Her throat bobbed like a wriggling fish as she swallowed. Thanking Rentarō, she let her head fall back against the window again and closed her eyes.

The man in the dark glasses turned to Rentarō. "I imagine you folks have been doing pretty well for yourselves since the war ended," he said in an interested way.

"Oh, I don't know..." Rentarō said vaguely. He thought he could hear a Kyoto accent in the man's speech.

The truth was, it had indeed been a profitable time for people in his business. Not only had the earlier shortages in drug ingredients eased, but a law that banned taking kits from more than one vendor, which had been passed during the war to limit competition, had now been repealed, so peddlers like him were once again free to approach anyone. Add to that the fact that the war had depleted medical supplies in most households, and the market was ripe both for placing new kits and for on-the-spot sales. When the new yen was introduced the previous spring, all of Toyama's peddlers had filled their baskets and headed for the rice-growing regions of Niigata and the northeast. Thanks to the food shortages in the big cities, these areas were awash with money, so they'd all made out very well. Still, Rentarō was not inclined to discuss the secrets of his trade with a stranger. Raking in big profits didn't go with the image of the honest, hard-working medicine peddler any better than a flowery kimono with long, hanging sleeves went with a wrinkled old lady.

"There's really only so much you can make from selling medicines," he said evasively.

The man's mouth turned down and he scratched his chin. "Well, I suppose the rackets you really wanna be in right now are lumber and construction. That, and anything that caters to the occupation. I hear whorehouses for the Yanks are doing a booming business in Tokyo."

The crudeness of the remark left a sour taste in its wake. "But the Yanks won't be hanging around forever, either," Rentarō pointed out.

The man placed a hand on each knee and leaned forward with amusement on his face. "What makes life interesting is never knowing what might happen next. I wouldn't put it past them to decide they wanted to stick around."

"Not likely," Rentaro said, though on second thought he wasn't so sure. During the war, everybody believed Japan would win. The government put out nothing but upbeat reports. Once the war was over, they learned it had all been a pack of lies. The Potsdam Declaration supposedly promised that the occupying troops would leave once peace and freedom had been established in Japan, but was there any guarantee? The Americans could easily be lying to them, too, just as their own government had done.

While Rentarō was thinking about this, the man in the dark glasses added crisply, "Well, no matter what happens, the one thing you can count on is money. No woman's gonna take a second look at you if you don't have money."

He glanced past Rentarō at the dozing woman. She was now hunched forward in her seat with her head hanging like a rag doll.

"I don't know that women are all so cut and dried," Rentarō countered.

The man gave a crooked frown. "Women are a mercenary lot," he said, and then fell silent.

"By the way, are you perhaps from Kyoto?" Rentarō had been wondering about this since the man first opened his mouth.

Dark glasses nodded indifferently.

"Is it true Kyoto was spared from any air raids?"

"So I've heard," he said. When the indefiniteness of his reply elicited a puzzled look from Rentarō, he added, "I was away in the army, so I don't really know."

"And you haven't been home since you got back?"

He made a dismissive sound. Then, glancing outside the window, he said "Oh!" and quickly jumped to his feet. They were coming into Kamagafuchi Station. He pulled a large, empty rucksack from the luggage rack overhead. It was obviously homemade and had been repeatedly mended. One of the straps fell against his face as the bag came down and knocked his dark glasses off, exposing a gaping hole where his left eye should have been. The flesh around it looked inflamed like a burn.

The man hurriedly put his glasses back on. "So long, then," he said, and hopped off the train with the empty rucksack dangling in one hand.

The train started up again and continued on its way through the early spring countryside. Rentarō guessed that the man was probably a black-marketer. Most of those working in the black markets were demobilized soldiers. When he saw them in their tired old fatigues manning booths in front of Toyama Station, he got the feeling that a wide gulf lay between such men and himself. There was a different air about them. He supposed it had something to do with the difference between those who had been in the fighting and those who had not, but he couldn't put his finger on exactly what it came from.

He had served his country, too – for three years, starting when he was twenty. Stationed in Siberia, he'd spent his days staring at the sky over the frigid plains; he never saw any action. By the time the Greater East Asia War broke out, he had even finished his service in the Reserves, which meant he could continue living in Malaya without any fear of being drafted. He had little doubt that the war experienced by the man in dark glasses was a vastly different thing from the war he himself had experienced.

After a time the tracks fell in alongside the Jōganji River. The spread of cultivated land gradually grew narrower as the mountains rising beyond it closed in on the river. The houses in this area were still wrapped in their snow shields, as if they had yet to wake from hibernation, but the green of spring was popping out along the paddy dikes and among the trees nearest the foot of the mountains.

The passengers dwindled with each stop at tiny, deserted stations along the way. Almost no one new got on. Rentarō wondered about the woman beside him, who was still dozing with her head hanging forward. Wasn't she going to miss her station? But he felt it would be sticking his nose in too far to actually shake her awake and ask where she was going.

The clatter of the wheels grew louder and the car lurched from side to side as the train started across a steel bridge over the river. The woman slept on through the commotion. Rentarō stole glances at her from time to time. With her hair done up in the traditional style, the nape of her neck was exposed. It was smooth and slender, and very pretty. She had her hands folded in her lap: they were small, delicate hands. He saw that the fingers were chapped and wondered if it could be from doing outdoor work she wasn't accustomed to.

The train arrived at Awasuno Station, the end of the line. As soon as the coaches pulled to a halt, the woman raised her head and lifted the rucksack at her feet. It was as if she had been awake and alert the entire time. After shouldering her bag, she turned to Rentarō. "I'm feeling much better now. Thank you so much," she said with a bow, and then quickly stepped off the train.

By the time he hefted his bundle onto his back again and went through the gate, the woman was already disappearing up the street in front of the station. He felt a little disappointed, as if his kindness had been repaid with a brush-off. Oh well, he thought, as he moved on out of the station. Perhaps it was just another sign of the hard times everybody had been going through since the war.

The wood-frame houses around the station all looked quite new. The village, built on a shelf of land jutting out into the Jōganji River, was only about ten years old, and was made up mainly of employee housing for the region's electric power company and a trucking business, along with the homes of people who provided services for them. Rentarō headed up what appeared to be the only street, thinking this was as good a place as any to begin trying to place his kits, when he noticed a crowd of about twenty people gathered around the gates of a school up ahead, watching something in the schoolyard. He walked up behind them and peered over their shoulders to see what was going on.

It was a small school, with only a single wooden building. A flurry of activity was being directed by a man in the odd combination of a frock coat and black rubber boots – presumably the principal. Several men and women, perhaps parent volunteers, were helping to set up a speaker's platform, arranging chairs in rows, and hauling a reed organ out of the building. Through the windows could be seen the close-cropped heads and pageboy haircuts of students polishing windowpanes and wiping off desks.

"Is there going to be some kind of ceremony?" Rentarō asked the woman standing in front of him with a baby strapped to her back. The collar of the padded cotton jacket she'd wrapped around herself and the baby was shiny with drool.

"They say some occupation officials might be coming to visit," she said excitedly. "That's why they're in such a bustle." She had an upturned nose a little like a bat's.

"All the way out here?" he said in surprise. Right after the war, American troops in jeeps had made the rounds of schools in Senbashi and other nearby towns to search for banned textbooks and anything else they shouldn't have. On one occasion, they found three machine guns in a gym. When caught red-handed trying to hide the weapons in a closet, the principal claimed implausibly that someone had left them in his office the night before, he had no idea who. Thanks to one of the teachers, this ludicrous attempt at an excuse became public knowledge, and the man's reputation in the community suffered a fall.

"Well, nobody knows if they'll actually come to a little place like this, but the village office got word that a jeep was headed in this direction, and all the schools out this way were told to be ready just in case."

"I bet they're coming to see if the new system is working out," a man in rubber-soled workmen's socks put in from beside her.

Starting that year, the old "People's Schools" set up during the war had been abolished and replaced with a whole new system. The reforms had been pushed by occupation policy-makers, so there seemed a pretty good chance the man was right.

"I sure do hope they come," said a bright-eyed young woman with rosy cheeks. "I've never seen an American before."

A man wearing wooden *geta* on his feet emerged from the building with something under his arm and came trotting toward the gates. The crowd opened up to let him through. The object he was carrying turned out to be a framed slogan from during the war that said "Pray for the prosperity of the Greater East Asian Empire."

"Are you kidding?" someone called out. "The school still had one of those things hanging around? Don't you know you could be sent up for war crimes?"

"I'm thinking I saw a war poster still on the wall at *your* house, too?" the man retorted. He was apparently the school custodian.

The villagers burst out laughing as he trotted off toward the station.

When the laughter died down, the woman carrying the baby eyed the bundle on Rentarō's back and asked, "You a medicine peddler?"

"That's right," he said and, not one to miss an opening, quickly went on, "This is my first time out this way, and I was wondering if you've had any others of us coming by since the war."

"Oh, yes. The man we had before came back just about a month ago."

"Sounds like a dependable fellow," Rentarō said, disappointed. "But did you know that the one kit per household rule's been abolished, and you can take as many kits as you like now? Even if you don't think you'll use it, how about letting me leave one of mine with you too?"

Fingering the hand towel draped around her neck, she tilted her head as if to consider, when someone shouted, "Here they come!"

A single army jeep could be seen bouncing toward them on the bumpy gravel road out of the forest. The villagers watched it coming in amazement. They'd been talking about it all morning, but they hadn't quite believed anybody would actually show up in such a remote place. Voices rang out up and down the street: "They're here! They came!"

"You sure they're really with the occupation?"

"Look at that! They're coming right this way!"

People began popping out of doorways and yards in both directions – a woman in an apron with her kimono sleeves tied back; an old man who'd been hulling rice in the sun; a man with a hoe in his hand from working in the garden. All eyes were pinned on the green jeep as it drew closer. In it were two American officers and two Japanese men. The younger of the Japanese was presumably an interpreter; the other was an elderly man wearing a formal crested kimono. Noticing that some of the villagers were greeting the older man, Rentarō gathered he was someone prominent in the local community.

The jeep slowed to a crawl as it reached the main part of the crowd and turned to enter the school gates. Some forty or fifty children were now lined up in the schoolyard with their teachers and the principal, and they all bent at the waist as the visitors pulled up. The villagers quickly followed suit.

The two foreigners got out of the vehicle. Everybody stared at their pink skin and blue eyes and large noses. The principal stepped forward to greet them and thank them for coming. The interpreter translated what he'd said.

"Their skin really is a different colour."

"Look at those noses! They're like elephants!"

"As if you've ever seen an elephant!"

The villagers joked quietly amongst themselves while watching the officers' every move.

"So that's what the killers look like," came a low, sneering voice. A boy of fifteen or sixteen was glaring in the officers' direction.

"Shut your trap, Kiyo. You looking to get thrown in jail?" the man in rubber-soled work socks said.

"Gutless cowards," the boy spat back, then elbowed his way through the crowd and fled. Shaking their heads, the others shifted to fill in the spot where he'd been standing and turned their attention back to the two Americans now saying something to the interpreter.

With everybody so enthralled by this event, Rentarō doubted he'd be able to generate any interest in what he had to offer. Taking care not to bump people with his bundle, he edged his way out of the crowd.

As he looked around, trying to decide what to do next, he noticed a small general store across the street, where an elderly woman was busy dusting off the merchandise. She seemed oblivious to what was going on at the school as she flicked her duster over the rubber-soled socks, elastic bands, kerosene lamps, wax candles, and sundry other things arranged on the merchandise tables. With a glimmer of hope, Rentarō decided to approach.

"Hello," he said, and the old woman turned a face that looked as small and yellow as a kumquat toward him.

She barely glanced at him before saying, "I don't need no medicine."

In spite of the brush-off, he pressed on: "There's no need to be that way, Granny. It doesn't cost you a thing to let me leave a kit with you."

"Medicine's for them that cares to live. I reckon I've already lived all I want, so I ain't got no use for 'em no more. I plan to just go on and die when my time comes."

She evidently didn't believe in mincing words.

"But there must be others close to you who want you to go on living," he suggested.

She threw him a look from the corner of her eye. "I ain't livin' to make nobody else happy."

It was obviously no use. "I see," he mumbled, and turned to go.

"You could try up Mandala Road," she called after him. Looking back, he saw her rubbing her nose between her thumb and forefinger as she continued, "The villages out that way could probably use some medicine. A lot o' new people seem to've settled in since the war, and I had somebody come by durin' the winter askin' if I had anythin' for a fever."

Rentarō had never heard of Mandala Road before. When he asked where it was, the old woman lifted her duster and pointed up the road toward where the army jeep had emerged from the forest.

"That way," she said. "Turn left when you get to the Jizō statue. It ends up at Yakushidake. The mountain may be named for the Medicine Buddha, but I don't guess ole Jizō at this end is handin' out any powders or potions."

She opened her toothless mouth and laughed.

He heard the organ begin to play in the schoolyard, and then the children raised their voices in "The Apple Song." To the sound of the familiar tune, he trudged up the road toward where it was swallowed up into the forest.

20

Asafumi rounded the bend and saw a troop of monkeys sitting in the middle of the road. He slammed on the brakes and yanked the wheel sideways to avoid running them over. Barely missing the animals, the car came to a halt on the shoulder. The monkeys bared their teeth and screeched as they turned their red behinds and fled into the forest.

For several moments, he just sat wide-eyed, unable to move, but once the animals had all disappeared into the undergrowth, he put the car in reverse to pull back onto the road. As he began to turn the wheel, the rear of the car sank with a *thunk* and the engine died. When he restarted it, the wheels would only spin in place. With a frown, he took off his glasses and put them on the dashboard before getting out.

The outside rear wheel had fallen into a rut at the side of the road, which he'd failed to notice because the drop was hidden under a blanket of dead leaves. He tried lifting the car, but it was immediately obvious that he didn't have the strength. When he opened the trunk to find the jack, it was nowhere to be seen, apparently having been put somewhere else by mistake during the move. This meant he was probably going to be stuck there until he could get somebody's help. But he hadn't passed a single car in the half-hour since starting up Mandala Road. Thinking wearily that he might have to hike all the way back to where the road forked, he scanned the road ahead as far as he could see. A patch of something red caught his eye through the trees on the right. He took a few steps to one side for a better view and thought it looked like a thatched roof that had been roofed over with red tin.

Relieved to find a house nearby, Asafumi dropped his keys into his pocket and started walking. The left side of the road fell away into a deep canyon, but after walking just fifty metres or so, a cluster of about ten houses came into view on the slope to the right. Tin and tile roofs peeked from between plantings of persimmon, camellia, nandina, and other garden trees and shrubs. A narrow path angled up toward the houses, and next to the road at the foot of this path was a small Jizō statue in a little shelter. In front of the image were some small chrysanthemums just beginning to wilt and a chipped teacup full of water.

Taking heart in these signs that he might be able to find someone to help him, he proceeded up the path. The first house he came to had a yard overgrown with weeds and storm shutters closed tight. The next was stripped of all its doors and shutters, and when he walked up to the wide-open veranda, he saw that the tatami mats were gone as well and several boards in the subfloor had caved in. Was it an abandoned settlement? But somebody had to have placed that offering of flowers in front of Jizō. Clinging to the hope that someone still lived there, he continued on up the path. Stones had been piled up to form retaining walls between the path and the homesites, and where the slope was steeper, logs had been used to form steps. Stepping stones had been placed in a small creek that ran through the hamlet. This was no doubt once a busy footpath, Asafumi thought. He could picture women passing up and down it to share food from their gardens or kitchens, or to forward the community clipboard to its next station; children playing house along the wayside; old folks chatting on the retaining walls. But now the stone walls were crumbling, a broken dipper lay forgotten beside the path, a water faucet next to somebody's garden was rusted shut. And the houses themselves were all slowly falling to pieces – gables collapsing, eaves askew, windows missing their panes. Weeds grew unchecked in every yard, with washtubs, bicycle tires, sections of water hose, and decaying bamboo poles scattered among them. Asafumi was becoming worried. The hamlet appeared to be completely deserted. In which case his best bet was probably to walk back to the fork in the road before it got dark.

But as he turned to head back to the car, he saw what appeared to be a storage shed through some cedars standing next to the path. Under its eaves was some neatly stacked firewood that looked as if it had been cut quite recently. Beyond the shed stood a house with a tin roof over thatch. He recognized it as the one he'd seen from the road. He made his way toward it through the clump of cedars. The shutters were tightly closed, but the house and yard were well taken care of, as if someone still lived there. The doorpost bore a sticker indicating payment of a television fee. And there was a nameplate saying "Shōichirō Katsumura, Dobō, Ōyama." Asafumi was pretty sure he recognized the name Dobō from the sales register. He wished he'd brought his bag with him from the car.

He tried the door, but it wouldn't budge. The people who'd lived in this house obviously still came back from time to time, but they weren't here now. As he turned to go, it occurred to him to try the storm shutters along the veranda, too, and he pulled on the first panel. To his surprise, it moved without resistance. He slid it all the way open and peered inside. Through the glass veranda doors he could see a tatami sitting room. A *kotatsu* table without its quilt sat in the middle. Off in one corner, he spotted a black telephone on the floor. His heart leapt. He didn't know the Yasudas' number, but he could call his mother in Senbashi, and she could get in touch with them to come and pull his car out. Removing his shoes, he stepped up into the house. The air inside had the stale smell of time standing still. He picked up the phone and dialled his parents' number, but when he put the receiver to his ear he heard nothing.

Of course not, he thought. They wouldn't want to pay for standing service to a house they hardly ever visited. He dropped the handset back into its cradle. Before stepping down from the veranda, he paused for a look around. Through the open shoji screens on the front door side of the room was a dirt-floored entryway and kitchen. Next to an old-fashioned tile-lined sink stood a cement cooking counter. Atop it sat a small gas burner with an aluminium tea kettle on it. On a shelf above was a candle inside a hurricane glass. There was a propane tank for the gas burner. But no doubt the electricity had been shut off just like the phone, he thought, as he closed the shutter and turned to go.

The sun was already approaching the ridgeline. Remembering suddenly that sundown comes early in the mountains, he realized he didn't have much time left. He picked up a piece of wooden plank he found lying in the path and hurried back to the car.

Collecting some rocks to help fill in the rut, he wedged the board under the rear wheel, then got in and switched on the ignition. When he felt the car edging forward, he stepped hard on the accelerator, his heart pounding. The engine roared, but the car slid right back into the rut. After several more tries he decided it was no use. By now the sun had moved on past the mountain ridge, and a madder-coloured glow had come into the sky. The shadowy woods all around him echoed with the calls of birds.

Asafumi leaned against the car as he considered his options. Hoofing it back to a hotel or other lodgings near the Awasuno slopes would probably take three to four hours. He shrank at the thought of walking such a distance in the dark. It might be better to spend the night here and set out in the morning. He could sleep in the car. On the other hand, he wasn't so sure he liked the idea of sleeping more or less in the open at the side of a remote mountain road. What if he went back to that house? Even if the place was empty, he'd feel safer being inside a house. The hamlet was deserted, so there was nobody to object. Making up his mind, he retrieved his overnight bag from the trunk, locked the car, and headed for the path again.

Dusk was falling by the time he reached the Katsumura house for the second time. He opened the storm shutter and let himself inside. With the help of the dim light still filtering in from outside, he found the pull cord for the light fixture and tried it. As he'd anticipated, there was no power. Remembering the old candle holder, he stepped down into the kitchen and groped his way to the counter to get it. Next to it on the shelf was a box of matches. Relief flooded through him as the flickering light from the candle lit up the kitchen.

Candlestick in hand, he made a brief tour of the house. There were two more rooms on the other side of the sitting room, both of them devoid of any furnishings except tatami. He found a single set of bedding in the futon closet in one of the rooms. Whoever returned here from time to time apparently stayed the night. Back in the kitchen, he found a stoneware teapot and teacups under the sink, along with a canister of green tea. He turned the cock on the propane tank and tried lighting the burner. There was some gas left. Rejoicing at the prospect of some hot tea, he went to fill the kettle, only to discover that the tap was dry. The water had been shut off, too. But if the people here were making themselves tea, there had to be another source of water somewhere. Perhaps there was a well outside.

Searching outside in the dark with nothing but a hurricane candlestick wasn't going to be easy. But he was thirsty. If only there were a vending machine somewhere, he couldn't help thinking. Then for a mere hundred yen or so, he could not only save himself the trouble of finding a well, drawing the water, bringing it to a boil, and finally making some tea; he could have his choice of a whole selection of hot or iced teas on demand. But to sit there wishing wouldn't make the thing appear. With heavy feet, he carried his light to the front door, unlatched it, and stepped outside.

Instead of a well, he found a trickle of water drawn from a nearby rill filling a small cistern behind the house. He had no way of telling whether it was safe to drink, but he knew boiling would take care of that, so he promptly filled the kettle.

Back inside, he heated the water and made his tea. As he sat at the kotatsu table sipping it, the deep silence all around him began to make the room feel uncomfortably close. He needed some music, he thought. Not the keening of insects or soughing of the wind, but the sound of the human voice, or notes produced by human hands.

Shizuka claimed he was a music addict. He'd always shrugged off the accusation before, but considering how he was feeling now, he had to admit that she might be right.

How had it happened? When had he gotten so he simply couldn't stand being without music. He'd begun listening regularly when he was thirteen or fourteen, after receiving his first boom box. It was right around the time he began studying for his entrance exams to high school. He remembered spending long hours at his desk with music playing in the background.

The music habit had been with him ever since. He'd studied to background music all through high school and college, including the preparation periods for his college entrance and employment exams, and to this day he put music on whenever he could.

Now he found himself in a place where no man-made sounds were to be heard. He felt as though an irreplaceable part of his world had collapsed and he was staring into a void.

He tried singing songs aloud to himself, but he quickly discovered that he didn't know many of the words. Even though he'd played the songs countless times, he'd never really listened to the lyrics.

The realization sent a chill through him, and he got to his feet. He felt restless; he needed something to do. For no particular reason, he opened the closet where he'd seen the futon and peered inside. Next to the bedding was a medicine kit box. He pulled it out and opened the lid. It contained no medicine, only a collection of buttons and safety pins and such.

He carried the box into the sitting room and set it on the table. The outside of the box was plastered with stickers bearing the names of various well-known remedies.

He went to get his overnight bag and pulled out the sales register. Thumbing through it, he found Dobō listed second to last. *On mountainside above Mandala Road, fifth house at back, Kamezō Katsumura*, read one of the entries. He guessed Kamezō was probably Shōichirō's father. It said there were five children in the household. Altogether there were fifteen families in the hamlet, each with seven or eight members. He tried to imagine what the place would have been like then. It must have bustled with activity.

He looked about the house. The removal of all furnishings and belongings had left it a colourless place. Once upon a time, a large family had lived and laughed between these walls, but now they had all moved away.

The quietness pressed in on him again. He sat back down at the table.

Cobwebs on the ceiling. A square spot on the wall where perhaps a calendar had hung. The worn-out *tatami*. A room furnished with only a *kotatsu* table and a phone.

Was his music merely a device to avoid having to look at things like this?

He thought back to his teen years again. The home where his father was always away, and his unflappable mother called the shots. The endless days he'd spent preparing for tests and entrance exams that came at him one after the other. When he pictured himself then, all he could remember was listening to music. The tunes came back to him, but the lyrics had failed to leave an impression.

He stretched out on the tatami. The dimly lit ceiling spread out above him.

Even after getting married, he'd gone on listening to so much music that Shizuka called it an addiction. What was he trying not to see now?

He lay contemplating this question as the murmuring of the mountain outside the house gently pressed in around him.

21

Shizuka stared into the darkness, her eyes wide open. Night had come without any word from Asafumi. She'd crawled into bed feeling peeved. Couldn't he at least have called when he knew he would actually be staying overnight?

How far had he gotten, she wondered. Had he found a hot spring inn to stay at somewhere along Mandala Road? Had he been able to reconnect with some of the old customers listed in that notebook? When she got tired of speculating uselessly about her husband's day, she turned her thoughts to the conversation she'd had with Miharu on Cloth Bridge.

The business about women being destined to fall into Hell's Pool of Blood had made a strong impression on her. That name had immediately brought to mind the way she'd continued sleeping with both Hiroyuki and Asafumi for so long. Alternating between them had been tremendously exciting to her during the first year of her marriage. But the edge eventually wore off, and sex lapsed into little more than a mechanical exercise no matter whom she was with. Then, once the thrill of the illicit had dulled, the sense that she was doing something genuinely wrong began to weigh on her conscience.

From time to time, she had considered confessing the affair to Asafumi. But the words kept digging in their heels when they reached her lips. Revealing the truth would bring the entire world she'd constructed for herself crashing down around her. She didn't have the courage to widen her horizons by pushing aside the walls holding up that world. All she could imagine finding in their place was absolute emptiness and ruin, not a new life.

So now she'd come to hoping that she could somehow muddle through by simply leaving well enough alone. Give it a few years, and they'd both lose interest in sex. The problem would simply go away. That was what she told herself to keep from falling apart.

She rolled over in bed. She longed for someone to wrap her arms around.

On nights when she was alone like this, she didn't find herself longing for sex with Asafumi; it was sex with Hiroyuki that she missed. Especially the sex she'd had with him soon after getting married, when the knowledge that she was being unfaithful lifted her to previously unknown heights. Sex where she felt as if she'd been thrown into a red-hot crucible and her consciousness was melting into the far beyond. But times like that gradually grew fewer, and the fewer they became, the more she clung to Hiroyuki in pursuit of the pleasure she'd known before.

"You know," he said with a look of distaste during their last assignation before the move, "you've been acting like a greedy old maid lately."

As usual, she'd joined him at a hotel on a Saturday afternoon, informing Asafumi that she was meeting a woman friend.

"Well," she said a little testily, "when I want to do it, I want to do it."

"They say that's the flip side of frigidity, you know."

A chill went through her. She hadn't heard that before, but it sort of rang true. Still, she wasn't about to back down.

"So you're telling me I'm frigid?" she said, sitting up in bed and fixing him with a furious look.

A smile tugged at his lips. "Yeah, that's right. If you can't get enough no matter how much you do it, then you're frigid. You never even come."

"I do too," she said, thinking of the sensation that exploded inside her when they made love.

"That's bogus," he said, clasping his hands over his head. He lay watching her through slit eyes as she sat fuming. Then he added, "I can tell. I know what happens to a woman when she comes."

That did it. Everything crumbled to dust inside her. He had in effect told her that she wasn't a real woman. She wanted to snap back that she was as much of a woman as anyone. But she also knew deep down that she couldn't entirely deny faking her orgasms.

She got out of bed and started putting on her clothes.

"So you're running away?" Hiroyuki said.

"That's right, I'm running away. You're so cruel," she said icily. She felt as though she might fall apart if she didn't keep up a stony front.

"Running from me isn't going to help, you know," he said quietly, as if trying to soothe her.

But she'd had all she was willing to take. Having divided women up between those who came and those who didn't, he'd placed her among the losers who didn't. She felt humiliated. From getting into the high school and college of her choice to landing a job, she'd always been a winner. At every milestone in her life, she'd been one of the chosen. No selection process had ever given her the bump.

"Go fuck yourself with all those happy comers," she spat out, and hurried from the hotel. She had not seen Hiroyuki since.

She thought at first that ending the affair might make things better with Asafumi. But that proved to be wishful thinking. The guilt she felt over her two-timing never went away. And sex with Asafumi had even less spark to it than before.

If she was frigid, then Asafumi had to be impotent. An impotent man would be incapable of sensing a woman's frigidity. They both shared a condition that prevented them from ever actually getting all the way there. And thanks to that, they inevitably came away unsatisfied no matter how many times they made love.

Shizuka slid her hand under the elastic of her underwear and reached into the dampness between her legs. She felt for her pearl, then gently began massaging it with her index finger. A warmth began to spread around it, and she let out a soft moan.

The image that invariably came to her when she touched herself was of the penis she'd seen standing erect in the shrubbery as a child. She could no longer recall who she was playing with at the time, but they were in Yokohama's Yamashita Park. She happened to turn toward the thicket, and there it was – a glistening male organ gripped by a fist, growing larger and stiffer with each stroke. That was the cock she longed to hold deep between her thighs. That purple-pink menhir rising among the foliage, bursting with virility.

She was stroking harder now. A powerful surge welled within her, as if the ground were splitting open. She rolled over and arched her back. An intense quivering filled her body, then faded away like mist.

Sleep always came easily after she did this. And the sleep that came was more restful than after sex with Asafumi.

Why should that be? she wondered. Why was she filled with such desire for that organ from long ago, while her husband's left her cold? Why had Hiroyuki's cock once made her nearly melt away with pleasure but in time lost that effect?

As she continued to turn these questions over in her mind, she drifted peacefully off to sleep.

22

With his large bundle weighing heavily on his shoulders, Rentarō hiked up the gently sloping road carved from the mountainside with frequent half-moon cut-outs. The branches that arched overhead were just beginning to sprout new leaves, their shadows drawing intricate lines on the roadbed. From every direction came the gurgle of melting snow as it formed rivulets in the woods.

He'd had no difficulty finding the road. It was right where the old woman had said, and there had even been a signpost to mark it – a log with an arrow pointing this way labelled "Mandala Road". But it had turned out to be such a narrow track that he found himself wondering whether there could really be any villages ahead. He marched along the deserted road half doubting he would ever find anything.

To a ripe red apple I press my lips
Under the quiet gaze of the blue autumn sky

Snatches of the song the schoolchildren had been singing for the American officers kept running through his head.

What a change, he thought. Barely more than a year ago, these same people were cursing the Brits and Yanks as incarnations of the devil and bracing for their impending arrival on Japanese shores; now they were pulling out all the stops to make them feel welcome – even though they hadn't exactly arrived under the friendliest of circumstances by dropping atom bombs on Hiroshima and Nagasaki after carpet-bombing Tokyo and dozens of other cities. To the sound of air raid sirens, city folk had fled in every which direction, frantically trying to escape the showers of firebombs falling from the sky. Yet now those teachers and villagers were all but waving the American flag as they greeted an inspection team – even bringing out a reed organ to entertain them with songs. The obsequiousness of it all was sickening. But it did not go so far as to induce loathing. The soil in which his current feelings grew was far too mixed up to produce genuine hostility.

In the days following Japan's defeat, everything Rentarō had believed in until then suddenly took on a new shape. The emperor was transformed from a living god into a tiny Japanese man standing stiff as a mannequin beside General MacArthur, and the Great Japanese Empire that everybody had been so sure would win the war and become leader of all Asia was now being called a fourth-class nation. The divine origin of Japan, regarded as an absolute truth during the war, was declared a lie, and democracy was presented in its place as the greatest treasure known to humanity. Newspapers and radio stations under occupation control declared that the Allied Powers had come as saviours, bearing democracy to free them all from military tyranny. Just as they'd once believed that the Japanese Empire would save Asia, people now believed that the United States of America would save Japan. But it was still, at heart, no more than a matter of belief. And having had their previous beliefs betrayed by the abrupt demise of emperor worship at the end of the war, few could feel completely secure in their new faith. Rentarō himself had the awkward sense that he didn't quite know where he ought to stand.

The day the war ended had found Rentarō in Osaka. He'd arrived there the morning before to visit a customer near Kyōbashi Station.

After making that stop, he bought a box lunch at the station with a meal coupon. Just as he finished eating and started walking up the street away from the station, a preliminary alert sounded. Over the last six months, he'd been hearing these things on a daily basis, no matter where he happened to be, so he paid little attention at first, but then the alert was upgraded to an air-raid warning. Throngs of workers, mobilized students, and Women's Volunteer Corps members came pouring out of the sprawling Osaka Armory complex nearby. Thinking this definitely didn't look good, he turned back toward the station. A formation of B29s appeared in the blue summer sky and began releasing bombs. The target was obviously the armoury, but now and then one of the bombs would stray closer to the station. The large bundle he was carrying prevented him from moving very quickly, so he found a sheltered spot beside a nearby store where he could take cover. The explosions came in waves, and the ground shook with each blast. Smoke and debris filled the air above the armoury with a dense cloud that blocked the sky. Suddenly he heard an explosion behind him, and turned to see that the station had been hit: the main building had caved in, and the rails of the Katamachi Line were bent like a snake rearing its head. Hearing people crying for help, he headed toward their voices. When he came to the elevated tracks of the Tōjō Line, he found handbags and shoes and such scattered about on the ground – and the people they belonged to buried in the wreckage of the spot where they thought they'd be protected. A woman with only her bloodied head showing was groaning in pain; a writhing arm protruded from beneath the rubble; a man with a large chunk of concrete across his belly was squirming like a crushed frog. Rentarō threw his bundle down and ran to help pull victims free.

Station workers and members of the local civil defence unit soon arrived on the scene. Rentarō used medicines from his baskets to treat the injured. He did this without the slightest hesitation. There was no sense in hoarding what he had when he might be killed in an air raid himself tomorrow. All his supplies quickly disappeared – both the new medicines he'd brought with him, and the old ones he'd retrieved at his customer stops so far. His pride in being a medicine peddler had never been greater. The victims took what he offered with trembling hands. Some were unable to speak, but he could see the gratitude in their eyes and on their faces. He was a ministering angel to them, offering succour in their time of need. Everything he handed out became like Hangontan, the miracle cure his ancestors claimed could even raise the dead. Any medicine given when all other hope is lost takes on the power of Hangontan.

Even after his supplies were exhausted, there remained much more to be done – pulling people from the rubble, carrying the injured to the hospital, recovering the dead. His own family was in far-off Toyama, and he had no immediate cause to worry about them or go rushing home, so he continued helping with rescue operations until after the sun went down. That night, a station worker found a place for him to sleep in the shadow of the damaged building. He lay down with a deep sense of satisfaction at having done something truly valuable for the first time in his life.

The following day he shouldered his empty baskets and started on foot toward the next station down the line, which was now as far as the trains could come. Along the way he saw massive craters left by one-tonne bombs in the riverbed. Smoke from cremation fires rose among the rubble. Victims of the bombing recognized his trade from the bundle he was carrying and begged for medicine. A child with his leg covered in blood lay half-conscious under the eaves of a building. A woman clutched the limp body of a baby to her chest. A man called out the names of his family as he walked along. An elderly woman with an air-raid hood over her head squatted in the remains of what must have been her home, staring vacantly into space.

Lacking anything more that might serve as Hangontan, there was nothing Rentarō could do for these people. How had it come to this? he wondered bitterly. When the war began, everybody took victory for granted. But reports from the battlefront just kept getting worse. By the time he got back from Malaya, there were very dark clouds on the horizon. And yet every newspaper and radio station continued to insist that Japan would come out on top. Something didn't add up, though he wasn't quite sure what. The whole country was engaged in the effort. People persevered through hunger and scarcity. They clung to the belief that the sacrifices they were making would one day be rewarded. But Toyama had been bombed, Tokyo was said to be a wasteland, and he'd heard talk of some new kind of weapon destroying Hiroshima and Nagasaki a few days ago. Now Osaka had taken another massive hit. The much-rumoured Allied landing sounded more likely every day. Faced with that threat, the government was beating the drums for all hundred million Japanese to fight to the death. Somehow, victory was supposed to emerge from that final pitched battle.

He noticed a crowd in front of a half-broken building up ahead. As he approached, wondering what it could be, he saw that many of the people were hanging their heads in tears. Some were on their knees, sobbing without restraint. He thought someone must have died, but when he poked his head through the crowd, he discovered they were gathered around a slightly singed radio. The national anthem began flowing from the speaker, accompanied by heavy static.

"What's going on?" he asked a man standing as stiff as a rod beside him.

Glaring at the radio with his eyes peeled back, the man said, "We lost the war."

That's not possible, thought Rentarō. But the man's face was filled with rage. And from the young woman hunched over in sobs, to the old crone with a hand towel pressed to her face, to the youth walking dejectedly away, the behaviour of everyone in the crowd confirmed the truth of what the man had said.

In stunned disbelief, he looked around. The city laid waste by bombs and fire looked even flatter in summer's midday sunlight. It was an all black-and-white world. Bedraggled figures covered in dust and dirt came and went along the street through the surrounding rubble – weeping, heads hanging, steps heavy with dejection, every one of them looking ready to collapse in a heap.

What he saw was like a picture of the afterworld. He felt as if he were watching departed souls wandering about on the other side of the great divide, and thought he must have died. But he had no more Hangontan with which to bring anyone back to life. There would be no more miracle cures here.

It was a moment seared permanently in his memory.

From that day onward, the entire country put the war behind it, and the words "recovery" and "reconstruction" were on everybody's lips, including Rentarō's. But whenever he thought back to that scene in the burned-out ruins of Osaka on the day of Japan's surrender, he would invariably find himself wondering if perhaps he, too, had died in that final air raid.

Everybody knows that nobody lives forever. But somewhere deep inside, most people feel as if they themselves will somehow be spared. Rentarō was no exception. Could it be that he merely *believed* he was still living, while in fact he had died on the day the war came to an end? Occupation troops had arrived and their jeeps roved the streets. Talk of democracy filled the air. GIs tossed gum and chocolate bars to clamouring children, while men young and old scrambled to pick up the cigarette butts they dropped. Schools welcomed occupation officials like VIPs. But as he watched all of this going on around him, everything seemed to belong to somewhere far away. Was it because he had passed into the realm of death?

He looked at the mountain road now stretching before him. Bright sunlight poured through the branches coming into leaf overhead. It could hardly be called a landscape of death. And yet there was that same faraway sensation he couldn't quite dispel.

No medicine was needed in the realm of the dead. He no longer felt the same enthusiasm when he shouldered this trademark baskets. Gone was the satisfaction and the sense of contributing to society that came from helping people get well. The day before the war's end, he had experienced the greatest sense of fulfilment he'd ever known in his work, only to lose that feeling forever at the moment of Japan's surrender.

The steep slope to one side fell back from the road, and some terraced rice paddies came into view ahead. He could see farmers at work turning the hardened soil. Here and there a thatched house was tucked out of the wind against a stand of cedars or at the back of a rice terrace – ten or so houses altogether.

Rentarō turned from Mandala Road onto a footpath leading toward these houses. He came to the first immediately after crossing a bridge that spanned a small stream. Rectangular strips of *daikon* radish, strung up to dry last autumn, still hung under the eaves, and chickens running free in the front yard pecked at the ground for grubs. A dog chained to a persimmon tree was curled into a ball, asleep.

As he walked across the yard toward the house, he noticed a plaque on the doorpost inscribed in ink-brush with the phrase, "Home of a Fallen Soldier". He gazed at it for several moments before turning to the open door and calling into the darkness beyond. "Hello? Is anybody home?" He could hear the *tonk-tonk-tonk* of a knife chopping vegetables on a cutting board, but he received no answer. He raised his voice to call two or three more times, until the chopping finally ceased and an old woman with a muslin hand towel wrapped around her head emerged. When she saw Rentarō with his large bundle, she broke into a broad smile that revealed several missing teeth.

"Oh, the medicine man! It's been such a long time! How have you been?"

She was obviously mistaking him for another peddler who'd come to this village before.

"Actually, I'm new to these parts," he explained. "Looking to drum up some new business. I'm not the man you've had before."

"It certainly is good to see you looking so well," she said nodding her head up and down. "You can't imagine how we've been looking forward to you coming by."

He gathered she was hard of hearing. She gave no sign of having understood a word he'd said.

She directed him to the veranda, and went back inside cooing with delight. Smiling wryly to himself over her confusion, he lowered his bundle onto the veranda. Almost immediately the shoji screen opened behind him, and the woman handed him a large medicine kit envelope. Emblazoned across the front was her previous supplier's business name: "Sankatsudō." Worn corners, torn edges, and brown stains attested to its long service. He looked inside to find it completely empty.

Clearly, the man who used to keep the envelope stocked had not been here in a very long time. Perhaps he had died in the war or been forced to move away after losing his home to Allied bombing. Or maybe he had simply lost his records for this route. Whatever the case might be, it boded well for Rentarō's chances of establishing his own clientele out this way. With his hopes rising, he repeated that he had come looking for new customers and took out a similar envelope labelled "Nonezawa Pharmacy."

"That's very kind of you," the woman beamed. "This other one's in such tatters."

He decided to give up trying to explain. Taking a fresh notebook from his top basket, he asked her the name of the hamlet and of the master of the house. With the book open to the first page, he wrote: "Ōyama Village, Magawa. By way of Mandala Road from Tateyama Line Awasuno Station. Hachisoko Hamlet. Yoshizō Kitagawa, first house on right across wooden bridge."

He filled the large envelope with packets containing the most commonly used medicines – restoratives, fever powders, cold remedies, and so on.

"Does anyone in the family have a chronic condition in need of a special preparation?"

He glanced surreptitiously inside the house as he spoke. On the wall of the front room adjoining the veranda were portrait photos of Emperor Meiji as well as the reigning emperor. The sliding doors were open to a sitting room beyond, where a wood fire burned in the sunken hearth, sending wisps of white smoke into the air. On the nearer side of it was a round bassinet made of straw, with a baby still too young to walk lying in it. The next room along the veranda was the altar room, with an imposing black-lacquer Buddhist altar set against the wall. Displayed on the altar shelf was the portrait of a still relatively young man, framed in black – no doubt the fallen soldier of the plaque on the doorpost. Had he been the head of the family, or an unmarried second or third son? Rentarō wondered.

The woman interrupted his thoughts. "I wonder if you might have some Hangontan you could leave us?"

"Hangontan?" he echoed in surprise, his heart skipping a beat.

"Yes," she said, holding his gaze with a hopeful look from beneath her creased eyelids. "It does my palpitations good."

Hangontan is history, and we'll never have it again in Japan. The words were on the tip of his tongue, but he held them back.

Her face fell at seeing his expression. "You don't have any?" she asked.

"Oh, yes, I certainly do," he said quickly. "You just caught me by surprise because these days most people seem to go for the Western medicines, and it's not very often I get asked for old standbys like Hangontan."

As he explained, he drew a packet of Hangontan from his well-organized baskets. The name appeared in thick black brushstrokes on the front, with "Special formula of the Nonezawa Pharmacy" written in smaller letters after it. It would be different from Sankatsudō's preparation, but that clearly hadn't occurred to the woman. As she took the large envelope with the Hangontan added to it, she raised it in front of her and bowed her head in a gesture of gratitude.

"This is such a relief," she said happily. "You feel so vulnerable when there's no medicine in the house."

Restacking his five baskets, Rentarō tied the cloth around them and got up from the veranda. The old woman gave a deep bow with the envelope still clutched to her chest. He told her he would come again, and left the farmhouse behind.

There was no sense to it, he knew, but he couldn't help feeling as if he'd given the woman a supply of phony Hangontan.

23

As two, then three days went by after Rentarō's departure, a growing sense of emptiness and loss came over Saya. To distract herself, she spent the time hoeing the garden. Once she had worked the soil into soft furrows, she planned to plant the squash and cucumber seeds she'd obtained from a neighbouring farmer. Every seed was precious.

She enjoyed the sponginess of the earth beneath her bare feet as she broke up the soil and shaped the rows. It brought back memories of walking through the jungle in Malaya with Rentarō. She'd always gone barefoot in those days, whether walking through ferns or spiny rattan. Following behind in his thick-soled shoes, Rentarō had been amazed at the way she padded along in her bare feet. This was before he took her to live with him in Kota Bharu – before she'd adopted the custom of wearing shoes. He'd been surprised by a lot of other things, too: her ability to identify animals by their tracks; her knack for finding shelter from sudden showers; and most of all, her extensive knowledge of the plants that grew in the jungle. Even when he seemed unimpressed by something her brother had done, if she did the same thing, he'd suddenly be full of admiration.

"What's this called," he would ask, crouching over a plant he hadn't seen before. "Tiger's paw." "What's it good for?" "You drink it in hot water when you're having a baby." "Oh? What's it taste like? Is it anything like tea?" "What's tea?" "A plant you put in hot water and drink for refreshment."

Conversations with Rentarō had been unlike those with any other man. The men of her tribe never paid any attention to what the women said. Except when they had to tell them something important – about a tiger lurking nearby, maybe, or about the tribe moving tomorrow – they only talked among themselves. The women ignored the men, too, generally going about life in their own separate world. Men and women would escape from their groups to be with someone they liked only when they felt a certain itch inside. If they were married, they did it with the person they were married to; if they weren't, they chose someone else who wasn't.

Rentarō had shown Saya a completely different way for a man and woman to behave with each other. They'd roved about the jungle together to collect medicinal herbs; in Kota Bharu, they'd gone to the market side by side to do their shopping; they'd spent long hours sitting and talking together about all the little things going on in their lives. Until she met Rentarō, men had existed only on the other side of a wall; they were like a different species to her – creatures who thought about completely different things and behaved in completely different ways. They made demands of one kind or another from their side of the wall, and the women usually jumped to serve – though sometimes they ignored them if they weren't in the mood. When a man spoke to a woman, it was as a command, and the woman's only response was to say yes or no. The two sexes were as alien to each other as dogs and chickens.

Only one person had ever been any different: the healer. He treated men and women alike. He talked with them both in exactly the same way – sometimes gently, sometimes sharply. When he was teaching the young Saya about plants, he always spoke gently. "See this," he said, pointing to a redfoot plant. "If you steep the flowers in hot water and drink it, you feel aroused." "What's aroused," Saya asked. He pressed his hand to his crotch. "If you're a man, this grows big, and if you're a woman, you get hot down there," he said, gesturing between her legs. She put a hand on her crotch. She couldn't imagine what he meant about it getting hot. The lines around his mouth deepened as he smiled. "I'll show you when you're a little older," he said.

And he had indeed been the one who taught her the way of man and woman. She was just playing one day, straddling a fallen tree trunk and bouncing up and down, when he beckoned for her to follow. He led her behind some trees and told her to put her hand under his loincloth. She felt his limp penis. While she was rolling it between her fingers, feeling what it was like, he said, show me yours. She lifted her loincloth for him, and he touched the little bump between her legs. A charge went through her body.

"This here," he said, "is a woman's seed." He took his finger away. "If you water it well and make it happy, the woman inside you grows and becomes a beautiful bloom."

"What about this?" Saya asked, wrapping her hand around his penis. It had begun to grow hard.

"This is a man's heart," he said. "It swells when he's with a woman. When the woman's seed grows moist, and the man's heart fills to bursting, it makes the woman want to swallow his heart up. Then the two of them put their bodies together."

Saya knew what putting their bodies together meant. She had seen people joined like that many times, in a thicket somewhere or the darkness of a hut.

"But you must be careful," the healer went on. He put his hand over Saya's as she held his stiffening penis. "For some men, this ceases to be their heart. They turn it into a sword. Both here in the jungle and outside."

This was harder for her to follow. Even a little later, when he put his own heart into the hollow beneath her seed, his words remained a puzzle to her. Only long afterwards, in Kota Bharu, did she finally understand.

There, at the P-house, she encountered hundreds of men whose hearts had turned into swords. They plunged their blades deep into her body, planting the seeds of hatred in her wounds. As she lay limp with exhaustion on her flea-bitten mattress, she would think of the medicine man: if only she had listened to him and not brought Rentarō into the jungle; if only she had stayed where she was instead of coming to live in Kota Bharu. Then she might have been spared ever knowing what he had meant.

Leaning with both hands on the handle of her hoe, Saya looked absently across the landscape around her. She could see fuzzy green mats of sprouting rice where seedbeds had been prepared in the paddies. Blossoming cherry trees glowed pink on the embankment of the river in the distance. A warm breeze carried the scent of flowers and spring leaves.

Which had Rentarō given her? she wondered – his heart or a sword. She had found a shared warmth in their connection, much like the warmth she'd felt with the healer. And she was convinced she had found his heart, too. During all those happy days in Kota Bharu, he had watered her seed with his bursting heart – yes, surely it had been a heart.

Yet it was this very same man who'd opened the door to those hordes of men flashing swords instead, and she could not stop blaming him for it.

Why did she persist in hating him so? He was the one whose heart had swelled for her. He was the one who'd led her out of the jungle and introduced her to a whole new life. Why should he have to bear the burden of other men's sins? How could he have known what lay in store for her on the other side when he opened that door?

Don't be fooled!

A voice rang out nearby, and she turned to see the figure of Kim Suk-hwa planted like a tree in the furrow she'd just finished shaping. A pool of blood darkened the soil where her torso disappeared into the ground.

Remember what he did to you, she shrieked, her face twisted with hate. *He used you and tossed you aside like a banana peel. That's what men are like. This stuff about a man's heart is all a load of crap.*

158

Saya threw the hoe at her to silence her shrill voice. It fell across the furrows and Suk-hwa disappeared. For several moments Saya just stood there, staring at the spot. A small white butterfly flittered past.

Then, picking up her hoe, she raked over the place where Suk-hwa had been. Once the furrows were in proper shape again, she took the tear-shaped squash seeds and began pushing them into the ground one by one.

24

Rentarō continued his journey on foot along Mandala Road. Every village he came to were glad to take his medicines, and they happily put him up for the night when he asked. The road following the Kanoko River narrowed and grew more rugged as he went.

Toward evening on the third day after leaving Senbashi, he arrived at another hamlet. This one was nothing like the others he'd visited. There were no large thatched farmhouses here – only crude log-frame huts with shingle roofs held down by stones. Eight such huts were clustered together on a sloping patch of cleared forest, with several newly cultivated farm plots nearby.

He had heard talk along the way about a pioneer group carving a new settlement out of the wilderness farther up the valley. This had to be the place.

About twenty men, women, and children were busy in a field that was still strewn with a good many rocks. The men were working to remove a tree stump, while the women broke up the soil with hoes and the children pulled weeds or picked up stones. No one looked over thirty. The deeply tanned men with close-cropped hair and scruffy beards all wore old military fatigues or the wartime civilian uniforms, and the women, too, were dressed in the half-kimono and *monpe* style that had been standard wear for them during the war. Rentarō felt as if he had stepped back in time.

The entire group stopped what they were doing and eyed him warily as he approached. He gave them a friendly smile and bobbed his head in greeting.

"Oh!" came a female voice from among the figures leaning on pickaxes and hoes. "It's the medicine man."

Behind a round-faced man with heavy eyebrows stood a woman of more slender appearance, smiling his way. It was the woman he'd met on the train. His smile broadened at the sight of a familiar face.

"Have you licked that cold you had?" he asked.

She nodded and whispered something to the man in front of her. The man's eyebrows rose like a pair of wings and his expression relaxed a bit.

"My wife tells me you gave her some help," he said, and bowed his thanks. At this, the tension ebbed from faces all around. The others had clearly been waiting for his cue, which suggested he was their leader. He looked a little older than the others, too – probably pushing thirty.

Rentarō looked around the group as he explained that he had been placing medicine kits in hamlets along the way, and he was hoping he might do the same here. He saw eyes lighting up among several women standing a short distance apart. But the man with the heavy eyebrows had regained his cautious look. He kept his eyes fixed sharply on Rentarō but didn't immediately respond.

When prospecting for new customers, peddlers didn't always receive a warm welcome. Get too persistent and people might peg you as one of the high-pressure hucksters who give door-to-door sales a bad name, and threaten to call the police. But this was a time of shortages, and Rentarō knew the settlement had neither a doctor nor a regular supply of medicine. They should be leaping at the chance to take care of an important need, but for some reason their apparent leader seemed reluctant to let down his guard. Rentarō was beginning to think he might be difficult.

"You say we don't have to pay till next time?" he finally asked.

"That's right," Rentarō assured him. "You pay only for what you use, and not until after you use it."

It was hard to believe there could be anyone who didn't know how his business worked. The feeling he got was more that the man actually did know, but wanted to make doubly sure. Maybe they were short of cash.

"If it's pay later, it sure sounds good to me," a man with a small moustache said cheerfully. He had a hand towel looped around his neck.

The leader gave a grunt that sounded like agreement. Encouraged, the other men chimed in to say they'd feel better if they had some medicine in the house. The women nodded, too, relieved that the men had come around.

"Well, in that case, I suppose it makes sense," said Heavy Eyebrows, as if yielding to the general consensus.

"Then I'd like to begin making the rounds right away," Rentarō said.

"But it'll be dark before you can get to us all," came a worried voice. It belonged to a woman with smallpox scars on her forehead.

"That's right," said Small Moustache. "Where were you planning to spend the night?"

When Rentarō said he'd go on to the next hamlet and ask for lodgings there, the woman turned to a tall man with a broad nose and said, "He could stay at our place."

The man bunched his lips, obviously hesitant. "But we don't have a spare futon."

As if drawn by a magnet, all eyes turned toward Heavy Eyebrows.

"He can stay with us," he said quickly. He thumped his pickaxe on the ground a couple of times to shake off the dirt before turning to the men. "What say we call it a day? You can all come over to my place later and we'll share some sake with our visitor here. It'll be a good chance to find out what's going on in the rest of the world, too. He can pass out the medicines then, and you can just take them home with you."

One of the cardinal rules of those in Rentarō's business was to always go personally to each house where they left a kit. It was part of how they built a relationship with their customers. So he would definitely have preferred to make the rounds of the houses one at a time. But he didn't want to disturb the goodwill he finally felt developing, so he held his tongue.

The others quickly agreed and began picking up their hoes and baskets and heading back to their houses. Dusk was gathering over the valley. The murmur of the Kanoko River below seemed to stir the chill that had come into the air.

"How long have you folks been in this place?" Rentarō asked the man with the moustache.

He slowly swept his eyes over the cleared fields. "This is our second year," he said. "We were in the army together, all of us men, a bunch of city kids from around Tokyo. When the repatriation boat brought us back from down south, the war had taken our homes, there weren't any jobs, and we were pretty much at the end of our rope, so we decided to move out here and go back to the land. Ohara there," he said indicating the man with the heavy eyebrows, "has some relations in the area, and they're letting us use the land for free."

"Must be pretty tough, not being used to this kind of work."

He stuck out his lower lip. "It's nothing compared to what we had to do in the army," he said. "Digging trenches and marching day after day with packs that weighed a tonne on our backs. Now *that's* what you call tough."

Rentarō asked where they'd been stationed, and he said the Philippines. Then, glancing toward his buddies, he remarked, "Considering that more than half the troops died, we count ourselves lucky to have survived."

"Mr. Medicine Man!" It was Ohara calling to him from the doorway of one of the houses.

"See you later," Small Moustache said and headed for the house behind it.

The Oharas might be the only ones who had bedding enough for guests, but their house looked no different from the others. Stones held the roof in place, and the walls were of old clapboard that looked like salvage from an abandoned house somewhere, with the bottom half covered in swatches of cedar bark to help keep out the cold. Inside the door was the usual earthen area and just one room with a raised wooden floor. This was covered with a thin rush matting that was beginning to look pretty threadbare.

"Water, Fumiko," Ohara called out on entering.

As he went to set his hoe and pickaxe in the corner, his wife hastily dipped some water into a small wooden bucket and placed it on the edge of the raised floor, together with a washrag.

"Here you are, dear," she said.

"Guests first," he prompted gruffly.

"I'm sorry," she said. She turned to Rentarō and bowed, gesturing toward the water.

He thanked her, lowered his baskets onto the floor, and washed his feet. Then he untied his bundle and took out a cloth bag.

"Here's some rice you can use."

When you depended on the hospitality of your customers for lodging, it was essential to bring along your own rice. Fumiko glanced toward her husband for approval before accepting it.

The woman was behaving like a mouse in the presence of a cat. She seemed to cower before her husband's every word and move. It made Rentarō feel uneasy as he sat down again on the edge of the floor. After changing the water for her husband, Fumiko began stirring the embers in the kitchen stove to get it going. Ohara sat down next to Rentarō and washed his feet.

The splash of water and the crackle of kindling filled the darkening cabin. When his hands and feet were clean, Ohara stepped up onto the floor to light an oil lamp, then went to get two teacups, which he filled with some bitter tea. The two men sat on the edge of the floor sipping their tea as Fumiko hurried to prepare dinner with no time to stop and wash her own feet.

"Have you been coming out this way long?" Ohara asked.

"No, this is the first time." He paused several moments before adding, "Thanks to the war, I'm basically back to square one."

Ohara nodded. "That's pretty much what brought us out here, too."

"I understand you were in the Philippines."

"Yes, among other places," he said, and then fell silent.

Fumiko was using a bamboo blowpipe to fan the flames. With the conversation stalled, Rentarō looked around the cabin as he drank his tea. Apart from two large wicker containers in a corner of the room behind him, and the spade, hoe, and other digging tools leaning against the wall of the dirt-floored room, there wasn't much to see. For lack of anything better to do, he turned to his baskets and started preparing the envelopes he would hand out when the others came to join them later on.

Ohara finished his tea and went outside. Rentarō soon heard the sound of wood being split.

He was just finishing the eighth envelope when Fumiko called to her husband, "Dinner's ready." A moment later Ohara appeared in the doorway.

The meal consisted of *daikon* rice, some wild vegetables simmered in a sauce, pickled red turnips, and weak miso soup. The couple had no meal trays or table, so it was served on the floor, with the rice pot and soup pan placed in the middle and each person's bowls and plates arranged around them. They sat down at the three places Fumiko had set and ate in silence. The rice was cold and dry, a low-grade Chinese variety, apparently left over from morning; she hadn't used what Rentarō brought. He watched as the two of them began shovelling in big mouthfuls of rice, stuffing a bite of pickle or vegetables in after, and wolfing it all down. Ohara dragged the plate of pickles toward him using his chopsticks.

It was like watching dogs feed. They were both eating only to survive. It reminded him of the families he'd seen in the ruins of Osaka, gathered around a pan or two outside whatever crude shelter they'd managed to patch together after their house burned down; or of the orphans huddled under the eaves of the station building bolting down some scraps of food they'd scrounged up somewhere. This was what it meant to lose your home, he thought. You went back to living purely for survival. When the Oharas' house burned down in the firebombing of Tokyo, all the ways a home has of humanizing things had gone up in smoke for them as well.

With the meal over in practically no time at all, the two men remained where they were, drinking tea, while Fumiko cleaned up. Before long, there was a knock at the door and a chorus of voices called, "Good evening."

"Ah, here they are," Ohara said brightly.

His wife went to open up, and the men filed in, with Small Moustache in the lead. Each brought a small offering of sake or something to nibble on prepared by their wives. Gatherings like this no doubt took place with some regularity. Fumiko arranged their contributions on the floor in the middle of the room and set out teacups for them. While she returned to cooking something at the stove, the men sat down in a circle and began pouring for each other, quickly getting into a party spirit.

"So tell us, Mr. Medicine Man," said Small Moustache. "The cherry blossoms must be popping open down in the city."

"I suppose they're at about twenty percent."

"That means we shouldn't have too much longer to wait out here, either," said a man with a burn scar on his cheek.

"We'll have to have a picnic under the flowers again, like we did last year," Ohara boomed to the enthusiastic agreement of the others. The man seemed to have suddenly come alive. "We need to get the millet in before that, though. Those millet cakes everybody liked so much at New Year's were all thanks to the good crop we took in last year."

"The Tashiros and Moriyamas are going to have new mouths to feed pretty soon, too. There'll be more of us by January, so we actually need to do better than we did last year."

Talking about the future was a way of forgetting about current hardships. With a sparkle in their eyes, the ex-servicemen began sharing the plans they had for their pioneer village. They would draw water from the Kanoko River to make rice paddies. If they cleared some trees higher up the slope to plant mulberry bushes, they could raise silkworms, too. It wouldn't be all that long before they needed a school. In the minds of these eight men, their little settlement would someday be a bustling community with a school and town hall – a hub of activity for others who lived up and down Mandala Road.

"So the watchword is still 'Be fruitful and multiply', even with the war over," said Small Moustache. "We need all the hands we can get to rebuild the country." There was fervour in his voice.

"You got anything to perk us up for baby-making?" a small man with big ears sticking straight out asked, turning to Rentarō.

"Absolutely!" he said with some gusto, buoyed by the gaiety in the room. "There's a tonic called Kinkontan."

"Speaking of which," the man with the scar on his cheek said, as he reached for a slice of pickled *daikon*, "remember Sergeant Major Yamazoe crowing about the stuff he used to take before trips to the P-house?"

"Right, right, something he'd 'requisitioned' from some Chinese shop."

"The Korean girl he always went to told me once she hated the days he came in," said a light-skinned man with bulging eyes. "She said he never let up all night long."

"You know what I think, Tashiro. I bet that was her way of telling you you couldn't hold a candle to him?"

Tashiro's cheeks turned red and he scowled. "Hardly. She was just saying how scared she was of him."

"Oh, I get it," Ohara said with mischief in his smile, "You were in love with her, weren't you?"

Tashiro looked flustered and pursed his lips. The others laughed.

"Hey, it was serious," someone said.

"Kayo's not gonna like it if she finds out," said another.

"Forget it," said Ohara. "It wasn't really love, it was just the war. When you live knowing you might have no tomorrow, any girl who's the least bit nice to you looks like the Goddess of Mercy."

"Yeah, definitely, you got that right," said Small Moustache. "I remember getting hard-ons all the time. Anybody who gave me a place to put it had to be the greatest goddess there was."

"Not that you ever got much time to worship your fine goddess, 'cause *wham*, *bang*, your pecker'd shoot off and it'd be all over."

Starting to get quite drunk, the men threw their heads back and laughed.

"But you know," said Tashiro, "I can't believe we dragged those girls all the way from Korea and then just dumped them when we had to get out."

Small Moustache poured some sake into Tashiro's cup. "Hell, it's not like we had a choice. Besides, bitches like that, even if they're stuck in the Philippines, they've got built-in wares to sell. I'm sure they're doing just fine."

"The only reason we're here today is because we dumped our excess baggage. That's how war is," said Ohara bluntly.

Silence fell over the room. After several moments, Scarface spoke up a little more loudly than necessary.

"So how about that pine stump we dug up today? That was one big root system. You suppose we can get some pine-root oil out of it?"

"Great idea," said Small Moustache. "I even remember talk about flying planes with that stuff during the war. I bet there's some good oil in it."

"Yeah, we deserve some payback after all the trouble it gave us getting it out."

"No kidding. Those roots refused to let go of the ground no matter how hard we pulled."

"Kind of like the way those Korean girls wouldn't let go of our truck," said Tashiro. Ohara told him to give it a rest already, but he seemed not to hear and went on, both hands wrapped around his teacup and a tremor in his voice. "I can still see them now, grabbing at that tailgate, begging us to take them with us – those eyes, those hands. Then the sergeant major swings his sword and a hand goes flying. The very girl he always went to see! I can't get it out of my mind – the sight of that hand tumbling through the air."

"I said enough!" barked Ohara.

"He's right," Small Moustache put in soothingly. "You've got to forget about all that. It's ancient history now."

"Look, Tashiro," Scarface said, with some irritation. "That girl wasn't the only one who lost a hand. Our own guys were losing arms or legs or getting their guts blown out, too. It was war. You did what you had to do to survive – everybody did. You didn't have a choice. There was a lot of ugly stuff, but the best thing now is to just forget about it."

Tashiro shook his head. "How'm I supposed to do that? I dream about it all the time. Those pleading eyes. That hand flying through the air."

"Shut the fuck up!" Ohara abruptly stood up and clouted Tashiro hard enough to send him rolling backwards. He looked up from the floor with quivering eyes. Ohara glared down at him. "Nothing you saw in the Philippines was worth a dog's whimper. I was in China. I slogged it out on the front lines for seven goddamn years. What you got was a couple of tenderfoot years and then home sweet home. You never saw shit. So stop your snivelling over some whore's hand. You call yourself a man?"

Tashiro hung his head in tears. Ohara sat back down with a thud and crossed his arms. "Fucking cry-baby," he muttered.

Not surprisingly, this threw a damper over things. The men sipped their sake in silence. The mood was now more like a wake than a party.

Left out of the conversation, Rentarō's mind had begun to wander. Back in the days when he was posted to Siberia, the army didn't provide what it referred to as "comfort women" and what everybody else called "P-girls." With no real fighting to speak of, and nothing to do but stand watch under endlessly dull gray skies, there'd been frequent incidents involving the rape of local women by troops bored out of their minds. More and more of the men began making furtive visits to the infirmary with VD symptoms, and headquarters had to send out notices calling on them to exercise better judgment. Thanks to his trade, Rentarō already knew enough about VD to refrain from risky behaviour, but without that background, he might well have been among those who failed to contain their impulses at the sight of women. Despite the absence of almost any fighting, troop strength dropped drastically due to the large number of men who became infected. He once heard that that was exactly why the army had eventually decided to bring in its own women.

The "comfort houses" set up for this purpose had been mentioned from time to time by some of the Japanese officers who visited Rentarō's home in Kota Bharu. He could only put together a vague picture of what they might have been like based on those conversations.

"Well, I think I'm ready to hit the sack," Scarface said with an exaggerated yawn. Since everyone was feeling uncomfortable under the heavy pall that had fallen over the room, they all quickly chimed in with similar remarks and began getting to their feet.

"Hey, what about the medicine?" Small Moustache called out over the hubbub. He looked expectantly toward Rentarō, who sat toying with the cup in his hand.

"Let's let that go till tomorrow," Ohara said glumly. "He can do the rounds."

He seemed to have forgotten that he'd rejected the idea of Rentarō going from house to house earlier. Of course, Rentarō himself preferred the individual approach anyway, so he had no objection.

Tashiro was so drunk he had to be held up on both sides as the men crowded through the door.

Silence returned to the cabin. Fumiko began clearing cups and bowls away and cleaning up, but Ohara continued to sit cross-legged, drinking – which gave Rentarō no choice but to stay where he was as well. Ohara alternated between staring into the darkness in the corner and crushing bugs on the floor with his finger. There was something murky and black in his expression that seemed to come from a deep, festering anger.

Drying her hands as she stepped back up from the kitchen, Fumiko began laying out the futons. There were just two, which she placed against opposite walls of the small room, as far apart as they could go. So the business about spare futon merely meant that the Oharas had two sets of bedding. Which implied, presumably, that the other houses had only one.

"Shall we turn in then?" Ohara said when Fumiko finished laying everything out. He went outside. Rentarō followed him out to relieve his bladder before bed. Avoiding the cloud of ill humour that surrounded his host, he chose a spot some distance away and opened his trousers. No light came from any of the other huts; he supposed everybody had gone straight to bed to conserve lamp oil. Bright stars spread across the clear sky overhead.

As he listened to his pee splashing among the weeds, Rentarō thought of his family in Senbashi, and of Saya.

What if he were to just keep travelling on from here and never go back? The silent treatment from his wife was tiresome, and now there was Saya's pregnancy to complicate things even more. If only he could get away from them both and make a fresh start of it somewhere. Seeing how these ex-soldiers were building a new life for themselves on this mountainside made him feel all the more that way.

The country was still turned upside down from the war. Given the way things were, he could go missing now and barely cause a stir. Like these men pulling up stakes in Tokyo and coming to Tateyama, he could simply go somewhere else to settle, and nobody would think anything of it. If he said he'd moved back from overseas, they'd just take him at his word.

Rentarō turned these thoughts over in his mind as he walked back to the house. Ohara was already in bed. Rentarō went to the other bed and removed just his gaiters before pulling the covers over himself. Even with the advent of spring, the temperature still dipped pretty low overnight in the mountains.

Fumiko closed up behind him and turned out the lamp. A moment later he heard her crawling in beside Ohara. Then the house fell silent.

25

Whooo oo-oong, whoon whooo oo-oo-oong.

The sound of someone humming came drifting through the darkness and drew Shizuka from her sleep.

Whooo oo-oong, whoooo oo-oo-oong, who-oo who-oo whoong.

It was a deep-throated sound that seemed to emerge through pursed lips, coming from somewhere out in the garden. She folded back the quilt and slowly sat upright. It had to be the middle of the night by now. The utter stillness made the tune sound all the more forlorn.

Had Asafumi finally returned? But surely he would just come inside instead of staying out there humming to himself... And the last thing a burglar would want was to make any kind of noise...

The sound continued like a single thin strand, sometimes rising, sometimes falling nearly to the point of dying out.

Of all the times for Asafumi to be gone, she thought, feeling her resentment return over the lack of any word from him.

She sat still for a time, listening, but the voice went on without pause. Finally, she rose from the futon and crept through the dark into the front room, taking care not to make noise. She slowly pulled back the curtain and peered outside.

Deep shadows lay over the shrub-filled garden. Here and there the face of a leaf reflected the glint of moonlight.

Shizuka turned her ear toward the sound. It seemed to flow from the darkness among the trees and shrubs. The gentle voice now came clear as that of a woman. She thought about going for the flashlight, but she was afraid that might make the voice stop. There was an eerie quality to it that frightened her, but it also beckoned to her.

She unscrewed the lock and slid the glass door aside. The chill air of the early autumn night washed over her face. She stepped out onto the veranda and then down into the slip-on sandals they kept at its foot. The dew on the grass dampened her toes as she started down a meandering stepping-stone path.

Whooo oo-oo-oong, whoooooon, whoo-whoo-whoo-whoonng.

The voice was coming from somewhere deeper in the garden. Thanks to the time she'd spent pulling weeds and pruning overgrown branches during the summer, it was now much easier to pass among the shrubbery. Enough moonlight broke through the taller growth to softly light up the winding path.

Around a bend she came to where the great old tree stood. Its gray trunk stretched tall and straight, and large leaves with wavy edges filled its branches.

Whoonnnng nnnng. Whooo oonnnng.

The sound came from beneath this tree. As she peered through the shadows, Shizuka saw the figure of a woman walking slowly around its thick trunk, her arms folded across her chest as if lost in thought. Long black hair fell down the back of her small but well-proportioned figure. Her face caught the moonlight. Round, with a dark complexion. Two big black eyes as shiny as obsidian. A neat little nose. Thick lips. Like the face of a Hindu goddess.

Saya.

The name came to her in a flash. But the woman appeared to be no older than herself. She couldn't possibly be Saya. Saya would have to be over eighty by now – if she was even alive.

The woman came to a halt. She raised her black eyes in Shizuka's direction.

"Did you get his heart?" she asked. The words were not very clear, and Shizuka was barely able to make them out.

"Pardon?" she asked back. But she felt as if she was in a dream, and couldn't be sure she had even said the word aloud.

"Or did you get a sword?" came the voice a second time.

She was about to repeat her first response when she noticed that the woman's eyes were not focused on her; they were looking right through her. Then the woman abruptly turned her head and resumed her circuit of the tree, picking up her soulful tune again as well.

Whooooo oo-oong, whoon, whoon, whooo-nnnnng.

As she slowly circled on around the tree, she melted into the shadows of the surrounding garden and disappeared.

26

A mass of pendulous white mandala flowers hung amidst the foliage. *Here, sir. How about right here?* A Chinese man with a camera slung around his neck beckoned enthusiastically. *Okay. Looks good*, said Tamiya, the boss, a gold chain dangling from his fob pocket. He turned to the six apprentices behind him. *All right, guys*, he said. *Let's take the picture here.*

Weighed down by large cloth-wrapped bundles on their backs, Rentarō and the other budding peddlers lined up for the shot.

Here goes. Everybody ready? The Chinese man held the camera up in front of his face. A crowd of Malay spectators had gathered behind him – dark-skinned men wearing black caps, high-collared shirts, and sarongs. With all these other eyes besides the eye of the camera staring at him, Rentarō felt himself tensing up.

Show your Toyama spirit! Tamiya called out, without looking away from the camera.

Rentarō and the others pushed their chests out and braced their legs. The scorching sun beat down from above.

Show the pride of your trade! Tamiya added. *Working to keep all Asia healthy!*

The apprentices thrust their chests out even further. If they weren't careful, the weight of their bundles would topple them over backwards.

Smile! Nice big smile! shouted the photographer, flashing an exaggerated smile of his own. The onlookers burst out laughing.

No, don't smile! Tamiya barked, and the apprentices stiffened with a jolt. That was when the camera's eye opened and closed.

The clack of the shutter startled Rentarō awake. He was surrounded by darkness. For a moment he thought he'd been blinded by the flash, but then remembered that the picture had been taken a very long time ago.

He was lying in bed on the floor of the Oharas' hut. Through the thin walls, he could hear the trees stirring in the wind outside.

Even after waking, he continued to drift in and out of his dream for a time.

"Stop it!"

A whisper hissed through the darkness and broke through his semi-consciousness. He opened his eyes. He could hear Ohara and his wife jostling under the covers.

"Not now!" Fumiko hissed again. It seemed her husband was in an amorous mood. At his age, he no doubt found it difficult to contain himself once he got aroused. Rentarō decided he would pretend to be asleep.

But Fumiko continued to protest. There were more tussling sounds, and then she rasped out in a tearful whisper, "This isn't fair. I'm not some P-girl, you know."

"Watch your tongue, woman," he snapped. "When did I ever call you that?" He kept his voice low, but it was thick with fury.

"You didn't have to. It's the way you—"

There was the sharp slap of a hand on a cheek. Rentarō no longer felt he could remain silent.

"Best to avoid violence, sir," he said.

"Mind your own damn business!"

He heard the sound of covers being thrown off and the man getting to his feet. Then came a dull thud, followed by the sudden pressure of Fumiko falling against him. Ohara had apparently kicked her across the floor.

"Mouthy bitch! This is why they're all laughing at us for never having any kids," he spat out, before stamping down into the entryway, throwing the door open with a bang, and storming outside.

Past the open door, Rentarō could see the faint light of stars in the sky. The sound of Fumiko's ragged breathing, rapid as a heartbeat, filled the darkness. She seemed unaware that she was pressed against his body through the quilt. He took his hand out from under the covers and laid it on her back. She was curled into a ball.

"Are you all right?"

She gave a little start. "Yes," she said, straightening her back and pushing herself upright. Rentarō's hand fell to the quilt as she rose.

She remained sitting half-on and half-off his futon as she added weakly, "He's never been the same since coming back from the war. He's so on edge all the time..."

Rentarō sat up too. "I imagine he had to go through some pretty awful things," he said.

"I know that. But it's like... I don't even know him anymore." She let out a long, deep breath. It was a sigh filled with sadness, and yet somehow it seemed to clear the air in the room and brighten the atmosphere.

Half hoping he might hear another such sigh, Rentarō said softly, "He wasn't violent with you before?"

"No, nothing like this," she said, shaking her head. A wisp of her hair brushed against his neck and then lifted away.

"You poor thing," he said, raising his hand to her cheek. It was wet with tears. He gently stroked it with his palm. Suddenly the strength seemed to go out of her and she fell against his chest, sobbing quietly.

Moving from Tokyo to remote Tateyama must have come with a thousand misgivings for someone like her. Yet the man who was supposed to be her strength remained too full of rage to offer any relief from her worries. Rentarō felt genuinely sorry for her, and moved a comforting hand slowly back and forth across her back

"Everything's going to be all right," he said. "It's only because times have been so hard since the war. Things'll get better soon."

He realized that what he was saying to Fumiko applied just as much to himself. That's right. Things'll get better soon, he told himself, as he continued stroking her thin back. She nodded her head like a child against his chest.

An angry bellow broke through the darkness from just inside the door. "What the hell's going on in here?"

Ohara had returned. Even without any light in the room, he must have been able to see their dim shapes huddled close together. Fumiko pushed herself away.

"You son of a bitch! Putting the moves on my wife the minute I'm gone. I knew it. You were after my woman all along."

Wood knocked on wood in the corner where the tools stood. Just as Rentarō realized that Ohara was grabbing a hoe or spade to use as a weapon, he heard something whoosh through the air. He gave Fumiko a hard shove in one direction as he dove away in the other. A garden fork landed right where they'd been sitting, its prongs digging deep into the bedding.

"Stop it! It's not like that!" Fumiko screamed, but Ohara showed no sign of hearing. He pulled the fork out and lunged at Rentarō. Rentarō jumped down off the raised floor and tore out of the house in his bare feet with no time to even grab his baskets.

"Come back here, you son of a bitch!" Ohara yelled behind him. "You're gonna pay for this!"

Rentarō glanced over his shoulder. He could see Ohara coming after him in the moonlight, brandishing the fork in his hands.

"I'll fucking kill you, you bastard!"

Ohara's fury rang out in the night air.

"What's going on?" somebody called. Other men were apparently emerging from their houses to see what the commotion was about.

"It's the fucking medicine man. He was getting it on with my wife," Ohara shouted.

"Catch 'im!" came another voice. "We'll teach him a lesson he won't forget!"

That was all Rentarō needed to hear. He took off as fast as he could. The stones on the path dug painfully into his unprotected feet, but he couldn't be worrying about that now. With his pursuers clamouring after him, he ran for dear life down the path toward Mandala Road.

These ex-soldiers were still waging battle, he thought, as he tripped over rocks jutting from the side of the path and winced at branches slapping him in the face. The war hadn't ended yet for them.

Before long he realized that the voices behind him had died away, and the only sounds he could hear were the rustle of trees and murmur of the river. Gasping for breath, he stumbled to the side of the road and collapsed onto some grass. He had no idea how far he'd come. The cold spring sky glittered with stars overhead.

He hugged his knees to his chest and dropped his head in front of him. Having hightailed it without his precious wares, he was now sitting somewhere along Mandala Road with nothing but the clothes on his back. A rueful smile came to his lips as it sank in that he was alone in the Tateyama wilderness with no shelter for the night and completely stripped of his bearings.

It had been the furthest thing from his mind that he might actually get lost on this road. He was a disgrace to his trade.

He rolled over onto the ground and curled up on his side. As the chill of the night settled in against his back, he worried that he might catch a cold, but it was not long before sleep overcame him.

27

In his semi-consciousness before waking, Asafumi was trying to work out where he was. He started out thinking he was in the apartment in Yokohama, before remembering that he didn't live there anymore. It was galling to be reminded that he'd lost his comfortable home in the city. His life with Shizuka there had been filled with high hopes for the future – at least in the beginning. When exactly had their prospects begun to fade? Bit by bit, as they repeated their daily trip to work and back, the shine had worn off. And in the end they'd been forced to move to Toyama. Which meant he must now be at his grandfather's place – the house where he'd retired to live out his final years after a life of peddling medicines. Asafumi had never once imagined that the place might one day become his, or that he'd end up in the same line of work.

Images of his classes at the training centre, his parents' Ferro concrete home in Senbashi, his father and brother laughing over cups of sake, and Miharu chattering away in the passenger seat of his car burst across the dark skies of his mind like a display of fireworks. Finally it came to him that he had set out along Mandala Road in search of the places listed in his grandfather's sales register. The car had gotten stuck and he couldn't go home, so he'd decided to spend the night in an empty house in a village called Dobō.

The moment this fact registered in his brain, his eyes popped open like a startled bird's.

He found himself gazing up at a soot-darkened ceiling with cobwebs in the corners. He was lying on the bare tatami of the sitting room, wrapped in a quilt he'd dragged from the futon closet next door. The slightly more lived-in feeling of this room had made it seem a more inviting place to sleep. Narrow streaks of sunlight filtered in through cracks between the panels of the storm shutters along the veranda.

Asafumi got to his feet and slid the first panel open. Bright morning light tumbled into the house like an avalanche.

In this new light the anxiety and the sense of utter isolation he'd experienced the night before seemed like the product of an overactive imagination. There'd never been any need for such unease. If he still couldn't get his car out of the rut this morning, all he had to do was walk straight back down Mandala Road. He could probably be at the ski area before noon. After that it was a matter of making one simple phone call.

He went out to the cistern behind the house and splashed some water on his face. As he listened to the birds singing overhead, last night's fretting about being addicted to music began to seem rather silly. He had nothing to worry about. There was nothing wrong with him. Everything was okay. Slipping the old notebook back into his overnight bag, he returned the quilt to the closet, put everything else back where he'd found it, and closed the storm shutter behind him.

The village of Dobō was just as deserted as it had been the day before. But this morning Asafumi was in an altogether different frame of mind, where even an abandoned village could have a certain charm. He reached the bottom of the path and set off down Mandala Road.

The dew glistened in the sun like a thousand teardrops on the grass. Through the treetops on the downward slope he could see the brightly lit mountainside across the valley. Birdsong came from every direction. The sigh of the wind, the rustling of leaves, the gentle gurgle of the river below – all the sounds of nature now seemed more musical than any of the man-made music he was constantly feeding his ears. He listened in delight. The colours of nature had taken on a new vividness as well – the sky a blue so deep it might swallow you whole; the trees a green so brilliant it might dazzle your eyes. The light bounced off the leaves with a silvery glint that seemed to radiate from within the plants themselves. Bathed in that same light, Asafumi felt as if his body had become a vast reverberation chamber that captured each and every sound spilling from the mountains all about. He was filled with a quiet symphony of nature. Stopping short, he closed his eyes and drew in a deep breath to savour the smell of the green hillside with his whole body. For a brief moment, his head swam. Feeling the warmth of the sun on his eyelids, he opened his eyes again and looked at the road stretching ahead.

He gave a start, as if he'd been touched on the shoulder from behind. The road had changed. The pavement was cracked and broken, and weeds grew thick from every patch of exposed ground beneath. There were no guardrails, and here and there the roadbed had crumbled away. The trees on either side stood tall and dense, their branches tightly intertwined. His recollection from yesterday was of a road in much better shape, with white guardrails lining the sloping edge. Had the fading light hidden its actual condition? Even then, this seemed far too different from what he remembered.

As he puzzled over the change, he realized he was uncomfortably warm and pulled off his jacket. He still felt hot, so he pushed the sleeves of his sweatshirt up. A deliberate survey of his surroundings revealed that the foliage was different from the day before as well. Trees in full autumn colours yesterday were now a vibrant green. The grasses along the roadside grew thick and tall, and even the sunlight filtering through the forest canopy seemed much brighter. It was as if summer had come back to the mountains.

Had there been an extreme weather event of some kind? But that couldn't explain the state of the road. He was beginning to feel a little uneasy. In an attempt to shake off his growing agitation, he set out at a half-trot to find his car.

With each step, the transformation of his surroundings grew more pronounced. The orderly forest of white oak, chestnut, and beech trees he'd seen yesterday had given way to a dense mixture of species. The hillsides were dominated by tall trees with large, thick, glossy leaves unlike any he'd ever seen before. Vines with amazingly big yellow-green leaves clung to their trunks, and long tendrils dangled from their branches. On the deeply shaded forest floor grew oversized ferns and plants with huge pink and white flowers.

It was as if he had entered a different world. But the road was still the same road. He remembered it curving exactly this way around this very same bend.

When he reached the spot where he had left the car, he nearly fainted in shock. The car was gone, and in its place he found a man of about fifty lying on the ground, curled into a ball against the cold. Oddly, he was dressed in a khaki outfit like he'd seen in pictures of civilian's during World War II. His hair was in a tangle, and he had no shoes.

A vagrant, perhaps? But remote mountain roads weren't where you expected to see men like that.

"Excuse me," he said.

The man opened his eyes and looked up at him. He had a rugged, angular face with thick eyebrows and bulging eyes. He reminded Asafumi of his grandfather – though this man was considerably younger than his grandfather had been when he knew him.

Seeing that he had company, the man sluggishly pulled himself upright. He eyed Asafumi warily as he began rubbing his arms for warmth.

"Would you by any chance know what happened to the car that was here?" Asafumi asked.

"A car?" the man said, looking perplexed.

"A blue Volkswagen. I got stuck in a rut yesterday and had to leave it overnight."

Still bleary-eyed, the man shook his head.

Asafumi stepped to the edge of the road and peered down the steep drop-off toward the river. There was no sign of a car having rolled down the hillside. He couldn't find the rut he'd been stuck in, either, nor any of his tire tracks. The Volkswagen had vanished into thin air, and this man who looked as though he came from a different era had materialized in its place.

He studied him out of the corner of his eye as he shifted to a spot in the sun and rubbed his face vigorously with both hands. The possibility that he had stolen the vehicle could probably be ruled out. A car thief wasn't likely to return to the scene of the crime and fall asleep.

Asafumi made a full circuit of the area, looking for any sign of the car, peering up and down the road and searching among clumps of trees, but he found no trace of it anywhere. The man watched his movements with an increasingly dubious look on his face.

"Are you sure you really had a car?" he finally asked, with a distinct note of scepticism. The dialect he used marked him as someone from the region.

"Yes, I really did," Asafumi said, deliberately using Tokyo speech as a way of distancing himself from this man who was beginning to strike him as a little odd. He fished the key from his pocket. "See?"

The man studied it curiously. "That doesn't look like any car key I've ever seen," he said.

Asafumi wasn't sure what to make of this remark. It was a perfectly normal key, the same as anybody's. He began to think the man must really be missing a screw or two. Perhaps he'd escaped from a mental institution, or from a house where he was usually kept confined. That might explain his curiously old-fashioned appearance, too. It was probably best not to get involved any further with somebody like this.

"Well," he said, picking up his overnight bag, "I guess I'll be on my way."

He started back in the direction he'd come the day before. Trying to regain his earlier composure, he told himself that if the car had indeed been stolen, he needed to reach the nearest house as soon as possible to call the police. If he stayed in this place any longer, he might get swallowed up by all the strangeness going on and turn funny in the head himself.

"Wait! Hold on a second!" the man called, and came running after him. When he caught up, he said, "I wonder if I could ask you a little favour."

Without slackening his pace, Asafumi turned to look at him. He really did remind him of his grandfather.

"I'm in a fix. I got caught in a bit of a stew at the village just up the road last night," he said quickly, keeping pace with Asafumi, "and I had to make a quick escape with no time to grab my stuff. It's what I make my living with, so I can't very well leave without it, but there's no telling what they might do to me if I go back to get it myself. Could you maybe run up there and retrieve it for me? I'd be happy to pay you for your trouble."

The man talked as if he had a proper job. If the bit about having to run from some kind of trouble was true, it would explain the bare feet. Maybe the man's head was screwed on straight after all, Asafumi thought, and pulled up short.

"When you say it's what you make your living with, what exactly are we talking about?"

"Baskets of medicine," he said. "I'm a medicine peddler. I've been trying to drum up some new customers along this road."

So this person who looked so much like his grandfather also happened to be in the same business. An odd, spiralling sensation came over Asafumi.

The man evidently thought from Asafumi's expression that he didn't believe him. "It's the truth," he said. "I'm not trying to pull anything suspicious here. I work out of Senbashi, and my name is Rentarō Nonezawa."

Asafumi stared at the man, his jaw hanging. His cry of astonishment came out as no more than a choked gasp.

Was this supposed to be some kind of a joke? But how could a man he'd never met before know his grandfather's name?

"I... know someone by that name, too," he said haltingly. "The person I know was born during Meiji, and he lived in Southeast Asia for a number of years, before—"

"You mean in Malaya? If so, that would be me. Have we met somewhere before?"

"But the person I'm talking about is dead!" he nearly shrieked.

Asafumi's cry left the man bewildered for a moment, but his unshaven cheeks soon loosened into a grin.

"Well, I guess you must have picked up some bad information," he said. "There's been an awful lot of that going around since the war, so it's not hard to imagine. I suppose there was bound to be somebody who thought I'd been caught in an air raid and killed somewhere while I was out on the road."

"No, no, no, the man I'm talking about died at the age of eighty-five."

"Well, in that case, I guess it has to be somebody else." He pressed a palm to his forehead and shook his head back and forth. "So there was somebody else with exactly the same name who also went to

Malaya? Strange things do happen. Your man must have been born at the very beginning of Meiji then." He obviously believed another Rentarō was involved.

"What year were you born?" Asafumi asked.

"Me? That'd be Meiji thirty-three. I'm forty-seven."

Asafumi quickly calculated the years in his head. He couldn't remember just how long the Meiji and Taisho periods were, but if the man claimed to be forty-seven now, it meant he thought this was still sometime in the first half of the Showa period.

"This may seem like a strange thing to ask, but could you tell me what year it is right now?"

The man gave him an odd look. "Showa twenty-two, of course."

So he had to be out of his mind after all. Asafumi still couldn't explain why the man claimed to have the same name as his grandfather, but to all appearances he seriously believed this was the twenty-second year of Showa, which by Asafumi's calculation would be 1947. It might not be smart to hang around in such an isolated place with someone who was off his rocker.

"I'm sorry, I'm actually in kind of a hurry," he said, abruptly breaking off the discussion. But as he turned to go, the man grabbed hold of his arm.

"I'm begging you, please. I really need your help. The place is just around the bend."

Asafumi shook his arm free. "I'm sorry, but—"

Just as he began to repeat his refusal, there was a sudden movement in the underbrush and three dark figures bounded onto the road a few steps ahead. At first glance, Asafumi thought they were monkeys, but he immediately realized they were much too big for that. They were the size of men, with long, mane-like hair and tattered loincloths wrapped around their waists, their faces and bodies streaked with dirt. They appeared to be humans, not apes, yet their eyes didn't seem to hold the slightest spark of intelligence. Their feet were bare, and they carried crude wooden clubs in their hands.

One of the three let out a growl and lunged forward. As if this were their cue, the others joined the attack.

Rentarō spun on his heels to flee, and Asafumi turned to follow. But he had gone only a few steps before he felt a tug on his right hand. One of the attackers had caught hold of the overnight bag he was carrying. Asafumi gripped the handles with both hands and tried to hang on, but his adversary wrested the bag from his grasp with much greater strength.

Car key, wallet, credit cards, the sales register. An inventory of the bag's contents flashed through Asafumi's mind as he dove after it. A long, dark shape swung across the periphery of his vision, and the next instant a searing pain shot through his head as he crumpled in a heap on the ground.

28

Shizuka had worked up a bit of a sweat by the time she rode through the gate of the Senbashi house on her bicycle. After getting lost on the way, she'd wound up pedalling all over town before finally arriving.

Still breathing hard, she pressed the bell, and her mother-in-law appeared at the door. Takiko looked ready to go out, in lipstick and earrings and an attractive blue, yellow, and green knit dress.

"Sorry to be so late," she apologized. "I got lost."

Having said she would be there at three, it turned out there were no buses at the right time, so she had decided to come by bicycle and get some exercise while she was at it. Then she made the mistake of taking what she thought would it be a shortcut through the paddies, only to come out somewhere completely wrong and not know where she was. She'd more or less had to circle around the entire town, and it was now well past three.

"Oh, don't worry about that," Takiko said lightly. "My meeting isn't until five anyway. We have plenty of time."

There'd been no word from Asafumi in two full days and Shizuka was starting to be seriously concerned. When she called the Nonezawas, Takiko had urged her to come by the house so they could talk.

The shoe cupboard and floor in the entryway were polished to a high sheen. As Shizuka removed her shoes and stepped inside, Miharu appeared down the hall.

"Hi, Shizuka," she said. She had on the jacket she wore for work, apparently having just returned from her shift. "Still no word from Asafumi?" she asked as she took the jacket off.

Shizuka shook her head and removed her jacket, too. Takiko suggested they all go into the kitchen. Shizuka took a seat at the large table, while Miharu went to the counter and measured out some tea for the teapot. Warm sunshine filled the spacious room, its soft light brightening the white plates and bowls filling the dish drainer, the coffee maker sitting out on the counter, and the plastic tablecloth covering the table. Two weeks after Kikuo and Kōichirō left on one of their usual sales trips, the more comfortable atmosphere of an all-female household had settled in.

"He mentioned before he left that he thought he might stay over somewhere for a night, but then he didn't come back last night either," Shizuka said, trying not to show how worried she was.

Miharu cocked her head thoughtfully as she poured hot water into the teapot. "It certainly didn't look like a particularly dangerous road," she said. "I mean, where he could wind up crashing or something."

Takiko was slicing some *yōkan* she had gotten from the refrigerator. "I'm sure it's nothing to worry about, Shizuka," she said with a smile. "When the men go off on a trip, we often don't hear from them for as much as a week at a time."

"But this wasn't really like that. He just wanted to see if the houses listed in that notebook were still there."

"Well, maybe it put somebody in a nostalgic mood when he showed up, and they urged him to stay." Takiko set a plate of sliced *yōkan* in front of Shizuka and sat down at the table. "Somebody brought us this as a gift. It's from Kawadaya. Have a bite."

Yōkan was not one of Shizuka's favourite things. She preferred the lightness of cake to the cloying sweetness of this dense adzuki-bean jelly. But wanting to be polite, she took a piece.

"Grandpa was saying there're several different villages out that way, so I'm sure he'd call if he ran into trouble," Miharu said as she brought the tea to the table.

Shizuka was a little taken aback by how they both brushed her worries aside so casually. Maybe it was understandable in Miharu's case, since Asafumi was only an in-law, but for Takiko, this was her son they were talking about. How could she be so calm when her own flesh and blood had gone missing?

Noting Shizuka's surprise, Takiko quickly finished chewing her bite of *yōkan* and washed it down with some tea. "You have to understand, Shizuka," she said with a pat of her chest, "when you're married to a travelling salesman, you can't be getting into a tizzy every time your husband's been gone a couple of days. After all, he spends at least two hundred days out of the year away from home."

True enough, if you took two hundred days as the norm, two days was a mere one percent.

Shizuka was hesitating over whether to say anything further when Takiko leaned forward in her chair and asked in a more solicitous tone: "Actually, I've been more concerned about you than about Asafumi. How are you faring out there in that house all by yourself?"

Shizuka thought of the woman she had seen in the garden two nights before.

Takiko noticed the shadow that crossed her face. "What?"

"Well," she said haltingly, "I was just wondering if anybody's ever talked about seeing ghosts or something in the garden." It didn't escape her attention that the two women quickly exchanged a glance. "Because I saw something two nights ago that I don't know how else to explain. It was a woman." She watched them both closely for their reactions.

Takiko reached for her cup and took a sip of tea before answering as if it were the most ordinary question in the world. "The Yazakis who lived there before said they sometimes thought they heard somebody in the garden, but they went on renewing their lease for fifteen years, so I guess it couldn't have been anything that really bothered them."

"That's right," Miharu chimed in, "any time I was out there, they just seemed like one big happy family, no problems at all."

Shizuka suspected they were only trying to reassure her, and in fact at that point both of them seemed at a loss for what else to say. An uncomfortable silence settled over the room. In search of something more concrete to latch onto, Shizuka decided to plunge ahead.

"Did anybody ever find out what happened to the woman called Saya?"

A faint cloud came over Takiko's plump face, too. "She just disappeared." This was the same answer Asafumi had given. "No note or anything. We pretty much figured she must have gone to live with Isamu, since he was her only family, but we never heard from him either... Anyway, that just sort of became the end of it."

She gave the side of her teacup a quick stroke with her fingers as she finished.

The woman's disappearance was no doubt considered a blessing by one and all, Shizuka thought to herself.

"Oh, yes, yes," Takiko said as if suddenly reminded of something. "Later on, when we were making arrangements to rent the place to the Yazakis, I had to file a missing persons report with the police because she was still officially living there. I couldn't quite believe my eyes when I saw her registry card. Saya wasn't even her real name. It was Kim something-or-other. It turned out she was Korean."

"She wasn't from Malaysia?" Shizuka asked in surprise. Miharu had pricked up her ears, too. She apparently didn't know this part about Saya.

"That's what we'd always thought, certainly, so I can tell you, we were all pretty bowled over. Since the registry card gave her legal domicile as someplace near Shimonoseki, the police said they'd check to see if maybe she'd gone back there. But the area had been hit hard during the war, and all the addresses had changed when they rebuilt. They couldn't find out anything."

Takiko stared off into space for several moments as if trying to recall something from those days, then pressed her lips together in a frown. "I certainly never would have guessed she was Korean from the way she looked. She had such a dark complexion, with big, round eyes and a double crease in her eyelids. I thought she looked more like someone from Kyushu or Okinawa."

Shizuka thought of the woman she'd seen in the middle of the night in the garden. Takiko's description of Saya seemed to fit exactly.

Did you get his heart?

The woman's words echoed in her ears. What could that have been about?

"When it really comes down to it, I'd have to say we never actually knew much about her," Takiko said, placing both hands in front of her on the table with a little slap.

"But didn't things about her background come up in the course of conversations?"

A crooked smile formed on Takiko's face. "The fact is, we hardly ever saw her. I mean, the children all took an instant dislike to her, right from the start – I'm talking about Kikuo and his siblings. And none of us ever went to that house if we could help it. For special occasions like New Year's, and Bon and memorial services, we'd bring Father here. We always held things like that at this house."

"But you still must have seen her *some*times," Shizuka said.

"Well, of course, when Father asked us to come, or when we'd go to fetch him for those special things, we might exchange a few words. But nothing more than the usual greetings and some meaningless chitchat – never anything of substance. I occasionally saw her around town too, doing her shopping, chattering away with various groups of housewives. She actually seemed to be pretty well known locally as a kind of a folk healer."

"A folk healer?" Shizuka said in surprise.

"When people complained about stiff shoulders or some other nagging problem, she brewed up these therapeutic teas for them and gave out health advice. I guess she made a little extra spending money that way, from people who wanted to show their appreciation."

Shizuka tried to think of the woman from two days ago as a folk healer, but had difficulty making the label fit. For her, the term conjured up an image of someone old and wizened, and maybe a bit unsavoury – none of which agreed with the lively-looking woman she'd seen in the garden.

"Do you have any pictures of her?"

Takiko shook her head. "Not a one," she said.

Saya had had a connection with this family for some four decades, beginning shortly after the war. And yet, today, she had been effectively erased from the family history. A shudder when through Shizuka as she realized how completely the family had shut the woman out.

"It's perfectly understandable if you consider what happened to Mother," said Takiko, making excuses. "I don't think she ever knew a moment's peace after the day Saya showed up. It took a terrible toll on her heart, and she died without even seeing fifty. I mean, by the time I came to this house as a bride, her husband had basically abandoned her. He moved in with that woman at the other house as soon as her boy finished high school and went away to a job in Osaka. Kikuo and the other kids all blamed Saya for their mother's early death. They couldn't stand her."

She let out a short, clipped breath and looked up at the clock on the wall.

"Oh, my," she said, "look at the time. I'm sorry, but I have to be going. I got dragged into this big fancy campaign to beautify the city, you know. They even made me vice-president, and it's just awful."

She actually sounded rather proud of her role. Getting to her feet, she hurried up the hall. Moments later, she returned with a cardigan thrown over her shoulders and a purse in her hand.

"It was so nice to see you, Shizuka. Come see us again soon."

Shizuka started to get up, but she motioned for her to stay and hurried off toward the front door. When they heard the door close, Miharu reached for a piece of *yōkan*.

"Actually, at least half the purpose of these committee meetings of hers is to have a party afterwards," she said with a chortle. "As soon as Dad's out of the house, Mom suddenly gets busy-busy." She popped the slice of *yōkan* into her mouth.

Shizuka was still thinking about what Takiko had said. "So basically, Saya went permanently missing," she murmured.

Miharu widened her eyes. "You're not thinking that could happen to Asafumi, are you?"

Her heart skipped a beat. As a matter of fact, she wasn't thinking that at all. But now that Miharu mentioned it, it seemed entirely possible.

"If he's still not back tonight," Miharu said, "I'll call my dad and ask him to drive out to see what he can find."

"Thanks, I'd appreciate that."

Miharu washed the rest of her *yōkan* down with a swallow of tea before going on. "It's better for us wives not to think too much about what they might be doing on the road, you know."

"Why do you say that?"

Miharu gave her a sharp glance. "Men will be men," she said. "There's no telling what they might be getting into."

"You mean like sleeping around?..."

Miharu twisted her freckled face into a frown. "Maybe... Why wouldn't they, after all? You'd be surprised at some of the things I see and hear when I'm driving my cab. Men in town on business trips chatting up some local bar girl. Couples asking me to drop them off at hotels in the middle of the day, obviously sneaking around."

She poured some fresh tea into both their cups. Shizuka felt a twinge in her chest as she thought of her assignations with Hiroyuki.

"Doesn't that make those two hundred days when they're away even harder to bear? Not knowing, I mean."

Miharu thought for a moment before shaking her head. "No, not really. In a lot of ways it's easier on us when they're gone. You saw Mom. When Dad's not here, she gets to go out more. For the hundred-odd days when the men are home, the house belongs to them, but the rest of the time it's ours, and we get to sit back and relax."

"Except you have to do without 'relations,'" Shizuka said, remembering her mother-in-law's words.

Miharu gave a rueful smile. "Sounds like something Mom must have said. I got an earful, too, when I was first married. From the way she harps about it, she must have missed her husband's attentions something awful."

"What about you, Miharu?"

She blushed. "It wasn't so bad when the kids were small. But these days?" She broke into a broad smile. "I can hardly keep the lid on it sometimes."

Shizuka nodded.

"And you know what?" Miharu gave her a mischievous look. "I actually get turned on when I'm driving men around in my cab. I think about how I'm alone in the car with a guy I don't even know, and it makes me feel all tingly. I figure maybe it helps take the pressure off."

"Maybe I should start driving a cab, too," Shizuka said with a playful grin, though she was secretly half serious. She could well imagine that being with men she didn't know in the confines of a cab might be a turn-on.

"I may be married, but I'm not made of stone," Miharu said, her elbows on the table and chin cupped in her hands. "So it's only natural that I get the urge for it sometimes. Especially when he's away on a long sales trip. Times like that, if I pick up a cute guy in my cab, I fantasize about driving straight to a hotel and going to bed with him." She stroked her cheeks with her fingers as a dreamy look came into her eyes.

"Have you ever actually done it?"

Miharu's eyes popped wide open, and she waved her hand back and forth in front of her face in denial.

"Are you kidding?" she said. "In a small town like this, there's no telling who might see. If anybody found out, my marriage would be over, so I wouldn't dare. What about you? Don't you sometimes get the hots for a guy and want to go off somewhere with him?"

An image of Hiroyuki flashed through her mind, but she sidestepped the question. "Well, sure I do, but when you're married, you know..."

Miharu nodded as if to say, *So there you go.* "You hear about women out there having these wild love affairs, but for the woman in the average marriage, the whole idea of sleeping with another man is, well, basically pure fantasy."

And it's precisely because it's pure fantasy that she can sit here talking so candidly about it with me, Shizuka thought to herself. If her daydreams ever became reality, she'd no longer speak so openly about being turned on by other men. It was fine to talk about daydreams, but you couldn't talk about what was real.

Even now, Shizuka still found herself lusting after Hiroyuki from time to time. Despite what he'd said about her being frigid, she longed to sleep with him simply because he was someone other than Asafumi. Perhaps all she really wanted was to prove to herself that she could still sleep with other men even after being married.

Miharu went on, her eyes drifting off into space. "I think Mom must have had some pretty strong urges when she was young, too. She once told me that on nights when her husband was away and she was home alone, she actually slept with her legs tied together."

"Her legs tied together?"

"Uh-huh," Miharu nodded, throwing her a provocative look. "With some kind of cord around her knees. She said it was something her mother-in-law taught her to do."

"But why would she do a thing like that?"

"Well... maybe she thought it'd be indecent to sleep with her legs apart."

"Which would have to mean she was afraid of somebody seeing her. But who in the world could she have been worried about?"

Miharu blinked. "You're right," she said. "She must've had reason to think somebody might peep."

"Who?"

They looked at each other. For Takiko to be so self-conscious about masculine eyes during the night implied a secret desire for just such an intrusion. The thrill of having glimpsed something about their mother-in-law's private fantasies brought a sparkle to their eyes.

"I'm home," came a child's voice from the front door. Miharu quickly got up from the table.

"Would you like to stay for dinner, Shizuka?" she said. "I can drive you home later."

"But I have my bicycle..."

"We can take the truck and throw it in the back."

Dinner with the Nonezawas sounded much more inviting than an evening spent all by herself, waiting anxiously for Asafumi to return.

"All right. That sounds nice."

"We women have to stretch our wings a bit while we have the chance, you know."

Shizuka watched her disappear down the hall, feeling as though some of her sister-in-law's irrepressible cheerfulness was beginning to catch.

29

Rentarō stopped running. He gasped for breath as he turned to look back the way he'd come. The wild men with their wooden clubs were now out of sight beyond a bend. Dropping heavily onto the seat of his trousers in a clump of grass at the roadside, he opened the front of his khaki shirt to let in some air while he tried to bring his breathing under control.

As his panic began to subside he wondered what had become of the man he was walking with. He'd heard him cry out, but he'd been too scared to do anything but keep on running. The guy could easily have been bludgeoned to death.

Who were those men, anyway? Another bunch who'd found refuge here after being left without food or shelter by the war? At any rate, with brutes like that roving about, it would be too dangerous to go any farther into these hills.

Yet even if he was eager to move on, he couldn't very well leave his baskets behind at that settlement. They were his livelihood. No matter how riled up that Ohara guy might be, he had no choice but to go back for them. He would simply explain that nothing had happened between him and Fumiko: all he'd done was offer comfort in a moment of distress; his intentions had been perfectly honourable.

With a plan set in mind, he immediately felt more at ease. He looked up and down the road, trying to puzzle out which direction the settlement might be. In the scramble to escape last night, he'd completely lost his bearings. In fact, he wasn't so sure this was even Mandala Road anymore. Not only was it wider than the track he remembered from the day before, but the roadbed had been levelled and paved at some point – though the pavement was now badly broken up, with grass and weeds flourishing in the cracks. Since when did they pave mountain roads so far outside the city? He'd never heard of such a thing. Had he stumbled on some secret military route constructed during the war? He could think of no good reason why they'd choose remote Tateyama for something like that.

As he turned his head back and forth trying to decide which way to go, he felt a warm sense of recognition that nearly brought tears to his eyes. Giving a little shake, he bunched his eyebrows and took a closer look around. Aha, he thought. It must be the scenery. A fiery sun beating down from above. Thick vines waving their big heart-shaped leaves. The deep tropical green of the foliage on the trees. Giant ferns spreading their fronds like peacocks' tails... It all reminded him of the jungles he'd trekked through as a young apprentice in Malaya, with his heavy baskets digging into his shoulders.

He realized it must have been like this from the time that fellow shook him awake, but he'd been too busy worrying about how he was going to get his medicines back to notice.

What was going on? It was as if he'd somehow been transported back to those jungles. But he knew that wasn't possible. He got to his feet and walked across the road to where he could get a better view of the valley. There was a river flowing below. Both from its size and from the terrain it wound its way through, he recognized it as the Kanoko. He also saw the familiar shape of Yakushidake rising beyond the ridge on the other side, confirming beyond any doubt that he was still in the Tateyama foothills. But the slopes were thick with the kind of lush vegetation he'd known only in Malaya.

He stood dumbfounded, utterly stumped by what to make of the change. All he could imagine was that maybe the war wasn't over after all, and another newfangled bomb had been dropped – one that somehow turned Toyama into the tropics overnight, or scattered a hallucinatory gas that made you think that had happened. Or had he actually died and entered the afterworld? He tried giving his cheek a hard slap. When everything around him remained the same, he abandoned any further attempt at an explanation.

With Yakushidake to give him a rough fix on where he was, he knew that every river and stream on this side of Tateyama ultimately drained into the Jōganji. So even if the river he saw below wasn't the Kanoko, all he had to do was follow it downstream and he would end up at one of the stations on the Tateyama Line.

He craned his neck to see which way the river flowed. Downstream was back the way he had just come, toward where he'd been attacked. He found a fallen branch nearby and broke off a piece to use for protection, then started retracing his steps.

His muscles and joints were stiff from having been forced to run pell-mell for his life twice in short order, and from sleeping on the bare ground in between. He was still working out the kinks when he reached the place of the attack. The fellow from before was lying naked and unconscious in the grass at the side of the road.

Stripped of all his clothes, it was easy to see that he didn't have any serious wounds.

Rentarō stood studying the man's pale skin and feeble build, with ribs sticking out. He had to have been of draft age during the war, but it was all too obvious that this wasn't a body hardened by military service. On top of that, even with the current food shortages, he had the beginnings of a spare tire around his middle. Recalling the man's Tokyo dialect, Rentarō decided he was probably some big-city tycoon's soft and pampered son who'd come to Tateyama on holiday; but not having the heart to just leave him lying there, he reached down to shake his shoulder. The man's eyes fluttered halfway open. His glazed gaze fell first on Rentarō, then slowly began to take in the area around him.

"Are you all right?" Rentarō asked.

He lifted a hand to his head. "I've got a bump," he said.

"Consider yourself lucky that you're alive to complain about it."

Rentarō was still speaking when the fellow shot upright. He'd suddenly realized he was stark naked. Putting a hand over his groin, he looked frantically about as if searching for a place to hide.

"Relax," said Rentarō with a crooked smile. "I've got a pecker, too."

The naked man kept his hand where it was, but stopped looking for cover. "Can you believe it? Those guys were like Pithecanthropus or something," he said. "If we reported this to the university, these hills would be crawling with anthropologists in no time flat."

Despite his joking tone, Rentarō couldn't help feeling sorry for him. He fumbled in his pocket and pulled out a folded muslin hand towel.

"Here. Why don't you use this to cover your precious jewels there," he said.

The man sheepishly accepted the offering and staggered to his feet. Stretching it across his front, he reached around to tie two corners together behind him. He looked like someone in the changing room at a public bathhouse.

Rentarō stifled a laugh. "I figure I'll keep on going the way we were," he said. "What about you?"

The fellow seemed to consider this as he looked up and down the road. Then he pointed in the direction Rentarō had just come.

"There's an abandoned village back that way, with a bunch of houses still standing. I'm wondering if I might be able to find something to wear."

"An abandoned village?" Rentarō said in surprise. "I don't think so."

"Sure there is. I spent the night there."

"But I just came from that way. If there was any kind of village, I'd have seen it."

"No, really. I stayed there. Just hold on a second, okay? I'll be right back."

He started up the road at a trot. Rentarō watched his pale-skinned butt bouncing up and down as he receded into the distance. The guy was probably disoriented from being hit on the head. But then again, maybe there really were some houses up that way that he hadn't noticed. He kept his eyes on the spot where the naked figure had disappeared.

It wasn't long before he came trotting back. Rentarō could see the disappointment written on his face long before he arrived, so it was no surprise when he blurted out, "I don't get it. It's gone!"

"Well," said Rentarō, "they say travel is best with a companion. Why don't you come with me?" If he was going to continue on down this road, he knew he would feel safer to have company.

"Thanks, I think I will." After accepting the invitation, he turned to face Rentarō directly and said in the tone of a formal introduction, "My name is Asafumi."

His eyes seemed to drill into Rentarō, as if looking for some kind of reaction. Not entirely sure what to make of the intense stare, Rentarō simply replied, "Is that right? Nice to meet you."

"Likewise," Asafumi replied. There was a look of letdown in his eyes. He picked up a branch he found lying at the side of the road and broke it across his knee to make a club like Rentarō's for himself. "Shall we be going, then?"

They set out along the broken pavement together. The *slap slap* of their four bare feet rose from the asphalt like the patter of a small drum. Dappled sunlight fell through the branches overhead onto the road, mottling their skin.

For his part, Asafumi was feeling as if he'd wandered into someone else's dream. When he jogged back up the road just now, he'd found the village of Dobō gone without a trace. The spot where it had stood only hours before was overgrown with vegetation as thick as a tropical jungle, without the slightest sign of any houses ever having been there. Meanwhile, Mandala Road was crumbling beneath his feet as if it had seen no traffic in decades, and wild bushmen resembling *Homo erectus* roved the hills it travelled through. And to go even further beyond the bounds of comprehension, he'd run into a man who seemed to be none other than his dead grandfather.

Something very strange was going on – that much couldn't be clearer. But he didn't have the first clue what it might be. What he did know was that his car and clothes and overnight bag were gone, he'd acquired a bump on the side of his head that throbbed like hell, and he was hiking down Mandala Road with nothing but a flimsy hand towel wrapped around his waist.

"When I was in Malaya," Rentarō said as he rolled up his khaki sleeves, "there were times when I had to travel roads where tigers or panthers or bandits had been reported attacking people. I remember walking along with my heart in my throat and a hunting knife in my hand."

The mention of Malaya made Asafumi feel as if he were listening to the grandfather of his childhood across the distant passage of time.

"All by yourself?" he asked. Without even thinking, he had phrased the question in the Toyama dialect.

Rentarō opened his mouth in surprise. "Oh, so you're a local boy, are you?"

Embarrassed, Asafumi acknowledged that he was, hastening to explain that he'd become accustomed to using Tokyo speech most of the time from having lived there so long.

"Did you travel alone?" he asked again, continuing in the local dialect.

"No, I went with other peddlers and our Malay interpreters." The corners of his eyes crinkled as he gazed ahead along the time-ravaged road. "For hours on end, we'd trudge along the red clay roads stretching through the jungle, lugging our huge bundles in the tropical heat – shirts sopping, backs aching, mosquitoes whining around our heads. It was pretty punishing."

Asafumi thought of the delegation from the Planet of the Toads in his grandfather's photo.

"Why would you want to travel so far away to sell your medicines?" he asked.

It was a question he had never verbalized as a child, but as he heard the words coming out of his mouth, he realized it was something he'd always wanted to ask.

"Why?" Rentarō repeated the question as if taken aback. "It was my work."

"But couldn't you have done perfectly well just in Japan?"

Rentarō seemed to sink into thought for a time. The gentle rise and fall of the road continued. Asafumi realized that he had been driving too fast on his way out yesterday to notice the ups and downs. On the other hand, he thought, how could he be sure this was even the same road?

"I guess I was looking for adventure," Rentarō finally said, appearing to be amused by the idea. "In those days, the whole country was looking outward, across the oceans. It wasn't only drug makers. As we moved on into the Taisho Period, all the talk was about it being time for Japan to get out into the world, and everybody was just bubbling with excitement. The famous medicine peddlers of Toyama were right in there with the rest of them. One after another, they started taking their business to Taiwan and Korea and Sakhalin and China. Some even set their sights on Hawaii and South America."

"I never realized they'd gone so far afield."

Rentarō's face glowed with pride, as if he himself had travelled to those more distant places.

"Basically, our people followed wherever Japanese emigrants had gone. As soon as the country opened up in 1868, people started moving abroad to put down new roots in no small numbers. Malaya had its share, too – most anywhere you went, the barber and photographer would be Japanese. As it happened, one of my dad's cousins, a man named Yoshikatsu Tamiya, had moved to Singapore to open a drugstore, so I took advantage of the family connection and got hired as an apprentice in 1917. I was seventeen at the time. Sure, I could have stayed home to sell medicines here, but I took it into my head to go to Malaya – I suppose because I wanted to see what the world was like someplace else."

That was still long before it became possible for people to travel all over the globe at the drop of a hat, thought Asafumi. If you had a youthful itch for adventure, you pretty much had to connect it with work somehow. Today's incessant flow of tour groups dragging heavy suitcases behind them to foreign destinations had its origins in the medicine sellers who went abroad with tall cloth-wrapped bundles strapped to their backs.

"Those were good times. During the rainy season, from September to February, we worked at the shop in Singapore, and then when dry weather came, from March through August, Mr. Tamiya would take five or six of us apprentices out on the road with him. We'd travel in a group to various parts of the peninsula before splitting up to go door-to-door. I remember how heavy and hot it was lugging around the big five-tiered baskets in that climate. But the boss said we had to look our best in order to uphold our good name, and he insisted we always wear a coat and tie."

Rentarō rambled on as they continued down the decaying road. Once he got started, the memories seemed to come rolling back to him one after the other without interruption. For Asafumi, it was as if he'd returned to his childhood – except that this time the stories actually held together instead of being disjointed fragments repeated at random on automatic rewind. Here, under the blazing sun on a remote mountain road, he was finally getting to hear his grandfather's stories the way they were meant to be told. Even the sharpness of the gravel beneath his bare feet was forgotten as he was drawn completely under their spell.

"A lot of towns in Malaya had Japanese communities by then. So, naturally, we asked those people to let us leave kits with them. But we also did some wholesale business with Chinese herbalists, and we went door-to-door looking for Malayan customers, too. At first I had to have an interpreter with me, but eventually I learned to speak the language well enough to get by on my own."

Having grown uncomfortably hot, Rentarō removed his rumpled khaki shirt. His undershirt had been washed so many times you could almost see right through it. After a moment he remembered Asafumi's plight and held the shirt out to him. "Want it?" he asked.

Asafumi was dripping with sweat, too, and in any case, even if he put the thing on, he'd still be no better off down below, so he shook his head.

"How long were you there?"

"About three years that first time," Rentarō said as he tied the shirt around his waist. "Just when I finally had the language down and was starting to feel at home, I got my draft notice. So I sailed back to Japan, and the army shipped me out to Siberia. When I came home the next time, after my tour, my parents had arranged a match for me, so I met the girl and got married. Since I couldn't very well take off for Malaya again after that, I stayed put and helped my dad and brother with the business here in Toyama. But then after the Manchurian Incident an anti-Japanese mob of local Chinese destroyed Mr. Tamiya's shop in Singapore, and he asked me to come help him rebuild. That got me back to Malaya for a brief second stretch, and pretty soon I was making the trip about once a year, delivering remedies prepared in Japan to Mr. Tamiya, and picking up Malayan raw materials to bring back home with me."

"Every year?" Asafumi said in surprise. The boat trip in those days must have taken a good month. You had to be pretty fond of a place to spend that kind of time travelling there year after year.

Rentarō rested his club on a shoulder and nodded happily. "That's right. Those were the days. So long as I kept on the go, the money just kept rolling in. Tamiya's shop did well too, and eventually he set up his own little factory and started making medicines locally. With labels touting their benefits in the local language, of course."

"Is that right?"

"The Malay trade was still in its infancy at that point. The Korean Peninsula and Taiwan were both Japanese territory, and Manchukuo practically belonged to Japan too, so Toyama's drug makers were already well-established in those areas, sending stuff from here as well as setting up new factories locally. Like I say, with packaging tailored to each language. Since expanding into Asia was official state policy, the government was offering a whole raft of incentives and helps. At any rate, business just kept getting better at Mr. Tamiya's shop, and I guess it was around the time full-scale war broke out in China, he said he wanted to open up a branch in

Kota Bharu and asked if I'd be willing to run it. It sounded like an interesting challenge, so I said yes."

"But you had family here in Toyama," Asafumi said, thinking of his father and uncle and aunt.

"A travelling salesman's gone from home eight months out of the year anyway," Rentarō replied with a shrug. "And when you're away, there's not much difference between being off somewhere in Japan or somewhere overseas. Plus I was being called on to serve my country."

"Serve your country?"

Asafumi couldn't imagine how selling medicine had anything to do with that. Rentarō blinked as if realizing something for the first time, then gave a crooked smile.

"The war's over now, so I don't suppose I need to keep it secret anymore. When we were getting ready to open the branch, some officers from the intelligence service visited us at the shop in Singapore and said they needed our help. If we were going to open up in Kota Bharu, they wanted us to use our presence there as a base for gathering information and helping with their pacification efforts. They presented it as a request, but coming from the government, it was effectively an order, of course, so we really had no choice."

This was the first Asafumi knew of his grandfather's time in Malaya having anything to do with the government. Noticing his interest, Rentarō went on.

"At first it was a matter of relaying any information I happened to pick up on my rounds of the villages, and handing out free remedies for common things like malaria and scabies to build up goodwill. Then the army landed in Kota Bharu and swept down the peninsula to take Singapore. After that, the officers left in charge of the city started visiting regularly, pumping me for all sorts of information."

"So now you were working directly for the army?" Asafumi asked, not quite sure what to think of the revelation that his grandfather had played a role in Japan's war of aggression.

Rentarō nodded proudly. "That's right. I did my part during the war too, as a patriotic citizen."

30

There was a sudden commotion on the road out front and Saya looked up from the laundry she was folding. Three boys were ganging up on Isamu, pounding him with their fists and kicking him in the shins. Even with his arms and shoulders pinned down, he was butting his head and pumping his legs to fight back.

Dropping her laundry, Saya jumped down from the veranda into the yard and raced toward them, the hem of her dress kicking up behind her. As soon as they saw her coming, they took to their heels, but after running a safe distance turned back to shout with their hands cupped around their mouths.

"Your mother's a whore!"

"Go back to the jungle, you darky bastard!"

Saya picked up a stone from the gravel road and hurled it at them. It hit one of the boys on the shoulder. He looked stunned.

"You fucking shit!" Saya screamed and threw another stone. "Take that, you fucking shit! You fucking shit!"

She repeated the same curse over and over. As the boys turned tail and ran, she laid a comforting hand on Isamu's shoulder. He was breathing hard. His shirt was torn and she could see fresh scratches on his cheek and arms.

"Those kids are always—" he started to say, but his mother stopped him with a quick, "I know, dear," and led him back toward the house with an arm wrapped around him.

Ever since school started, Saya had noticed that Isamu often came home showing the scuff marks of playground fights. Most of the time he refused to say anything, and even when the wounds were too obvious to ignore, he would insist they were from a fall, so she thought it best not to press him too hard about it. But there could be little doubt that he was being bullied. His broken Japanese and unfamiliarity with local ways stood out, and it made him an easy target. She was proud of him for not whining about it.

She led him into the dirt-floored room and had him take off his clothes so she could wash his cuts. Then she brought him a clean shirt and trousers from the pile of fresh laundry, and gave him a steamed potato as a snack. While he sat on the edge of the veranda to eat it, Saya went back to folding clothes.

Spring had now arrived in earnest, and the direct sunlight was warm enough to raise a film of perspiration on her skin. The seeds she'd planted in the garden were beginning to pop up.

"Heh heh," Isamu chuckled.

"What?" his mother asked.

He looked up at her with his round, dark eyes. "You said, 'You fucking shit.'" Then he chuckled again as if he couldn't get over it.

Saya broke into a smile, too, but it quickly faded when she realized how easily the words of her Japanese tormentors in Kota Bharu had slipped from her own lips. That had been their constant refrain as they ranted at her and beat her and pressed their sword blades into her: "You fucking shit. You fucking shit." It was like a chant they used to egg themselves on.

From the time she was first detained and tortured by the Kempeitai, and throughout her months of serial rape at the P-house, she had never gone long without that phrase being yelled in her face. She'd learned to hate it like no other, for it was invariably a prelude to pain. And yet, now, those same words had come from her own mouth without her even being aware of it. It sent a shudder through her.

The evil spirits in those men must have jumped over onto her, she thought. Hadn't the healer said that's what spirits did – took possession of the very people who despised them most? And there was no doubt in her mind that the soldiers who'd bellowed "You fucking shit" at her had been the very embodiment of evil.

They're evil to the core.

Her brother had said it too. In exchange for Saya's freedom, he'd had to agree to work for the Japanese, so his words carried the weight of someone who knew.

After escaping from the P-house, Saya moved back to the jungle with Isamu, who had been in her brother's care while she was in captivity. But it wasn't long before they returned to Kota Bharu. She couldn't sit still for worry that if they were away from the city when Rentarō came back they might never see him again. It was her involvement with him, she knew, that had brought charges of spying on her, but she hadn't yet begun to doubt his word. It had never entered her mind that he might have abandoned her.

Their former landlord's wife blamed Rentarō for her husband's death at the hands of the Kempeitai, and she wouldn't hear of renting the house to Saya again. The place was nearly uninhabitable in any case after what the arresting officers had done to it. So Saya and Isamu moved into the shack where her brother lived on the outskirts of town. By this time, Kekah had begun working as a guard at the Japanese prison to earn a bit of money. He left for the prison early each day, and returned after dark looking utterly drained.

"The place is a jungle filled with evil spirits," he said venomously. "It's even turned me into one." He would scarcely touch the dinner she prepared, and sat staring at the starry sky with dark, cloudy eyes.

The Japanese hauled off anybody they suspected of spying, and tortured them until they confessed. They forced Kekah to help.

"I can't stand the things they make me do, but what choice do I have?" he moaned. "If I don't do what I'm told, it'll be me next in line." Once he'd agreed to work for the Japanese, there was no backing out. His eyes grew hollow, his body emaciated.

The things he witnessed were far too heavy a burden to keep bottled up inside him. He began emptying his heart of the day's events when he came home each night: tales of men young and old, Malayan and Indian, driven to their knees and forced to talk with a knife-edge at their throats; or found dead in their cells with faeces stuffed in their mouths; or writhing in pain as their penises were seared with a branding iron. Every day brought descriptions of new barbarities.

"And the worst of it is," he said through sobs, "I'm one of the torturers. I kick women in the face. I stuff mouths with shit. I burn pricks with hot irons. I yank out fingernails. I scream 'You fucking shit' in their faces."

Kekah longed to go back to the forest, to heal his tortured heart in its stillness and warmth. It would be a refuge where he could pour out all his cares, all he had seen and felt – something he could not find in the city. If he'd had a girlfriend, she might have been able to offer some solace. But their neighbours looked down their noses at Saya and her brother. They considered the jungle people no better than slaves. No city girl would have anything to do with Kekah. So it fell to Saya to be his refuge. She had to provide the stillness and warmth of the forest. As she listened quietly each night, he would let the horrors of his day spill out, and it would bring him a few brief moments of peace.

But everything he told her also became engraved deep in Saya's own mind, adding Kekah's hatred for his Japanese masters to the bitter feelings she already bore them. Saya's forest sanctuary quickly became overgrown with rancour. As it soaked up the rage that Kekah brought home, it was transformed from a place of stillness and warmth into one of festering hostility.

When the war came to an end and British forces returned, many of those who had worked for the Japanese were made to stand trial for collaboration. But they could be considered the lucky ones, for many more were hunted down by their victims and given summary justice on the spot. In this climate of revenge, Kekah naturally feared for his life and wanted to go back to the jungle. Saya told him he could go if he liked, but she would stay behind. With the war over, she was surer than ever that Rentarō would return, and she wanted to be in Kota Bharu when he arrived. Kekah insisted he could never leave her and Isamu in the city by themselves. They argued heatedly back and forth – you go without us, no, you have to come with me – right up until the day Kekah was killed. There was no way of knowing who had done it. His body was found beside a road on the edge of town with all four of his limbs broken, his throat slit open, and his eyes gouged out.

As she laid her brother to rest, Saya made a vow: she would not return to the jungle; she would find revenge. To her mind, Rentarō was the one responsible for his death. If he hadn't taken her to live with him in the city, if he hadn't invited those army people into their home, Kekah wouldn't have had to die.

With this thought, her hatred for the soldiers and Kempeitai swelled to include Rentarō as well. And that feeling was still with her now. She still lived in its grip.

Having finished folding the laundry, Saya sat staring vacantly out into the yard. Butterflies fluttered about over the furrows in the garden. On the road beyond the front hedge, she saw one of her neighbours slowly leading a cow her way. He saw her too and bobbed his head in greeting. She smiled back. In the distance, farmhouses surrounded by protective stands of trees dotted the landscape now turning green. Isamu finished his potato and hopped down into the yard to chase after the hens.

Hatred seemed utterly out of place on such a tranquil spring day. More than half a year had gone by since her bitterness had brought her to Japan. In the train to Singapore and throughout the sea passage, she'd thought only of revenge as she tested the edge of her secret knife. But she had failed to grasp what it really meant. The moment she laid eyes on Rentarō again, she realized she didn't hate him enough to plunge a blade into him.

And in fact, as she sat there on the veranda, she found herself wondering if she really hated him at all anymore. She certainly had when she stood over her brother's dead body. It was the fury she'd felt then that had fuelled her journey to Toyama. If Rentarō had tried to turn them away, she intended to hold her ground and kick up the biggest fuss he'd ever seen; she would have shouted to the whole world everything he had said, everything he had promised, and then put her knife to use.

Instead, however disturbed he may have been by her unexpected appearance on his doorstep, he had not thrown her back on the street. He'd taken her into his home for a time, then gone to the trouble of finding her a separate house to live in. These things had begun to soften her feelings.

Yet, they were not enough to dissipate entirely the rancour that clouded her heart.

It was still there. The hatred she felt for the men who'd abused her, and who'd put her brother through a living hell. The hatred she felt for the blood Rentarō shared with them. Yes, it was for being Japanese that she hated him. The malice she bore was not for the man; it was for the people and country he was part of. But the army that overran Malaya had been dismantled, and the empire that stood behind it was gone. By the time Saya landed in Japan, all she found was a people picking up the pieces of their defeat with remarkable good cheer. The warm smiles that greeted her held no trace of the cruel sneers she'd been given by the soldiers in Kota Bharu. The enemy she came to confront seemed to have vanished like the mist, and she was left with nowhere to direct her loathing.

Saya stacked the folded laundry and carried it inside. After putting everything neatly away in the closet, she opened the suitcase she had brought with her from Malaya and took out the finger-hole knife. Gently, she rubbed her thumb along the edge of the sleek, curving blade.

Just whose throat was this knife supposed to be for? she asked herself, as she inserted an index finger through the ring that served as its handle and stared at the glinting steel.

31

Through the green tunnel arching over the road came the distant sound of a flute and percussion.

Teedle-eedle-ee, pang pang pang.

"I think something's coming this way," Asafumi said in a low whisper, pointing down the road in the direction they were going.

Rentarō gave him a doubtful look, but then turned to listen for several moments and nodded.

"Might be a good idea to take cover," he said.

Asafumi was not inclined to argue. After the attack of the wild men a while ago, they had good reason to be leery of who they might encounter, and in any case he wasn't particularly eager to be seen dressed in nothing but a cotton towel. They quickly hid themselves behind some trees in the thicket by the road.

Teedle-eedle-ee, pang pa-pang pang.

It sounded rather like a festival parade – except the lack of any clear melody made it closer to the cacophony of the little bands hired to draw attention to store openings and other special events. As they watched the road from behind some trees with their clubs at the ready, a very odd-looking procession came into view.

A man wearing a ragged plastic string shirt and nothing else, his flaccid penis dangling beneath the ends. A woman whose hair stuck out like a bamboo broom, dressed in a gunnysack with holes cut out for her head and arms. A giant of a man who had to be over two metres tall, pulling a wooden cart piled high with rags. A dwarfish man tooting on a flute made from a length of metal pipe. A one-armed woman beating on a large aluminium pan lid hanging around her neck. A bald old man with a bright red rabbit strapped to his back, muttering something under his breath as he walked. A man with a bad case of scabies, who looked like a walking clump of dirt. A woman with a prominent bump in the middle of her forehead, rapping on a piece of bamboo with a stick. A man who was white as chalk from head to toe. A woman bent nearly double at the waist. A man no taller than a boar and almost as furry.

Asafumi and Rentarō watched in astonishment as the twenty or so men and women straggled by, oblivious to their presence. A murmur of voices rose among them like a bubbling stream, blending with the music of the makeshift instruments to spill across the road.

Huddled in the foliage, Asafumi and Rentarō were praying that the ragtag troupe would simply move on by without incident, when a black dog leapt from their midst and began barking at the thicket where they'd taken cover. The creature had two heads and barked with equal ferocity from both of its mouths, flashing two sets of menacing fangs. The entire group stopped short.

"It seems we have company," shouted the man in the string shirt. All eyes turned to look directly at the trees where they were hiding. Asafumi broke into a cold sweat. Rentarō poked his head out from between the branches.

"Sorry, but could somebody please restrain this freakish beast?"

A stir went through the crowd, and a girl of twelve or thirteen stepped forward. She had curly dark hair and a round face, with big, black, inquisitive eyes. Like nearly everyone else in the party, her feet were bare. She had on an adult-sized dress that was much too big for her, hiked up around her waist with a length of vine.

Walking up to the two-headed dog, she slapped it on the back behind the split in its neck. The animal quickly settled down – though a low growl continued to rumble in its throat.

Rentarō stepped out into the open. Offering a friendly bob of his head in greeting, he said, "Might I ask where all you folks are off to?"

"Where're we off to, he wants to know," said the woman in the gunnysack, bursting into a laugh as she glanced around the group. The others laughed, too. It was a listless, hollow laughter – like the laughter of the dead. As if to liven things up, the dwarfish man tooted a string of notes on his flute, and the one-armed woman *panged* out a beat on her improvised cymbal.

"We could ask the same of you. Where'd you turn up from?"

This voice came from a fine-featured youth clad in a colourful array of loosely tied cloths. The person's androgynous good looks and long locks gathered at the back of the neck left Rentarō uncertain whether he was looking at a he or a she.

"From Senbashi," he said, maintaining the same genial tone.

Somewhat reassured by Rentarō's composure, Asafumi stepped nervously out from behind his tree. Given the bizarre appearance these people presented, he no longer felt so self-conscious about his own state of dress.

"Where's that?" the androgynous youth shot back.

Thinking maybe they'd come from another prefecture, Rentarō explained, "Right next to the city of Toyama."

"Toyama?" the youth said. "Never heard of it."

Several of the others exchanged glances and asked, "Where's that?"

In his travels around Malaya, Rentarō had grown accustomed to the unexpected – from flowers as big as tatami mats, to dead bodies tied high in the trees, to processions of Hindus scattering petals as they walked – so the group's outlandish appearance had hardly fazed him. But how could anybody travelling in the foothills of Tateyama not know about Toyama or Senbashi?

"You've never even heard of Toyama?" he said, his voice rising nearly to a shout. "Where in the world did you folks come from?"

"I've heard of it."

The voice came from on top of the wooden cart. What until now had appeared to be only a pile of rags suddenly stirred, and a head popped up from its midst. It was wrapped like a mummy in a dirty scarf, with openings only for the eyes and nose, and the shoulders to which it was attached were cloaked in a gray blanket-like robe.

"I remember hearing that name somewhere or other, a long time ago," continued the voice.

The wrinkled eyes and the voice belonged to a woman of very advanced years. Rentarō looked into the elephant eyes peering from beneath the fabric. There was a wariness in them as they returned his gaze. He had the odd feeling that they had met somewhere before, though at the same time he felt sure they never had. But as he stared back at her, trying to puzzle out where these contradictory feelings came from, any possible clues seemed to slip elusively away.

"Is that true, Granny Uba?" several of the others called out.

The scarf-wrapped head gave a nod. "It was a long time ago. A long, long time ago." The word "long" seemed to take forever to roll off her tongue as she repeated it.

Holding back a mounting uneasiness, Rentarō declared emphatically, "I'm not talking about a long time ago. I'm talking about a big city that's just a hop and a skip away from here right now."

"The cities and towns are all gone," came a voice just as emphatic. "Every last one."

It was the old man with a rabbit on his back. His cheeks shone nearly as much as his hairless head. He fixed Rentarō with the look of a man prepared to defy anyone.

"Your town is gone, too," he said.

"That's not poss—" Rentarō began to say, but the old man raised his voice and drowned him out.

"It's the calamity! It's all because of the calamity!"

Rentarō stiffened. When he had first noticed the change in climate, he'd wondered whether some new kind of bomb had been dropped, and whether the war might still be going on. Maybe he'd been onto something. But he wasn't sure how far he could trust those instincts.

"I thought the war was over," he said.

"War is never over," the old man erupted in scorn. The red rabbit was staring over his shoulder with big round eyes. It was as if he had a ball of fire strapped onto his back.

"It's war, war, war no matter which way you turn. That's what brought the calamity."

"What's this big calamity you keep talking about?" Asafumi asked.

The old man looked at him in surprise. "Are you kidding?" he said.

The other eyes turning to look at him seemed to join in saying, *How can you not know that?* He sensed in them also a disapproval of his near nakedness, which made him feel self-conscious again.

"*We* are the calamity," the beautiful youth said, gesturing with his left hand toward his chest.

Asafumi began to wonder if these people were some kind of religious cult. Maybe the woman they called Granny Uba was their spiritual leader. But that still didn't explain the talk of calamity, or the claim that all the cities were gone.

"We need to be on our way," the tall man said after several moments of silence. "Otherwise the sun will be down before we get to the next place."

The old woman wrapped in rags slapped the side of the wooden cart. "It's a half-day's journey to where we stop for the night."

The carter lifted the handles. The rusty iron wheels creaked as the wagon lurched forward. The rest of the group began to fall in behind.

"Where is it that you're going?" Rentarō asked.

"We're off to find Yakushi," the man in the string outfit said in a singsong voice.

"Yakushi?" Rentarō said.

"That's right. Yakushi. The Healing Buddha. He's going to fix our troubles."

"Want to come along?"

"He can mend your troubles, too."

Several of the others chimed in as they all turned to go.

Before the woman in the gunnysack could fall in step, Rentarō pointed in the direction the group had come from and asked, "Could you tell us what's down that way?"

As she swung around to look where he was pointing, the neck of her sack was pulled to one side, revealing a skin covered in gray fish scales lower down.

"The city," she said, shrugging the gunnysack back into place.

"But nobody lives there anymore," said the man whose features were completely obscured by scabies.

"It's the calamity! It's all because of the calamity!" the man with the red rabbit shouted from near the front of the column.

"Let's be going, let's be going," called the old crone on the cart. "We're on a pilgrimage to Yakushi!"

Teedle-eedle-ee. The dwarfish man blew into his flute again. *Pang pang pa-pang.* The one-armed woman beat on her cymbal. With sluggish footsteps, the procession moved off.

Rentarō tried to gather his thoughts as he watched the ragtag pilgrims receding up the road. From the sound of it, the war had indeed started up again and led to some great disaster that left Japan in ruins. This seemed to confirm that the overnight transformation of the mountainside had come from some unimaginable new weapon.

Even the atomic bombs the Americans had dropped on Hiroshima and Nagasaki two years before had been beyond his comprehension. When it was explained that scientists did something with atoms so they could destroy a city of a hundred thousand or more using just one bomb, he understood all the words, but he couldn't quite put together what they really meant. The bombs supposedly emitted some special kind of heat rays that sank into the earth and continued to harm people long after the cities had been flattened. Some accounts said that nobody could live in the bomb zones again for eighty years, and peddlers who went to areas nearby were still coming back with stories about the after-effects making people suddenly lose their hair or spit up blood and die, even after all this time, or about women who'd been exposed to the mysterious rays giving birth to deformed babies.

The emperor told the people that Japan had accepted the terms of the Potsdam Declaration and surrendered, but if you wanted to be suspicious, you could find plenty of room for doubt. For one thing, now that everybody knew the government had been lying through its teeth during the war, what guarantee did anybody have that it wasn't still doing the same? Maybe they had only pretended to surrender. And then when it came out that they were somehow carrying on, one of the Allies dropped another newfangled bomb on the country.

If it turned out that the war wasn't over, then his first concern had to be survival. Quickly making up his mind, he turned to Asafumi, who stood lost in his own thoughts beside him.

"I'm going with them," he said.

"What?"

"It sounds like maybe the war isn't over. At times like this, there's safety in numbers."

"But those people are nuts," Asafumi shot back. "How could the entire population of Toyama suddenly be gone? That's crazy talk."

"They say Hiroshima and Nagasaki vanished in a single flash. Maybe some new bomb like that got dropped on Toyama, too."

Asafumi flinched at the thought, but then immediately shook his head. "I'll believe it when I see it."

"You could get yourself killed first."

"I'm going home," he said resolutely.

Rentarō decided there was no point in arguing with him. He retrieved his club and started up the road after the pilgrims.

"Grandpa!" Asafumi cried after him.

Rentarō threw a dirty look over his shoulder. "I'm not that old yet," he growled. Who did he think he was anyway – treating him like some old geezer? He walked on.

Asafumi stood rooted to the spot. The word had popped out before he could even think, and he was at a loss what to say next.

Please don't leave me, Grandpa!

Those might have been his next words if he had been any more befuddled than he was. They were on the very tip of his tongue. But somehow he managed not to blurt them out.

He wavered a little as he watched Rentarō hurrying off after the procession. To go down this dangerous road alone might not be such a good idea. But after coming this far, he just couldn't see himself turning around again and heading back deeper into the mountains with that gang of weirdos.

What he wanted was simply to get on home as quickly as he could – assuming, of course, that the house was still standing where he'd left it. But what if those people were right, and the city really *was* gone? Then what? Between the extreme weather change and the return of his dead grandfather, there was definitely something very strange going on. Was it actually a mistake for him to think that Toyama remained intact at the end of this road?

Torn between the desire for company and the urge to hurry home, Asafumi found himself stymied, unable to make a move.

"Better get going."

Startled, he turned to see the girl with the two-headed dog standing among the trees on the far side of the road.

"What're you doing here?"

She smiled. "You wanted to go back to the city, right?"

He gave her an uncertain nod.

"I'll go with you. I've always wanted to see what it's like."

She stepped from the underbrush onto the road. The dog followed close behind, panting noisily with both of its tongues hanging out.

"You've never been to the city?"

She shook her head. "Come on, Kekah," she called to the dog and, without waiting for Asafumi, started walking in the opposite direction from her companions.

"But... you just came from this way," he said as he hurried after her. It would be nice to have someone to travel with, but he was also concerned that he was taking her away from where she was supposed to be going.

"It doesn't matter. All I ever do is go up and down Mandala Road with Granny Uba."

"So this really is Mandala Road?"

In his relief, he almost whooped.

Without interrupting her leisurely pace, she gave him a look that said, *What a weird thing to ask.*

"But wait a minute. What do you mean – all you ever do is go up and down Mandala Road?"

"We show the pilgrims the way to Yakushi. That's what we've been doing for as long as I can remember."

"You and Granny Uba, you mean?"

"Yes," she said brusquely, as if getting tired of his questions. But he was not inclined to shut up when there was more he wanted to ask. As a scientist, coming up against something he didn't understand made him want to find out everything he could about it.

"Then won't she miss you and be worried if you're not there?"

"There's no reason for her to worry. She knows we'll eventually meet up again somewhere along the road."

"Why are you and Granny Uba doing it, anyway – showing pilgrims the way to Yakushi?"

"How should I know?"

In the annoyance that crossed her face this time was a flicker of the wildness he'd seen in the three bushmen. He shrank back, deciding to hold his tongue after all.

As he replayed the encounter with the pilgrims in his mind, he couldn't help getting the sense that none of them really knew why they were doing what they were. But the girl and the dog seemed well-acquainted with the road, and he silently fell in step. Kekah walked several paces ahead, wagging his tail as he led the way. Apparently forgetting that anyone was walking beside her, the girl began to hum a tune. *Whoooon, whoo-whoo-whoo-whoong...* Her thick lips were puckered as if to blow soap bubbles, and her eyes seemed to drift blankly through space. Asafumi immediately thought of Saya. She had hummed a tune like this, too – or rather, something like a tune that never quite settled into any fixed melody.

"What's your name?" he found himself asking.

This time she gave no sign of irritation. Her deep black eyes sparkled brightly as she replied with a lilt, "Kesumba."

32

The sky was a solid sheet of mackerel clouds as the SUV approached the spot where the smaller road headed deeper into the woods. Miharu was in the front passenger seat, and her father Yoshitaka was driving.

"I sure hope it doesn't rain," she said.

"I reckon it'll hold off till evening," he said, taking the fork.

Shizuka was in the back, hoping and praying they would know what had happened to Asafumi by the end of the day. It was now nearly four full days since he'd left on his trip.

When there was still no word from him the day before, Miharu had phoned her father and asked him to drive out to Mandala Road and see if he could learn anything. Her father called back late in the evening to say he'd found a blue Volkswagen parked at the side of the road. In order to make sure that it was actually Asafumi's car,

Miharu had taken a day off and driven Shizuka out to her parents' place this morning.

The forest road was wrapped in gloom under a cloudy sky. Apprehension gripped Shizuka as she peered up the tunnel-like roadway winding through the trees. Reforested cypresses gave way to mixed old-growth, and then, as they rounded a long bend, the Volkswagen came into view. Yoshitaka pulled to a stop in front of the squat little car.

Shizuka was first out of the SUV. As soon as she spotted the toy rabbit dangling from the rear-view mirror, she knew the car was theirs. It was a souvenir from a day she and Asafumi had spent browsing the shops in Yokohama's Motomachi district. Then she saw his glasses sitting on the dashboard.

"This is it all right," she said, a slight quiver in her voice.

Miharu circled the car checking each door and the trunk. Everything was locked up tight.

Yoshitaka made his way around the vehicle, too. "You can see here how he got his rear wheel caught in this rut and couldn't get back out," he said. "He took his keys with him, so I suppose he must've set off one way or the other in search of help." In a khaki jacket, with a hand towel looped over his belt, he carried himself like a man used to backwoods terrain. Between farm tasks, he often worked as a mountain guide for visitors to Tateyama.

"But walking back to Awasuno from here shouldn't take more than a couple of hours," said Miharu, folding her arms in puzzlement. "We know the car's been here for at least one night, so he should have been able to get through to Shizuka or the house in Senbashi long ago."

"When I found the car sitting here yesterday, I thought maybe he'd gone in search of help, so I drove on all the way to where the road ends, but I didn't catch any sign of him," Yoshitaka said. Then, perhaps to set Shizuka's mind at ease, he added, "Of course, it was in the evening and getting dark, so it's possible I just didn't see him."

"Maybe he decided to just leave the car here and check out Mandala Road on foot," Shizuka said. She didn't actually think Asafumi was that intent on finding the villages in the book, but she said it anyway in an attempt to keep her hopes up.

Miharu, in her upbeat way, quickly lent her support. "Yeah, I bet that's it," she said. "I think we should drive on to the villages up ahead and ask if anybody's seen him. What do you say, Dad?"

"Sounds like a plan," he nodded.

They got back into the SUV and pushed on. Almost immediately they came to a cluster of houses on one side. Yoshitaka slowed the car to a crawl. Miharu opened her window and leaned out for a better look.

"It looks completely deserted," she said. The doors and shutters were either firmly closed or completely torn off.

"When the economy took off in the mid-fifties or so, people from villages out this way starting leaving for the city right and left," Yoshitaka said as he glanced at the receding houses in his rear-view mirror. "Actually, some weren't even what you'd call villages – just five or six families helping each other out. A lot of the places abandoned in those days have since been completely swallowed up by the forest, and you can't even tell where they were anymore, but from the looks of this one, people must have lived here till pretty recently."

"You can hardly blame them for wanting to leave," Miharu said. "Life in the city's a whole lot easier than up here in the snowy mountains."

"It's amazing how things have changed," Yoshitaka said. "When I was a kid, we went to school in clothes full of patches and sneakers that were falling apart, but you never see kids like that these days. Back then, only rich people could afford a colour TV, but now practically any family has two or three of them scattered around the house. And it's not just the way we live, the people are different, too. Like when groups come to climb Tateyama, I always used to get the sense that they were real people, but these days it's like they're TV sets that got up to walk. The scenery just flickers across their blank eyes without ever really registering."

"So you're showing walking TVs the way up the mountain?" Miharu laughed.

He gave a rueful smile. "That's about the size of it. It's pathetic."

Shizuka listened to their talk in silence, wondering what the difference was between the scenery she saw pictured on a TV screen and what she was seeing outside the window right now. Whether it was the distant view of the mountain ridge or the trees turning colour on the roadside, it seemed essentially the same as what you would get on any modern TV set with a decent picture. There wasn't anything about seeing the scenery first-hand that particularly appealed to her. She did think *Oh, wow, that's pretty*, or *Ah, the air smells so fresh*, but underneath it all it really didn't take hold of her in any special way. Deep down, she felt indifferent.

And to be honest, her concern for Asafumi's safety right now was nearly as superficial. If she dug very far beneath the surface of her worries, what she found was indifference. She considered the possibility that he might actually have died somewhere out in these mountains. It didn't seem very likely, and yet off in one corner of her mind, plans were already starting to take shape for if it turned out to be true: she would pack up the house in Toyama and move back to Yokohama to begin a new life as a widow there. But like the scenery flowing by, these thoughts, too, felt as if they belonged to someone else's life in a drama that was unfolding on TV.

In sudden horror at what she was thinking, she tensed the muscles of her folded arms as hard as she could.

"Oh, there's a house! Over there!" Miharu cried out.

Shizuka looked through the trees in the direction she was pointing. On the other side of the Kanoko River stood a house with smoke rising from a bonfire in the front yard.

"Let's see if they can tell us anything about Asafumi," Yoshitaka said as he found a lane that appeared to lead that way and made the turn. The gravel track descended to an old concrete bridge before starting to climb again on the other side. It led between a stand of cedars and some mixed growth. The SUV bumped up the hill. The area where the cedars grew was terraced with stone retaining walls and had obviously been farmland once. Here and there a wall had collapsed, or a heap of lumber and roof tiles lay where a house once stood. It appeared to be yet another abandoned village.

Only a small patch or two next to the house with the rising smoke remained under cultivation, appearing to be planted mainly with Chinese cabbage and eggplant. The single-story building had a tiled roof and was not very large. Ears of corn had been hung in rows beneath the eaves to dry. Firewood was stacked against the side wall, and closed storm shutters blocked off half the windows. Yoshitaka drove just inside the front yard and stopped.

A bald-headed old man was bent over a stick, pushing dry leaves into the fire. He lifted his head to reveal puffy cheeks, arching eyebrows, a hard line of a mouth, and deeply tanned skin. His trousers were dark with grime, his sweatshirt frayed at the cuffs, and the toes sticking through the thongs of his rubber *zoris*, blackened with dirt. He eyed them warily as they got out.

Yoshitaka made a polite bow. "Sorry to bother you, but we were wondering if a fellow about thirty years old might have stopped by here."

When this only seemed to put him more on his guard, Shizuka remembered the snapshot she'd thought to bring along and dug it out of her purse. "His name is Asafumi Nonezawa," she said, holding the picture out. "He's been missing since four days ago."

The old man rounded his lips in surprise as he looked at Shizuka, then broke into a smile. "You must be from Tokyo," he said. There was no Toyama accent in his speech.

"Yes, I am," she said. "It sounds like you are, too."

He nodded. "Born and raised in Arakawa Ward."

"Then what brought you to live in a place like this?" Miharu broke in with her usual lack of reserve.

"I came out here to settle after the war," he said, leaning on his stick with both hands. "A bunch of us who lost our homes in the air raids, we all came out together, but..." He squinted off toward the abandoned fields for a moment. "I guess this is what you call 'the aftermath of brave soldiers' dreams,'" he said, wistfully repeating a famous line by the haiku poet Bashō. After a brief pause, he turned abruptly back to Shizuka and said, "Anyway, if you're from Tokyo, maybe you can tell me how the reconstruction's going. Have they started to clear the ruins and rebuild yet?"

Bewildered, Shizuka looked at the other two. The ruins were gone long before she was even born.

"It's been over half a century since the war, sir," Yoshitaka said. "The rebuilding was finished decades ago."

"Ah, yes," he nodded, "that's right, isn't it."

Seeing that he was back to responding normally, Shizuka held out the photo again. "So, we were wondering if you'd seen this man."

He studied the picture with a furrowed brow. It was a snapshot taken during a hiking trip. Asafumi had a daypack on his back and was smiling a bit stiffly into the camera.

"The face does sort of ring a bell..." the old man said. The muscles in his face twitched as he continued to study the photo.

Shizuka was buoyed by the hint of recognition. "Did he come here?"

He took the picture from her and scrutinized it more closely. "No," he said after several more moments. "I'm afraid I can't place him."

"It would have been in the last few days," she said, not ready to give up. "He came out this way to see about some medicine sales."

The skin on his head twitched. "He's a medicine peddler?" he asked sharply.

"Yes, that's right," Miharu said, stepping closer. "He was visiting old customers."

Shizuka didn't really think of Asafumi that way yet, so she was caught off-guard by her remark. But Miharu pressed on, excited that they might finally have a lead.

"He wasn't travelling like in the olden days with all the baskets on his back, but he should have had an old notebook with him called a 'Medicine Kit Register.' It originally belonged to a peddler who came out this way right after the war, and he was..."

The old man had gone completely stiff. Every line in his creased, round face was drawn tight. Noticing the change and worried what it might mean, Shizuka was about to interrupt Miharu, when a loud *pop!* split the air. Everybody jumped and looked toward the fire. Realizing it was only a piece of bamboo bursting in the heat, they turned back to the old man for his answer. But he just stood there like a terra-cotta statue, not moving a muscle, his eyes fixed on the flames.

"Sir?" Miharu said, reaching for his shoulder. He recoiled from her touch, his right arm convulsing in an odd way as he did so, and then suddenly the stick in his hand came whipping through the air and hit her in the neck. She cried out in pain as she sank to her knees.

He raised his stick to strike again.

"Stop!" yelled Yoshitaka, quickly stepping between them. But with astonishing swiftness, the man changed his grip and thrust it into Yoshitaka's belly like a bayonet. He doubled over and fell to the ground.

It was all happening too fast, and Shizuka stood paralyzed with fright as the man now raised the stick in both hands like a sword and brought it down on Yoshitaka's back. Yoshitaka rolled onto his side. Swinging the stick high over his head, the man brought it down again, and then again, each time letting out a sharp shout. His face had turned a deep crimson, with veins standing out on his forehead, and there was madness in his eyes. Clearly it was no longer Yoshitaka he was seeing, but something else, and he was striking at that thing with every bit of strength he had in him.

When she realized he might beat Yoshitaka to death, it finally brought Shizuka out of her spell. "Stop it!" she screamed, throwing herself at him with all her might. He reeled off balance and tumbled into the fire. Flames shot up around him. With a howl, he rolled out onto the ground. White swirls of smoke rose from the back of his shirt and trousers. Shizuka leapt for the stick he'd dropped and held it poised to knock him down again if he started to get up. But he was too busy rolling back and forth, trying to stop his clothes from burning.

"It's hot! It's hot!" he cried.

Miharu staggered to her feet and went to check on Yoshitaka, who lay on the ground with his head wrapped in his arms.

"Are you all right, Dad?" she said, shaking his shoulder. "Are you all right?"

Yoshitaka gave a nod. He was still gasping for breath, and blood trickled from the corner of his mouth, but he managed to push himself upright. He looked at the old man still rolling about in his smouldering clothes.

"We should probably tie his hands while we have the chance," he said.

Miharu turned to Shizuka, who had begun to shake as she stood there holding the stick. "See if you can find some rope," she said.

She dashed toward the house. Looped loosely over a bamboo laundry rod under the eaves, thick with cobwebs, was a length of rope for hanging ears of corn up to dry. She grabbed it and brought it back to Yoshitaka, who got to his feet with a grimace.

He stood over the groaning man. Miharu stepped up beside him, keeping the stick at the ready.

The man offered no resistance as Yoshitaka wound the rope tightly around his wrists. He lay curled in a foetal position, his whole body trembling like someone with malaria.

Yoshitaka studied the blackened back of the man's sweatshirt. "Looks like it burned right through to his skin," he said. "I think we'd better get him to a hospital."

"Suppose he might have some family around?" Miharu asked, looking toward the house.

Her father looked at the dilapidated building, too. "I have a feeling he's on his own," he said, "but there must be somebody we can contact to turn him over to. The man's obviously unbalanced. It's not safe for him to be living by himself."

"Maybe we can find an address or phone number inside," Shizuka said, turning to Miharu in the hope that she would go in with her. The thought that Asafumi might have been murdered by the madman brought visions of stumbling across his mutilated body somewhere in the house. She didn't think she had the courage to face that prospect alone, and wanted her sister-in-law's company.

Much to her relief, Miharu quickly agreed. "Good idea," she said as they both started toward the house.

Removing their shoes at the veranda, they stepped inside. The front room had a futon laid out in the middle of the tatami floor. Plastic shopping bags, empty snack bags, and an assortment of dirty clothes were scattered about. The place looked more like the lair of a wild animal than a human habitation. Behind this was a sitting room, separated by sliding doors, which had been left open. There was a traditional low folding table here, with a teapot and teacup sitting on it. A television was positioned to be visible from the futon in the front room. On beyond the sitting room was a dirt-floored kitchen area. A pan thick with simmer sauce sat on a clay brazier. After glancing briefly around this space, they circled into a third tatami room situated next to the sitting room, and a fourth that looked out onto the veranda next to the front room where they'd first entered. It appeared that this half of the house had not been used in quite some time. The badly worn tatami mats were thick with dust. Opening the closets, they found nothing but storage boxes and an old kerosene heater. Shizuka breathed a sigh of relief that their quick tour had not turned up Asafumi's body.

Of course not. What real reason did she have to think he might have been killed? She felt like a fool for letting her imagination run away with her. But then the chilling thought came to her that, somewhere deep down, she might actually have been hoping he was dead.

That was ridiculous. Why would she want that? She brushed the idea aside and started to step back into the room with the futon in it, when she noticed three framed photographs mounted on the wall above the sliding doors. The one on the right was obviously from when the village still had a substantial population. A large group of men and women stood holding sickles and hoes and other farm implements, and there were a good many children as well. They all stood smiling proudly with a newly planted rice paddy behind them. The centre picture was a family portrait. In the front yard of this house, a man and woman stood staring stiffly into the camera with their two children – a boy and a girl, both looking about ten years old, give or take. The man's arching eyebrows and hard set lips identified him as their mad assailant in a younger day. The woman's hair was freshly permed, giving her a refined air. With a hand on her son's shoulder, she was trying to smile but without too much success, and there was a vague aura of sadness about her. The boy had close-cropped hair and stood ramrod straight in his bare feet with a look of defiance on his face. The girl, apparently the younger of the two, held her brother's hand, smiling. In the picture on the left, the siblings were fully grown, now looking about thirty. Next to the brother was a woman with a baby in her arms. The sister was in a miniskirt and had become quite tall, nearly the same height as her brother. The young people were gathered around the old man as he sat on the edge of the veranda. His wife was not present.

As Shizuka stood studying these photos, trying to glean any clues she could about the old man's relations, Miharu called out from the sitting room.

"I think his name is Manzaburō Ohara."

Shizuka quickly went to join her. She was sorting through some postcards and envelopes in a letter holder on the wall.

"This one's from a Katsuichi Takatomi in Ōyama," she said. "Maybe we can find out something from him. His phone number's here, too."

It was a New Year's card from this year with only the pre-printed "Happy New Year" message – no handwritten note. They apparently weren't on particularly close terms.

"The pictures in the other room show him with a son and a daughter," Shizuka said as she began flipping through the rest of the mail. The postcards were all impersonal notices – an invitation to a veterans' gathering, an appointment reminder for his annual checkup, and so on. The letters had old postmarks, with return addresses in Tokyo or Osaka. None were from anybody named Ohara, so they offered no leads on the whereabouts of the son or daughter.

"Oh well," said Miharu. "At least we didn't come up completely empty-handed." She slipped the New Year's card from Katsuichi Takatomi into her pocket.

They went back out to the veranda. As Shizuka stooped to put on her shoes, Miharu said, "Oh, here's another closet."

There was a door at the end of the veranda about the width of a tatami mat. She pulled the door open to look inside and let out a gasp.

"Look at this!" she exclaimed. "It's a set of medicine baskets!"

Shizuka peered over her shoulder. Sure enough, in the closet sat a stack of five baskets, brown with age. The tools of the trade.

"What in the world are these doing here?" Miharu wondered aloud as she pulled the baskets out and opened the small one on top. It was packed full of notebooks, photos, letters, and other odds and ends.

"Here's an address book," Miharu said, fishing out a small notebook with a navy blue cover. The addresses and phone numbers were written in a woman's hand. They were obviously very old. Returning it to its place, she said, "What's this?" and pulled another notebook out from under the pile.

Shizuka felt her heart contract, and a sensation of numbness swept through her all the way to her fingertips.

It was an old-fashioned notebook bound with thread around the outside of the spine. The label on the cover bore the title "Medicine Kit Register," and the date "April 19, 1947".

"But Miharu, that's..."

Tensely, she opened it to the first page and read aloud, "Ōyama Village, Magawa. By way of Mandala Road from Tateyama Line Awasuno Station..."

It was the very register Asafumi had taken with him in his bag.

33

The glaring sun beat down relentlessly from above. Even in the shade of the overhanging branches, its heat seemed to press in from all sides. A clamour of shrilling cicadas and birdsong rang out from among those same branches. Giant ferns crowded the roadside, and thick vines curled about the trunks of the trees. Rentarō felt as if he was back in the jungles of Malaya.

Day after day he had travelled by train through terrain thick with vegetation just like this. He'd made the rounds from one palm-thatched house on stilts to the next, explaining the efficacy of his remedies. When he used the placement system, he tended to find the kits chewed up by rats or the family gone by the time he next returned, so to avoid such losses he generally stuck with on-the-spot sales.

His job was relatively easy in the cities, where people already knew about the use of medicinal preparations from the British chemists and Chinese herbalists who had preceded him. But purveying to outlying villages was far more difficult. The natives were accustomed to taking their problems to witch doctors, whose treatments consisted largely of incantations and prayers, so it was no simple matter to make a sale. Witch doctors who saw him as a threat to their own business would sometimes run him off. If he forgot the Islamic prohibition against consuming pork and let slip that a remedy contained something from a pig's organs, his kits would wind up torn to pieces and scattered on the ground. Then again, there was the time the villagers thought he was another witch doctor, who simply happened to come from a far-off place called Japan, and asked him to exorcise some evil spirits that had been making trouble. He shook a tree branch back and forth as he'd seen Shinto priests do in purification rituals, then told them they needed to buy his remedies. He and his co-workers at Tamiya's store in Singapore had laughed about that for a long time afterwards.

Memories of those days spun through his mind one after the other. Everything had seemed so fresh and new then. He wasn't even twenty. A life of endless possibility stretched before him.

Except for being drafted and forced to return to Japan, he might well have decided to stay on permanently in Malaya. He could picture himself married to a local girl and running his own pharmacy. At the very least, he wouldn't have wound up caught between Yōko and Saya, not knowing which way to turn. At this thought, a sense of deflation displaced the fond memories, and his mind came lurching back to the present, where he found himself without his wares, tagging aimlessly along behind a bunch of freaks in a landscape transformed overnight by what he could only imagine was some new kind of bomb.

The pilgrims continued their plodding progress up the mountain road. Now and then they would hear a commotion in the undergrowth, but fortunately it always turned out to be just some monkeys or birds, and the wild men did not reappear. Perhaps the size of the group kept them away.

He felt sorry for that fellow he'd parted company with. If he'd had a little more sense, he would have understood what the dangers were. Travelling back down this road all by himself was pure folly.

He noticed he was walking beside the woman with a big bump in the middle of her forehead. The bump rose high enough to look not unlike a horn.

"Where're you from?" he asked.

"The city," she said blandly. The way the bump stretched the skin on the rest of her face gave her quite a forbidding appearance.

"Which city would that be?"

"The city is the city. What else is there besides the city?"

Rentarō decided to try a different approach.

"Where does your family live?"

The woman turned to stare at him with widened eyes, which combined with the bump on her forehead to make her look like a classic ogre.

"What's family?" she asked.

"Your father and mother... and any brothers and sisters you might have. You know – the people you're connected to by blood."

This answer appeared to vex her even more. He half expected her to sprout fangs.

The androgynous youth walking a few steps ahead was listening in.

"It's no use asking us things like that," he turned to say.

"Why's that?"

"We don't remember anything."

A faint smile made his face even more beautiful.

"We used our brains too hard," came a gravelly voice from behind them. It was the old man with the red rabbit. "We used them so much they broke."

"But what about the stuff you said a while ago about some kind of catastrophe? And this lady just told me she came from a city."

"That's basically as much as we can remember," said the youth. He spoke in a voice as clear as a spirit medium relaying a message from the gods. "And even then, we only remember it dimly, like an image on water. The fact that we're talking about it with you now will start to blur pretty quickly, too, and it probably won't be long before we've forgotten the whole thing."

"It's the calamity. It's the calamity," sang out the man in the string outfit, shaking his arms and legs. The horned woman quickly joined in, gaily swinging her hips back and forth as she clapped her hands. "It's the calamity. It's the calamity." They were repeating the old man's words, but Rentarō got the feeling they had no idea what "calamity" actually meant.

It was like when he first arrived in Malaya, he thought. People would speak to him as if he were no different from them, but he couldn't understand a word they said. Since everybody there looked pretty much the same as people back home, he felt as if somehow he alone had suddenly been cast out of the world he knew into the wilderness.

As he watched the pilgrims clapping their hands and shaking their bodies about, he realized that the two-headed dog and the girl it seemed to belong to were missing. Yet nobody appeared the least bit concerned. Or maybe they hadn't even noticed. He considered asking about them, but figured he'd just get another incomprehensible answer and decided against it.

The trees fell away to the right and the view opened up. A river flowed below, with a small village on the other side. Ramshackle houses were scattered among terraced fields, whose stone retaining walls were in need of repair here and there. People could be seen working in the fields, pulling up weeds or turning the soil. In some ways it reminded Rentarō of the settlement where he'd left his things the night before, yet the houses themselves and the state of the fields looked completely different.

On the cart, Granny Uba drew a staff from among the rags around her and pointed it toward the village.

"Go there," she said.

The procession started down a small lane toward the river. The dwarfish man began playing his handmade flute, which prompted the one-armed woman to beat on her pan lid and the horned woman to rap on her hollow bamboo. The man in the string shirt started dancing, and the others quickly got in the spirit too, clapping their hands and raising high-pitched cries of *Hey, hey!* at random intervals. They all trooped noisily to the bottom of the grassy lane, where they came to a bridge. The railings were half gone, and the entire structure looked as though it could tumble into the river at any moment, but they made their way across and proceeded up the other side. *Teedle-eedle-ee, pang pa-pang pang*. At the sound of flute and percussion, the people working in the fields stopped what they were doing and like a rising tide began converging on the lane leading into the village.

With faces darkened by the sun, the villagers all had long hair gathered at the back of their necks, and the coarse, homemade garments they wore offered no means of telling male from female. Their farm tools were of extremely crude construction – little more than scraps of metal lashed to sticks. Something in their eyes reminded Rentarō of the bushmen he'd encountered earlier, and he stiffened with caution.

"We're on a pilgrimage to Yakushi!" Granny Uba announced from her place atop the cart, and the assembled villagers quickly opened the way to let the procession through. With the cart and its giant puller in the lead, they resumed their progress up the lane through the fields. Leaving a short gap, the villagers fell in behind.

The house to which Granny Uba directed her carter stood at the highest point in the settlement and was noticeably larger than the others – though to call it a house was in fact being generous. It looked more like a heap of refuse – wooden posts and crossbeams, rusty steel poles, battered tin sheeting, and who knew what else, obviously salvaged from old houses somewhere, cobbled together just well enough to offer shelter from the elements. A solitary figure stood waiting in front of it. The curve of the chest and thickness of the hips told Rentarō it was a woman. She was dressed in the same coarse, shapeless garment as the others, but with one difference: she also wore a string of shiny glass beads and stones around her neck. The woman watched the procession approach with a stern look on her face.

The tall man brought the cart to a halt and Granny Uba got down. Leaning on her sturdy staff, she walked toward the woman, who greeted her with a nod of the head.

"We're on a pilgrimage to Yakushi. We'd like to ask shelter for the night."

The woman gestured toward the door of the house. Granny Uba proceeded inside, and the rest of the party followed.

The building had one large room and no flooring. Spread directly on the ground at the back was a small carpet braided from strips of cloth. Walls of haphazardly overlapping boards stretched between the four blackened corner posts. The structure lacked any windows, but a certain amount of outdoor light filtered in through gaps between the boards.

Granny Uba lowered herself onto the braided carpet. Even indoors, she did not remove the scarf wound about her head. Her ragged robes seemed to blend right in with the carpet as if it was all part of a single long train.

The woman who had greeted them out front came in behind them and seated herself on the ground facing Granny Uba. She seemed to think it only natural that her visitor should have the seat of honour. Granny Uba waited for the other members of her party to settle in against the walls.

"How have things been for you here of late?" she asked when the commotion had subsided.

"The millet is doing reasonably well, but we're having trouble with bugs in the soybeans. And though we've lost one of our able-bodied men, two new little ones have arrived."

Like the pilgrims, the woman spoke without an accent and punctuated her sentences with frequent pauses. Rentarō found this puzzling. The absence of dialect made sense for the pilgrims, who had presumably come from farther away, but it seemed odd in the speech of someone who lived right here at the foot of Tateyama. Her neglect of the usual polite forms surprised him, too — almost as if the language was still new to her. Her entire manner showed that she regarded Granny Uba with respect, yet the words she spoke sounded quite rough. Of course, the pilgrims were pretty rough-spoken too, but since they were all such eccentric characters anyway, it hadn't bothered him so much to hear them skipping the usual courtesies. Had these villagers moved here from some other part of the country as pioneers too — like the old soldiers at that other settlement? But from the look of things, they'd been here a good many years already, not just since the war. To live here that long and not pick up even a hint of the local dialect suggested that they must have been completely cut off from the outside. But it was hard to imagine how they could have managed that.

"So you have a net gain of one. Not a bad outcome," said Granny Uba, kneading her hands together. Her skin was as wrinkled as the bark of an old tree.

The woman lowered her eyelids in acknowledgment, then opened them again. "We'd like you to take one of the little ones with you to Yakushi."

When Granny Uba nodded her assent, she rose and moved to the corner of the room. There, in a box, lay two cloth-wrapped bundles. She lifted one of them and started back, cradling it in her arms. It was a baby. It began fussing as soon as it was picked up. She handed the infant to Granny Uba. Its flat nose was turned up and thick hair grew on its face, giving it the appearance of a baby boar. Granny Uba promptly passed the child to the woman in the gunnysack. The entire transaction took place as if they were handling a piece of merchandise.

With these formalities out of the way, the woman went back outside. The pilgrims made themselves comfortable, some stretching out on the ground to rest, others taking turns holding the baby.

Rentarō moved closer to Granny Uba. "Does a pilgrimage to Yakushi mean climbing all the way to the top of Yakushidake?"

She gave him a hard look from between the layers of her scarf. "What is Yakushidake?"

"A mountain. Right up that way," he said, pointing in the direction of the peak.

"You don't find Yakushi by climbing a mountain," she told him. "The only way is to keep travelling Mandala Road."

"So this really is Mandala Road," Rentarō said as relief flooded through him. Knowing for certain that he was still on the same route might be a first step toward figuring out what this baffling place was.

"If Yakushi isn't up the mountain, then where exactly is he?"

She looked at him as if he couldn't have asked a sillier question. "Yakushi is on Mandala Road," she said. "You just have to keep walking until you find him."

It sounded entirely hit or miss. He wondered if he might have more success taking a different tack.

"You said before that you'd heard of Toyama a long time ago. Could you tell me more about that?"

"Did I say that?"

"Yes, you did. The name is Toyama... To-ya-ma."

Granny Uba narrowed her eyes. "Oh, yes. That's right. I believe I did hear that name somewhere or other... a long, long time ago. But I'm afraid I can't recall where or how it might have been."

His heart sank. The old woman was clearly a figure of respect, not only to the pilgrims travelling with her but to the people in this village as well, and yet she appeared to remember no more than anyone else. In that case, maybe that other woman was a better bet for knowing something – the one who seemed to be head of the village. He made his way outside.

The villagers had returned to their work in the fields. Rentarō found the woman by a small pond next to the house, fed by a conduit from a nearby stream. Squatting on some rocks at the water's edge, she was rinsing some herbs.

"Rabdosia," he said.

She turned to look over her shoulder. She had very dry skin from exposure to the sun, but apart from that she was quite attractive, with well-defined features. She stared at him evenly, without blinking.

"That's its name – the plant you have there," he said before lowering himself onto his haunches and taking a stem from the pile at her side. The leaves were bigger and thicker than any he'd seen before, but both their fragrance and the fine hairs on their surface marked the plant clearly as a member of the species. "Some also call it the resurrection plant because it's been known to bring people back from the brink of death. Do you folks make infusions with it?"

The woman studied the bunch she had in her hand as if seeing it for the first time.

"I don't know about any of that. We just drink it in hot water because it makes us feel better."

She stole a glance at him out of the corner of her eye before going back to her rinsing. Gathering four or five stems at a time from a pile on the other side of her, she dipped them in the water and shook them briefly, then set them on top of the others lying in a pile between her and Rentarō.

From where he was squatting, Rentarō let his eyes drift slowly across the village. Every house in sight was patched together from an assortment of lumber, corrugated iron, and other building materials, gathered from who knew where, like a bird's nest. In the fields, villagers were turning the soil with their primitive implements. At the edge of the woods, several men were clearing some new land for crops, removing felled trees and digging out stumps. Everywhere that adults were at work, children were also doing what they could to help.

"It must get pretty cold for you folks when the snow flies," he said in a veiled reference to the crudely built houses.

"Snow?" she said without pausing in her task.

"Yes, snow."

She looked as if she didn't have the first idea what he was talking about. How could she live at the foot of Tateyama and not know what snow was? he wondered, but then he remembered the changes he'd observed earlier: those huge ferns and rampant vines. He'd never seen such lush, jungle-like growth in Toyama before, even at the height of summer.

Until now, it had seemed possible to him that a new weapon had somehow made plants grow to massive proportions in the space of a single night. But if this woman had never experienced snow, then it couldn't have been just last night that the climate turned tropical.

He raised his eyes toward the distant mountains. The jagged peaks marching across the sky were unmistakably those of the Tateyama Range. But they looked different from the way he remembered since he was a little boy. Before, the summits had been devoid of vegetation, with snow lingering all year round in the alpine valleys, but now the mountains were covered in dense green forests from foothill to crest. If he'd been wrong about the change being caused by some newfangled bomb, then how was it to be explained? If this place had always been this way, did it mean he'd wandered into an altogether different world? Like the ships that took him year after year to tropical Malaya, maybe this time some unknown power had taken him to a tropical Tateyama.

As a new unease stirred in his chest, Rentarō became aware of a ticklish sensation ascending his inner thigh. He looked down to find the woman's hand softly stroking his leg. With a suggestive smile tugging at her lips, she moved her fingers slowly toward his groin. The strong scent of a woman came to him. She felt for his penis, then took hold of it through his trousers and began gently massaging it. He was too startled to move. When he began to grow hard, she took his hand and pulled him to his feet.

With both his loins and his curiosity aroused, Rentarō followed the woman into the thicket behind the pond, where she led him to a grassy spot well hidden from view. She lay down on her back and pulled him toward her. What she wanted was obvious; there was no need for words. As he unbuttoned his trousers, she raised the skirt of her scratchy tunic up over her waist. He lowered himself between her legs. His thickening penis slid inside without resistance, growing even harder in the hold of her warm, moist sheath. She lifted her hips against him. With the pungent smell of grass all around them, he thrust vigorously in and out. Her moans merged with his grunts, and the green of the forest, the blue of the sky, the songs of the birds, and the far-off voices all receded into the distance. It was a brief, convulsive coupling. He came to a climax, withdrew, and rolled over onto his back. With a look of contentment, she pulled her tunic back down to cover herself.

"Won't your husband be angry?" Rentarō said.

"Husband?" she asked, her puzzled eyes peering through a tangle of black hair.

"Your man."

She let out a little snicker. Bringing herself upright and rising to her feet, she looked out over the shrubbery and pointed toward the figures working in the fields. "They are all my men," she said.

"Don't the other women get upset if you claim them all for yourself?"

Wiping himself with some grass, Rentarō stood up and began fastening his trousers. She eyed the buttons curiously.

"I don't," she said. "It's the same for all the women. Everyone will say they are her men."

Rentarō didn't know what to think.

The woman slapped a hand on her belly. "But I'm number one," she said, "because I've made the most babies."

"Including that child?" he asked, pointing toward her house, whose roof was level with the shrubbery.

"Yes," she nodded proudly. "I've made three offerings to Yakushi."

Her mention of offerings made Rentarō think of the giant eight-tailed serpent of myth that devoured one young girl each year until it was finally hacked to pieces by a god. He began to wonder if Yakushi was some kind of child-eating monster, like that serpent.

"Who exactly is this Yakushi anyway?"

"The one who heals calamity and affliction," she said as if growing impatient with his questions. With her sexual needs satisfied, she seemed to have lost interest in him. Brushing grass from her clothes, she started back toward the pond.

Rentarō hurried after her. "But how does he heal? What medicines does he use?"

She frowned. "I wouldn't know."

"Then how do you know he heals?"

"Just look," she said. They were now back at the pond, and she motioned with her arms to indicate the houses and farmland spreading between them and the river. "Bugs eat our soybeans, and we lose somebody now and then, but our land continues to grow bit by bit, and we have more newborns than we have people dying. It shows that things are getting better."

"What's this big calamity everybody keeps talking about?" Rentarō couldn't help asking.

Looking annoyed, she took her time before answering. Finally she said slowly, "You shrivel up and die... right where you are."

34

Saya caught her breath when she saw the tiny pairs of leaves poking out of the dirt. These were the seeds she had brought with her from Malaya, which she'd planted as soon as the ground had thawed. She dropped onto her knees and gazed lovingly at the dozen or so different baby trees that were sprouting to life.

Rentarō had insisted that Malayan plants couldn't possibly grow in the Japanese climate, but she refused to believe him. *See? They came up just fine*, she was itching to tell him, but he had not yet returned from his trip.

She looked up at the mountains, which were beginning to turn green. Rentarō was somewhere out in those hills now. Unless, perhaps, he'd gone right on past them to somewhere farther away. As her eyes traced the line of tallest peaks, forming a white edge against the blue sky beyond, she had an awful feeling that Rentarō might never come back.

Rising slowly to her feet, she began placing sticks in the ground as a fence to keep the chickens away from her nascent jungle. A warm breeze rustled the grass nearby and filled Saya's dark, slightly curly hair. Her belly was already beginning to show a small bulge.

Isamu was at school. The laundry she'd hung out to dry rippled gently under the eaves. The veranda stood waiting for a visitor, its dark floorboards brightened by the sunshine. Saya pictured Rentarō sitting there in his usual spot.

What would she do if he really did fail to come back? she asked herself gloomily. When he'd stopped by on his way out of town, she had told him she would find him no matter where he went. But she was in a foreign land, and if the man decided to disappear somewhere, she knew she would have little way of finding him. So really, what would she do if he was gone for good? She'd have nowhere to direct her fury anymore! In a fit of pique, she threw down the stick she had in her hand.

Why wasn't Rentarō with her now? How she hated him, despised him, loathed him! She absolutely loathed him, and missed him – oh, how she missed him. She missed him so much that she hated him.

She was rapidly working herself into a frenzy, her mind going around in circles. When she finally came out of it with a start, she found her hands filled with broken to pieces of stick, and quickly tossed them aside. Sinking to the ground, she sat staring at her tiny tree sprouts as if in a trance.

Her mother, her aunt, and her sisters had all assured her that no matter who you married, once the man was your husband, you began to feel for him like family. Saya had always believed it would be that way for her as well: love would grow as she and her husband had children and shared their daily meals and worked alongside each other. So when she followed Rentarō to Kota Bharu, she didn't have the slightest doubt that they would someday become family. He had never set fire to her heart and body the way boys her own age had done, but she saw the man who'd given her the paper balloon as the one who could make her dreams come true. If somebody had told her then that after loving him she would come to hate him, or that even when she hated him she would feel bereft without him, she wouldn't have thought it possible.

She wondered what words of wisdom the medicine man would have had to offer if he were here. The conflicting emotions she felt were as bewildering to her as when she'd seen her first automobile.

Don't ever let yourself fall in love.

The warning Kim Suk-hwa had given her one day came back to her. The two of them were resting in the shade of the palm grove behind the P-house after a lunch of watery rice gruel. Saya asked what "fall in love" meant, which made Suk-hwa look surprised. But after a moment she explained that it was when a man made you feel like your chest was being squeezed so tight you couldn't breathe. Saya told her she'd never known anything like that. Suk-hwa gave her a sad smile and said it was better that way.

Saya quickly began to suspect Suk-hwa herself had fallen in love. In the past, after the tide of soldiers had ebbed for the day, or during the brief breaks between waves, she used to rant and rave about them all, but now she just sat there silently. She fingered a square red bag someone had given her, pressing the fabric to her cheek and jingling a little bell on its string over and over. Saya could feel her sadness as she listened to the tinkle of the bell fading into the moist shade of the palm trees.

But not very much later, Saya had escaped from the P-house, so she'd never found out anything more about it.

The next time she saw her was after the war ended. The Japanese occupiers were gone, as well as the Thai troops who had initially taken their place, and the British had returned. Kekah was picking up some money for essentials as an errand boy for a Malay family, and Saya was helping some of their neighbours with housework in exchange for small amounts of fruit and vegetables. Then, thanks to a connection made through one of those neighbours, she was hired as a maid by an Englishman.

Her new employer had bought a rubber plantation near Kota Bharu and moved into a rented house in town. A paunchy man with a reddish-brown beard, he had lived in the country before the war and spoke fluent Malay. Now that the fighting was over, he'd come back to start up a new business venture. When Saya arrived at his house on her first day, he introduced a large woman with high cheekbones and a shapely nose as his companion. Despite her fancy clothes and superior manner, Saya recognized her instantly: it was her friend from the P-house. Suk-hwa treated her as a stranger, so Saya did the same, but she wondered whether this was just for show or if the woman had actually forgotten her.

Except to give her instructions in broken Malay about cleaning the floors or doing the laundry, Suk-hwa spent most of her time sitting in the parlour next to the front door, gazing idly out the window. An air of unhappiness seemed to hover about her angular profile.

Ten days or so went by, and the Englishman left to visit his plantation. As soon as it was just the two of them in the house, Suk-hwa switched to Japanese.

"So you managed to get your life back," she said. She'd known all along that her new maid was Saya.

"You made it out alive, too," Saya said, which brought a curl to Suk-hwa's thin lips.

"Thrown out is more like it. When the war started going badly for them and they took to their heels, they just dumped us Korean girls wherever we happened to be. For me it was Singapore, which is how I got picked up by an Englishman. I'm still nothing but a toilet hole. But at least it's easier being a privy for one man than for a mob of soldiers. What about you? How've things worked out for you since you got away? Did your Mr. Wonderful from Japan ever come back for you?"

Saya shook her head. "But war is over now, so he coming back soon. I'm sure he miss his boy."

"I can't believe you're still saying things like that," she scoffed. "What makes you think anybody'd come back all this way for a shithole? Even the kid – to your man, he's just a dump he took in that hole. When're you going to get that through your head? That's all you were to him – a convenience to do his business in. And a foreign one at that – not even his own kind. Japanese men always prefer Japanese privies, no matter where they go. It's only when they can't find any of those that they'll make do with ones from other countries."

"You wrong, you wrong. It not like that with Mr. Ren. I know you wrong," Saya cried out.

"Your fine Mr. Ren's no different from anybody else," Suk-hwa shouted back, as if Saya's burst of anger had released her own bitterness.

"They're all the same, those bastards. They may say nice things, some of them, but in the end they just shut the privy door and walk away. The better ones might say thanks on their way out, but that's the only difference. They still leave you high and dry. You were just the guy's private P-girl. You were his Malayan toilet. A hole to polish his pole in."

Saya threw herself at Suk-hwa with such force that the chair she was sitting on toppled backwards onto the floor. Astride her, she grabbed her hair with both hands. Suk-hwa dug her nails into Saya's cheeks. Saya bit hard on one hand with her teeth. Suk-hwa cried out in pain. She kneed Saya in the stomach. Saya doubled over, gasping for breath. Burning with fury, she put both hands around Suk-hwa's neck and began to squeeze.

If the Englishman hadn't returned at that point, Saya might well have choked her to death. He shoved Saya away from Suk-hwa and demanded an explanation. They both refused to speak or look at him.

He told Saya she was fired. Getting to her feet, she dusted herself off and walked out the door.

That night, lying under the palm roof of her hut with an arm around Isamu, she thought again about what Suk-hwa had said. Kekah had gone out after supper, and hadn't yet returned. The sleeping boy's quiet, rhythmical breathing was the only sound in the darkened hut. But Saya couldn't fall asleep. Suk-hwa's words had lodged like thorns in her heart.

It didn't especially bother her to be called a pole polisher for the men who came to the P-house. But she was furious at being told that's all she was to Rentarō.

It simply wasn't true. Rentarō couldn't have seen her like that, she told herself. But she could hear another voice saying maybe Suk-hwa was right. The voice grew louder and louder, buzzing in her head like flies around fish.

Unable to lie still any longer, she took care not to wake the boy and slipped outside. All up and down the street, people were sitting in front of their houses enjoying the cool of the evening. Since Muslim women never went out alone at night, she could feel the heat of everyone's gaze. And with this came a sudden realization. Rentarō had chosen her because she was neither a Muslim nor a local girl. He could live with her in Kota Bharu without the slightest worry that her people might raise a stink. On top of that, she knew all about plants with healing powers. She'd been a convenient choice in so many different ways.

You were his Malayan toilet. The thorns from Suk-hwa's remark dug in deeper, and the blood they drew left a trail of drops behind her.

The lights were ablaze in her former employer's house. The sound of English-speaking voices and music spilled from inside. Suk-hwa sat alone at the top of the porch steps, hugging her knees. Her master and his guests were drinking and having a good time, but she'd been shunted outside with only herself for company.

Saya called to her softly from under a *plumeria* tree covered with blossoms like white puffs of breath. Suk-hwa stiffened for a moment, but then saw Saya and relaxed. She came down the steps to join her beneath the tree.

"What's up?" she asked.

"What you say before, you truly believe?"

Saya wanted to know just how serious she had been.

"I believe it with every bone in my body."

Tears came to Saya's eyes.

Suk-hwa had calmed down since earlier in the day. It was as if their little scuffle had released something toxic that had been building up inside her.

"Your man's not coming back," she said. "If he's still alive, he's at home in Japan, carrying on with his wife and kids as if nothing ever happened here. He just used you, so forget about him."

Her eyes drifted off past the porch to the bamboo grove rustling in the darkness beyond.

"I'd like to forget, too, if I could," she went on. "Wipe my mind clean of all those men who used me for a pot. But I doubt I ever can. You were lucky. You were only there for a little over two months. For me, it was nearly two years, living like that. My body's shot all to hell, and I detest every last man on earth. There's no way I can ever know the joy of being a woman. Not for as long as I live."

"It make me mad," Saya blurted out. "He never plan to come back, but he promise he will. I was believing him."

Suk-hwa fixed her with a sour look. "What you need is revenge," she spat out.

"Revenge?" Saya said, not recognizing the word.

"It means to get back at him," she explained. "If someone hits you, you hit back. If someone kicks you, you kick back. If you just keep your mouth shut and take it, then you're a loser. You'll have nobody but yourself to blame, and you'll spend your life squirming around like a worm with its head in the ground. The answer is to get revenge."

Saya shrank from the virulence in Suk-hwa's voice.

"But what about you?... You not get revenge?"

Suk-hwa filled a cheek and let out a scornful *pff*. "I'm already dead, honey. I was a P-house toilet for so long, I fell into the cesspit and drowned. This is a corpse you're looking at. You have to be alive to get revenge. And you still are. Listen. If you do it now, you can get to Japan for free. Just sneak onto one of the repatriation boats. The word is that all the remaining Japanese are being taken to a camp in Singapore and sent back to Japan from there, so all you have to do is get yourself to that camp. Use my name. Tell them you're Korean but you were living in Japan and got dragged down here against your will."

There was a fierce intensity in her eyes as she peered into Saya's face, swollen with welts from their fight.

"Take your boy and dump him in his father's lap. Show all the wives and families in Japan just what their men were up to while they were away from home."

"But if I use your name," said Saya, "what you do?"

Suk-hwa looked away. "I can't go home anymore anyway," she said. "They'd all say I'm dirty – Japanese and Koreans, both. People like to keep their toilets out of sight. They don't want to see them walking around in broad daylight. And I'm not about to go through life letting the very people who made me into a toilet tell me that I stink."

Barely-contained emotion distorted her face. It reminded Saya of a monkey baring its teeth against a tiger even when it knows it doesn't stand a chance.

"What about the man you fall in love?" Saya asked.

Her face tightened.

"He was nice, and he tried to run away with me." Her voice had turned husky, as if something was caught in her throat. But there was a distinct note of sarcasm in the way she said "nice".

"We didn't even make it to Kota Bharu before we got caught. He got beat up by his captain and said I'd sweet-talked him into it. You don't want to know what the P-house boss did to me. Believe me, I thought I'd die for sure that time…"

She turned abruptly and went inside.

Left standing by herself in the yard, Saya wondered if Suk-hwa had gone because she found it too painful to continue with her story. But reluctant to leave, she decided to wait where she was for a while.

Upbeat music and cheerful voices continued to come from the house. The scent of *plumeria* was all around. She thought back to her days with Rentarō. Like Suk-hwa tonight, whenever his friends came to visit, she'd been sent outside to kill time alone on the porch. Suk-hwa was probably right about what she'd been to him, she thought wearily. That would explain why he didn't want her out in front of his friends.

A creaking step broke through her thoughts, and she saw that Suk-hwa had returned. She came with a piece of paper pressed to her chest, which she held out for Saya to take. The anguished expression from before was gone, and in its place was a look of resolve.

"I wrote down my name and the address where I was born," she said. "If anybody asks, just show them this. If they want a passport or ID of some kind, tell them you were a P-girl. They know no Korean P-girl was given anything like that. They're still too busy sorting stuff out from the war. Just keep quiet, and nobody'll question a thing. You can go back to Japan as me."

Saya took the paper. It was only a single thin sheet, but it felt almost heavy in her hand.

"I do that," Saya said.

Suk-hwa broke into a smile. "You're me now. Go to Japan and get back at all those men who treated us like shitholes."

The hands that clasped Saya's felt bony and dry, and she noticed for the first time that her friend was missing two fingers on her right hand.

35

The road leading back to the city was blocked in several places by landslides. As he scrambled on all fours around the blockages with only his skimpy hand towel for protection against the encroaching brush, Asafumi's soft, pale skin quickly became covered with scratches. Worse still were the red welts from the endless swarms of mosquitoes.

It was like a survival game on a video console, he thought to himself. Like being a character inside some virtual adventure. As his alter ego battled one difficulty after another, his real self seemed to be watching his every step at one remove.

But where exactly was that real self? He began probing through his consciousness for an answer, only to discover that it was like sticking his hand in a bucket of mud: there was nothing for him to latch onto.

He thought back to different periods in his past – when he worked at the lab; when he and Shizuka were dating; when he lived free of cares in an apartment by himself; when he was just getting settled in his grandfather's old house. But whatever point in time he returned to, the self he found there seemed to be living inside a video game – just like now.

As the sun rose in the sky these thoughts were increasingly interrupted by the sting of ants biting his bare feet or the pain of stubbing his toe on a rock or a bulging tree root. By the time the sun was directly overhead, he was drenched in sweat, and as hunger gnawed ever more insistently at his stomach, his mind became more and more preoccupied with his desire for food and rest. It was no wonder. He'd had nothing to eat since lunch the day before. But the dog and the girl walked briskly on.

"I'm famished," he finally called out.

"Me too," Kesumba shrugged, without slackening her pace in the least. So long as *she* wasn't complaining, Asafumi apparently had no choice but to keep on walking.

The road seemed to be on a very gradual descent, but the going never got any easier. With knee-high grass and weeds growing thick in every crack of the broken asphalt, it was almost like walking through a meadow. Some of the weeds had sharp prickles. From the way the road wound along, he thought they ought to be back among the reforested cypress trees by now, but the hillsides continued to be dominated by broad-leaved evergreens, with not a conifer in sight.

In the course of the morning, Asafumi had begun to wonder if he might have gone through some sort of time warp. Thanks to Kesumba's earlier remark, he knew he was still on Mandala Road, but this obviously wasn't his own time at the beginning of the twenty-first century anymore. And the dramatic difference in climate and vegetation could never have occurred in a mere ten or twenty years. So where in time had he come to? Was this some century far in the future after climate change had utterly altered the globe, or had he returned to some distant past when massive beasts still roamed the earth?

But in the end, the notion of travelling through time was simply too fantastic for him to accept. It felt more as though he was wandering through a dream.

He thought of the day in August when he and Shizuka had driven to Senbashi for dinner with his family. He remembered joking that the planet might succumb to neutron bombs or an alien attack long before global warming or desertification finished off the human race. The flippancy of the remark now made him cringe. After shooting off his mouth about imaginary catastrophes with hardly a care that day, here he was, caught up in something just as crazy, flailing about without the faintest idea how to fend for himself.

He wondered what Shizuka might be doing. She had to be going out of her mind with worry. Or did time here on Mandala Road move at a completely different pace from back at home where she was – like in the legend of the fisherman taken to an undersea palace by the turtle he had rescued?

He continued to turn these questions over in his mind as he walked, but all to no avail. It served only to confirm the sense that he'd wandered into the alternate reality of some virtual survival game.

Kesumba stooped to pick up a dark purple object about the size of a tennis ball. Many more of the same hung from the branches arching overhead. She split it in two and handed a piece to Asafumi. He stopped the mental wheels he'd been spinning and examined the strange-looking fruit. It had a white, jelly-like substance in the middle, surrounded by a layer of lavender-coloured flesh about a centimetre thick.

"Eat just the white part," she said, demonstrating with her finger how to scoop it out.

He followed her example and took a bite. It had the mild sweetness of milk jelly. When they finished, they searched the ground and found four or five more lying among the leaves at the side of the road. After making short work of these, they looked up at the tree. Kesumba picked up several stones and began throwing them at the hanging fruit. Even when the stones found a target, the fruit didn't drop very easily. With Asafumi joining in the effort, too, they finally managed to knock just three more to the ground after a great many attempts. The first of them was worm-eaten, and the next one shrivelled and dry. Only the last was edible, so they split it between them.

"I've never had any fruit like this before," Asafumi said, his lips now purple. "What's it called?"

"I don't know."

Kesumba abruptly started off down the road again. Asafumi had been hoping to rest awhile, but too embarrassed to say so, he dragged his tired legs back into motion.

"Don't you have a home?" Asafumi asked as he came up beside her.

"Mandala Road is my home," she said in a singsong voice, then stopped short again at the side of the road.

Before them was a patch of brambly stems with a sprinkling of red berries growing on them. Kesumba popped one into her mouth. Asafumi followed suit. The burst of sweet-sour flavour seemed immediately to ease his fatigue. His companion appeared to be well acquainted with the edible plants along this road.

"And I guess the roadside is your refrigerator," he said cheerily, feeling reassured by the prospect of food to be had for the taking along the way. He moved farther into the thicket, picking and eating more berries.

"Refrigerator?" she asked. The look on her face told him she had no idea what it referred to.

"I just meant it provides you with things to eat," he said.

She gave him a dismissive look. "Not enough to fill anybody up."

Right. A little bit of fruit here and there wasn't likely to sustain them. He realized the stupidity of his remark.

"Then where *do* you get your food?"

"When you're on a pilgrimage to Yakushi, they feed you where you stop for the night. That's the rule."

"The rule?"

She fluttered her black eyelashes. "Uh-huh. That's how it works."

Kekah suddenly began to growl. He had been waiting quietly at the side of the road while they picked berries, but now his four ears twitched and white fangs showed in both his mouths. Asafumi looked in the direction the dog was growling and caught a glimpse of several mane-like heads among the trees: more of the same people who'd attacked him and stripped him naked that morning.

"Ape-men," Kesumba said.

He stiffened as the terror of the earlier attack came back to him.

"Don't worry," she said, laying a hand on his arm. "Come on, Kekah. Let's go," she called, and started slowly away. Asafumi edged after her, keeping one eye on the spot where the dog's growling was directed.

Kekah protected their rear for a time as they moved down the road, still turning to growl into the forest now and then. Finally he fell silent and stepped out into the lead again. With the berry patch now some distance behind them, Asafumi relaxed as well.

"Are there a lot of those ape-men along Mandala Road?" he asked.

"Uh-huh," she said. "They live in the hills all up and down the way, and they go after travellers – to steal things from them. For food, they normally hunt animals or feed on nuts and wild fruit, but if they can't find anything else, they'll attack villages and kill people to eat."

Asafumi shuddered at the thought that he could have been made into a meal. He was lucky that they'd been distracted by his bag and clothes, or didn't happen to be hungry at the time.

"Aren't you scared of travelling in such a dangerous place?"

"They're actually afraid of the pilgrims," she said. "Because they look so different from them. And Kekah, too, with his two heads – they're definitely afraid of him and keep their distance. So we're safe if we have him with us."

The dog heard his name spoken and turned to look. Two heads with gleaming fangs and four alert eyes extended from a single thick neck. It was enough to make anyone tremble. Asafumi realized how lucky he was to have Kesumba and Kekah with him.

The road narrowed and broadened and narrowed again as they went. It had been clear for some time now that this was no longer the way he'd come the day before – not as wide overall, and obviously never paved. There was no sign that it had ever seen a motor vehicle, but trampled grass attested to relatively recent foot traffic. Kesumba seemed to know the way well and strode on without faltering, walking several steps ahead of Asafumi in her oversized dress, a cloud of wiry curls surrounding her head, humming her strange tune: *Whooooon, whoooon...* He watched her from behind as she paced along, enchanted by her little figure.

She was making her way through a vast green universe with just a two-headed dog for company. Even though she walked only a few steps ahead, it somehow felt as if she was thousands of light-years away. He couldn't imagine why this was.

Whoooon, whooooo oong... came her voice across light-years of space.

Then she stopped and pointed to a gray stone marker at the side of the road with only its top visible among the tall grass.

"This is where Mandala Road begins," she said.

An arrow was carved on the face of the stone, labelled in fading characters with the name. A short distance farther on, the narrow track came to a broad asphalt road in no better condition than the one they'd been on earlier. At the junction stood a small hut – a crude, makeshift structure with a thatched roof. On the ground next to it were some half-burned logs left over from a fire.

"When we reach this place, we rest awhile," she said, "and then we turn around and go back the way we came. We keep going back and forth."

Hardly even listening, Asafumi started down the wider road. The sight of the stone marker, and then of a road that had obviously carried substantial traffic in the past, convinced him they must be most of the way back to town, and he was eager to get there. A moment or two later he realized Kesumba wasn't with him and turned to see what the problem was.

She was still standing beside the hut, hesitating. Kekah sat at her feet, peering anxiously up at her.

"What's wrong?" he asked.

She smiled sheepishly. He remembered her saying that she'd never been beyond Mandala Road and wondered if she was too afraid to come, but just then she tightened both hands into fists and started forward, almost as if she were plunging into water. After several resolute steps with her eyes held wide, a whimper from Kekah brought her abruptly to a halt.

"Come," she called.

She had to repeat her command three times before the dog finally lifted his hindquarters to follow.

"Did you think something bad might happen if you left Mandala Road?"

She gave him an annoyed look. "Course not," she said, pointing her lips in a pout beneath her slightly upturned nose.

Asafumi smiled as he stole a sidewise glance at her innocently girlish profile. She might know everything there was to know about Mandala Road, but she was still only a child. She no longer felt light years away; she was an ordinary twelve- or thirteen-year-old girl, walking right there beside him.

"Were you born on Mandala Road?" he asked.

"I don't know."

"Is there anything you *do* know about yourself?" he said with a touch of exasperation.

"My name is Kesumba. I've been going up and down Mandala Road with Granny Uba as long as I can remember. What else is there to know?"

It was the longest answer she'd given to any of his questions about herself.

"There's plenty more to know," he said quickly, wanting to keep the ball rolling. "Like about your mother and your father, or the world outside, or the future..."

Her uncomprehending frown made her look a bit like a piglet.

"You're here because somebody gave birth to you, right?" he said. "That person is your mother. The person she's with is your father. Together, they're your parents. Where are your parents?"

"I was found growing like a sapling in the middle of Mandala Road," she said cheerfully.

She made it sound like the tale of the Bamboo Princess, Asafumi thought.

"Who told you that?"

"Granny Uba."

He fell silent. There seemed little point in asking her anything more.

As the sun tilted toward the horizon, the shadows of their three forms on the crumbling, weed-ridden asphalt grew longer. The road levelled off, and they began to pass the occasional broken concrete building or rusty hulk of a car. Skeletons of steel poked like dead trees above the forested hillside. The view of Mount Tateyama in the distance and the shape of the nearby hills suggested they had reached the Awasuno area, but the slopes where the ski runs should have been were covered with full-grown trees.

The road turned gently uphill again for a time, and then at the top of the rise the view opened up. They found themselves looking out over a river with broad, rock-strewn banks. It was the Jōganji. But the beautiful scenery Asafumi had driven through on the river terrace the day before was nowhere to be seen. The mountainsides then covered with trees coming into colour were now buried in rubble nearly to the top. Even from afar, he could tell it was the remains of countless ruined buildings. Not one of them stood intact: even at best, the roofs had caved in; some retained only a wall or two; others had been reduced to nothing but corner posts. The ruins spread out much too far to be those of a mere town. They continued along both sides of the river all the way down the valley to the Toyama Plain. And the distant plain, too, appeared like a wasteland of shredded plastic debris.

During his last spring break in college, just before he joined the working world, Asafumi had travelled to Istanbul. The city was his final stop in a month-long backpacking tour of Europe. While there, he visited the Galata Tower, where a man who lived in the Ottoman Period was said to have strapped wings onto his back like Icarus and launched himself on a flight across the Bosporus. He remembered how he'd gasped when he reached the top of the tower and looked out over the city.

Every hill in sight was a mass of little houses. The tour guide spoke of the endless flow of people who had moved to Istanbul from points near and far. The city had grown continuously to accommodate the influx, edging up the hills, filling in the flatlands, extending its amoeba-like tentacles further and further from the centre.

In the same way, the Toyama Plain through which the Jōganji flowed must have spawned a massive metropolis, growing like some kind of giant organism, expanding its reach in wave after wave of development. But at some point the organism had expired, and the city withered and died. The people were gone, and where once the din of human activity had filled the air, the only sound to be heard now was the wash of water in the riverbed below.

"Is that what they call the city?" Kesumba asked.

Asafumi simply nodded, still unable to believe his eyes. The declining sun shone across the devastated city, its red glow brightening only the western face of each wall that remained standing. It was like a child's toy city, destroyed by too much roughhousing. Everywhere he looked, the fragments of buildings shimmered in the reddish light. Flocks of crows flapped about the ruins like flurries of black snowflakes being tossed in the wind.

"It used to be," he finally said.

His own voice seemed to come from somewhere far away.

36

"I'm afraid he just won't listen to reason. No matter what his family says, he absolutely refuses to leave that place."

Perched on the edge of the bed with a hand on each knee, Katsuichi Takatomi let out a heavy sigh. Miharu had called him from the hospital in Ōyama using the number on the New Year's card they'd found at Manzaburō Ohara's house. Luckily, he was at home, and came as soon as he could. Wearing a brown jacket and sneakers, he had the muscular build of a man hardened by farm work. He looked about sixty.

Ohara had been treated for his burns and was now resting, knocked out by the sedatives he'd been given. According to the doctor's estimate, he would need to stay under care for about a week. He lay next to the window in a mixed, six-bed ward. At the moment, his ward-mates included a man with a bandaged leg strung up in the air, a gray-haired woman who appeared to be asleep, and a child sitting upright on his mattress engrossed in a Game Boy. The other two patients were away from their beds. Since this was during official visiting hours, Miharu, Yoshitaka, Shizuka, and now Takatomi had no need to worry about disturbing the others as they talked in the corner by Ohara's bed.

"May I ask how you know Mr. Ohara?" Miharu asked Takatomi. She was wearing a bandage where she'd been hit on the neck.

He turned toward the man lying asleep with his mouth partly open.

"We're distantly related," he said. "It was my grandfather who provided the land for him and his army buddies to settle on out there after the war. As I understand it, he felt sorry for a bunch of discharged soldiers without homes or jobs, and he agreed to let them use the land for next to nothing. But then MacArthur's land reforms classified him as an absentee landlord and turned title over to the people actually living there. He used to grouse about no good deed going unpunished, but in the end he basically figured there was nothing he could do about it."

"And after all that, the place is deserted now," Yoshitaka put in. He'd cut his lip during Ohara's thrashing, and there was a slight slur in his speech.

"I suppose it was a sign of things to come when they went on a dam-building spree in the mid-fifties and village after village started being swallowed up by the rising waters. That set off a general exodus from the area, including from the villages along that road. Ohara's settlement was no different. One by one, families pulled up stakes and moved out. They were all originally from the Tokyo area and had family there, so they basically went back where they came from. But even after everybody else was gone, Ohara refused to leave."

"I suppose he'd become too attached," Yoshitaka said sympathetically.

Takatomi frowned. "Actually, more than that, I suspect he just couldn't adapt to a new situation anymore. He'd always been stubborn and short-tempered, and I guess every time another family said they were pulling out, he'd curse them up one side and down the other – even the ones who were with him from the start. His kids must have had all they could take of him, too – they couldn't get out of the house fast enough once they grew up. When his wife died – bless her soul, she bore the brunt of his temper all those years while she went on looking after him – when she died, there wasn't anybody else to take him in, so he just stayed on in that house all alone. Eventually the electricity and water got shut off and he went back to living in backwoods style. I think it was around that same time, there started to be more incidents where something would set him off and he'd behave erratically. I heard all kinds of stories. Not recognizing a mail carrier and giving him hell for trespassing. Chasing a district social worker away with a stick for suggesting he move to a care facility. But I never imagined he would go this far."

Shizuka listened with growing trepidation. Finding the sales register at Ohara's house meant Asafumi had to have been there. So before they all left for the hospital, she'd asked Miharu and Yoshitaka to help her make a more thorough search of the place, inside and out. They'd found no further trace of him. But from what she'd just heard, it seemed hard to rule out the possibility that her husband might have come to harm at Ohara's hand. She gazed down at the sleeping man, lying with a sheet pulled up to his neck, his breath rising and falling in a raspy snore. His eyelids twitched now and then, and his lips seemed to be mouthing something in between the snores. She resisted an impulse to shake him violently awake and demand to know what he'd done with Asafumi.

"One time his two kids went out there hoping to bring him in for a psychiatric evaluation," Takatomi continued, rubbing his hands over the threadbare knees of his trousers. Shizuka got the feeling he was trying to compensate for the injury done to Miharu and Yoshitaka by emphasizing the man's mental instability. "But the minute he heard the word psychiatrist, he flew off the handle and said he was disowning them. Well, he knew how to work the fields and make his meals and basically take care of himself, and living in that abandoned settlement was pretty much the same as being in an isolation ward anyway, so in the end they figured why push it."

"I've still got my wits about me just fine," came a low, husky voice from the bed. They all turned to look at Ohara. Through half-open eyelids, his gaze was fixed on Takatomi. "I'm no Tashiro. I never let the war touch me in the head like he did. Forever beating himself up over things he'd done, till finally he throws himself in the river – what a disgrace! Nobody every heard any apologies from me. I moved on with my life. I kept my eyes on the future."

They all stared at Ohara as if a corpse had come back to life. He looked angrily from one to another.

"But then what? Just because we got beat, the whole country starts saying the war was a mistake. Nobody's proud of serving anymore. Where does that leave the ones who died believing the country would fight to the very last man to make sure they didn't die in vain? The men who came back alive ought to be ashamed of themselves. I certainly am. And that's why I'll bite my tongue off before you'll ever get me to say it was a mistake to go. We had to win the war if we wanted to protect our wives and daughters. That's what we were all fighting for. Not to save the country, but to keep our families safe. How else were we going to do that? If anybody made a mistake, it's the bastards who started the whole thing. The rest of us who got drafted into it – we just did what we had to do. But then we got beat, and suddenly the whole country's going around like a dog with its tail between its legs. And with losers like that for parents, the kids and the grandkids turn into namby-pambies, too. That's why the settlement fell apart. Because it was a bunch of namby-pamby losers. They decided it was too tough for them out there and went slinking back to town."

"Well," said Takatomi in a mollifying tone, "you have to understand that the times have changed."

"The times have changed all right," Ohara said, thrusting his jaw forward. There was fire in his eyes beneath his drooping eyelids. "Ever since losing the war, this country's been acting like a gutless coward, hiding behind America's skirts all the time. What the hell did we fight for, anyway? I thought we wanted to keep their filthy boots off our soil. Millions of men gave up the best years of their youth, threw down their lives even, to keep the foreign devils out. But look at our young people today. They're like trained monkeys, eating right out of America's hand – watching American movies, listening to American music, wearing American clothes. Hell, for all intents and purposes, they might as well *be* Americans."

"Not American. International," Miharu put in lightly, but Ohara brushed her off.

"What would a woman know? Women have never had a clue what war's about. That's how they could go sashaying up to those Yanks the minute the war was over. What the hell were we fighting for? I thought it was to protect our women and children. So what do they do? They cosy up to the bastards just like that. They sold us out. First our country sold us out, and then all our women and children did too."

His voice quivered with rage. For several moments nobody said anything, held silent by the ferocity in his words.

"Naturally, none of us can know what you had to go through out there," Yoshitaka finally said quietly.

"Of course not!" Ohara snapped without lifting his head from the pillow. "I was deployed at the front right through the whole thing. I spent my entire twenties crawling through mud. My unit was sent into Hebei after what they called the Marco Polo Bridge Incident, and then from there to the Battle of Shanghai. We fought tooth and nail for three long months, figuring we'd get to march home in triumph when we won. A lot of men died, but we finally took the city. Hooray, time to go home, we thought, only to find out we had to march to Nanjing next. To add insult to injury, the quartermaster corps couldn't keep up, so we had no food, we had to fend for ourselves locally they said. It was unbelievable. Sometimes we ate, sometimes we didn't, and either way we had to keep slogging on toward Nanjing under all our gear..."

He paused, sunk in his memories.

Enough with the war stories, thought Shizuka, and jumped at the chance to change the subject. She brought out the sales register they'd found at the house.

"Mr. Ohara, I was wondering if you could tell us what happened to the person who had this with him."

He eyed it warily as he took it from her. Apparently in need of reading glasses, he held it at arm's length to make out the label on the cover, and lay squinting at the date 1947 for several moments as if lost in thought.

"He was looking for the people listed in that book," Shizuka went on. "Trying to find the houses where it says medicine kits were left a long time ago."

"Medicine kits?"

"Yes. The kind a salesman leaves with you and then comes back to refill. My husband had that notebook with him when he left home a few days ago, and today we found it in your house."

The rising urgency in her voice fell on deaf ears. Ohara had begun flipping pages, but his eyes were not focused on the book; they seemed to be somewhere else.

"Surely you remember the man who brought it," she pressed.

"You're damn right I remember." His voice was suddenly deep. "The bastard put the moves on my Fumiko."

Shizuka was stunned. Her husband? Going after another woman? The Asafumi she knew would never do that.

"I'm sorry. What exactly are you saying?" she demanded, but Takatomi broke in.

"Come on, Mr. Ohara. You know this lady's husband couldn't have had anything to do with your wife."

Ohara lay glaring at the sales register with his lips locked in a thin, hard line as if to contain his fury.

An announcement came over the PA system in the hallway. "Visiting hours will be ending soon. Visitors are asked to—"

The rest of the sentence was lost in a burst of static, followed by a high-pitched squeal.

"Incoming!"

Letting the notebook fall, Ohara leapt out of bed and ducked low to the floor, any pain from his burns apparently forgotten. Scanning his surroundings, he patted himself with both hands and shouted, "Where's my gun? Sawa! Moriyama! My gun! Get me my gun!"

"Now take it easy, Mr. Ohara," Yoshitaka said, moving in to calm him down, but he was shoved roughly aside.

"Stay outta my way! Can't you see we're under attack?"

Ohara's eyes were now fixed on the ceiling, as if watching for enemy warplanes. An outstretched arm groped for his gun.

Miharu lunged for the call button. The other patients and visitors in the room were looking their way with mouths agape. Patients passing by in the hallway heard the commotion and began crowding around the door.

Shizuka bent to pick up the notebook, which had dropped at Ohara's feet. But before she could reach it, he grabbed her by the hair and yanked her head back. She let out a cry. He thrust his sun-darkened nose at her, his face twisted in a murderous rage.

"Fucking P-girl! Somebody get me my sword! I'll stick it up her filthy cunt!"

Her mind went white with terror. She felt as if Ohara might drag her right into his madness.

"Let go! Let go of me!" she shrieked at the top of her lungs. Yoshitaka and Takatomi stepped in to restrain him from behind, but they couldn't break his grip on her hair.

The more she squirmed and screamed, the angrier he became.

"Howl all you want, you fucking she-dog! Lettin' any cur that comes sniffin' around stick it in you! How about I stick mine in too, Fumiko? That's what you want, isn't it? Huh?"

A heavyset, bespectacled nurse with a take-charge manner hurried in carrying an injection tray. Asking Yoshitaka and Takatomi to hold Ohara's arm, she quickly administered the sedative. Slowly, the man's grip relaxed, and Shizuka's hair came free, but he mumbled deliriously on.

"Cross me and I'll make sure you regret it. Who do you think you're dealing with? I slashed and burned my way through the whole Pacific War. I chopped off enemy heads. I strung those Chinks together with wire and torched 'em with gasoline. I threw little girls to the ground and jammed my big fat rod in their tight little cunts. And when I took a mind to, I cut 'em in two and skinned 'em with my sword. That's right. That's what I did. You got a problem with that?... See the enemy, take 'em all out... That's what they trained us to do... So what's the problem?... I was fighting for my country..."

He seemed to be ranting at someone who wasn't even in the room.

The nurse put the empty syringe back in the tray. "There's something called 'posttraumatic stress disorder,'" she said. "I guess it's pretty common among Vietnam vets in America. There'll be some kind of trigger event and then suddenly they start reliving what they went through during the war. They say it can flare up years and years later, so maybe that's what's going on here, too."

"He's a sick man. That's all there is to it," Takatomi said, as if the matter was now settled. Once again, Shizuka got the feeling he was trying to absolve Ohara's violent outbursts by attributing them to mental illness.

She looked down at the old man, who had now drifted off into a stupor and lay with his eyes closed. His lips were still moving, but no sound emerged.

"Are you okay, Shizuka?" Miharu asked as she retrieved the sales register from the floor. "Did he hurt you?"

She ran her fingers over her scalp. It still stung, but she forced a smile and said, "I'll be okay."

The nurse parted her hair to take a look. "I don't see any injury. But you should probably go on home and try to take it easy for the rest of the day. With something like this, it's often the shock that's the bigger problem."

"Yeah, let's get out of here," Miharu said, sounding only too happy to be able to leave. She motioned her father and Shizuka toward the door. They all moved out into the corridor with Takatomi.

As the crowd that had gathered during Ohara's outburst began to disperse, the four visitors walked down the shiny linoleum hallway toward the front entrance. They passed a lounge area where patients were talking and watching TV, and then a voice came over the PA system again to announce that visiting hours were over and lunch was on its way. As she took in the sights and sounds of all the normal activities going on around her, Shizuka finally began to feel like herself again.

She turned to Takatomi. "Who's Fumiko?" she asked.

He rubbed his nose with the flat of his fingers in a gesture of awkwardness. "Mr. Ohara's dead wife," he said in a low, deliberate voice. He seemed as bewildered as she was by the way Ohara had reacted to the medicine kit register.

How could that be? she thought. If the woman was already dead, Asafumi couldn't possibly have done anything to her.

While Shizuka was still puzzling this over, Miharu spoke up. "Maybe something happened a long time ago involving his wife and a medicine seller." She nodded to herself as if to say that had to be it. Her usual self-assurance had returned as they put the hospital room behind them, and now she turned to Takatomi to ask, "Were you implying before that he was violent with his wife?"

"Yes, I've heard it said so," he confirmed a little hesitantly, then quickly added, "Well, I understand there's some admissions paperwork I need to take care of, so I'm afraid I'll have to say goodbye here." With a quick bow, he hurried off toward the reception window.

It seemed pretty obvious that he wanted to avoid any further discussion of the subject. Having witnessed another of the old man's fits up close, he probably thought it better not to air the family's private affairs too openly with outsiders.

They emerged from the hospital's spacious foyer. The mackerel clouds that had filled the sky earlier in the day were breaking up, and the pale sunshine of autumn shone through here and there. With purses clutched under their arms, staff members going on their lunch break were scattering toward the town's small shopping district down the street. This was officially the centre of Ōyama, but it was a sparsely populated place still surrounded by rice paddies, with only a handful of larger buildings, like the town hall and library, to anchor it.

"I'm thinking maybe we need to file a report about Asafumi with the police," Yoshitaka said as they headed for the parking lot.

37

With the light starting to fade in the sky, Asafumi and Kesumba crossed a rust-encrusted bridge and proceeded into the ruins lining the far bank of the river. It was even clearer from close up that these were indeed the remnants of a major city. The road that stretched ahead in a straight line was intersected by others, and despite being littered with crumbling walls, steel girders, and other debris, they retained the appearance of city streets. The smaller houses had been reduced to little more than rubble, with only parts of their steel skeletons left to mark where they'd once stood. Only buildings of four or five stories had kept much of their original shape, some appearing sufficiently intact to be habitable. Their roofs had collapsed and windows had blown out, but ragged pieces of cloth hanging in the openings, or greens and vegetables strung up to dry, were evidence of occupancy here and there.

They did not actually see anyone else in the streets, however. Now and then, when Kekah lowered his head and growled, they thought they saw a shadowy figure flit between heaps of rubble, but it was gone before they could call out to it. If there were indeed people inhabiting these ruins, they were obviously living in fear and taking care to keep out of sight.

In the absence of a human population, plants and animals had laid claim to the territory. Weeds and creeping vines flourished wherever they'd been able to find a bit of dirt in which to put down roots. The dearth of both water and soil no doubt explained the absence of larger shrubs and trees, but Mother Nature was nevertheless slowly stretching her green fingers across the sterile landscape. Mice skittered about among the vegetation. Here and there a cat lurked in the shadows or a dog lay motionless on the ground, eyeing the mice for their next meal. Every creature they glimpsed was skeletally thin and appeared to be near starvation.

From time to time they came across sun-bleached bones – some recognizable as human, others as animal – typically scattered about the charred remains of campfires, over which the meat had presumably been cooked. The white bones stood out eerily in the semi-darkness, not so much frightening Asafumi as making him feel as if he'd wandered into a surrealist painting. It was like nothing he'd ever seen before. The only human remains he'd confronted in the past had been tucked into caskets and surrounded by flowers.

Beside him, Kesumba was busy taking in the unfamiliar landscape, her eyes darting about as they walked. Their pace had slowed since entering the ruins. The concrete debris strewn everywhere dug into their bare feet, and Asafumi had already gashed his big toe on a shard of glass. He needed to watch his step or he might hurt himself more seriously next time.

Where the road was paved with cement or asphalt, the ground was still warm, even though the sun had gone down. With neither trees for shade nor ready water, the ruins had to be almost unbearable in the heat of the day. That alone would be enough to drive people away.

What in the world could have happened here, Asafumi kept asking himself. A once-thriving city had somehow been destroyed. The pilgrims had talked about a calamity. What exactly had taken place?

Some of the walls that remained upright were scrawled with graffiti. *Asshole. Drop dead! I'll kill you. This is hell.* The words were fading and difficult to make out in the dim twilight, which probably meant they had been there a long time. Still, the writing represented the only communication of any kind they had encountered, so each time he spotted more markings, Asafumi paused to read what they said. In some cases all he found were hastily painted X's or handprints rather than proper characters. There was a persistent suggestion of violence and disorder. He couldn't suppress a growing unease about being in a place like this with nothing but a small towel around his waist.

He found it worrying, too, that nothing changed no matter how far they walked. All they saw was one broken building after another and endless heaps of rubble. It seemed increasingly unlikely they would find anything different up ahead.

"I'm thirsty," Kesumba said, which made Asafumi realize how parched his own throat was. Kekah was panting hard with his two tongues hanging out. When they were on Mandala Road, they'd been able to drink from little streams along the way, but they'd seen no water at all since entering the ruins.

"I guess we need to go down to the river."

They turned toward the Jōganji and soon found themselves following a path worn through the rubble by human feet. No doubt the few who still lived here came this way for water, too.

Buildings had once crowded down to the edge of the riverbed. Then, it seemed, there had been a powerful flood, which left the areas closest to the river strewn with boulders and hunks of concrete.

The spaces between them were filled with low-growing shrubs, and giant ivy climbed over the rocks. A chorus of insects rang out from among the ground cover. This, and the sound of rushing water, washed soothingly over Asafumi as they approached the river. He began to relax, and all at once the fatigue of the day seemed to bear down on him.

They made their way across the river rocks to the edge of the water. The collective flow from deep in the Tateyama Range was rippling by. Without removing his towel, Asafumi walked into the current and lowered himself in.

"Ahh," he called out. "This feels great!"

Kesumba pulled off her dress to follow. She had nothing on beneath. Asafumi turned away, feeling awkward at the sight of her pubescent breasts and little tuft of hair. Oblivious to this, she stepped into the river and, splashing herself on the way, came to stretch out next to him in the shallows. The dog followed close behind and lay down beside her.

A cool breeze moved across the water. They looked up at the bleached ruins above them, glowing wanly in the lingering twilight. The city of rubble continued on up the hillside and melted into the inky darkness near the top.

"Is this all there is to the city?" Kesumba asked after drinking her fill of water. "There's nothing here."

"Well, once upon a time there were lots of big houses here, with lots of people living in them."

"What's 'once upon a time'?"

Asafumi wasn't sure how to answer. "Before now," he said. "Lots and lots of days before now."

She blew a thin stream of water from her mouth. "So, not today?"

"No, not today. Today is now. Once upon a time is before."

"But no matter what day it is, isn't it always today?"

"Not really. Time goes by. There was a today before now when you were a little girl. But today, now, you've turned into a big girl."

She made a face. "Nuh-uhh. This is how I've always been. Not little and not big."

Asafumi was at a loss. Had he entered a world where there was no before or after – only an eternal present?

Kekah had wandered off to explore the riverbank, and now he suddenly started barking, his tail whipping furiously back and forth: obviously he had found something. Kesumba rose from the water to see what the fuss was about, throwing on her dress as she went. Asafumi quickly followed.

The dog was clamouring in front of a large pile of debris. Beneath the jumble of moulded plastic and corrugated iron and such there appeared to be an opening just big enough for a person to squeeze through. That was clearly where Kekah's excitement was directed. As they came nearer, they saw a stick poking out of the hole, jabbing at the dog. By the time they reached the spot, he had managed to grab the stick in his jaws.

"Come, Kekah! Sit!" Kesumba commanded. He went on growling, but obediently padded over to his mistress and settled at her feet. The stick stopped moving.

Asafumi bent low in front of the opening. "Who's there?" he called.

A stone came flying out, and he jerked aside. It was accompanied by the high-pitched voice of a child.

"Go away!"

Telling the dog to stay, Kesumba stepped up to the opening. "We promise not to hurt you," she said lightly. "Why don't you come on out?"

Another stone landed at her feet, but then there were no more. She crouched over the hole. "Really. It's safe to come out. We promise we won't hurt you."

A small head edged cautiously into view. It was a boy of perhaps ten, with sunken cheeks but big, blazing eyes. His eyes darted nervously from Kesumba to Asafumi to Kekah. When he saw the dog's two heads, one staring straight at him, one looking the other way, he began to shrink back inside.

Asafumi quickly spoke up. "Is this where you live?"

The boy slid a little forward again and dipped his head.

This was the first person they'd met in these ruins. Asafumi squatted down beside Kesumba and asked as gently as he could, "Can you tell us what happened here? How did it all end up like this – such a complete wasteland?"

The boy looked at him blankly for a moment before saying, "I don't know."

261

His heart sank. It was the same answer he kept getting from Kesumba. But he wasn't ready to give up. "Why are you living in a place like this?" he tried again.

Still showing only his head, the boy was keeping a wary eye on Kekah. "Because everybody else is gone," he said.

"What happened to them?"

"They died," he shrugged. "They got sick... or they got eaten..."

Asafumi was stunned. The boy had said this as if it were the most ordinary thing in the world.

"Eaten by what?"

He thought he knew what the answer would be, but he still felt compelled to ask.

The boy motioned indifferently toward the ruins with his chin. "The ones who were left."

That would certainly explain why he was hiding by himself inside this hole, Asafumi thought. Suddenly aware of the threat they might face, he quickly scanned their surroundings. With stars now beginning to dot the sky, he could make out no more than dim shapes in the darkness.

"Where'd you two come from?" the boy asked back, finally showing some curiosity of his own.

Asafumi was still considering how to answer this when Kesumba pointed across the river and said, "Over that way." The range of peaks leading to Yakushidake loomed black against the deep blue night.

The boy looked up toward the distant mountains. "That's where all the strong people went," he said. "The only ones left here are old folks and kids."

"Maybe you should go, too. There're people living in the woods," Asafumi said.

"Really?" For the first time, his voice had perked up.

"Yes, really," said Kesumba. "And they have plenty of food."

At this, the boy finally came crawling on out of the hole. He wore a woman's dress that was much too big for him. Even with it hiked up at the waist with a length of cord, it hung down to his knees. His bony shoulders looked barely wide enough to hold it up. The fabric was torn in several places, and the bare skin beneath was black with dirt.

"Would you go with me?" he asked, his hopeful eyes bouncing back and forth between them.

Asafumi didn't know how to respond. He had assumed that once he reached the city, he'd be able to find his way back home. These ruins that seemed to go on forever had pretty much dashed those hopes. But he couldn't really see himself going back the way they'd come.

"Sure," Kesumba said.

The boy's face lit up. "Just give me a second, then," he said, and turned to duck back inside. He seemed eager to be on his way.

Kesumba grabbed the back of his dress. "Not right this minute," she said. "We walked a long way getting here. We need to rest."

The boy pointed to the hole he'd come out of. "You can use my place."

Asafumi wasn't so sure about burrowing inside the tiny opening, but Kesumba happily accepted the invitation. "Thanks," she said, then added, "We're hungry. Do you have anything to eat?"

Asafumi was surprised at her. It seemed an odd question to ask someone who was skin and bones and obviously hadn't had much to eat in quite a while. But the boy wasn't bothered in the least.

"I'll get you something," he said.

Disappearing into his lair, he emerged a minute later holding a stick in one hand and something they couldn't see in the other.

"What's that?" Asafumi asked.

The boy opened his fist. In his palm was a fishing line with a hook fashioned from a bit of wire.

"My fishing stuff," he said. "I already have a trap set up, so I'll check that, too, to see if I've caught anything. Wait right here, okay? Promise not to leave me behind," he pressed, before heading upriver.

"The kid really seems to have it together for as young as he is," Asafumi said with admiration.

Kesumba sat down by the entrance to the boy's hiding place and Kekah came to lie beside her. "What does 'have it together' mean?"

"Have it together means... well... that he's got a good head."

"Why do you say that?"

"Think about it. He's so little, and yet he's managed to survive by himself in the middle of all this, figuring out how to fish and everything."

"What do you expect?" she said, biting back a yawn. "It doesn't matter whether you're big or little, everybody has to figure out how to feed themselves."

"But children are still weak, so they often can't make it without someone to look out for them."

"That's only natural. It's the same with trees. The weaker seeds and nuts get blown away in the wind or washed away by rain before they have a chance to grow. Only the strong ones are left to get big."

At a loss for a response, Asafumi also sat down on the stony ground. Kesumba leaned over and laid her head on Kekah's furry black back.

"You must be tired," Asafumi said.

"I feel heavy," she said softly. "When I start to feel heavy, I close my eyes, and pretty soon I'm somewhere else and I've become another me. My other me goes to lots of different places, and sees lots of different things, and does lots of different stuff, and then when I open my eyes again after that, I feel light again."

After mumbling all this as if to herself, she closed her eyes and pressed her face deeper into Kekah's back.

What kind of dreams did Kesumba dream, Asafumi wondered. And what about the people who still lived in these ruins, or those pilgrims on Mandala Road searching for Yakushi, or those ape-men who roamed the hills? What kind of dreams did they all dream?

A crescent moon had come into the sky. The Big Dipper and Orion stood out among the stars. The ruins lay perfectly still in the pale light. As he sat looking across the landscape of broken buildings, jagged walls, and teetering uprights, Asafumi found himself recalling the day his parents visited Yokohama to have dinner with Shizuka and her mother at the Landmark Tower. He remembered gazing down over the endless city stretched out below and feeling an inexplicable sense of desolation come over him. At the time, he'd regarded it as nothing more than pre-engagement jitters – that he was simply unnerved by the approach of one of life's major milestones. But he now wondered if that hadn't been it at all. He wondered if the sensation might in fact have been a presentiment about the future. And he wondered if perhaps the diners who filled restaurants on the top floors of skyscrapers and the tourists who rode up to the

observation deck atop Tokyo's Metropolitan Offices were all drawn
to such vantage points by visions of the city's end held somewhere
deep in their subconscious.

Clasping his knees, Asafumi contemplated the flattened city
stretching before him. The place must have once been home to
hundreds of thousands of people. Yet now it was a ghost town. Had
he been swallowed up inside his own vision of the future?

Whooooon whoon whoon whoong.

Almost inaudibly, Kesumba began humming. Her eyes remained
closed, but her lips moved with each note. He couldn't tell whether
she was awake or humming in her sleep.

Needing to relieve himself, Asafumi got to his feet. While he was
peeing on some large rocks a short distance away, he realized that
what looked like a slope rising next to where he stood was actually
part of a fallen Ferro concrete wall. The building it was once part of
had apparently toppled over onto its side. As his eyes drifted across
the fallen slab, he spotted some scratch marks between the tendrils
of ivy creeping over it. They seemed to be from a nail or some
other sharp object, leaving little doubt that they had been made by
design rather than by accident. He thought it might be some kind
of writing, but he couldn't see the marks well enough in the dim
light of the moon to be sure. After shaking himself dry and fixing
his loincloth, he pulled the ivy aside and traced the scratches with
his fingers.

SHRIVELLING DISEASE

In characters as awkward as a child's, that was what it said.

What did it mean? he wondered, with his fingers still resting on
the barely detectable grooves. It wasn't a name he'd ever heard before.
Did its being carved here mean it was something particularly bad?
Come to think of it, the boy who'd gone fishing had mentioned
people getting sick and dying...

As he was puzzling over the unfamiliar name, there was a
movement behind him. He spun around to find a half-naked old
man coming at him with an iron bar poised to strike. A completely
hairless pate and deeply wrinkled face showed his considerable age,
but there was nothing frail in the way he swung the bar, his deep-set
eyes blazing. Asafumi tried to twist away, but the sound of the bar

whipping through the air was followed by a sharp jolt in his side. He fell to the ground. His assailant raised his club for a second strike, this time aiming for Asafumi's head.

Graaarrrr!

The old man pitched forward onto his face as Kekah fell on him from behind. The iron bar clanged harmlessly to the ground. Climbing onto the man's back, the dog reached for his arm with one set of jaws while pulling at the soiled cloth around his waist with the other.

"Get off me! Get off me, you damn brute!" the old man cried, twisting to break free. With only a filthy loincloth to cover himself, his ribs stuck out sharply from his emaciated body, making him look like an Indian ascetic. But the way he was fending off the dog showed that his bony limbs still had a good deal of strength in them.

"Off, Kekah! Off!" Kesumba commanded as she hurried up.

The dog reluctantly let go with both sets of jaws and backed away. The old man sat up and stretched his lips into a tense smile.

"Does this monster belong to you?"

Kesumba nodded. He got to his feet and looked down at Asafumi, who was still clutching his side.

"This one's got some mighty juicy-looking meat on his bones," he said. "Let me finish the job and I'll share him with you."

"I'm not your dinner!" Asafumi tried to yell, but thanks to the pain in his side it came out sounding more like the last croak of a dying chicken. He worried that he might have broken a rib.

"He and I came here together," Kesumba said. "I'm not going to eat him."

The old man spat on the ground. "Fine. I've got other grub," he said as a parting shot, then retrieved the iron bar and picked up a drawstring bag together with something black lying beside it in a heap. Looking more closely, Asafumi saw that it was three dead crows with their feet tied together.

"Wait," said Kesumba. "How about sharing those?"

"Forget it," he snapped, raising his cudgel. "And don't get any ideas about sicking that freak of nature on me again. It caught me off guard before, but next time I'll beat it to a pulp." Then he pointed at Asafumi with his chin. "Of course, if you wanted to trade for this nice piece of white meat here, I'd be happy to give you the whole lot."

Kesumba shook her head.

"Then I'm not about to hand out any eats for free," he said with a snort, fixing his eyes back on her. He looked her up and down, pausing as he took in the small mounds of her budding breasts and the curve of her hips. A faint smile came to his sphincter-like mouth. "You can have one bird if you'll let me use your slit."

"Get lost, pervert," Asafumi broke in. Holding a hand to his side, he tried to stand up, but a stabbing pain made his knees buckle under him and he dropped back to the ground.

"Make it two," the girl said.

"Are you crazy, Kesumba?" Asafumi burst out, but she ignored him. She stood challenging the man with her hands on her hips like a middle-aged woman haggling over the price of vegetables.

The man thought for a moment. "Sure, why not," he shrugged. "I can catch more crows anytime, but this kind of bird's a lot harder to come by."

He set the dead crows down at his feet. Finding a flat rock nearby, he sat down on it and beckoned to Kesumba. She told Kekah to stay and stepped forward.

"Don't do it, Kesumba. Do you even know what he's asking?"

She gave him a disbelieving look. "Of course I do," she said. "I do it with the pilgrims too, sometimes."

Asafumi watched in silence as she went to stand in front of the old man in the dim moonlight. She gathered the skirt of her dress up over her waist. Her small, dark-skinned buttocks were all Asafumi could see from where he sat. The old man put a hand on each of them and pulled her toward him.

"Wait," she said sharply. Her tone brought Kekah to his feet with a warning growl. The old man wasted no time letting go. Dropping to her haunches, Kesumba lifted his grimy loincloth to take hold of his penis, and began playing with it as if she were making a mud pie. This obviously wasn't what the old man had expected, and he straightened in surprise, but then he quickly relaxed again, leaning back on his hands to let her do as she pleased. As she pulled and stroked, she hummed her strange little tune: *Whooo oo-oong, whoooooo oo-oong...* His penis soon began to respond. The look of perplexity on his wrinkled face gave way to one of dreamy-eyed pleasure as she continued her gentle massage. Finally, she rose to straddle him, and slowly lowered herself onto his hardened cock. Wrapping an arm around his neck, she looked more like a child offering her doting grandfather a hug.

Asafumi sat dumbstruck as he witnessed the copulation of an old man and a pubescent girl. The girl was moving her bottom up and down, faster and faster. Abruptly, the man took her by the hips and rolled her onto her back. He pushed into her from above, and her small body began to rock like a boat beneath his thrusts. Her teeth flashed, and Asafumi realized she was enjoying it too. The old man pumped his hips, utterly lost to the world. With the moonlit ruins as their backdrop, the two of them continued their coupling in a quickening rush of grunts and moans.

The people here had all gone back to the wild, thought Asafumi, only to realize in dismay that his own penis was erect as well.

38

"I have to admit," Mitsuharu said with a sigh, "I had a bad feeling when he said he wanted to visit Mandala Road."

After leaving Ohara at the hospital, Yoshitaka, Miharu, and Shizuka had decided to stop at the house in Ashikuraji for a bite to eat before going to the police. Miharu had just finished recounting the events of the morning to her grandfather over a lunch of grilled fish and taro simmered with devil's tongue.

Mitsuharu was sitting a short way back from the table with his legs crossed and an ash tray on the tatami in front of him. He took a drag on his cigarette and exhaled.

"The road actually has quite a long history," he said, waggling his head. "It started out as one of the routes used by old-time Shugendō ascetics on their pilgrimages through these mountains, and even in my day it still didn't see much general traffic. There've been all kinds of stories since way back about strange things happening or people disappearing."

"You didn't say anything about that when I asked you before," Miharu said reproachfully.

Mitsuharu's stubbly cheeks tightened awkwardly as he tapped the ash from his cigarette. "Well, you know, I didn't want to alarm you youngsters with a bunch of old rumours."

Miharu threw Shizuka a guilty look, as if she blamed her grandfather for Asafumi's disappearance. Meeting her glance with a weak smile, Shizuka turned toward the old man.

"Did the people who went missing eventually return?"

"I don't know as I can say. All I can tell you is that I heard stories about weird things going on out that way. Not so much among the locals, but with people from outside – people who came to climb. Some of the old guides used to say Hell Valley only got its name as a tourist ploy, and the real gateway to hell was Mandala Road..."

"I never heard about any of this before," Yoshitaka said.

"Well, they're just stories, you know," he shrugged.

"In any case, what we need to concentrate on right now is Asafumi, not old legends," Miharu said, bringing the conversation back from the realm of strange tales to the situation at hand. "I'm sure that man knows something. We need to get the police to question him."

Her father didn't seem so enthusiastic. "I doubt it'll do any good. You saw what he's like."

"All they have to do is avoid mentioning the war or his wife."

"Better add medicine sellers to that list," he said.

"But that'd prevent you from asking anything about Asafumi," his wife broke in, which brought them both up short. Satoko began freshening everybody's tea as she went on in a sympathetic tone, "I suppose he must've had to go through some really awful things during the war."

"Well, if he did, he had it coming," Miharu snorted. "The way he brags about all the killing he did, the old goat."

"Miharu!" her mother scolded under her breath.

Yoshitaka and Shizuka looked at each other awkwardly. As firsthand victims of the man's madness, they'd have liked to call him some choice names themselves.

"You were in the war, too, weren't you, Grandpa?" Miharu said, looking at him.

"That's right," he said lightly.

"See?" Miharu turned to her mother. "Grandpa must have had a hard time, too, but he doesn't go around hurting anyone."

"We-e-ell, I don't know that comparing him with Grandpa really tells us anything," Satoko said with a strained smile.

"Whereabouts were you sent?" Shizuka asked.

Mitsuharu stubbed out his cigarette and looked out the sliding glass doors to the veranda. Beyond the garden spread a chilly autumn landscape. The harvest was over, and rice paddies reduced to stubble stretched in every direction, looking rather like schoolboys with fresh haircuts.

"It was an awful long time ago now," he said slowly, as if trying to trace his way back. "But I remember going from Nanjing to Hunan... and then from there to Indochina."

"You were in Nanjing?" Miharu's voice rose in surprise. "Ohara mentioned being there too."

Shizuka stiffened as she recalled the man's description of events in the city. Mitsuharu reached for another cigarette.

"That's hardly surprising. There were tens of thousands of us there."

With a click of his lighter, he lit the cigarette.

Miharu arched her neck forward. "Ohara was going on about stringing people together with wire and burning them alive, and raping little girls, and chopping off people's heads. You never did anything like that, did you?"

He took a drag on his cigarette. "I imagine I did, at least some," he said, to everyone's astonishment. Then a little smile came into his eyes, and he added, "Youthful indiscretions of a sort, I suppose."

The stunned Miharu asked again, "So you tied a whole bunch of people up with wire, too?... And killed them?"

He avoided a direct answer. "Killing's what you do in war."

"As they say, war is hell," Satoko began in a mollifying tone, but Shizuka broke in again, unable to keep silent.

"But killing in such horrific ways? And even raping children?"

Mitsuharu abruptly turned to look at her, his face impassive but his eyes flashing. Shizuka realized it was the same look Ohara had had when he grabbed her by the hair in the hospital, and her heart stopped. But a moment later, his eyes softened.

"It was so long ago now, I can't remember. I just can't remember," he said. Then slapping himself on the side of the head, he added jokingly, "I'm getting so feebleminded in my old age."

39

The red rabbit hopped about the ring of light cast by the bonfire in front of the headwoman's house. The man in the string shirt was spinning like a top nearby, his arms spread wide and a trancelike smile on his face; the strings rose in a circle around him as he turned. The carter was tossing the dwarfish flute player into the air and catching him in his arms; the little man squealed each time he was hurled toward the darkened sky. The horned woman drummed a familiar beat on the pan lid hanging around her neck, *pang pa-pang pang*. The androgynous youth was belting out a tune without lyrics in a high-pitched voice. The rest of the pilgrims were twisting their bodies every which way, dancing to the beat.

In a wider circle around the fire sat the villagers, drinking a wine made from barnyard millet. Their dogs wandered about behind them, on the prowl for any scraps of food tossed aside. At first glance, the darkly tanned faces glowing red in the light of the flames appeared to be thoroughly enjoying themselves, but there was also something ambiguous in their expressions, as enigmatic as the smile of a dog.

Sitting cross-legged on the ground, Rentarō nibbled on some nuts as he took in the festive scene. Until a short while before, he had been up there with the rest of them doing a fish-scooping dance, using a large leaf in place of the wicker scoop. But he had worn himself out and decided to take a break.

In exchange for their night's lodging, the pilgrims were expected to provide an evening of entertainment. Not that they had any special talents to offer, as he quickly discovered. They merely clapped their hands and danced about, doing whatever amusing or silly thing came to mind. But to judge from the pointed fingers and frequent laughter, that was apparently all it took to tickle the villagers' funny bones.

The headwoman sat next to Granny Uba, to all appearances enjoying the party as much as anyone. Her earlier roll in the grass with Rentarō seemed long forgotten, and not even a casual glance came his way.

Beyond them, the black mountain ridge cut across the bottom of a sky lit with thousands of stars and a sickle moon. Every now and then the distant howl of a wild dog could be heard from the dark valley below.

Someone stepped across his field of vision and plopped onto the ground beside him. It was the androgynous youth.

"I was standing up there singing away just now," he said, "and all of a sudden I had no idea where I was anymore." Seeing Rentarō's uncomprehending look, he gave a pretty smile and went on. "I've had it happen to me before. It's as if everything inside me empties out and floats away into thin air."

"I guess you must really like singing."

The youth considered this for a moment. "I don't know," he finally said. "It's just that this voice comes pouring out of me and it feels so good."

Rentarō looked up at the people still dancing in the light of the fire. That probably applied to them all, he thought. It wasn't a question of liking it or not; they were simply doing what felt good in the moment. When you've lost your memory, what else do you have? He looked at the village chief again. Their coupling had no doubt been like that for her – something that felt good in the moment, only to be clean forgotten once time had moved on.

Maybe travel was like that, too: doing what feels good from one instant to the next; cutting yourself off from both past and future and living for the pleasure of the present. It was under these conditions that Saya had come into his life. As with the village headwoman earlier in the day, the time they spent together was supposed to be only for then and there – a feel-good moment that was meant to be forgotten once the moment had passed.

But she had failed to see it that way. She had followed him all the way back to Japan, brandishing their past like a knife to threaten his peaceful life.

He thought again how easy it would be to simply keep on going and never turn back. The days of putting up with resentful looks from his wife and Saya would be over. Just as he'd left Malaya to break it off with Saya, he could now leave Senbashi to free himself from them both.

Suddenly he realized that that was effectively what he'd already done – what had gotten him to wherever he was now. Maybe like the people in this strange place, all he really needed was to forget. Memory was a pair of leg irons shackling him to the past. He looked at the pilgrims again. These people had somehow managed to escape the hold of memory. How had they done it?

Thinking of what the headwoman had told him, he said, "This calamity thing – is it true that you shrivel up and die right where you are?"

The youth looked blank for a moment, then nodded. "That's the way some people put it."

"What does it mean?"

He folded his slender hands together in front of his face as if in contemplation. It reminded Rentarō of a Buddha he'd seen at one of Kyoto's famous temples – he wasn't sure which. The youth's perfectly chiselled profile glowed red in the firelight.

"I remember just a tiny bit," he finally said. "I remember somebody saying people weren't acting like people anymore... Back in the city."

Rentarō leaned forward at this mention of the city.

"What was it like there?" he asked.

He winced a little. "I was scared... I remember crumbling walls... people screaming... a lot of killing going on..."

A look of fear flashed in his eyes and he stopped short.

Rentarō hesitated for a moment but then jerked his chin toward the dancers and said, "Were all the people there like you folks? A tad unusual, I mean."

"We were different from the others," he said, as if it was a complicated question. "That's why we couldn't stay... People told us *we* were the calamity... The only cure was a pilgrimage to Yakushi, they said. So we started looking for Mandala Road, and pretty soon we ran into others who were looking for it, too."

"The city's gone."

The heavily bearded villager sitting on the other side of the youth looked up from the roasted sparrow he was working on.

"That's what one of our village elders always used to say, until he died not so long ago. The city's gone. He escaped and helped start this place."

"What exactly happened?"

"Everything began shrivelling up and dying right where it was," he said, echoing the headwoman's words. He took a sip of his wine. "Plants, and people, too. Once they start doing that, it's all over. Because they go without leaving any seed."

Rentarō sighed and raised his nearly empty cup to his lips. He was getting nowhere.

Where in the world had he wandered off to? he asked himself again. He was a seasoned traveller; he had ranged far and wide from the time he was fifteen without ever losing track of where his feet were taking him. But this was different. He had no idea where he was anymore.

Grrrrr, grrrrar.

All of a sudden the dogs were on their feet growling into the darkness. The villagers froze. There was a rustling in the thicket beyond the reach of the firelight. The dogs shot off in that direction, barking in a frenzy. Just then, a wave of dark figures leapt out of the underbrush.

"It's the ape-men!" somebody shouted.

Rentarō instantly recognized the hairy, nearly naked figures as the same kind who had attacked him and his companion that morning. Swinging clubs with hunks of metal lashed to them and raising a wild battle cry, they swooped into the circle of light and fell on the villagers. The dogs sprang at them with open jaws, but the raiders easily fended them off, bashing them on the head and spine. The stronger of the men and women fought back with whatever they could find at hand; the elderly and children ran away into the darkness, crouching low. The air was filled with the thud of body blows and the crack of breaking bones. Cries of pain and panic rose all around.

The frightened pilgrims were about to follow the fleeing villagers, when Granny Uba stepped forward and swept her staff in a circle.

"Everybody gather round! Stand behind me here!" she cried.

They all quickly pressed together at her back. Hesitating for only a second, Rentarō raced after the youth to join them. Granny Uba stood as if shielding her threatened brood.

An ape-man with wild hair and a bushy beard came up waving a bloodied club, his eyes flashing with menace and his large teeth bared. He let out a roar as he raised the club over his head, but then stopped in midair, seeming somehow cowed by the group's weird appearance. Granny Uba swiftly unwrapped the scarf around her head and thrust her face toward him. Since her back was to the pilgrims, Rentarō couldn't see, but her adversary froze stock-still for a moment, then spun on his heel and fled.

Granny Uba went on standing guard between the pilgrims and the mayhem around them as the savages pressed their attack, bludgeoning villagers, wolfing down food from the feast, and ransacking the houses for meat and vegetables that had been hung up to dry.

Soon some of those who'd escaped the initial attack came back armed with hoes and cudgels. Not yet ready to withdraw, the ape-men met this resistance fiercely. A woman bleeding heavily from a split head lay writhing on the ground. An ape man who was pushed into the fire let out a piercing howl. Feral shouts and cries of distress rose above the din. But the raiders had come only to take, not to destroy. Having stolen what they could, they now retreated into the woods, dragging the bodies of dead villagers behind them.

When peace had returned, the dazed survivors quietly surveyed the damage. Soon one, then another began dropping his stick or hoe to help the wounded, or to begin cleaning up the food and dishes strewn about the ground.

The fire was still burning. Like birds poking their heads from their nests, the pilgrims edged out from behind Granny Uba. She had already wrapped the tattered scarf back around her head.

There was a heaviness in the air. But the villagers went mutely about the task of cleaning up as if they'd merely come through a sudden storm.

"It's the calamity. It's the calamity," chanted the one-armed woman in a low voice as she began beating the metal disk around her neck, *pang pa-pang pang.*

40

The three crow carcasses with their pinfeathers singed off were skewered on spits over a small fire, their dark red flesh sizzling as it browned. Asafumi, Kesumba, and the old man sat around the fire watching with eager eyes, hungrily licking their lips. Every so often the old man or the girl reached out to turn the birds so they would cook evenly. Asafumi was still nursing the blow to his side from the old man's club. He didn't think he'd actually broken a rib, but a bruise appeared to be forming, and there was some swelling.

At the moment, though, it was not pain but pangs of shame that bothered him most – the shame of accepting food for which Kesumba had had to sell her body. His gnawing hunger had won out over his sense of honour: he'd been unable to refuse her invitation to share in the meal. With a shudder, he wondered if this meant he, too, might stoop to eating human flesh if nothing else was to be found.

When the old man handed over the promised pair of birds, Kesumba had been quick to ask if he could also get a fire going. Still in the glow of sexual gratification, he'd taken a firestone and touchwood from the bag tied to his hip, gathered up some dry leaves and driftwood for tinder, and set about making a fire with a practiced touch.

A skinny yellow moon smiled down from the penetrating darkness of the sky. The ruins lay as quiet as a necropolis, lit by its pale light. The boy who'd gone fishing had not returned. Kesumba sat scratching Kekah's head and gently humming her strange tune, obviously in high spirits. The old man was absorbed in getting his own bird cooked just right.

"Crows are smart little buggers, and they're no easy bird to catch," he said proudly as he adjusted his spit again. "But they're tasty. Much tastier than any stringy human flesh you might come across around here."

Having been called a juicy piece of white meat earlier, Asafumi found the remark unsettling.

"So what's your trick?" he asked, hoping to steer the conversation away from cannibalism.

The man gave him a hard look, his lips set in a firm line. "I'm not fool enough to tell you that when I know every new crow trapper will mean less for me to catch." Then out of the blue he asked, "You ever fought in a war, young fella?"

"No," he said, not sure what to make of this sudden turn.

"It figures," he sneered. "When perfectly healthy young men don't go to war, they turn into a bunch of gutless pansies like you."

Asafumi didn't like being called a pansy, but he wondered if the stock the man seemed to place in war for building character might actually mean he knew what had happened to the city.

"So would I be correct in thinking that *you* must have gone to war?" he asked politely.

"Damn right I did."

"Which war would it have been?"

He was hoping to hear about the conflict that had reduced this city to ruins, but the answer caught him by surprise.

"The Greater East Asia War."

"The Greater East Asia War?... You mean, as in the Pacific War?"

"The Greater East Asia War is the Greater East Asia War," he said adamantly.

"But... in that case, how did you wind up here?"

He blinked as if a big soap bubble had burst in front of his face. Then, as though searching for something that wasn't there, his eyes moved from Asafumi to Kesumba and to the moonlit ruins beyond before he finally said, "I don't know."

"You don't know?"

"No, I don't. I feel like I was still at the battlefront till just a little bit ago. Like I was in Nanjing, raping girls and ramming bamboo sticks up their cracks. Except it's all kind of murky. When I stop to think, it seems like maybe I was in Hankou instead, lopping off people's heads. Or maybe I was wading through a Philippine jungle with my bayonet fixed."

He wrapped his bald pate in his hands for a moment, then abruptly took them away and stared at his companions in bewilderment.

"But if I was just there, then I should still be in my twenties. I shouldn't be a hairless old geezer. That's the part I can't figure out."

"I guess you've been here a lot longer than you think."

He screwed up his face in puzzlement, before turning to gaze across the ruins again.

"I wonder. Maybe so. But still, somehow, I can't help feeling like I just got here. On the other hand, I also have this vague sense that it was after the war and I was living in a small village somewhere, but I can't really make anything out. It's like trying to see something in a murky pond. All I actually remember is stuff from the war."

The look of puzzlement had gone, but exasperation had entered his voice.

In much the same way as the Yakushi pilgrims, this man had lost his memory, too, Asafumi thought. He was wondering what the reason could be, when Kesumba, who had been absently turning the birds from time to time, said they were ready. Coming back to the present, the old man removed his spit from the fire and brought the roasted meat to his mouth.

Kesumba took the other two and laid them down in front of her to twist a leg off each. "We'll save these for the boy," she said, before lifting the now one-legged birds again and holding one out for Asafumi. He still had qualms about accepting it, but he did.

With her healthy set of teeth, Kesumba quickly tore off several bites to fill her cheeks, then sat chewing quietly, savouring the flavour. Having several missing incisors to compensate for, the old man went at his piece with a noisy series of sucking and smacking sounds. Asafumi gently pulled off a strip of the skin with his teeth. It tasted of burned feathers, so he quickly spat it out, and Kekah pounced on it. He took a small bite of the dark red meat underneath. It had a bit of a gamy smell, but it tasted pretty much like chicken. Once he'd chewed up this first morsel, his wariness went. He ate greedily, digging his teeth in all the way to the bone. Some salt would be nice, he thought, but soon even that was forgotten. For a time all three of them were too busy eating to speak.

When he was about half done, Asafumi paused and turned to the old man. "Have you heard of something called the shrivelling disease?"

The man had moved on to the liver or heart. With his mouth full, he gave only an ambiguous grunt in response.

"I found the words scratched onto a collapsed wall over there," Asafumi explained.

The old man chewed the sticky mess in his mouth quite a few more times before swallowing, as if reluctant to be rushed through a tasty bite. When it was gone, he let out a belch that sounded like a squashed frog and said, "It's what you've got."

Asafumi was taken aback. "Me?"

"That's right," he said, as he inspected the carcass in the light of the fire for any bits of meat he might have missed. "You're still young, but you act like some decrepit old geezer who's got nothing but talk left. Even your pecker's got less pep than mine. It's like you're still walking around but you've already shrivelled up and died."

It came as quite a jolt. Never would Asafumi have guessed that somebody might see him this way.

"Wow. Spare my feelings, why don't you," he quipped, trying to conceal his shock by turning it into a joke. But the old man wasn't through.

"It makes me sick to my stomach just looking at you. You depend on a little girl to save your sorry ass. How can you call yourself a man? You're only half a man. If you went into the army, you'd be the first one picked as brownie queen. It's a damn shame I can't turn you into some good eatin', 'cause that's really all a guy like you's good for."

The usually even-tempered Asafumi felt his blood starting to boil. "I can't believe I'm being insulted by an admitted child rapist," he bristled.

"Oh?" the man retorted. "Are you so sure you wouldn't have done the same? I'll bet you've secretly been hankering to get it on with this girl, too. I expect that pecker of yours got pretty jumpy when you were watching us bump and grind a while ago."

He'd hit a nerve. Asafumi's entire body flushed with heat. He noticed Kesumba eyeing him curiously and cringed with shame.

"Like hell!" he shouted. "I'm not some lowlife pervert like you."

"Oh, you're not, are you?" the old man scoffed. "Well, la-di-dah. Don't think I don't know your type. You're all talk and no walk. You put on such fine airs, but the first time you see real action, you go blank in the head and lose control. The next thing you know, you're running totally amok, killing people right and left – in a lot worse ways than I ever did – and raping every little girl in sight like a maniac."

Asafumi leapt to his feet. "You keep talking like that and I'll make you regret it!" he shouted.

The old man reached for the iron bar lying on the ground beside him. "Oh yeah? You wanna fight?" he boomed. "You gonna show some grit after all?"

Asafumi felt his legs turning to jelly. Blood rushed to his head as he fought to control his panic. He balled his hands into fists, intending to punch him in the face, but his iron bar and menacing glower held him back. He could not move.

"Aaaghh!"

With a frantic yell, he bolted. He had to get away. The river rocks caught at his feet, but he ignored them and stumbled on. It was actually from himself that he was running: from the man inside him who'd lusted after Kesumba; from the coward who couldn't even stand up to a guy twice his age. He ran on in utter humiliation, fiercely gritting his teeth.

He'd never seen himself this way before. He was supposed to be one of the elite, hired by a topflight company for a plum research position straight out of college. It was through no fault of his own that he'd been laid off when the firm had to retrench. He was a victim of the sick economy. In all his life, he'd never once had dirty thoughts about little girls, or quaked in fear before an elderly man.

How can this be happening? This can't be me! he cried out inwardly as he fled. But no matter how far he went, he knew he'd never be able to blot from memory the face-off he'd just lost.

He bashed his knee against a boulder in the dark and reeled to the ground. As he landed, a piece of driftwood dug into his bruised side, and he let out a yelp. Lying on a bed of rocks, he struggled to catch his breath.

The chill of the river air brushed across his nakedness. Grass growing along the water's edge rustled in the breeze. Vacantly, he gazed up at the cold, starry night. It was a spectacularly clear sky.

What if the bastard was right? he thought. What if he really was the kind of gutless creep who raped little girls at the front? What did that say about the life he'd lived until now, unaware of his hidden nature? Had it meant anything at all?

He lifted his hands from his side and spread them over his face.

41

With a shopping bag made from a torn sarong in her hand, Saya paused in front of the general store to see what was on display: some scrub brushes, several kitchen knives, an army-helmet cooking pot, a washbowl, and a few other meagre offerings. She had come into Senbashi because of word that there was to be a distribution of fish, but by the time she arrived the supply was sold out and she'd turned back disappointed.

Her eyes lingered on the army helmet that had been converted into a kitchen pot, thinking how much nicer it would be if she had two pans to cook with. The Nonezawas had given her just one when she moved out. Even meals consisting mostly of potatoes and *daikon* would be far more satisfying if accompanied by some hot soup. But with only a single pan, she could never serve hot food and soup at the same time.

She picked the pot up for a closer look. The top of the steel helmet had been flattened to make a stable base, and the holes originally intended for a chin strap had been fitted with a metal handle. It would be perfect for soup. But she was running low on money. A month had gone by since Rentarō left on his trip. If he didn't come home soon, she wouldn't know what to do.

Wooden sandals scraped the floor, and the shopkeeper emerged from somewhere in the back wearing an apron. Her top was patched, and the *monpe* she had on were obviously refashioned from an old kimono.

"That's seven yen," she said. "It's the last one we have, so now's definitely the time to buy."

Saya quickly put the pan down. "Just looking," she said.

The woman didn't look very old, but some prematurely gray hair showed in the bun at the back of her head.

"All right, then," she said, her tone distinctly cooler, as she turned to go back inside.

"No sale?" came a man's voice from the dark interior.

"It's that woman from down south. You know, the mistress. She knew she wasn't buying, but I guess she couldn't keep her dirty hands off it."

As if propelled by the nastiness in the woman's voice, Saya hurried away.

Malice is like a poisonous snake. Hang around too long and you might get bitten – and the venom will spread through your body.

She made her way along the shopping street without slowing down. Drab structures with low-hanging eaves followed one after the other. Housewives were clustered in front of the rice shop, the sake shop, the greengrocer – getting help with their purchases or simply chatting among themselves. They glanced at Saya as she passed but went right back to their conversations. People in Senbashi had been friendly to her as long as they thought she was one of their own, home from the south. But because Rentarō had registered her for ration coupons under Kim Suk-hwa's name, word eventually got around that she wasn't actually Japanese, and a chill came over their friendship. The fact that Saya didn't look Korean continued to fuel interest in her identity however, and soon, no doubt abetted by the Nonezawa women, talk began to circulate that she was actually from Southeast Asia. Ironically, the misunderstanding that she had "returned" from the south, which Saya was happy to encourage at first, had eventually led them to the truth.

She could see the change in people's eyes once they learned she was not Japanese. They became like the occupying forces in Malaya. Those troops had looked on her people like fish in a pond – a lower form of life that could never climb out of the water into their world. In the same way, the locals here had quietly come to regard Saya as someone who didn't belong among them.

For to them, you had to be Japanese to be human.

Japanese men always prefer Japanese privies, no matter where they go.

Kim Suk-hwa's words rang out in her head.

Saya realized that Suk-hwa had been right. A bad taste spread down through her body, as if she'd taken a bite of bitter-tongue.

With no Japanese toilets to do his business in, Rentarō had simply used a Malayan substitute. That was all she had been to him. In a burst of renewed hatred, the desire to kill him returned.

He'd run away again – suddenly she was sure of it. Just as he had abandoned her in Malaya, he'd now left her in that old farmhouse in the middle of nowhere. For all she knew, he'd simply gone back to his house here in Senbashi; he might not have gone away anywhere, only stopped coming to see her and the boy.

Once this thought had lodged in her head, she could no longer just go home. She found her legs taking her in the direction of the Nonezawa house.

This was her first trip back since moving out, but she had no difficulty finding the two-storey house with the roof that curled up at the corners. She stopped in front of the gate and peered up the gravel driveway. The sliding front door stood open. She slowly started toward it. As she drew near, she heard the sound of a door opening and closing somewhere inside, then some muffled women's voices. They seemed to be busy with chores.

"What're you doing here?"

A voice from behind caught her by surprise. She turned to find Rentarō's wife holding a wooden tub full of freshly washed laundry. Her sunken cheeks appeared to have filled out a little since the last time she'd seen her. But her feelings toward Saya apparently hadn't changed, for she looked as though she might throw the laundry tub at her at any moment.

"Mr. Ren, he come home?"

"No," she said curtly, a spasm of hostility moving across her cheek. Saya eyed her suspiciously.

Yōko shook her head in exasperation. "You need to learn when to quit," she said. "You left my whole family in a shambles. Haven't you had enough?"

Had enough? What could the woman think she'd had enough of? As far as revenge on Rentarō was concerned, she certainly hadn't had enough yet.

Yōko apparently mistook the disbelief in her eyes for unhappiness. "Of course, I can understand why you might feel upset," she said, softening her voice a little. "After all, the cheating bastard used you and then tossed you coldly aside."

An image of Suk-hwa superimposed itself on her, and Saya's chest tightened painfully.

"We women always get the short end of the stick," Yōko went on. "We're pretty much at the mercy of whatever the men decide. But each of us has to find a place for ourselves in spite of that. Rentarō belongs in this house. This is where his family is. It's where I've made a place for myself – where I belong. It's not where you belong. You have to make your own place somewhere. And you really can only do that back where you came from."

Saya considered this at some length without saying anything. Yōko seemed encouraged that she was taking her suggestion seriously.

"If you had a mind to go home, I'd be willing to help you out," she offered in a much kinder tone. "I could give you the boat fare and enough to live on for a while. I've got some money squirreled away for special needs."

But Saya was barely listening. "Your house, it is toilet," she said slowly.

Yōko's eyes blazed. "What kind of talk is that all of a sudden?"

"I am his Malayan toilet. You are his Japanese toilet."

Yōko's face turned to stone. Her hands holding the washtub began to shake, nails biting into the wood.

"I suggest you watch your filthy tongue," she snapped back.

Her anger gave Saya a perverse sort of satisfaction. That was right. She wasn't the only toilet here. This alligator lady was one, too.

"For Mr. Ren, woman's this place is toilet hole," she said, patting her hand between her legs.

"Get out!" Yōko screamed, hurling the tub at her. It glanced off her shoulder and scattered its damp contents on the ground. "Get off my property!"

Saya wheeled around and marched out the gate, a faint smile tugging at her lips.

Yes, she was thinking. To Rentarō, the space between a woman's legs was a toilet. Saya's customers at the P-house hated the toilets they had to use; they were incensed at how they had to do their business after being dragged all that way to Malaya. The difference with Rentarō was that he actually liked the facility he'd found. But a toilet's still only a toilet, and once he got back to Japan, there was a Japanese one waiting for him.

Basically, Saya had been a wayside hut that Rentarō stumbled on in the jungle – a brief stopping place that appeared to him as no more than an outhouse. For Saya, it was a shelter furnished also with a bed and a cookstove, but these other amenities never even entered

Rentarō's vision. After all, even the wayside hut he called home in Japan had been only a privy to him.

In the same way plants and rocks and driftwood that have gone gray and dusty appear fresh and crisp after a rain, something that had remained murky in Saya's mind until now had finally come into focus. Even if the truth she now saw was an unpleasant one, it was refreshing to have gained this new clarity.

Making her way from one quiet residential lane down another, she soon reached a small river. A profusion of wild plants grew on its banks. Wondering if she might find some edible greens among them, she stepped out of her rubber *zoris* to make her way down to the water's edge.

The crystal-clear snowmelt flowing out of the Tateyama Range seemed to highlight every stone on the river bottom. Plants of all kinds crowded the bank – most of them varieties new to her. Some reminded her of things she'd known in Malaya, but with subtle differences in the size or shape of their leaves. She remembered how the healer used to say that plants growing beside rivers were more potent, so you needed to be especially careful that you didn't get something poisonous instead of medicinal.

Saya began examining each one more closely, sniffing their leaves and taking tiny bites. When she found something that looked, smelled, and tasted similar to a plant her people used as food or medicine, she picked some to take home with her.

With the smell of growing things filling the air around her and the spring sunshine warming her from above, she waded along the edge of the icy water in her bare feet, moving from one plant to the next. As she added to her small pile of greens, a growing sense of contentment settled over her.

Whoooon, whooo oo-oo-oo-oong.

She began humming to herself. It was the music that her people made as they moved from one temporary settlement to the next – phrases and notes that never quite formed a fixed melody.

Whooooon, whooo oo-oo-oo-oong, oo-oonnng.

As she continued humming and picking, she heard a voice call out to her.

"What are you doing there?"

Saya looked up to find a woman with a small cloth bundle clutched in her arm standing on the street that ran along the levee. She appeared to be a little younger than Saya, and she had on a pretty, if slightly faded, flower-print dress. Her shoes were made of leather and had tall heels. She wore a scarf around her hair – something Saya associated with Muslim women back home – which made her round, chubby face look like a moon floating in a sea of polka dots. It was a style of dress Saya had not seen before in Senbashi, and she couldn't help staring as she showed her the things in her hand.

"I pick plants for eating," she said. "For medicine too."

"Really? For medicine?" The woman took two or three steps down from the street toward the river. "When my grandmother was still alive, she used to go out and find plants that made stomach-aches and fevers go away just like that."

Saya nodded and went back to her picking. But the woman didn't leave.

"Do you know a lot about healing plants?" she asked.

Saya raised her head again. There was an earnestness in the woman's crescent eyes that caught her attention.

"Some things I know," she answered.

"Then maybe you could help me," the woman said, before slipping out of her high-heeled shoes and stepping through the grass down to the water's edge. She lowered her voice. "I get these awful gnawing pains in my stomach that wake me up in the middle of the night. My grandmother knew what to give me, but she's dead now, so I can't ask for her help anymore..."

She pressed a hand to her stomach directly beneath her breasts and winced.

Only a few minutes earlier, Saya had noticed a plant that reminded her of one the healer gave people who hurt in that spot. She pushed her way back along the bank, trying to find it again. A round leaf with a shiny green surface. There it was. Except for being a little smaller than in Malaya, it looked the same. Nibbling a piece to make sure it tasted right, she pulled up ten stalks or so by the roots and gathered them into a bunch. With a quick rinse in the river, she handed them to the woman.

"Let roots dry, then mix little bit in hot water and drink every day."

For several moments the woman simply stared at the leaves in her hand. Then she smiled and dipped her head in gratitude.

Saya pushed the last of the other things she'd picked into her homemade shopping bag and stepped from the river onto the bank. As she made her way up to the street, the woman came climbing after her.

"Wait a second," she said.

Saya stopped when she got to the road. Catching up to her, the woman dug a hand into her bundle and pulled out an onion. She pressed it into Saya's hand.

"A token of my appreciation," she said, then put her shoes back on, gave another quick bow, and hurried away.

Saya stared at the onion, feeling as if the herbs she'd picked had magically changed shape right in the palm of her hand. After a few moments she put it in her bag on top of the rest of her harvest and turned toward home. As she started down the road that shimmered in the warm spring sunshine, the music of her people began flowing from her lips again.

Whoooo oong, whoooo oo-oong...

42

The falling leaves had formed a carpet of red and yellow over the brown earth around Rentarō's old house. Shizuka went to get the rake and began gathering them into a pile. With two-thirds of the property covered in trees, she knew the postage stamp yard would be spread with leaves again by the next day, but any time she had nothing to do, her thoughts quickly turned to Asafumi, so she preferred to keep herself occupied.

Six days had gone by since she last saw her husband. She'd reported him missing to the police the day before yesterday, but they had yet to get back to her. When she went to the station with Miharu and her father to file the report, the officer in charge seemed to lose interest the moment it came out that the missing person was a medicine salesman, so she wasn't really counting on hearing anything. They obviously didn't consider it the least bit worrisome for a salesman to be out of touch for a few days. Miharu had gone to fetch the Volkswagen for her yesterday using the spare key Shizuka had at the house.

After raking the dry leaves into a heap, she set them ablaze with a cigarette lighter. They crackled as they began to burn. The wind pushed the billowing column of smoke into the trees that hemmed in the yard. The smoke caught the afternoon sun filtering through the branches in diagonal shafts of light.

Shizuka leaned her rake against the veranda and walked up the path through the garden. Now that autumn was upon them, the plants were entering their dormant phase and the shrubbery appeared rather forlorn. But as she continued on, breathing in the smell of damp fallen leaves, she soon found herself surrounded by lush foliage again. The deciduous trees had given way to evergreen species with thick, glossy leaves filling their branches. Almost none of the trees in this part of the garden were ones Shizuka recognized – though her knowledge of plant varieties was admittedly quite limited. As she moved deeper in among the dense green growth, she began to feel as if she were travelling somewhere far away; she was only walking through a modest little garden wood, but it felt as though she were wandering endlessly through a vast, deep forest. She thought of the mountainsides along Mandala Road that she'd visited with Miharu and Yoshitaka two days before.

Where had Asafumi disappeared to in those hills? She wished she could go back to that hospital and demand some real answers from Ohara. But the impulse quickly faded when she remembered the wildness in his eyes.

She'd been quite shaken by the atrocities Ohara described in his ravings. Although her paternal grandfather had died, her mother's father was still living. He'd been a soldier in the war, too: she knew he used to go to meetings of the Veterans Association. But he'd never spoken about his experiences in front of his grandchildren. To her, he had always been a friendly, mild-mannered old man. How could someone like that ever have killed anybody? Yet, if he was deployed at the front, he pretty much had to have done it. Even Miharu's grandfather had admitted to it – the gentle mountain guide who you'd never imagine could hurt a soul. In fact, though it had never really occurred to her before, virtually every man over the age of eighty she passed on the street had lived through the same experiences.

Until now, the Second World War had been little more to her than some lines in a history textbook. The August 15 anniversary marking its end was just another day in the middle of the annual Bon holidays, and when she came across an item about the war in the newspaper or on TV, it registered only as an event that had taken place long ago and far away. Yet it was something that people still living had been very much a part of. That's what seemed so strange to her now – because she'd always had trouble thinking of it as something that really happened.

And she could say the same about her husband's disappearance: it had yet to sink in as real. A chill went through her at the thought that he might actually be dead. But it lasted only for an instant before she was brushing the notion aside as simply not possible. Yet, the next moment she found herself thinking that if he *was* dead, she had become a widow, and she'd need to go back to Yokohama and find someone else to live with. To her surprise, she discovered that she was oddly excited by the prospect. She suddenly wondered if she'd ever really loved Asafumi.

She reached the tall gray tree deep in the garden. Branches filled with large, wavy leaves stretched overhead. Even on such a sunny afternoon, the light was dim in the shade of the tree. She came to a halt.

Did you get his heart?

The words she'd heard the woman speak here on the first night her husband was away echoed in her head.

Had she? she asked herself. Had she gotten Asafumi's heart? She wasn't sure. To begin with, what did she even know about his heart? Their relationship had been built on the easy camaraderie of colleagues in the workplace. She enjoyed his company, and felt she could let her hair down with him. It was like being with her best friend in junior high. They might argue about something from time to time, but it never blew up into a major to-do. Their mutual friends all commented on how compatible they seemed. To be honest, she felt so completely at home with him that there was no thrill of being with a man. Having sex was like holding hands, except with a different part of their bodies. There was none of the all-consuming desire pulsing up from somewhere deep inside that kept her hungering for more in her assignations with Hiroyuki. On the other hand, the passion had eventually begun to fade with Hiroyuki as well. Considering how quick she'd been to walk out when he called her frigid, maybe her bond with him hadn't been anything all that special either.

Shizuka's gaze drifted past the thick gray trunk to the dense growth beyond. Next to a shrub with leaves in the shape of an open hand grew a cluster of long, slender blades, rising out of the ground like water from a fountain. Instinctively, her eyes began searching for the penis she'd seen in the park as a child. That arched pillar among the foliage, reaching vigorously upward. Was that what she'd been looking for all these years? she wondered – the gorgeous penis etched into her retinas that day, silently dribbling white semen from its tip as it came to a climax.

She was still gazing into the undergrowth when, like an optical illusion changing shape, the figure of a man came into focus. A dark-skinned man, with large black eyes, a flat nose, and thick lips. His slightly curly black hair was mixed with gray, and there were wrinkles both under his eyes and around his mouth.

The sight of him standing there almost like another tree in the garden gave Shizuka a start. But there was a harmlessness in his look that kept her from crying out in alarm. When their eyes met, the man bobbed his head lightly in greeting.

"Sorry for trespassing," he said.

It was an apology, but he didn't sound particularly sorry.

Shizuka nodded warily. "Who are you?" she asked.

He stepped out of the underbrush. He was stockily built, with thick, muscular shoulders that brought to mind a well-inflated tire. He wore a green linen jacket over a polo shirt, and his trousers were a light brown – a combination that had camouflaged him well where he'd been standing. In his hand was a navy blue overnight bag.

"My name is Nonezawa… Isamu Nonezawa."

Shizuka quickly sorted through the names her husband had mentioned. Then it clicked.

"So you're Saya's son?" she said.

He smiled, revealing a healthy-looking set of teeth between his thick lips. "Did you know my mother?"

Why on earth would she run into Isamu here? Wasn't he supposed to have disappeared?

"Only from what I've heard," she replied, as questions spun through her head. "I'm Shizuka Nonezawa. I'm married to Asafumi, Rentarō's grandson."

"Ah, so you're Asafumi's wife, are you?" he said with easy familiarity. "I never actually met him as a boy, but I knew he used to visit his grandfather a lot. Can I conclude, then, that you live here now?"

She nodded.

"Well, well. If only I'd known that, I wouldn't have had to come sneaking around the way I did," he said airily.

"What in the world prompted you to...?"

She'd been about to say "sneak in like a thief", but she trailed off. The man had once lived here.

"It was my mother's last wish," he said.

"She passed away?" Shizuka asked in surprise.

"Yes, about a month ago. She'd been gradually getting weaker for quite a while, and then she began keeping to her bed more and more... I tried to get her to see a doctor, but she kept telling me never mind, it was her time, and she just kind of withered away like a flower."

He sounded a little like a father talking about a naughty child.

"So she was living with you? My husband told me she'd vanished after his grandfather died, and nobody knew where she was."

"That's right. She came to live with me. My dad supposedly said he was going to sign this house over to her, but I guess he never got around to doing the paperwork. When she realized this after he died, she decided simply to leave. I don't think the Nonezawas did anything to drive her away, but she didn't want to be beholden to them."

But didn't they go looking for her? she was about to ask, before realizing they'd have done no such thing. Considering what Asafumi's mother had said, they had probably thought good riddance. She claimed they didn't even know where Isamu lived. But if Saya went to join him shortly after Rentarō's death, she must have been in contact with him all along.

"Wasn't it hard for her to give up the home she'd lived in for so many years? She must have grown pretty attached to the place."

"Actually, no," he said, his voice suddenly louder. He scratched his head for a moment. "She shrugged it off as being just another wayside hut and never seemed the least bit put out by the move. Even after coming to Osaka, she never made a big deal about missing Toyama. She used to say the old merchant quarter where I live reminded her of the city back in Malaya, and I think she liked it there. But..."

He paused and looked down at the blue bag in his hand.

"To tell the truth," he went on, "I'm not really so sure. Near the end, she asked me to do one last thing for her after she died. She wanted me to bring her back here to the house in Toyama and put her up in the tree of the dead."

"Tree of the dead? Here?"

Isamu reached out and laid his hand on the trunk of the gray tree. "This tree. I remember her telling me when I was little. In her tribe back in Malaya, when someone dies, they tie their body to a branch high in the tree of the dead. It's supposed to be so they can watch over the ones left behind."

Shizuka looked up at the tree. It was tall, with branches reaching broadly out to the side. Perched high in a tree like this, the dead would indeed be able to see far and wide.

"But you can't really mean to put her body up there."

He threw his head back and laughed. "Of course not," he said. He raised the overnight bag in front of his chest. "But I came here thinking I could at least scatter her ashes from up there. I didn't know that Asafumi lived here now, and I didn't want to spook the people who did, so I just snuck in." Then, as if it never even occurred to him that she might turn him down, he added, "Do you mind?"

It seemed a little unsettling to think of somebody's ashes being scattered around where she lived, even if the person was a relative, so her first thought was to refuse. But the fact that it was Saya's last wish made her reconsider. Why not? she decided. The residue that remained after cremation was basically just carbonized calcium: not only was it unlikely to do any harm, it would probably enrich the soil a little for the plants. Nor would Asafumi object, she told herself, since he had actually known Rentarō and Saya.

"No, it's fine," she said.

"Thanks."

Isamu squatted on his haunches and set the bag on the ground. Opening the zip, he reached inside to take out a white cloth bag. It was small enough to fit in one hand, but he cradled it in both as he rose to his feet again.

"This is what my mother's come to," he said. "So tiny, and weightless."

Shizuka wasn't sure why, but she found herself reaching for the bag. He laid it in her hand.

It felt soft against her palm. From inside it came the voice she had heard before:

Did you get his heart?

43

Rentarō opened his eyes when he felt something tickling his nose. A bright mixture of brown and red fur filled his field of vision at point blank range. He jerked his head back with a start before realizing it was the rabbit from the old man's back, now on the loose and scratching at the ground in front of his face.

He sat up and looked around. The nearby ridges were beginning to light up. Farther away, the tall, snowy peaks of Tateyama glowed pink in the emerging sun.

The Yakushi pilgrims lay asleep on the ground around the heap of glowing embers left from last night's fire. The villagers had gone back to their houses to sleep after cleaning up. No sign remained of the upended food vessels and dead dogs that had been scattered about. The settlement stood quietly beneath a thin morning haze. Dark bloodstains colouring the ground here and there were all that told of the battle that had taken place.

Rentarō got to his feet and stretched. This was the second night in a row that he'd had to sleep under the stars. His joints were stiff. His skin was grimy, and he'd begun to smell pretty ripe. He longed to soak in a nice hot bath and sink into a soft futon. Back when he was travelling in Malaya, he'd often slept outdoors. But he was younger then. Now that he was approaching the half-century mark, sleeping rough took a much bigger toll on him.

So what was he going to do now? he asked himself, his head still fuzzy with sleep. Last night he'd been tempted to simply keep on going and never turn back. But he realized he had neither the courage nor the energy to give up his job and become an aimless wanderer. As a travelling salesman, he always knew exactly where he was going and why. It gave him satisfaction to visit customers and expand his business one home at a time. What would be the point of travelling without destination or purpose? He'd be like a child lost in the woods.

With the advancing edge of the morning sun creeping across the village, Rentarō took another look around. A few rough fields had been carved out of a small pocket among rugged mountains, and on the fringes of those fields the people had cobbled together some huts out of cast-off materials they'd found. This was where he'd ended up after somehow getting hopelessly lost.

As he stood there thinking, it occurred to him that this trip might have been all about getting lost right from the very start. Wasn't taking to the road when he found it too difficult to face Yōko and Saya merely a sign of how badly he'd lost his way in life?

He felt a sudden jolt. For an instant he wondered if it came from his heart, a pang of anguish, but then he saw something flying toward him from one side and realized he'd been struck in the back. He ducked and covered his head with his arms. A small stone skimmed past his elbow.

"Get out!" he heard someone shout.

He turned to see that several villagers had emerged from their houses and begun pelting the sleeping pilgrims with pebbles.

"You're nothing but trouble!"

"Get out of our village!"

"Scram, you damn freaks!"

A shower of invective accompanied the flying stones. Worn out from the attack and deprived of sleep by lingering fear, the throwers' eyes were bloodshot and baggy.

Startled awake by the hail of pebbles, the pilgrims jumped to their feet. The man in the string outfit began running in circles, shouting at the top of his lungs. The horned woman shielded the headwoman's baby with her arms as she tried to take cover behind the others. The old man scrambled to catch his red rabbit, crouching low beneath the barrage. The others searched frantically for an escape, but they were quickly surrounded as more villagers gathered to see what the clamour was about.

"Stop!" shouted Granny Uba through her headscarf. "There's nothing to be gained by throwing stones at us!"

"You brought the calamity with you!" came an angry cry in return.

"Beat it! Get outta here!"

"And don't ever come back!"

The stone throwers kept up the attack. Their fury spread to the bleary-eyed newcomers, and the volleys grew thicker. The night before, these people seemed to accept their misfortune with resignation, as if it had been an act of nature, but their suppressed anger was now bursting to the surface, and the strangers in their midst became the easy target. Yet not one of them had the courage to come near. Somehow, Granny Uba and her strange retinue still intimidated them.

"It had nothing to do with us!" shouted Rentarō as he picked up a stone and hurled it back. "It was the ape-men you should've told to get out! Instead you just ran around like chickens! Did you finally find your balls this morning?"

The villagers bared their teeth and sent a volley of pebbles in his direction. He took hits on his head, shoulder, and thigh as he curled into a ball trying to avoid them.

Granny Uba called to her carter that it was time to leave. He raced to get the cart from in front of the headwoman's house. Wasting no time, she climbed aboard and ordered the little flutist to play.

Teedle-eedle-ee. He blew into his metal pipe. *Pang pang pa-pang.* The one-armed woman beat her cymbal. As if a vengeful spirit had been exorcized by a priest, the hail of stones began to taper off.

"Move out!" Granny Uba cried, lifting her staff to point toward Mandala Road.

The carter stepped forward. The pilgrims fell in behind. The man in the string shirt began to dance. The others quickly followed suit, twisting and turning their limbs about. This seemed to reawaken the villagers' former deference: they fell back to open the way.

Walking with the pilgrims, Rentarō looked into each of the villagers' faces as he passed. He saw in their expressions a mixture of bewilderment, loathing, and fear. His eyes fell on the headwoman. A tangle of hair framed her face like the flames behind the head of a demon sculpture. Her arms and legs were black with dirt, and her whole body seemed to droop with fatigue. Like every other villager, there was hatred in her gaze. When their eyes met, she gave no indication that she recognized him; she simply stood there with her lower lip thrust out, eager for the group to be gone.

In the pale orange light of the morning sun, the pilgrims descended the gentle slope to the river. The grass along the narrow lane sparkled with dew. Birds hiding in the wayside grass flew up into nearby trees, startled by the flute and cymbal and rumbling cart. The music and dancing became more spirited as the procession moved away from the village. Soon the androgynous youth added his clear voice to the concert. The panic and confusion that had gripped the group only a short time before quickly melted away.

The horned woman was humouring the baby by bouncing it in her arms as she walked. Stepping along beside her, Rentarō asked, "Do things like this happen often?"

"Like what?" she asked, giving the baby a smile.

"Like getting blamed for that attack and being driven away."

She blinked several times and looked blank for a moment. Then her eyes drifted dreamily toward the bump on her head. "Oh, yeah," she said. "There was a ruckus, wasn't there?"

"Had you forgotten about last night already?" Rentarō felt a flutter in the pit of his stomach.

She inclined her head. "No, I haven't forgotten. It's just a little fuzzy is all." She looked down at the baby and gave it another big smile.

Rentarō turned to look back the way they had come. The villagers were re-entering their homes or heading off into the nearby woods. In the end, both they and the pilgrims would no doubt forget everything that had taken place. They would simply go back to doing the things they knew in their bones – for the villagers, working the fields, eating, and copulating; for the pilgrims, travelling along Mandala Road. Then an ominous thought came to him, and he quickened his step to overtake those ahead of him so he could catch up with the wooden cart.

"Granny Uba!" he called out, as he neared the cart from behind. The heap of rags shifted, and the two wrinkled eyes peering from within it turned in his direction. "Would you mind telling me how long you've been on this pilgrimage?"

"I don't know that I can say," she answered.

"Could it be," Rentarō said, swallowing hard before forcing the next words out, "that it's been going on and on without end? And so you've simply lost all track of when it began?"

She said nothing. After clattering across the bridge, the cart started up the other side. The slope slowed the carter's steps. Rentarō kept pace at the back as he spoke again.

"You don't actually ever find Yakushi, do you?"

"Yakushi is here," she declared forcefully. "He is somewhere along this road. If we keep walking, we will find him."

"Have you ever found him before?"

This time there was no answer. They came up to the road. Lifting her staff, Granny Uba pointed toward Yakushidake. The carter turned that way. A short distance ahead, the road wound back into a dim green tunnel through the forest.

"You've never seen Yakushi, have you?" he persisted, his voice rising to a shout as he moved abreast of the cart. Startled by his sudden outburst, the little flute player scampering along beside the giant carter turned to stare up at Rentarō.

Granny Uba finally broke her silence. "We each bring our own calamity onto Mandala Road. If we just keep walking, we will someday find the Healer."

"*I* don't bring calamity."

The heap of rags jiggled as if with laughter. "Don't you think your joining us shows that you do?"

"That was only an accident. I had no choice."

"I wonder."

There was a distinct note of mockery in her voice.

44

Something cold touched Asafumi's face. A hand gently slapping his cheek. He brushed it aside with a little moan. He wasn't ready to wake up. His entire body throbbed with pain. He turned over to go back to sleep, but then began to wonder whose hand it could be.

He opened his eyes. A gaunt-faced boy was peering at him. It was the boy he and Kesumba had found hiding in his burrow the day before. His heart sank to realize that he was still in the ruined city.

"Did you catch anything?" he asked from where he lay.

The boy nodded. "But I already ate it," he quickly added.

Asafumi's heart sank again. He pulled himself upright and saw that the sun was already climbing high. The rocks on the riverbed were beginning to get warm. Against the bright blue sky beyond, the shimmering air over the vast expanse of rubble suggested the rest of the city was also heating up.

Asafumi looked himself over. A large, swollen, black-and-blue mark had appeared on his side, and he had a number of smaller bruises and scrapes on his legs. Seeing how banged up he was reminded him of the old geezer telling him he was a prime example of the shrivelling disease. But perhaps because of the bright new day, the sense of despair he'd felt the night before did not return. If *he* had that sickness, then what about the others – his friends, his colleagues at work? Weren't they all pretty much the same? Everybody must have the disease. No, the violent old man was the one who had something wrong with him.

Once he thought of it this way, he immediately felt better. He turned to the boy hugging his knees on the ground next to him.

"You came to wake me up?"

"Uh-huh. The girl you were with went to look for food with that weird dog. She told me to come find you."

Asafumi took a dip in the river to clean himself and let the cool water soothe his wounds. Watching him from the bank with his sunken eyes, the boy looked so skinny he might almost have been mummified. Maybe the shrivelling disease was really just another name for starvation. That graffiti had probably been written by somebody who'd run out of food and knew he was going to die. Asafumi decided the old man had been full of hot air the night before.

"Did you see an old guy, too?" he asked as he wrung the water from his hand towel and wiped himself dry.

The boy squeezed his brow for a moment before saying, "A baldie?"

"Uh-huh."

"He tried to steal my fish," the boy said with obvious indignation, "so the dog chased him off."

Kesumba had apparently sicked Kekah on him again. Asafumi smiled as he pictured the old man trying to flee with the two-headed dog nipping at his heels.

Refreshed both in body and in spirit by his dip, he followed the boy back toward his burrow. Getting his first view of the riverbed in the full light of day, he could see that it was strewn not only with rocks and driftwood but also with disintegrating chunks of concrete, metal and plastic debris of every kind, and even a few rusted-out shells of old cars. Bones were scattered everywhere – many of them recognizably from humans. As he watched the skinny boy picking his way through this landscape ahead of him, Asafumi thought of the hungry ghosts in children's limbo, wandering about the Riverbed of Sai.

"What's your name?" he asked him.

The boy swung around. "Um... well," he hesitated, and then asked, "What's yours?"

"Asafumi."

The boy repeated the name slowly to himself once before starting to smile. "Then I'm Ami."

"You just now made that up," Asafumi said with a chuckle.

The boy nodded a little dispiritedly. "The truth is, I've forgotten."

Asafumi considered the possibility that he hadn't forgotten – that he'd actually had no name to begin with. He wasn't sure names went with the people who lived in these ruins.

Names were a product of civilization. But civilization appeared to have completely broken down here. The people had gone back to being animals. Everything civilization once gave them was now forgotten, and they had reverted to a world in which names weren't known.

He suddenly wondered who had given Kesumba and her dog their names. But if he were to put the question to her, he thought she would probably say she didn't know.

They reached the boy's burrow. The charred remains of last night's fire lay nearby. Seeing that Kesumba had not yet returned, the boy said, "I'll start getting some things ready for when we leave," and wriggled through the entrance hole.

Asafumi heard him rustling around inside. But then as he sat down beside the burned-out fire, he heard a shrill cry. Leaping back to his feet, he reached the entrance just as a dark head began to emerge. It was the boy. His skull was bashed in and yellowish brain matter oozed from the cracks. One whole side of his face was covered in blood, as if it had been doused with red paint. The boy's body slid slowly out behind his head like a turd being squeezed from someone's bowels. Frozen in shock, Asafumi watched the skeletal torso come fully into view, followed by his legs and feet.

Then a bald pate appeared. It was the old man from yesterday. In his hand was his iron bar, moist with blood. He rose onto his hands and knees and gave Asafumi a triumphant smile.

"You killed a child?"

It came out as a quivery whimper rather than a shout. The man ignored him. Using his weapon to haul himself upright, he promptly reached for the boy's limp arm and yanked it off the ground. When the torso lifted, too, the mouth fell open and released a trickle of blood. As the man began dragging the body away, Asafumi finally spoke again.

"Let go."

His voice was a little sturdier this time. The man turned to look at him as if he must be mad.

"You think I'd give up the grub I bagged?" he said, before resuming his steps.

Asafumi looked around and found a scrap of rusty metal nearby. As soon as he picked it up, the old man released his grip on the boy's arm. The lifeless body dropped to the ground with a thud. Lifting his club like a sword in front of him, he turned to face Asafumi.

"Finally ready to fight, after a good night's sleep?" he taunted.

The faintheartedness of the night before started to come back, but before it could take hold of him, he lunged forward.

Metal crunched on metal, and the rusty fragment Asafumi had picked up instantly fell to pieces. The old man swung his club again. It whipped past his ear, almost grazing his cheek as he arched his back to dodge it. The weapon came at him again before he could regain his balance, and this time he toppled to the ground. He grabbed the first rock he could lay his hands on and hurled it at the man. It struck him in the head, and while he was still trying to recover, Asafumi charged. His loincloth went flying, but that hardly mattered now. The old man crashed to the ground, and the iron bar slipped out of his hand. Asafumi pounced on him.

His opponent coiled up and bit him in the side with what few teeth he had left. Pain shot through him. He grabbed another rock and smashed it into his head. The rock hit home with a hard, dull *thunk*, but the man's jaws kept their hold on him. He could feel the teeth moving in his side, as if chewing on a piece of meat. The bastard was going to eat him alive, Asafumi thought in a panic. He brought the rock down again, and then again. Each repeated blow brought the same blunt sound to his ears. The old man screamed. Asafumi did not stop. He was in a frenzy. The bastard was going to eat him! He was going to eat him alive! But as he continued hammering at his skull, the terror in him became mixed with the exhilarating thrill of bone giving way to stone and sinking into the softness beneath. With brain matter beginning to fly, he went on pounding like a child gleefully splattering mud.

By the time Asafumi came back to his senses, the old man's head lay in front of him like a crushed watermelon. The brow had caved in, and the bald pate had been reduced to a bloody pulp. With his chest heaving, Asafumi tossed the rock aside. He unstraddled the old man and prodded his motionless body. A momentary spasm crossed the man's lips, and his eyelids twitched like tiny ripples in a pool of blood. Then he stopped moving.

Hearing a familiar bark behind him, Asafumi turned to see Kesumba and Kekah walking toward him across the river rocks. She had a bundle of greens in her hand. Seeing immediately that something was wrong, she broke into a run. He was still on his knees beside the old man's corpse when she reached him.

"The guy... he... the kid..."

He rose to his feet and tried to explain, but it was as if his tongue had seized up; he could barely even form words. The fear and excitement that had driven his frenzy still whipped about inside him, like the tailing winds of a violent storm.

Kesumba reached up and put her hand to his lips as if to say she understood. Her fingers smelled of the plants they'd been holding. The hem of her dress brushed against his exposed penis and he realized for the first time that it was erect, arching upward, as if he'd been in the midst of heated lovemaking. She gave it a playful poke. Together with an explosion of pleasure came a powerful impulse. The winds blustering inside him broke to the surface again. He grabbed her by the shoulders and shoved her to the ground. Lifting her dress, he exposed the thin tufts of hair beginning to cover her mound. Her crack beckoned.

Wedging himself between her legs, he gripped his penis and pushed his way in. He was met by a softness like that of the old man's skull yielding to the stone. A cruel excitement radiated through him. He pinned her shoulders to the ground and thrust himself deep inside.

"Kekah!" cried Kesumba.

With a snarl, the dog leapt at him, and he felt a sharp pain in his shoulder. He pulled away and rolled onto the ground. The dog was instantly on top of him, aiming his fangs at his throat. He struggled to push the muzzle away, but the dog sank his other set of teeth into that arm. He let out a scream.

"Off, Kekah! Off! That's enough!"

At Kesumba's command, the dog backed off, leaving deep bite marks in Asafumi's shoulder and arm, with blood coming from them both. He clutched the arm as he pulled himself upright. He was in a daze. Kesumba eyed him with a hand resting on one of Kekah's heads. He looked from her to the old man's battered head, and then to the boy lying lifeless beyond. His entire body went numb when he saw the boy. All that he'd done since witnessing the child's death began playing slowly back through his mind. It was as if a person he'd never known had risen from the dark recesses of himself to take possession of him.

"Forgive me," he rasped.

As his normal composure returned, the horror of what he had done sank in. He had murdered an old man and raped a little girl. He no longer knew who he was. He sat on the ground with his head clutched in his hands.

Kesumba got to her feet and walked over to the boy. She knelt down beside him and gave his body a shake. After confirming that he was indeed dead, she rose and went to check the old man for any signs of life as well. When she received no response from him either, she came back and sat down beside Asafumi. Kckah followed Kesumba around the circle, making his own inspection of the bodies, then began lapping blood from the old man's head.

"I'm not one whit different from that bastard," Asafumi moaned to himself. "I'm a murderer, too... And a rapist..."

Kesumba laid a comforting hand on his arm, stroking it gently back and forth. Her touch was soft and warm. He turned to look into her face. Beneath the dark eyes and flat nose, a sad smile hovered on her lips. When their eyes met, Kesumba quickly lowered her head and leaned her curly head against his arm. Then, like a small child stretching her arms around a gigantic stuffed toy, she wrapped her arms around him.

A surge of anguish rose from somewhere deep within him. It swelled into a great wave that pushed into every corner of his being, and almost before he knew it, he found himself sobbing without restraint.

45

Isamu was scattering his mother's remains from a branch high in the tree of the dead. Shizuka watched from below as the ashes drifted from his fingertips in the light of the setting sun. The white powder swirled like snowflakes in the wind, then slowly sifted through the garden shrubs and settled to the ground.

After first removing his shoes and socks, Isamu had scaled the tree and disappeared into the foliage with a remarkable display of agility. The soles of his feet dangling from the branch where he sat were like two restless leaves.

While the ashes fluttered down around her, Shizuka was thinking of Saya: The woman who'd come to Japan all the way from Malaya and stayed the rest of her life. The woman who wanted to return to dust in the place where she'd lived with her man. The woman who'd spent so many of her years coping with an alien language and culture. Was it all a testament to how deeply she loved Rentarō?

Yet the picture that emerged from the things Asafumi and his mother had told her was not of a woman filled with love. And if it was Saya's spirit that she'd seen in this same spot several days before, all she had sensed in her then was a deep sadness. There'd been none of the warmth you'd expect to feel from a woman in love.

So why had Saya chosen to live out her life in Japan, and why had she wanted this to be her final resting place?

When he was finished, Isamu stood motionless in the treetop for a time. Then he slowly climbed back down through the branches. On reaching the ground, he paused to look around at the trees and shrubs bordering the shaded space, almost as if he were taking stock of a strange planet on which he'd just landed.

"I remember my mother telling me that this place would turn into a forest some day... It really has."

"Was she the one who planted all these things?"

"Uh-huh," he nodded. "They're from seeds she brought with her from Malaya. My father was sure they wouldn't survive in this climate, but it looks like somehow they did."

So everything here had come from Malaya. Shizuka looked at the plantings around her in a whole new light.

"That's pretty amazing. Like your father said, you really wouldn't think tropical plants could make it here, with the climate being so different."

"No kidding," he said, kicking his feet into his running shoes and dropping to a knee to tie the laces. "Of course, if you know the difference, you can see that they haven't turned out as big, but they're doing perfectly all right. They didn't wither up and die like you might expect." He shook his head before adding, "Maybe there was some kind of magic spell she put on them."

"Magic spell?" Shizuka sounded dubious.

He nodded, his face completely straight. "Or if not that, maybe a special prayer. At any rate, her wish came true."

Standing up again, he brushed the dirt from his knees, picked up his bag, and prepared to go.

"Well then, thanks for being—"

"Can you stay for a cup of tea?" she broke in, before he could say goodbye.

He blinked, then smiled and glanced down at his watch.

"Thanks. That'd be nice."

As she led the way back to the house, Shizuka asked if there was any particular time he needed to be somewhere else. He said he planned to go straight back to Osaka.

"You're not stopping at the Nonezawas? They wouldn't be aware yet that your mother has passed away."

"That's okay," he said lightly from behind. "As she always said, so far as the Nonezawas were concerned, she was like some bad spirit they couldn't even see. She told me not to worry about telling them when she died. One day, *bang*, she appeared, and one day, *poof*, she was gone. That was good enough for them, she said."

Stepping along the damp path through the trees, Shizuka nodded to herself that news of Saya's death wasn't likely to affect the Nonezawas in the least.

"I heard something about your mother being Korean," she said.

Isamu made a sound that came out somewhere between a chuckle and a sigh. "That seems to have been her official status, yes. I found out about it when she came to live with me in Osaka – when I helped her file for a public pension. She told me her name was Kim Suk-hwa and she was Korean. I sent for a copy of her family registry, and sure enough, that's what it said."

"How in the world could that be?"

"That's what I wanted to know, but she just clammed up. All she would say is that she'd become Kim Suk-hwa, and that's the way it was."

The more Shizuka learned about the woman, the more of an enigma she became. What could she have been thinking and feeling as she made Japan her home for all those years?

They passed through the part of the garden where the trees were shedding their leaves and arrived at the house. Stepping into the room from the veranda, Isamu stopped short with his thick lips poised as if to whistle at the sight of the sound system, new carpet, and modern kitchen.

"This feels kind of weird," he said. He sat down at the low table. She saw his shoulders relax.

Shizuka went to put on the kettle. "I suppose it does" she said from the kitchen. "Since it's the house you grew up in."

"Yes, all the way through high school," he replied. "Then I got a job and moved to Osaka."

As she looked for something to serve with the tea, Shizuka wondered what the man did for a living, but she was reluctant to ask too many questions. Isamu gazed about the room curiously without saying anything.

She stood by the curtain between the kitchen and the sitting room while she waited for the water to boil. "Does it make you feel a bit sad to find someone else living in the house where you grew up?"

He seemed surprised by the question. "Oh, no, not at all," he said. He was probably only being polite, she thought, but then he added, "Since I got dragged around to a lot of different places when I was little, I can't say I became all that attached."

"Oh. I assumed you were born here."

"No, I was born in Malaya. My mother brought me to Japan when I was seven."

The kettle began hissing as the water neared a boil. Shizuka stepped back into the kitchen and poured the hot water into the teapot. She put some rice crackers given her by Miharu's family on a plate and took them in with the tea.

"Then coming to Japan must have been quite an adjustment."

"You can say that again. It was pretty tough at first. I didn't know much Japanese, and the other kids called me a barbarian, and said my mom was a kept woman. But probably the hardest part was being hungry all the time. We came right after the war when there were shortages of everything, and you couldn't find food anywhere."

If he was seven around the time the war ended, it meant he'd be nearing sixty now. But his sturdy build and easygoing manner made him seem much younger.

"Where were you in Malaya?"

"Kota Bharu. I was too young then to really remember much, but I do remember how scared I was of the Japanese soldiers. They came and took my mother away once, and she was gone a long time. When I asked her afterwards, she said they accused her of being some kind of spy. Anyway, they turned the whole place upside down when they came, and even today I sometimes have dreams about people forcing their way into my house in the middle of the night and busting up the furniture and stuff."

Shizuka thought of Ohara. Soldiers like him had fanned out all across Asia. There was no reason to think Malaya had been spared the atrocities he described. If Saya had been detained by the Japanese, it seemed doubtful that she escaped unscathed.

She placed a cup of tea in front of him. "Didn't that make you pretty embittered toward those soldiers?"

He took a sip and tilted his head, thinking. "Being only a kid, I was basically just frightened and didn't know enough to be bitter. But my mother was bitter all right. She hated them with a passion."

"But your father was Japanese too, and she apparently loved him enough to follow him all the way back to Japan. You'd think her hatred of the other people might get in the way of that."

"I've never quite been able to understand that either," he said, rocking back and forth in his seat like a tumbler doll. "I might only have been a kid, but there were times when I thought my mom must actually hate my dad. Except there also seemed to be more to it than that. I suppose there was an element of what you call a love-hate relationship. I remember the year I started school. I was eight by then, so they put me in second grade even though it was my first year. Anyway, a little bit after school started in the spring, my dad left on a sales trip. That's when I'd say the love-hate thing was the strongest. Of course, I was too young to think of it that way at the time; it wasn't until I grew up that I realized something like that must have been going on."

Shizuka waited for him to continue. He sat gazing at the trees with their thinning leaves outside the glass doors to the veranda. The pale blue sky showed through the branches here and there. His chunky hand moved across his thigh in a probing way.

"Every day when I got back from school, it was like coming home to a completely different person," he said after several moments, as if he'd finally fixed on the point from which to unravel his memory. "One day she'd be so prickly I knew I'd better stay out of her way, and the next she'd be waiting at the gate to hug me tight the minute I got home... She'd light into me for forgetting my father already, and then in practically the next breath she'd say, 'You poor thing, you must really miss him', and all of a sudden she'd be in tears. It was like there was some kind of storm raging inside her."

Shizuka thought of the figure she had seen circling the tree of the dead. Could that have been Saya at around the time Isamu just described? *Did you get his heart?... Or did you get a sword?* Were those questions expressing her own torment?

But imagining Saya's anguish was something Shizuka could do only in the abstract. She herself had never experienced such an intermingling of love and hate. She'd never been in that emotional place where you could hate the person you loved.

Or had she? Suddenly she wasn't so sure. If she dug down to the bottom of her frustration with Asafumi, mightn't she find hatred lurking there? Maybe she'd been too quick to dismiss the friction between them as a normal part of any relationship. A latent hatred could explain the speed with which she'd turned to thoughts of widowhood and going back to Yokohama, virtually as soon as she realized Asafumi might be missing. Hadn't she in fact been breathing easier with him gone? Somewhere deep down, wasn't she actually hoping that the yoke of her marriage might disappear?

Shizuka felt stunned. Was it really possible that she hated her husband? Did she bear him a grudge for binding her to a future in remote Toyama?

"Then something changed."

Isamu's voice broke through her thoughts, drawing her back to what he'd been saying about his mother.

"Do you know why?" she asked.

"I don't have a clue," he said with a frown. "I only knew something was different... Pretty soon, my dad came home, and there was a whole new feeling around the house – warmer, more relaxed. Until then there'd always been this tension, stretched tight as can be, but it was like that tension had snapped and gone away... It was strange. That trip to Tateyama was definitely some kind of watershed."

Shizuka's heart skipped a beat at the word Tateyama.

"Your dad's trip was to Tateyama?"

When he confirmed that it was, she quickly got up to go into the next room. Against the wall stood a desk with a computer, and on it was the sales register she had brought back from Ohara's house. She picked it up and took it back to Isamu.

"Do you recognize this?"

"Wow," he said, sliding his fingers across it as though across a long-lost treasure. "It's one of the notebooks he used to take on his trips." The writing on the cover caught his eye. "1947?"

"Yes. If you take a look, you'll see lots of Tateyama place names listed inside. It seems to be from when your father was first trying to develop a new route out that way."

He opened the book and made a face at the twisty, stylized handwriting.

"My husband set out to retrace your father's footsteps as shown in that book," she went on. "But now... he's gone missing."

When she heard herself say "gone missing", the words suddenly seemed to hit home in a way they hadn't done before. It was as if something she'd only seen displayed on a computer screen until then had leapt out and thumped her in the chest. She became choked with emotion and couldn't go on.

"Gone missing?" Isamu asked with concern.

Pressing her fingers to her mouth, Shizuka simply nodded. She wondered why she should become so emotional all of a sudden. The moment she'd realized she might hate Asafumi, his disappearance had hit her with new force. It seemed utterly illogical, but she didn't have the energy to analyze it.

The telephone in the corner of the room began to ring, its soft chime sounding almost apologetic for the interruption. It rang again and again but Shizuka didn't move.

"Are you going to get the phone?" Isamu asked hesitantly.

She finally stood up and went to answer it. "Hello?"

"Shizuka!" came Miharu's agitated voice. "Mr. Takatomi called just now to say that Mr. Ohara died this morning. From a sudden brain haemorrhage or something. Which got me thinking, what if he hit his head when he fell into the fire? Do you suppose we could be held responsible?"

Shizuka was thunderstruck. She was the one who'd pushed him.

"Dad's heading to the hospital to find out exactly what happened. But I can't go with him because this is parent–teacher day at my kids' school."

"I'll go right away too," Shizuka promptly said. If it was something she had done, she couldn't very well leave it all to Yoshitaka.

"Right, I think that's a good idea. Do you know how to get there? If you're going by car—"

"I don't like to drive, so I'll take the train."

Miharu told her where she needed to get off and reminded her of the name of the hospital, then said she would call her father to let him know and hung up.

"Is something wrong?" Isamu asked, having heard the alarm in Shizuka's voice.

She did her best to smile. "The man we thought might know what happened to my husband died. He fell into the fire when I..."

Unable to keep her composure, she sank to the floor. When she managed to speak again, the words caught in her throat.

"It... It might be my fault..."

46

With Kesumba's help, Asafumi dragged the two bodies into the boy's burrow and sealed off the entrance with stones. No matter how desperate he might become, he couldn't imagine ever eating human flesh. The thought still repelled him, even after discovering that he was capable of behaving just as brutally as the old man. Yet there was no telling what he might do if things got really bad. Nothing said for sure that he wouldn't come back here, push the stones aside, and feed on the decaying meat.

He didn't know who he was anymore. He'd always thought of himself as a pretty level-headed guy – reasonably well-adjusted, with a strong sense of morality. But he'd begun to see this as only an outer shell, concealing an entirely different person inside. Still, he was reluctant to admit that he was made from the same mould as the old man. Maybe they had some things in common, but surely they weren't altogether alike. If only to sustain this belief, he was determined not to eat human flesh.

Kesumba picked up the old man's drawstring bag and tied it to her waist. Then, as if she'd completely forgotten about what happened earlier, she turned to Asafumi with a sweet smile and said, "Let's go back to Mandala Road."

He let out a long breath and gazed across the river at the mountains stretching off toward Yakushidake. He asked himself what going back there really meant. Presumably it would mean joining the pilgrims in their endless search for Yakushi, the Healing Buddha. And before long, just like Kesumba and the people in these ruins, he would forget all about killing the old man.

"I don't think so," he finally said. "I think I'll head on home."

Kesumba looked at him as if she didn't understand. He pointed downstream.

"If I follow the river that way, it'll take me to my house. That's where I'm going." He laid his hands on Kesumba's small shoulders. "Thank you," he said, and he meant it from the bottom of his heart. It had come as some surprise just how great a comfort she had been to him – even though she knew hardly anything to speak of besides her own name and that of her dog. Perhaps what a person knew wasn't really important in the end. After thinking all this time that he knew so much, he'd discovered that he didn't even know himself.

"Goodbye," he said, gently patting her shoulders, then turned to begin his trek down the river.

A moment later he heard a gentle clacking of rocks behind him and looked over his shoulder. Kesumba and Kekah were following.

"I thought you were going back to Mandala Road."

She shook her head as she came abreast. The dog was several steps back, sniffing at the ground with his two snouts.

"I want to go with you."

"Why?"

"I don't know."

"Haven't you seen enough of the city? It's only going to be more of the same."

Kesumba squinted at the river and the wasteland spreading out beside it. The sun had climbed high in the sky, and the stones on the riverbed were hot.

"Then why are you going?" she asked.

"Because..." Asafumi started, but immediately trailed off.

He didn't really think anymore that he would find his grandfather's house still standing. But he wanted to go back to where it had been. It probably came from a desire to return to his former self – to what he had been before losing his way on Mandala Road and killing someone; to what he had been when he didn't think he was that kind of person; to what he had been when he and Shizuka lived their easy life together. And suddenly he was thinking of his wife: the woman who could be such a thorn in his side, and so stubborn, yet whose prickliness, like that of a thistle, was part of her charm; the woman with whom he'd so often chatted and laughed for hours on end.

"I want to find the woman I love."

Kesumba was silent for a time before asking, "What's love?"

Asafumi stared out across the ruins. How could he explain love in a place where nobody had a family anymore, it was everybody for himself, and men hunted other men for food?

"You probably feel like you always want to be with Kekah, right?"

"Sure."

"Well, that's what love is. It means you love Kekah."

She pushed out her lips in a pout as she thought about this for a moment.

"If you always want to be with her, why aren't you with her now?"

His heart lurched. He had set out on this trip by himself precisely because he wanted to get away from Shizuka for a while. He'd become fed up with her being so irritable lately.

He had always thought he loved her. But if he didn't even know himself, then how could he say he loved someone else? He realized he couldn't be sure that he'd ever loved her at all.

It wasn't true, then, that he wanted to find the woman he loved. He was looking for something else altogether.

"I retract what I just said." The expression on Kesumba's face suggested that she didn't know what "retract" meant, but he didn't pause. "What I actually loved was the life I had. Listening to my music, going about my usual routines, avoiding any major disruptions. I loved that placid existence. But when I think about it now, I'm not so sure I loved even that. More likely, the belief that I loved it let me turn a blind eye to other things, and in actual fact I didn't love anything at all. That's why I always filled my ears with music."

Once he began putting into words what was in his head, one thought after another came bubbling out like a spring. Walking beside him, Kesumba listened without saying anything.

"I was born in a town near the mouth of this river. It was just my parents, my older brother, and me. We had a family business selling medicine, like so many other families in town. One thing different about us, though, was that my grandfather lived separately, in another house. As far as everybody else in the family was concerned, the woman he lived with didn't exist. I couldn't understand that. My grandfather was kind of in and out – sort of there and sort of not there. But the woman who lived with him was definitely there – it was just that everybody pretended she wasn't. Which made her like a ghost. When I went to visit my grandfather, there she was. But once I went home, she didn't exist. My family only ever asked how Grandpa was doing. Nobody wanted to know about her. Her name was Saya."

Kesumba repeated the name. "Saya."

"That's right, Saya. But the name belonged to a ghost. Nobody ever spoke it aloud. After my grandfather died, Saya disappeared.

Now she really *was* a ghost. All trace of her vanished from my world. I think I loved my grandfather. And I might have loved Saya, too. At any rate, one day these two people disappeared from my life, as if they'd gone up in a puff of smoke. That was when it began. After that, I always had to have music in my ears."

The sound of the river accompanied them as they walked, the stones on the bank clattering faintly beneath their feet. Asafumi gazed across the barren landscape, and at the clear blue sky above.

"I became a quiet boy. I studied hard while listening to music and never missed a day of school. My whole life since then has been inside a cocoon of music. Everything flows by like the tunes that play in my ears and leave nothing behind when they're over. Kind of like walking through these ruins – just the same empty waste no matter how far you go..."

A surge of memories from his grandfather's house washed over him. As a boy, it had been a place of enchantment. On the one hand there were the marvellous stories his senile grandfather repeated over and over; on the other there was the comfort that came from Saya's quiet serenity. The mingling of the two created a very special place. Asafumi invariably returned from his grandfather's house feeling as though he'd been visiting another world. But then one day that world had been denied him. He was told it no longer existed. To him, this was the same as being told it had never existed to begin with. And at that point, the life he'd imagined for himself also ceased to exist.

From that day on, he became the model son his parents wanted him to be. A son who did not run off to strange lands like Malaya or the Himalayas to take up with exotic women as his grandfather had done. A son who made his way through high school and college with honours and landed a plum position with a good company. A son who may have moved in with his girlfriend without the benefit of marriage, but who in the end did the right thing and made it official to spare his parents from embarrassment.

Ever since losing his grandfather, he'd merely been playing a role. He hadn't been living *his* life. It wasn't the life that the bright-eyed boy who listened to Rentarō's stories was supposed to live.

What he was now returning to that house to find was the person he'd left behind there all those years before.

47

Black kites whistled as they circled overhead. The pilgrims moved sluggishly along Mandala Road. There'd been mountain streams they could drink from along the way, but with nothing solid to eat all day, everybody's steps had grown heavy. The road had narrowed and steepened in the course of the day, and the broken asphalt had given way to a stony trail choked with weeds. All that distinguished it from the rest of the forest was the absence of trees growing there. The dwarf no longer played his flute and the one-armed woman's cymbal remained silent. The singing and dancing had long since broken off. They walked through the dim green tunnel like a lost army of the dead.

Just when Rentarō began to think he could walk no further, the path grew brighter, and soon they came out into the open where a section of slope had been cleared. Three crudely built huts stood among several small farm plots. Granny Uba directed the carter toward them with her staff. The anticipation of soon having something to eat brought renewed life to the group. The little man began playing his flute, and the one-armed woman resumed her beat. The man in the string shirt launched into a dance, which prompted the others to begin shaking their arms and legs about as well. But there was little strength in their movements, and they looked like marionettes jerking clumsily in time with the plodding steps of the carter.

The procession moved up a path that forked off toward the huts. The harvest from the fields had mostly been taken in, but there were still a few plants growing here and there. Behind the huts were some fruit trees, with chickens rooting about for bugs beneath them. There were no people in sight.

Granny Uba ordered her carter to halt in front of the first dwelling.

"Pilgrims to Yakushi!" she called out.

Nobody appeared from inside.

When several more attempts were still greeted by silence, she leaned on her staff and heaved herself down from the cart.

There were ample signs that the place was inhabited, but an ominous stillness hung in the air.

Granny Uba started for the hut, where a mat of woven thatch hung like a curtain in the doorway. The pilgrims shuffled after her as if they belonged to the train of rags she dragged behind her. She pushed the mat aside.

Rentarō was close by, peering over her shoulder. A foul odour came from the darkness within. He was immediately reminded of walking through bombed-out Osaka amidst the stench of bodies decaying in the heat of the summer sun. This was that same smell. The movement of the hanging mat had also set off a disturbance, and he realized it was the buzz of flies taking to the air. He followed Granny Uba as she took a step inside.

Wooden bowls and chunks of firewood were strewn about a dirt floor carpeted with cut grass. In the middle of the room was a pit containing the blackened remains of a cooking fire, around which lay three bodies. Granny Uba prodded them with her staff, then said, "They are dead." The pilgrims craning their necks at the door fell back. She retraced her steps outside and moved toward the second hut.

"Somebody check the other one," she said.

Rentarō and the androgynous youth veered off toward the third structure. Neither of them said a word. They could all feel the thickness of death in the air now, and no one felt like talking.

Here they found the thatch curtain in a heap on the ground. Inside, a man who was no more than skin and bones was propped against the wall with his mouth hanging open, dead. He sat in a thick, foul-smelling puddle of body fluids and faeces. Next to him lay another body, face down but obviously a woman, with one hand resting on the man's thigh. Rentarō gave her up as dead as well, until he felt something on his foot that made him jump. She had reached out with her other hand to touch his ankle.

"This one's alive," he called to the youth, who was bent over two small figures in the far corner.

"These two kids are still breathing too," he said, "though just barely."

Rentarō turned the woman over and studied her face in the dim light from the doorway. It was puffed up like spongy soil and covered all over with purple-blue spots. A pestilence, he thought, and jerked his hands away. The woman groaned as her head thumped on the ground.

"Water..." she said weakly. "Water..."

"Sure," he said, instinctively wanting to help. "I'll get you some in a minute."

He moved across the room for a look at the two children. They lay naked in each other's arms, their bodies peppered with the same purple-blue spots, barely breathing. Sitting flat on the ground beside them, the youth was stroking their cheeks.

"Better not touch," Rentarō warned. "Whatever it is, you can be pretty sure it's contagious." The youth seemed not to understand, so he explained, "You could catch their sickness."

"It's more of the calamity," he said, and withdrew his hand.

Rentarō didn't know what the disease might be, but it appeared to have struck the residents of the village all at once, so he had to assume it was highly infectious. The youth rose and left the hut as if he'd suddenly lost all interest. Rentarō picked up a wooden bowl he found lying on the floor and followed him out to look for water. Granny Uba was emerging from the second hut with several of the other pilgrims.

"Three in here are still breathing," he called out.

"Just one in here," rasped the woman who was bent nearly double at the waist.

"All the rest are dead as doornails," said the man in the string outfit as if he somehow thought it was funny.

The youth, who had stepped into the second hut as the others came out, re-emerged saying, "It's the calamity."

The others nodded in agreement. The man with the red rabbit seemed especially worked up. "It's the calamity, it's the calamity!" he cried.

Rentarō turned his back on the rising clamour to go in search of water. Behind the huts he found a cistern fed by a mountain stream. Filling his bowl, he returned to the third hut and held it out for the woman to drink. She hardly had the strength to swallow. Most of the water spilled from the corners of her mouth, but she did manage to wet her tongue and throat before slumping back with a heavy gasp.

He went to fill the bowl again for the two children. Like the woman, they were only able to get a few drops down. All three of them had become extremely weak.

Rentarō thought of the medicines he'd left behind – and the help he might have been able to offer if he had them with him. Frustrated, yet wanting to do as much as he could, he fetched another bowl of water and took it to the hut with the other survivor. The stench here was almost unbearable. There were four dead bodies, and the one man who was still breathing lay on his back some distance away. He drank greedily when Rentarō held the water to his mouth, but then immediately brought it back up.

"Don't... eat me," he forced out in a barely audible voice. "Will... suffer... calamity."

"I know," Rentarō said. That was probably how the disease had spread. The people ate the flesh of its victims. It was only a matter of time before the rest of the survivors died. With a sense of complete helplessness, he turned to go.

Back out in the open, he was greeted by the sound of gleeful whoops. Pilgrims were scattered about the fields, helping themselves to whatever they could find, straight out of the ground. In the orchard behind the huts the sound of trees being shaken was mixed with the frantic squawks of fleeing chickens. There was a new mood of merriment in the air, as if they were all getting ready for a celebration. The few surviving members of the community were dying inside the huts, yet the pilgrims could think only of stealing the last of their food.

Flushed with anger, Rentarō ran over to Granny Uba, who was calmly observing the scene from the shade of a tree.

"What kind of pilgrims are you?" he demanded. "You go from village to village begging for food, and if there's nobody to stop you, you just take whatever you want? Is that what your pilgrimage is all about?"

The head bound in rags rotated in his direction. "A Yakushi pilgrim is calamity itself. That's why we are on Mandala Road."

"And being calamity means you can do anything you please?"

She moved her head ever so slightly. "There are no cans or cannots to calamity. It simply makes its way on. It makes its way on along Mandala Road."

"What *is* Mandala Road anyway?" he asked, thinking of all the strange things that had happened to him since setting foot on it.

He was not actually expecting an answer, but her response came immediately, in the flat drone of a mantra:

"A road that goes on forever until the day you find Yakushi."

48

It was a lovely tin box, painted in lavender. Clusters of colourful flowers decorated the rectangular lid, with green vines framing the edges. Saya slid her fingers across its top, feeling the smoothness of the metal.

"Open it," said her visitor, sitting on the edge of the veranda.

It was the woman who had stopped to talk to her at the river ten days before. She'd somehow managed to find out where Saya lived and dropped in, introducing herself as Tami Takabe. A red ribbon was tied in her freshly permed hair, accenting the showy red-on-white floral print she wore. She'd brought the pretty tin as a gift.

A sweet smell rose into the air as Saya raised the lid. It was a box of cookies, with each of them wrapped in a thin paper sleeve. She hadn't had anything like this to eat in a very long time. Merely imagining the crunchy sweetness made her mouth water.

"How you get this?"

Ration distributions never included things like this. Maybe they were available in Toyama, but even then they had to be terribly expensive.

A proud smile spread across Tami's painted lips. "My sweet darling gave them to me," she said.

Saya thought Darling must be somebody's name. Certainly somebody wealthy. Whatever your reasons, you didn't give expensive things like this unless you had a lot of money.

"I've been taking that medicine like you said," Tami bubbled happily, "and the pain in my stomach's a whole lot better now. It's really working wonders."

Saya put the lid back on the tin, thinking how excited Isamu was going to be. If she kept it open any longer, she wasn't sure she'd be able to resist taking a nibble right away.

Up to this point, Tami had been sitting bolt upright, with her hands folded primly in her lap, but seeing that Saya seemed pleased with the cookies, she finally relaxed. Propping her hands on the floor behind her, she leaned back and let her eyes wander about the house and garden. Not that the sitting room inside the open shoji screens offered much to see. Besides the futon folded up in the corner, the only furnishings to speak of were a beat-up old folding table from the Nonezawas for eating on, and a small wooden crate turned upside down for Isamu to use as a desk for schoolwork. On this improvised desk lay two children's magazines Rentarō had brought along. Saya read them with her son whenever she had a chance, trying to learn more Japanese. A bare light bulb dangled from the ceiling in the middle of the room, and several items of clothing hung from nails on the wall.

Tami ran her eyes over these things for a minute before abruptly asking, "Is it true you're from some country down south? Why don't you go back?"

Saya didn't mind the woman's bluntness – even appreciated it. Whenever she went into town, she knew everybody she ran into was itching to ask her the same thing. But they only asked it with their eyes; nobody had the nerve to speak up. The unspoken question weighed the air down like lead and pressed in on her. It felt as if it was meant deliberately to suffocate her.

"My man live here."

Mentioning Rentarō made her heart ache. She couldn't help wondering if she would ever see him again.

"You mean the older Mr. Nonezawa. You met him when he lived down south, right?"

Tami seemed to know all about her.

"You know, I really admire you," she went on. "You followed him all the way back here to Japan. When I think about following my man back to America... I'm not sure I could ever do it." She giggled self-consciously.

Saya didn't know what to make of the compliment. This was the first time anyone in Japan had expressed approval of what she'd done.

"Your man is American?" she asked.

Tami gave her a long, hard look, as if trying to gauge how she might react. Then, fidgeting like a skittish bird when someone starts to come too near, she nodded her head.

"A GI stationed in Toyama."

When she was still at the house in Senbashi, Saya had overheard the women talking about girls who took up with occupation soldiers. They were such a disgrace, they huffed. They brought shame on all Japanese women. Now she finally understood about the cookies and the gaudy dress. This woman had become a GI's toilet hole. When the Japanese were on top in the war, they'd used Malayan and Korean women, and now that they'd lost, their own women were being used by the Americans in the same way. That was how it worked. A woman's lot was to be the victors' toilet.

As Saya's silence drew on, Tami defensively began filling in a few more details. "I'm originally from Senbashi, but I went to live with my husband's family in Toyama when I got married. Except he went off to fight right away and got himself killed, and then the house burned down in an air raid, so I'm left looking for a way to support my husband's parents after the war. The only choice I could see was to become a GI's girl."

Her story came pouring out as if she'd made these same excuses to herself countless times before.

"But people are so cruel, you know. Right away they start giving me the cold shoulder, refusing to speak to me. Even my own parents, when I take them cans of food and cigarettes and stuff, they look at me like they wish I hadn't come — though of course they never turn down the goodies I bring."

"Your American man, he is kind?"

Saya's interruption broke her train of thought, and she made a face like a squished rice cake.

"Kind?... Well sure, of course he's kind. He treats me real nice, and he buys me anything I want, and—"

"You fall in love?" Saya interrupted again, remembering the phrase Kim Suk-hwa had used.

Her cheeks turned bright red, and she grew even more flustered. "Fall in love?... I mean, that's not really the question, is it? I'm just trying to survive, you know... But he's nice, and he treats me right..."

She didn't really seem to know how she felt about him.

"He is from army that kill your husband, yes?"

The woman looked as if she'd been stung by a scorpion. She pressed her lips firmly together and said nothing.

Saya dangled her legs back and forth at the edge of the veranda. The warm May sunshine danced in the yard. She noticed a parade of ants crawling along the ground. They reminded her of Japanese troops marching through Kota Bharu. All stepping forward to the same beat; all swinging their arms at exactly same angle; all staring straight ahead with the same stern expression.

"What difference does that make?" Tami finally said. "It's the government that got us into the war, and it's their own fault for losing. Now, thanks to the Americans, the world's at peace again. We should count ourselves lucky. If my husband's going to make complaints from the grave, then he should never have let himself get killed in the first place. He should've come back alive to take care of me like he was supposed to. Instead, the others who came back don't want anything to do with me. The only person who cares anything about me is my guy. Everybody else points fingers, men and women both, but nobody's willing to lift a finger to help. If they've got a problem with America, they should speak up and complain. Instead all they do is whisper behind people's backs."

She paused and looked Saya in the eye.

"I'll do whatever it takes to survive. I'll even sleep with the enemy. What's wrong with that?"

"Nothing wrong," said Saya, thinking of the things she'd had to do for the same reason. Even with the war over, it was still a kill-or-be-killed world. "But it make you very tired, yes?"

As if a wire that had been stretched between their eyes had suddenly snapped, Tami looked away.

"That's for sure," she said. "Makes you wonder why we should have to go to such lengths just to get by, doesn't it? Men are the ones who start the wars, but all us women get dragged into picking up the pieces afterwards." She placed a hand on her stomach. "Actually, I came today because I needed to talk to you about something else."

Saya's eyes widened in surprise.

"I missed my period. I think I'm pregnant."

The expression was new to Saya, but it wasn't hard for her to guess that Tami was talking about the red flower that blossomed between a woman's legs. When it stopped coming, the woman's belly began to swell, and then a child was born. That was how Saya knew she was pregnant again, too.

"Very happy," she said, but Tami made a face and her cheeks flushed.

"Are you kidding? Do you have any idea what'll happen if I keep this baby? I already get no end of grief, but if now, on top of everything else, I have a mongrel kid, I'll have to leave town."

Saya was shocked. Among her people in Malaya, the whole tribe celebrated when somebody was going to have a baby. It didn't matter who the father was – even if he came from outside. Nobody cared about that. Any child born among them was welcomed by the others.

"So that's why I came," Tami said, lowering her voice as if afraid of being overheard, even though there was nobody else in the house. "I'm hoping you know some herbs to take care of it."

Saya frowned. "Take care of it?"

"Uh-huh, take care of it. You know, get rid of it." This time she swept her hands downward in front of her groin as she said it.

Saya was stunned to realize that the woman was talking about killing her baby. No woman in her tribe would ever think of doing that. It had certainly not been among the things the medicine man taught her.

"I not know plant for that."

Tami eyed her suspiciously. "I don't believe you," she said. "My grandmother knew something that worked. I remember her telling women in the neighbourhood what to take."

"Maybe," said Saya. "But I not know it."

Tami's plump face began to shrivel up like a mushroom. Tears welled in her eyes, and she drew a handkerchief from her purse to dab at them.

"Must not cry," Saya said in irritation. She didn't like feeling as though she'd done something mean.

"But what am I supposed to do?... If I have a mixed kid, I'll be branded for life. How am I supposed to bring up a child like that? I can barely manage for myself, so how am I supposed to manage with a mongrel in tow?"

"You say you do anything to survive."

"Sure, if it's just me, I can muddle through one way or another. But if I have a mixed kid, I'll get the cold shoulder no matter which way I turn."

This harping on mixed blood was starting to get on Saya's nerves. "My boy is mixed, too," she said.

Tami gave a start and looked up from behind her handkerchief.

"And another one I have in here now," Saya said, patting her tummy.

Tami gazed at Saya's stomach. "Then surely you understand." Clasping her handkerchief tightly in her hands, she twisted around to look her straight in the face. Between swollen lids, her little black eyes burned with emotion. "One thing about us Japanese is that there's pretty much nothing we hate more than mixed blood. Even if we lose a war, as long as our blood doesn't get mixed, we can keep pretending to ourselves that we came out on top. Mixed blood means the women slept with the enemy – that's how we see it. During the war, if you weren't patriotic enough they called you un-Japanese and treated you like a traitor, but now that the war's over, they treat you the same way just for sleeping with an American. Have a mixed baby and you're both un-Japanese. So what's the kid supposed to do when he's born in Japan but they tell him he's not Japanese? He's got nowhere to go."

"Then my boy is un-Japanese, too?"

Saya recalled how Rentarō had promised to recognize Isamu in the family registry as a child of his who was born outside his marriage. Would the boy still be told he wasn't Japanese?

"You're actually better off than me," said Tami. "Because the father is Japanese. We don't care so much if our men have babies with women from other countries. That's the same as if we won the war. But when a Japanese woman sleeps with a Yank, it has a whole different meaning. It means we lost. That's how our men think. And the whole world works according to how the men think. Talk all you want about democracy and freedom, but the way people think never changes. People like us, we're like fish trying to swim against the current."

"Fish?"

"That's right, fish. We wiggle happily about now that the war's over, but we forget that we're still in the same water. It may seem like we're free, but we're actually trapped in that same old current."

Saya listened in growing puzzlement. Until now, she'd always thought that as far as the Japanese were concerned, all foreigners were like fish – that they only saw themselves as people, and everybody else was down there in a pond. But Tami seemed to be saying that the Japanese were fish too. So all there'd ever been was fish dumping on other fish?

In her mind's eye, she pictured an underwater scene. Schools of fish are swimming about among wavy strands of seaweed. Striped fish, black fish, silver fish; long skinny fish and stubby fat fish – swaggering, cowering, fleeing, chasing, ignoring. None of them has the slightest idea that there might be another world beyond the see-through ceiling that stretches endlessly over their heads; a world where the sun shines, rain falls, and wind blows. When the rainy season arrives in the jungles of Malaya, a certain glossy-leafed tree that grows along the riverbanks drops seeds with two paper-thin wings onto the water. Her people called them "fish seeds." If you ground them up and scattered them over the water again, fish would soon come floating to the top with their bellies up. You could scoop them out as easily as picking low-hanging fruit from a tree. It never entered the fishes' minds that the seeds they saw floating overhead might have something to do with their deaths.

If people everywhere were fish, then who scattered the poison that led to their deaths? Who had scattered the poison that killed her brother Kekah? Who had scattered the poison that killed Kim Suk-hwa? Who had scattered the poison that killed Saya herself, over and over and over again, at the P-house?

Tami gave a little sigh. "Well, I guess it doesn't do me any good to spill my troubles on you," she said as she got to her feet, her handkerchief still clenched in her hand. "I'm sorry to have imposed." She picked up the purse she'd set down beside her and hooked it over her arm.

"What you do about baby?" Saya asked.

"I don't know," Tami said quietly.

The medicine man had warned them all severely to be careful never to eat the fish seeds. They would give them terrible stomach-aches, he said, and in the case of women with babies growing inside them, their babies would die. Saya knew she had some of those seeds in her drawstring bag: she was waiting for the rainy season to plant them. She considered whether to give them to Tami, but the horror of killing a child still held her back, and she said nothing.

Since she was turning the woman down, she no longer felt comfortable about accepting her gift, and she gently pushed the tin of cookies toward her. Tami quickly stopped her.

"No, no, keep them. It's all right. Your boy'll be happy," she said, motioning with her chin toward Isamu's makeshift desk. But there was a sad smile on her face.

Tami didn't really want to kill the child either, Saya realized. It was simply the only way she knew how to survive. Saya herself had killed the woman from the repatriation boat when it was the only way for her to survive, and her brother had tortured and killed Malays and Indians for exactly the same reason. The demands of survival might differ from person to person, but the end was all the same.

Tami had started to walk away when Saya called after her.

"I give you medicine," she said.

She turned in surprise.

"Medicine to kill baby," Saya added.

Tami's eyes widened and her chin began to quiver as the full weight of what she had come to ask for hit home.

49

In the morgue at the hospital in Ōyama, Manzaburō Ohara was wrapped in a white sheet, his body cold. The eyes that had flashed with fury now lay closed, but his jaw was still clenched. Shizuka studied the ashen face for several moments before pressing her palms together and lowering her head.

According to what Yoshitaka had been told, there were no signs of external trauma to the head, so the most likely cause of the brain haemorrhage was a psychological shock of some kind. But neither the attending physician nor the nurses could explain what might have disturbed a man resting in his hospital bed to that extent.

A load was lifted from Shizuka's mind when she learned that the man had probably not died as a result of the fire incident. Yoshitaka was obviously relieved as well, and as soon as he'd relayed the good news, excused himself so he could get back to the work he was doing when the call came in. Shizuka didn't feel comfortable leaving in quite such a hurry, so she asked if she could view the body and pay her respects before going.

"He must have been about the same age as my mother," Isamu said over her shoulder. The room's bare concrete walls made his deep voice boom.

When he'd seen how shaken Shizuka was after getting off the phone with Miharu, he offered to drive her to the hospital in Asafumi's car. He had been looking on from a short distance away while she paid her respects.

"I think they said he was eighty-four. How old was your mother?"

He gave a shrug. "Probably a little over eighty, though it's hard to say. Even she didn't seem to know exactly."

There were voices in the hall outside the door, where the nurse who showed them in had said she would wait. A heavyset woman getting on in years had come up to her and was saying something. She was dressed in a gray suit and held a black overnight bag in her hand. After bowing to the nurse, she turned to come into the room.

"This is a member of Mr. Ohara's family," the nurse raised her voice to explain.

The woman bowed again as she entered.

"I'm Junko Ohara, his daughter," she said.

Without giving Shizuka and Isamu any time to respond, she walked briskly up to her father's body and looked down at him. Almost as though his rigor mortis had transferred to her, she stood as motionless as a statue, gazing impassively. Then she turned around. They could see no sign of sadness or tears. Her face was like a wall, without expression.

She smiled awkwardly when their eyes met, as if suddenly coming back to herself. "May I ask how you knew my father?" she said.

Shizuka quickly replied that she had met him two days before in the mountains, but as she was hesitating whether to mention the trouble they'd had with him, Junko made the connection herself.

"Oh, yes, Mr. Takatomi told me about you. I'm so sorry. I understand my father became violent."

Isamu saw the nurse signalling that she'd like to close up, and motioned the two women toward the door. It seemed impolite to take their leave right away, so Shizuka and Isamu sat down on a bench in the hall. Junko thanked the nurse when she finished locking up, then lowered herself onto the bench beside them, placing her overnight bag on the floor at her feet.

"I guess my father behaved like that with pretty much everybody who came," she sighed. "It'd been going on for quite some time."

Despite growing up in Toyama, she had no accent, perhaps because her parents were both originally from Tokyo. Her round face and small, recessed eyes reminded Shizuka of Ohara, but her broad shoulders and full body contrasted with her father's slighter frame. To judge from her frizzy salt-and-pepper hair, cut in a simple bob, and her rumpled and shapeless gray suit, she wasn't one to fret much about her appearance. She seemed the sort of person who'd spent her life trying earnestly to fit into society, only to have life pass her by.

"But neither my brother nor I could do anything about it. As far back as I can remember, something would set him off and he'd go on a rampage. Something completely trivial, like a thunderclap, or a salesman at the door, or someone tapping him on the shoulder from behind. And not every time. Just completely at random..."

"The nurse wondered if it might be posttraumatic stress disorder, from what he went through in the war," Shizuka said, relaying the explanation given by the matron who'd injected Ohara with the sedative.

Junko's eyes widened for a moment as if this was something she'd never heard before; then she nodded emphatically.

"I suppose that must be it. Every so often, he seemed to suddenly go back into the war. It was like he had one foot in our house and the other in the trenches all the time... Like even though he was sitting right there beside us, he wasn't really there." She paused briefly before going on as if something had suddenly clicked. "He wasn't really living in our world."

To Shizuka it sounded rather as if she was trying to rationalize why she felt no grief at her father's death.

"I suppose he just couldn't stop dragging the war around with him," Isamu said, breaking the silence he'd kept up to this point. "When I was little, I saw Hiroshima from the window of a train. It looked like the pile of ashes you have left after burning some trash. I went again for my school trip in high school, and when they explained to us how it got that way, it struck me that that must basically be what the Americans thought of Japan – that it was just a heap of trash. One big mountain of garbage, crawling with ants and cockroaches. That's the only way they could drop something like the A-bomb and wipe everybody out in one blinding flash. Then afterwards they act like they did everybody a big favour by burning the filthy heap of garbage and cleaning up the world."

"But we did a lot of horrible things all over Asia, too," Shizuka said, thinking of the atrocities Ohara had described.

"True enough," he said. "But there's a difference. No matter how outrageous and shameful those things were, they were always person-to-person. What I'm saying is that the bomb wasn't dropped on people; it was dropped on trash. And it wasn't just Hiroshima and Nagasaki – the Americans treated the whole country as one big mountain of waste and vermin. Until that's recognized, I don't see how we can ever stop dragging the war around with us. And until then, we'll never be able to take proper responsibility for the things our troops did, either."

Realizing how heated up he'd become, he gave a wry smile.

"Actually, I work as a termite exterminator. Which means I go from one house to another spraying pesticide on the little buggers, right? Well, when I see them dying in droves under my wand, I feel almost like a god. Like I've acquired this enormous power. And it kind of scares me when I feel like that. I imagine that's how the Americans felt, too, when they dropped the A-bombs – like they were gods. But the thing is, they've never gotten scared of themselves for feeling that way."

It surprised Shizuka a little to discover that Isamu worked in pest control. But she felt as though the sketchy picture she'd begun to form of him had come into clearer focus.

Junko nodded pensively. "I know my father did some really awful things during the war. And I know it wasn't only him. But he basically just said there'd been nothing else he could do, and left it at that. His constant gripe was that once peace came, everybody went around acting as if they'd never had any part in the war. He didn't understand how people could do that. I think that's why, somewhere inside, he could never stop fighting."

She stared at the gray door to the hospital morgue.

"He might still be doing that even now, after he's gone."

A nurse was being paged on the PA system, and the bustle of people coming and going filled the hall in both directions, but a bleak stillness hung in the air near the gray door.

50

As Asafumi and Kesumba followed the Jōganji downstream, signs of human activity continued to diminish. The faint paths leading from the city down to the river grew fewer and farther between, then disappeared altogether. They saw no one else moving about the valley on either side of the river; there was only the jagged and uneven profile of a dead city baked by the scorching light of the sun. The water level was higher than Asafumi remembered. Judging from the devastation all around, he speculated that a dam must have burst somewhere in the upper reaches of the river and released the water it had been holding back.

They advanced over the burning stones, drinking from the current when they became thirsty, and stopping to cool themselves in it when they dripped with sweat. Kekah followed faithfully behind, panting rapidly. At noon they cooked a frog the dog had scared up and ate it with some greens Kesumba picked at the water's edge. But Asafumi had trouble finding much of an appetite. When he saw Kesumba using the old man's flint, it reminded him of all the morning's events, and he lost most of his desire to eat. After their meagre meal, they set off again.

The sun slowly tilted toward the west. The mountains rising on both sides drew away from the river, and the Toyama Plain opened out before them. The sight took Asafumi's breath away: it was as if a blanket of white ashes covered the earth all the way to the horizon.

The plain had become an utterly forsaken waste. Not a single house stood intact anywhere – only fragments of walls here and there, or lone pillars reaching up like thorns pricking at the sky. What once were bridges looked more like torn spider webs hanging over the river. Far in the distance, a thin bright line stretched across the horizon. Like an egg shell pressing against the bottom of the azure sky, it had a blue-white glow.

"What's that?" Kesumba asked.

"The ocean."

"What's the ocean?"

"A place with lots of water."

"Like in a pond?"

"That's right, a really really big pond."

Asafumi smiled. Yes, the ocean was a big pond, and the continents were big islands in it. The earth was a great globe covered with ponds and islands, and human beings were minute little creatures crawling around on its surface.

The wind was blowing toward them, but the distance was too great for the smell of the sea to reach them. The river widened as it emerged from the valley onto the plain. Floodwaters had eaten away at its banks, and here and there streets and broken buildings could be seen sliding into the riverbed. As they continued to follow its course, Asafumi got a rough fix on the direction of Senbashi from the orientation of the river and ocean and mountains. His home town was located at the mouth of the Takimizu River, which flowed parallel to the Jōganji.

Despite the wholly altered landscape, the path of the Jōganji did not appear to have appreciably changed. When he thought they had gone far enough, he climbed over some boulders and blocks of concrete to the top of the embankment and was able to pick out the glittering surface of the Takimizu some distance to the east. It bent around in the same gentle arc as the Jōganji before straightening out to flow on toward the sea. Seeing the familiar river felt like being reunited with a long lost friend.

"This way," he shouted down to Kesumba, and promptly set off across country. The ground here was overgrown with creepers and weeds. The fragments of rusting metal and disintegrating concrete that poked through this greenery were so far gone that they crumbled beneath their feet. No pillars or rickety walls remained standing at all, and the flattened landscape stretched before them without obstruction. The buildings that once filled the area had succumbed to the forces of nature.

Millions must have lived here. The city had expanded and then expanded some more, until one day it burst like a bubble of gum.

What in the world could have made this happen? he wondered yet again.

He saw no signs of recent human habitation. There were no remains of campfires, no sun-bleached skeletons. His best guess was that the people who used to live here had escaped into the hills, fleeing farther and farther up the valley. But when they came to where Mandala Road began, they stopped to consider. Only the more daring ones then plunged deeper into the mountains, to return to the wild, while the others stayed behind to wander the ruins like starving ghosts.

Did the shrivelling disease refer to what happened to those who stayed behind? Did it refer to being stuck with nowhere to go and nothing to do but wither and die where they stood?

"There's no mountain or trail, but this place is just like Mandala Road," Kesumba said, interrupting his thoughts.

He looked at her in surprise as she pointed a grubby finger at the ground.

"Look at all the stuff that's growing," she added.

Now that she mentioned it, he realized that what was left of the city they were walking through no longer fitted the description of ruins. Vines and grasses of every kind were reaching out of the ground to wrap their tendrils around the rubble. The area was well on its way to becoming a grassy, green prairie. On its distant edge, the ocean glowed red in the light of the setting sun. Asafumi thought of the houses in Dobō. With each passing day, the empty village was being reclaimed by the encroaching forest. No matter what the species of tiny, insignificant creatures known as humans might endeavour to produce on the face of this great globe called earth, it was all destined to be swallowed up by the irresistible forces of nature in the end.

Perhaps the people who had withered and died were simply part of that process. Every balloon of bubblegum bursts when it gets too big, collapsing into a shapeless wad. Maybe the shrivelling disease was part of that collapse.

"There's some trees," Kesumba said excitedly, veering to one side as she trotted several steps ahead. Asafumi looked the way she'd turned and spotted a thick clump of green rising from the ground like a mirage. He immediately saw that it was in the direction he needed to go and hurried after her. Sensing his mistress's excitement, Kekah dashed out in front of them both. He went a short distance, turned to make sure they were still coming, then raced on ahead again.

It was twilight by the time Asafumi and Kesumba stood on the edge of a small wood. Tall skinny trees and short stubby ones. Shrubs with twisty gray branches intertwined like a woman in anguish. Shrubs adorned with large white and orange flowers. Trees bearing star-shaped fruit, or bumpy yellow fruit as big as a handball, or fruit that looked like purple eggs. Birds twittered noisily among the branches. As the descending dusk drifted in among its verdant growth, the wood took on the feeling of a deep forest. Directly in front of Asafumi were some bushes covered in bright purple-pink blossoms. Oleanders. The olive-green leaves, long and slender, blinked at him like almond eyes. When he smelled the sweet scent of the flowers coming faintly his way, he knew he had reached the spot where his grandfather's house once stood.

51

A pointed crescent moon hung in the sky above the eaves. The shadowy hulks of mountains crowded close on every side. The pilgrims sat on the ground in front of one of the huts, buzzing with conversation. Thanks to the fruit and vegetables they'd helped themselves to, there was contentment in the air.

Rentarō was sitting a short distance away with his arms around his knees. He was bone-tired. He'd been running around carrying water to the dying or looking for mats and blankets to cover the dead. When he first saw the others pilfering food from the fields, his reaction had been one of disgust, but in the end he had given in to hunger and shared in a few greens, as well as two pieces of fruit that reminded him of the mangoes he used to get in Malaya. Unlike the rest of the group though, he was still feeling oddly dispirited, and he now sat apart with his back turned to them like a sulking child.

"What's wrong? You look unhappy," the androgynous youth said, coming to sit beside him. He looked his usual cheerful self.

"Has it ever occurred to you that your pilgrimage might be just an endless journey to nowhere?" Rentarō said sourly.

A blithe smile came to his lips. "So what? It's better than staying put and doing nothing."

"If you stayed put, at least you wouldn't have to steal other people's food."

The youth seemed taken aback, as if accused of something he hadn't done.

"It's not like we had a choice. The people we were with threw us out. They basically told us to drop dead. But how does anyone have the right to decide who lives and who dies like that?"

Rentarō looked over his shoulder at the other pilgrims. The one-armed woman was gently stroking the baby's cheek with her only hand. The horned woman watched from nearby with a smile. The old man with the red rabbit was feeding his companion some grass, and the giant carter lay flat on his back, snoring away. It seemed obvious that no one had the right to dictate these people's fate.

"They don't," he said.

"Exactly. And that's why we keep travelling Mandala Road. We don't know whether to live or die, so we just keep walking."

"But wait a minute. There shouldn't be any reason why you can't decide for yourself."

He let out a snort. "How do you expect people who forget everything as soon as it happens to make any kind of decision?"

That's what it meant to forget, Rentarō suddenly realized. He had set out on a sales trip in an effort to simply forget everything – his wife, his family, Saya. But to do that was also to give up being able to decide anything else about his life.

His life. The words sent a jumble of scenes from the past spinning through his mind. The first sales trip he'd gone on with his father, when he'd cried himself to sleep because his legs and shoulders were so sore by the time they stopped for the night. The gratitude on his customers' faces as they told him, on return visits, how some medicine or other had saved the day. Getting told off by his boss in Singapore for being stymied by the language barrier. The first time he met Saya, and the way her face lit up when he tossed her the paper balloon. The day the go-between introduced him to Yōko, and how he'd stared at the slender nape of her neck as she shyly averted her face. Holding his firstborn child in his arms – so light, so warm – feeling ready to explode with joy. Following Saya through the dense Malayan jungle, watching her grow into a woman as she skipped along on those tiny feet. Their days of endless lovemaking at the house in Kota Bharu. The crayon drawing of "Daddy" that arrived from his son and made him feel homesick.

Each of these scenes had shaped his life. Saya and Yoko and Asatsugu and Kikuo and Tano and Isamu were all part of that life, and so was the unborn child Saya now carried. He couldn't run away from any of them. He seemed to have been trying to cling to only the happy turns in his life and flee from everything that was painful. But life was inevitably a mixture of both.

By trying to forget, he was making himself no different from the pilgrims, destined like them to wander forever and no longer able to choose his own fate. He thought of the fellow he'd split up with when he decided to follow the pilgrims. He had pegged the guy as a fool, and reckless, but maybe he'd been wrong about that.

Maybe he himself had been the foolish one. Impulsively, he'd started back along Mandala Road, thinking it was safer, little realizing it was in fact a road to nowhere – a road of lost souls, winding endlessly through the wilderness. That other fellow had at least chosen his own path.

Rentarō got to his feet. "I need to go," he said.

The youth gave him a puzzled look. "Go where?"

"Home."

He wasn't entirely sure where that home was anymore. He just knew it was where he needed to go.

As he started to leave, the youth called after him. "It's dark. It's not safe to travel at night."

Rentarō looked up the path leading away from the huts. Lit only faintly by the moon, it quickly melted into the blackness of the forest. There was no telling what might lie in wait there.

But if he let such fears hold him back now, there'd probably be something else to hold him back tomorrow. And he would find himself trudging once again along the road that eternally arrived nowhere.

Turning his back on the youth, he made his way onto the dimly lit path.

52

Shizuka lay awake in the back room, which had been small to begin with but was made even more cramped by the writing desk and bookshelves that lined the walls. Through the thin sliding doors, she could hear the rhythmical rise and fall of Isamu breathing in his sleep. For the first time in days, she could feel the warmth that came from having someone else in the house.

By the time they got back from the hospital, night had fallen and the last express of the day to Osaka had already gone. So when Isamu said he would find a room at a business hotel in the city, Shizuka invited him to stay at the house instead. She hesitated a little about letting another man stay with her while her husband was away, but the man in question was Asafumi's uncle, after all. It wasn't as if she were letting some complete stranger spend the night. And besides, she felt bad that he had missed his train on her account.

Isamu politely declined at first, but allowed himself to be persuaded. "Since it's a house so filled with memories of my mom and dad," he said in changing his mind.

They drove to a roadside restaurant nearby for some dinner. When they returned, Shizuka laid out her own futon in the back room so Isamu could have the front room where she and Asafumi usually slept.

Thanks to a nightcap of whiskey before turning in, she drifted off almost right away. But then she'd woken up in the middle of the night and couldn't get back to sleep. Her conversation with Ohara's daughter at the hospital kept playing back through her mind.

Junko had told her she lived in Kyoto, where she worked in an accounting office, sending her father modest sums of money whenever she could. She remained single. Having grown up watching her father abuse her mother, she said frankly, she'd become too disillusioned with marriage to take the plunge herself. Her brother lived in Tokyo, and she was planning to wait at the hospital for him to arrive before deciding what arrangements to make.

As they were leaving, Shizuka had turned for a last look at her, now sitting all by herself in the main waiting room. It brought back an image of Ohara as she'd first seen him, standing alone by the fire in the empty village. The old man's inability to put the war behind him had had lasting repercussions on his daughter's life.

After lying awake for quite a while, Shizuka realized she needed to go to the bathroom. Since it would require passing through the room where Isamu was sleeping, she tried to ignore the pressure in her bladder, but that only seemed to make it worse. Finally she accepted the inevitable and got out of bed.

She quietly slid the door open and looked into the next room. Isamu had asked her to leave the curtains drawn so he could look out at the garden before going to sleep. A small amount of light from the outside lamp spilled in through the glass doors lining the veranda, allowing her to see just well enough to make out where the futon and furniture were. She tiptoed around the foot of the futon and slipped through the sliding door to the front hall. The regular sound of Isamu's breathing remained unchanged. She was glad that her movements hadn't disturbed him.

As she was relieving herself, she thought of Ohara. His death meant she'd lost the only lead she had in her search for Asafumi. It probably meant she would have to go back out there to look for new clues.

She missed her husband — there was no question of that. But even with him gone, she still got through the days well enough. It made her wonder again exactly what Asafumi had been to her. The disappearance of Hiroyuki from her life had been much the same. She felt a little lonely, but the days continued to go by. In that case, she'd figured it was because she still had Asafumi. He had become a stand-in for Hiroyuki. But now that Asafumi was gone, who would be a stand-in for him? Isamu?

A shiver ran through her. She'd spent less than a day with the man, and she was already thinking of him as a possible replacement for her husband. When she was in grade school, there'd been a set of monkey bars on the playground. She loved playing on them, dangling from the bars and swinging through the air from one rung to the next. Were men essentially like those bars to her – each rung merely a means of getting to the next, though in fact each one was exactly the same as the last?

She pulled up her pyjamas and flushed the toilet, then switched off the light and started back to her room.

What was she going to find when she reached the end of the bars? Her mother had swung across her own set of rungs with men. And now she lived alone in a condo in Yokohama, nursing her bitterness toward them all. Was that how Shizuka would end up, too?

Something caught her foot in the dark and she lurched forward, tumbling onto Isamu's futon with a thud. She heard the flop of a notebook falling on the floor. The sales register, she thought, as a little groan sounded in her ear and the smell of a man filled her nostrils.

"Blessings from heaven," Isamu said with a low chuckle.

"I'm so sorry."

Isamu touched her shoulder in the dark and asked, "Are you all right?"

"Yes, I'm fine," she said and started to push herself upright. But the warmth of his body next to hers felt so good that she stopped short after barely shifting position.

As if sensing her reluctance to move, he said, "Could we maybe stay like this a bit? It reminds me of when I was little."

Shizuka imagined he was thinking of the days when he used to sleep side by side with his mother in this very room. She remained where she was, lying next to him on top of the quilt. The bedding was soft and warm. An air of intimacy seemed to enfold them in the darkness.

"When I was little, my dad lived at the house in Senbashi, but he came to visit us here quite a bit. He and my mom would always tell me to go outside and play, shooing me out of the house. They had grown-up things to talk about, they said. One day I peeked inside, and they were both naked."

She flinched. Given how young he'd been, she expected him to tell her what a shock it was.

"They were locked in each other's arms like they were lost to the world," he said. "It was riveting, actually. There was this amazing heat between them, and I felt like some powerful magnetic force had grabbed hold of my eyes and wouldn't let go. I've always wondered what that force was."

"I know about that myself," Shizuka said, her face buried in the quilt and her voice far away. "When I was ten or eleven, I was playing in the park and I saw some guy masturbating. He was hiding in the bushes, so all I could see was his hands and penis, but it was like you said, like a magnet had hold of my eyes and I couldn't look away."

"That's it all right," Isamu agreed.

"I suppose maybe it's part of that same magnetic thing – the picture's still stuck in my memory, and I can't get it out of my head."

"Same here. My mom and dad have been burned onto my retinas like that ever since."

Shizuka couldn't quite believe she was talking so casually about such things with a virtual stranger. Whether prompted by the comfort of the futon, or the darkness of the room, or the house feeling like home to them both, the words seemed to flow out of their own accord.

"I guess it's just part of that attraction men and women have," he said, and then added in a more playful way, "Talking about stuff like this is giving me a hard-on."

Taken aback, she started to pull away, but he reached over to stop her. "Care to touch it?" he said.

Goodness, no! she almost blurted out, but the words caught in her throat as the childhood image from the park rose in her mind's eye. This could be that penis, she suddenly realized.

She moved her hand toward his groin and felt for it through his shorts. It was as stiff as a rod, but much warmer than any monkey bar. She could feel its heat and assurance pressing firmly back against her fingers as she squeezed.

Did you get his heart? Or did you get a sword?

The two might be hard to distinguish, but they were totally different things. What she had in her hand now was his heart, she felt sure. It was what she'd been looking for ever since she was a little girl. The same thing her mother had been seeking as she swung from one man to the next.

She slid her hand inside his shorts. After twenty long years, she'd finally reached for the penis standing erect among the foliage in the park and taken it in her hand.

53

After washing the dinner dishes, Saya stepped from the dirt floor of the kitchen up into the sitting room. Isamu was curled up like a caterpillar on the tatami next to their little folding table, sound asleep. The lavender cookie tin from Tami sat open on the table, completely empty.

When she brought out the box and removed the lid, the boy had whooped as if he'd been told he could have every sweet being sold up and down the aisles of the black market. He'd promptly begun downing the cookies one after the other, and they were gone in what seemed like no time at all. Saya had managed to get only three for herself. But as she watched her little boy chewing blissfully with big golden-brown crumbs clinging to his lips, she didn't have the heart to tell him he had to save some for tomorrow.

The boy deserved to really have his fill of something special once in a while, she told herself. She remembered how happy she'd felt, as a little girl, when she found a tree in the jungle heavy with ripe fruit and gorged herself until she thought she would burst.

Not just with food but with clothing and everything else, they were constantly having to do without. To let Isamu experience complete satisfaction for a change was one of the best gifts she could give him.

She draped a blanket over the sleeping boy and sat down beside him to take care of the laundry. The bare bulb hanging from the ceiling cast a yellow glow over the room, and she could hear the soft rise and fall of Isamu's breathing. As she folded clothes that still smelled of sunshine, she thought of the fish seeds she'd given to Tami. She had mixed feelings about the woman's gratitude for helping to kill her unborn child. It felt almost as if she'd decided to kill the baby in her own womb, too.

When faced with a life or death situation for themselves, people seemed quick to make life or death decisions for others. In order to save his own skin, her brother had tortured and killed people. In order to preserve herself and her son, Saya had silenced the woman from the repatriation boat. But if she rationalized acts like these in the name of survival, then she also had to accept the killing of Malays, Chinese, and Indians by Japanese troops on the same grounds. The same went for her own thousand deaths to the thrust of their ruthless man-swords.

But surely there was a line somewhere, she thought. If you wanted the vegetables in your kitchen garden to flourish, you had to remove any stray plants that encroached on the rows. If you went from there to eradicating every other plant in sight, though, you'd be left with nothing else in your yard to enjoy. That would be to cross a line. Much as you wouldn't want your garden to take over your entire surroundings, there were certain lines in life that you simply did not cross — weren't there?

The plots her people cultivated in the jungle had been just big enough to meet their basic needs. But there was nothing "just big enough" about the rubber and coconut plantations she'd seen from the raft on her way to Kota Bharu. When people left the jungle, they seemed to begin expanding their gardens without any sense of limits.

To go on hating Rentarō was to expand her own garden in the same way. Hatred was like a plough. People used ploughs to extend their gardens endlessly, pulling up every unwanted plant in sight, before soon starting cities. Cities where hatred thrived.

Saya stopped folding the clothes and rose to her feet. She went to the closet to dig out the finger-hole knife she'd stashed away in her travel case, rolled up in a piece of cloth.

As long as she held onto this thing, she thought, it gave shape to her rancour. It was time to get rid of it. She could bury it in the garden.

Sliding open a shoji panel, she went out onto the veranda. A moon like the curved tip of her knife hung high overhead, casting its blue-white light into the hedged yard. She stepped into a pair of wooden sandals and moved toward the vegetable patch, where the seedlings had now reached the size of her finger. But before she got to it, she saw her brother Kekah standing among the rows.

Don't you dare. Don't you dare throw that away.

He stood swaying like a hanged man, his eyes half out of their sockets and his four broken limbs dangling limply from his body.

You've got to kill him. Kill all the bastards who killed you and me.

Clutching the knife to her breast, Saya ignored him and stepped into the garden. As soon as her feet touched the softened earth, a deep darkness descended around her. Instead of her garden, she was in a forest, surrounded by tall trees in every direction, with only the faintest moonlight illuminating a narrow path in front of her. Beneath a tree along the path stood Kim Suk-hwa, looking pale and drawn as she gazed at her.

He treated you like a toilet. Get revenge.

Under another tree stood the woman from the repatriation boat. Blood ran down her neck.

You took my life. So now I'm going to take yours.

Kekah came up to her and yelled in her face.

You've got to kill him. You've got to kill Rentarō.

Over her brother's shoulder she saw a throng of soldiers with swollen penises poking from their trousers.

Kill the bitch! Screw her good!

Saya threw down the knife and began running. The chorus of voices came right with her, swirling around her.

Kill the bitch! Screw her good! Ram it up her cunt! Wring her fucking neck! Carve up her sorry ass!

Her sandals flew off as she stumbled over rocks and clumps of grass in the path. She dashed desperately on in her bare feet.

Kill the bitch! Ram it up her cunt! Wring her fucking neck! Carve up her sorry ass!

The voices echoed through the forest. The clamouring figures appeared and disappeared before her as she ran. Their shouts were like the drumbeats pounded out on bamboo and tree trunks as her tribe's warriors set off for battle.

Kill the bitch! Carve up her sorry ass! Kill the bitch! Carve up her sorry ass!

The voices throbbed through Saya's head.

"Leave me alone! Stop shouting at me!" she cried. But her voice was drowned out by the angry din.

Kill the bitch! Carve up her sorry ass!

Ahead was a clearing with several crude huts – three or four of them lined up in a row. They reminded her of the makeshift shanties her people built in the jungle. Relief flooded through her. Maybe someone she knew would be there. Maybe even the healer. If she could find him, she knew he would help her. Was this a Japanese forest or the Malayan jungle? She had no idea where she was.

In the brighter moonlight between the huts and the forest, she saw a man coming her way. She caught her breath and stopped short; the man halted, too. He had on a khaki shirt with a closed collar, much like a military uniform. A soldier, she thought, recoiling at the memory of the P-house.

Kill him, Kesumba!

Kekah was back beside her with the knife she'd tossed aside, pressing it into her hand.

Kill the man who betrayed you!

Taking a closer look, Saya saw that the figure on the path was Rentarō. A scruffy beard darkened his face and his clothes were filthy, but there could be no mistaking who it was.

"Mr. Ren..." she called to him. Speaking his name renewed her longing for him.

"Saya?" Rentarō said in surprise as he hurried up to her. "How in the world did you get here?"

Kill him, Kesumba!

As Kekah hissed furiously in her ear, she looked down at the dull shine of the blade. Rentarō saw what she had in her hand.

"What are you doing with a thing like that?"

Screw the bitch! Ram it up her cunt! Wring her fucking neck! Carve up her sorry ass!

The bamboo drumming of voices boomed in her ear. Suk-hwa and the woman from the boat and the soldiers all pressed in around her, keeping up their relentless chant.

"My name is Kesumba," she said, as if riding the wave of their voices.

"No, it's not. It's Saya. I gave you that paper balloon, remember?" He smiled as if recalling that distant day.

The paper balloon. She saw a globe of rainbow colours coming through the air, arcing slowly through the darkness toward her chest. She thought of the dreams she and Rentarō had shared. Why had they all disappeared?

Kill the bitch! Carve up her sorry ass! Kill the bitch! Carve up her sorry ass!

The chanting swelled around her.

These were the voices that crushed the rainbow globe, she thought. Voices filled with hatred.

Raising the finger-hole knife, Saya spun toward the figure of Kekah. The sharp tip ripped across his torso. With neither a cry nor a whimper, her brother disappeared.

Spinning the other way, she sliced through Suk-hwa, then the woman from the boat, and finally the troops with their jutting cocks, one after the other.

Suk-hwa and the soldiers vanished at the touch of her blade, melting instantly into the darkness. The drumbeat of voices weakened. But the woman from the boat remained like a shimmery pillar of smoke.

When Saya met the woman's gaze, she saw herself. It was as if the woman had become her, and her own eyes were blazing at her with fury and loathing.

You killed me, the woman said one last time, before shrinking slowly into the darkness.

54

From somewhere in the distance came the keening of insects, on and on like a stuck doorbell. Asafumi opened his eyes.

The surrounding darkness reminded him that he'd fallen asleep under the large tree with a gray trunk in the middle of the wood. Only a few slivers of moonlight filtered through the branches above. The cool night air and the thick scent of the shrubbery in his lungs was refreshing. Kesumba and Kekah were curled up together beside him, fast asleep. The girl and Asafumi had eaten their fill of fruit from nearby trees before sitting down beneath this one and allowing the fatigue from their long day of walking to carry them off to sleep.

The noise he made as he sat up woke his companions. Kekah promptly got to his feet and gave his body a hard shake. Kesumba lay staring off into space for a while before finally opening her mouth to speak.

"I'm going back to Mandala Road," she said.

"Yeah, I think that makes sense," he agreed. For her, that had to be best. But he remained unsure about himself.

In a vague sort of way, he'd thought that if he returned to his grandfather's house, he might be able to see himself as a child again. Of course, he knew all along that there was no assurance of this, so to discover nothing left but the wood had not been a particularly big letdown. Yet he was somehow reluctant to leave the place behind again. He didn't know what more he expected to find here, but returning to Mandala Road felt too much like going back to the man he'd been before.

"I'm staying here," he finally decided.

"Okay," she said lightly, and stood up. She turned toward the path. Kekah wagged his tail and ambled after her.

"You're going in the middle of the night?" Asafumi said in surprise.

"It's cooler when it's dark. I think I know the way well enough."

Thinking he would at least see her to the edge of the wood, he stood up to follow.

They pushed past the clump of oleander bushes and emerged into the open. A crescent moon shone down on the flattened ruins, now well on their way back to fields of green. As if proclaiming the ultimate ascendancy of nature, the cry of insects rang out across the deserted remains of the once-thriving city. The dark shadow of the Tateyama Range rose high in the sky, seeming almost to lean out over the Toyama Plain. Kesumba lifted her face toward the mountains like an animal sniffing the breeze.

"Why did you come all this way with me?" Asafumi asked.

She turned to look at him. "Because you were alone," she said. Then after a brief pause she added, "You can't walk Mandala Road all by yourself. You'll stumble to the ground somewhere along the way and end up with your bones picked clean."

"So it's your role to help anybody who's not with somebody else?" Since she seemed not to understand, Asafumi rephrased it. "If you see somebody walking by themselves, do you always go with them?"

She shook her head. "No."

"Then why did you come with me?" he asked, expecting only another "I don't know." But she pointed at her chest.

"Something inside here told me to."

She smiled. Her white teeth stood out bright against her dark skin. Then she walked briskly away, with Kekah bounding after her.

He was taken aback by the abruptness of her departure. "Thank you," he called after her shrinking figure.

She did not turn. She simply continued marching across the wasteland with her oversized dress flapping in the night breeze and the two-headed dog at her heels. Asafumi followed them with his eyes until they dwindled to tiny dots and melted into the darkness. He had lost his companion, and he suddenly felt lonely.

Not knowing what to do next, he turned back toward the woods and found himself looking at a house instead. From the shape of its black roof against the starry sky, he recognized it as his grandfather's. Since it was the middle of the night, the house was dark. Only the lamp by the front door was on, its dim glow falling on his blue Volkswagen and Shizuka's bicycle parked in the drive. Startled, Asafumi swung around the other way again. Beyond the low hedge bordering the property stretched the familiar grid of rice paddies; a light twinkled here and there through the stands of trees sheltering the neighbouring farmhouses. The flattened and overgrown remains of the fallen city had vanished.

Asafumi stood agape, his eyes skittering in disbelief across the landscape. Then it finally began to sink in that he had returned.

I'm back! I'm home! His strength seemed to desert him for a moment as an overwhelming sense of relief flooded through his body. He started for the front door, only to reconsider and change course toward the veranda. Shizuka would have locked the door before going to bed; it would be easier to wake her up by rapping on the glass. She had to be worried sick after so many days without word from him. What would she think when she saw him standing there with only a towel around his waist? How was he ever going to explain it? How was he going to explain about Mandala Road? Or Kesumba? His head swam with all the things that had happened. He felt as though he might explode.

He stepped up onto the veranda. The curtains had not been drawn. She should be more careful, he thought, as he peered inside and raised a hand to rap on the glass. He saw two dark figures moving slowly on the futon in the middle of the room. His hand froze.

A man and a woman. Naked. Copulating. Sturdy masculine limbs twined with slender feminine limbs. The man lay on top, his back flexing as he moved. Not enough light entered from outside to see their faces, but Asafumi knew from the lines of the woman's body that it was Shizuka.

His wife was sleeping with another man. She was moaning with pleasure.

He stood rooted to the spot, watching their movements, unable to tear his eyes away. Behind a pane of glass, he peered as if from another world into Shizuka's private realm.

So this was how his wife had been spending her time while he was away. The realization roared through him like a tornado. Far from worrying about him, she'd been getting it on with someone else.

If he were to be perfectly honest with himself, he had sensed from the time they were still dating that there were probably other men in Shizuka's life. She would take several days off from work, saying she was going on a trip with a friend, or he could tell there was someone in the background when he called her on the phone. Even after they got married, she used to go out on Saturday afternoons and come home with a faraway look in her eye. So he'd actually known all along. He had seen the signs; he simply hadn't let himself think about them.

He watched through the glass as Shizuka came to her climax, every muscle in her body quivering with pleasure. She'd never responded quite like that when she made love with him. He felt a great surge of rage. It was the same fury that had consumed him when he killed the old man.

55

Rentarō watched in stunned silence as Saya sliced the air with her tiny blade. She spun first one way, then another, the hem of her pale yellow skirt rising about her in the soft moonlight.

He'd been flabbergasted to see her suddenly appear in front of him on this remote forest path. As if that weren't enough, she'd then said her name was Kesumba, and began swinging a knife wildly about. It was simply too weird. It scared him out of his wits.

By this time the pilgrims had become aware of Saya's presence, and came up behind Rentarō to see what was going on. They, too, watched her strange dance with their mouths hanging open.

Finally she stopped. As if abruptly coming back to herself, she dropped the knife to her side and brought her feet to a standstill.

"Saya," Rentarō called to her.

She turned to face him. For a moment her eyes showed no recognition, but then something seemed to click and her expression softened. Stepping up to him, she said slowly, as if dredging each word from the bottom of a deep pool, "To you, I am only toilet."

He was bewildered. "What are you talking about?"

Saya appeared not to hear him. "You are coward. You try to run away from me always."

He'd never once thought of her as a toilet, nor of himself as a coward. Yet somewhere inside, he heard a voice telling him that what she said was true.

"But I..." He searched for the right words. There was definitely more to it than that. He was genuinely fond of Saya. When he'd been forced to leave her, it had saddened him to no end. Her arrival on his doorstep in Senbashi had put him in a bind, certainly, and he remembered wishing he could simply close his eyes and find her gone, but he had never contemplated throwing her out. Yet, whatever he might say, he felt as though he would only be making excuses.

He'd had his excuses when he first decided to live with Saya in Malaya without saying anything to Yōko, and he'd had his excuses when he left Saya behind to return to Japan. Then he'd made excuses again when she showed up at his house in Senbashi. The truth was, somewhere along the line, while he was busy making all these excuses, he had lost his way. And he had wandered onto Mandala Road.

"I'm done running away."

There was nothing else left for him to say.

Her lips trembled. "I..." she began, but faltered. Her face twisted into knots as she struggled for words. "I never leave you," she finally said.

Each time her tribe moved to a new settlement, all they actually did was go from one set of makeshift dwellings to another. Even after hiking for days through the jungle, the place they came to would invariably be somewhere they had lived before. By the same token, even if she were to leave Rentarō and go back to Malaya, she would merely end up at another temporary stopping place. All men treated women badly. But Rentarō had given her a paper balloon. That was why she'd decided to stay on at the makeshift hut he offered. Now she just needed to wait for him to realize that the makeshift hut she provided in return included not only a toilet but a bed and a kitchen as well.

This was what she wanted to tell him, but she didn't think she could get it to come out right in Japanese.

As the last of the menacing spirits whirling around her faded away, the tenderness she felt for Rentarō slowly began to reassert itself. Her hatred had been like the ice on a pond in winter: its cold, hard shell had sealed off the warm feelings that lay beneath, preventing them from rising to the surface.

There came a low gasp from somewhere behind Rentarō.

"It's Yakushi!"

For the first time she noticed the crowd of about twenty people gathered there. The moon gave just enough light for her to see how odd they all looked. There was a woman with a large bump on her forehead, a man white as chalk from head to toe, and someone covered all over in animal fur.

The furry man, no bigger than a wild boar, slipped past Rentarō and bounded up to Saya. "You're Yakushi, aren't you?" he said. "I bet that's who you are."

"No, not Yakushi," she told him.

"Yes, you are. I know you are," he insisted, jumping up and down around her like a grasshopper. "I saw you cutting those evil things down with your knife. *Whoosh, whoosh, whoosh* – you sliced them all down, one after the other."

"That's right, I saw it too!"

"You're Yakushi! The Healer! You have to help us!"

The rest of the crowd flocked around, repeating these names. A tangle of dirty hands reached out to tug at her hair and clothes, or to touch her on the cheek and arms and neck. With a scream, Saya tried to pull away.

"Stop it!" shouted Rentarō, as he began heaving people aside. But like flies to a corpse, they kept coming back.

A gravelly woman's voice rose above the din. "That person is not Yakushi!"

Saya looked up to see someone with her head wrapped in ragged scarves coming toward her down the path, leaning on a wooden staff. But nobody else was listening.

"I saw it! I saw what she did."

"That's right. She got rid of all the calamities."

"Heal us! Save us!"

They elbowed Rentarō aside as they fought to cling to her. Sharp nails dug into her skin and frantic hands tore at her clothes. She swept her arms around to brush them off, and then the knife in her hand began flying back and forth to cut down the supplicants. Like her brother and Suk-hwa, each of them fell from sight at the slightest touch of the blade – the small furry man, the man who was white all over, the woman with the bump on her head. Spurred on by what she saw happening, Saya sliced the air like a woman possessed.

"Stop it!" shouted the gravelly voice again. "You are not the Healer!"

"Help us, Yakushi!" the others still clamoured. "Save us, Healer!"

I'm the one who needs to be saved, Saya cried out silently. I'm the one who needs the healer's help. She continued swinging her blade to fend off the clinging hands.

Then suddenly the voices fell silent. She was standing alone in the middle of a wood. The people had all disappeared; even Rentarō was gone. The only sound to be heard was the rustling of the trees that lined the moonlit path.

She looked at the knife in her hand. The handle was clammy with sweat. She remembered slashing at people with it, but could see no trace of blood on the blade.

Her brother had said the knife was for driving off evil spirits. Is that what all those weird people begging her to save them were – malicious spirits from the forest? But why would spirits like that be begging to be saved? Maybe they were only made out to be evil by someone else – as the Nonezawa women had done with her.

She tossed the finger-hole knife aside.

There was a hut at the end of the path up ahead. She was sure she'd seen three or four of them before, but now it was only one. There was a light burning off to one side. Somebody apparently lived there. She started up the path.

As she approached, she soon began to see that it was more than a mere hut; though not large, it was a proper house. In fact, apart from the veranda lined with sliding glass doors instead of shoji screens, it looked very much like her own house. The light she'd seen was next to the front door, and a small car stood in the driveway. On past the building she could see rice paddies, spreading out across the landscape. She was no longer surrounded by trees. She approached the house with a sense of wonder.

A man stood on the veranda, naked except for a small towel around his waist. He was focused intently on something inside, and he remained oblivious to her approach. Thinking it all distinctly odd, she stepped up beside him.

He still seemed not to have noticed her. She could feel the hatred pouring off of him.

Peering through the glass, she saw a man and woman lying side by side on a futon. They were naked and appeared to be resting after the exertions of making love. She couldn't help smiling, reminded of

Rentarō and herself. When he came to visit, they would send Isamu out to play, remove all their clothes and make frenzied love, then fall back on the futon to catch their breath just like this.

Yes, she thought. She and Rentarō had joined their bodies together an untold number of times over the years.

She turned to look at the man beside her. His forehead was pressed fiercely against the windowpane. His fists were shaking as if he might smash his way through the glass and burst inside at any moment.

"No," Saya said, placing a hand on his shoulder. With a start, he turned his head to look at her. His mouth fell open. He had obviously been unaware of her until then.

"Miss Saya...?" he managed to say in a barely audible voice.

How did he know who she was? she wondered. His face was anguished. She didn't know why, but she felt a bond between them. Perhaps she saw herself reflected in the anger, and hatred, and sadness that vied in the expression on his face.

Gently she slid her hand from his shoulder down his arm. He followed the motion with widened eyes. Then she raised her other hand, too, and began stroking him on both sides, moving her hands from his back to his shoulders to his arms. Tears spilled down his cheeks. Reaching farther around him, she pulled him to her. He pressed his head against her shoulder. She began sliding her hands up and down his back.

Whooo oo-oo-oong, whooo oo-oo-oong.

A string of soft notes rose from deep in her throat. The music her people hummed as they moved through the jungle on the way to their next settlement. The meaningless song the women of her tribe sang to pacify their fussing babies. The gentle cadences that flowed directly from one heart to another.

The man clung to her like a child. She continued running her hands gently across his back. She no longer knew whether she was comforting him or herself.

Whooo oo-oong, whooo-nnnng.

As she went on humming, the man began to turn transparent beneath her gliding hands. Before long he had faded away to nothing, and Saya realized she was stroking empty air.

She found herself standing alone on the veranda in the light spilling from a bare bulb inside. The shoji screens were open. Isamu lay asleep on the floor next to the small folding table, wrapped in the blanket she'd laid over him. She stepped into the room.

There was a flopping noise as she felt something fall on her toes. Looking at the floor, she saw a long, narrow notebook lying at her feet. On its white cover were some bold black characters written with an ink brush. She couldn't recall ever having had such a thing in the house.

She picked it up and began flipping through it. The writing stopped after just a few pages. She remembered seeing books like this at the house in Senbashi. They seemed to have something to do with the medicine business. Maybe it belonged to Rentarō. She dropped it into the empty cookie tin and closed the lid on top of it.

56

Rentarō stood motionless in the middle of the path. The bodies of the pilgrims lay in heaps around him, lit by the quiet moonlight. The whirling figure of Saya was gone.

"I remember," came a voice from among the bodies on the ground. The androgynous youth sat up and stared off into space as he continued. "The population kept growing, and the city had to spread farther and farther out to make room. Endlessly, on and on."

"And it got hot." Pushing himself off the ground like an inchworm, the man with the red rabbit got to his feet. "We stopped having winter – all year round it was like mid-summer. Food wouldn't grow, and nobody had work. You couldn't worry about other people anymore."

"It got to be everyone for himself," chimed in the dwarfish man in his squeaky voice, pulling himself up on the old man's arm. "You took whatever you needed to survive, from whoever had it, and people started killing each other right and left. I lost my mom and dad and all my brothers and sisters."

"Nobody could hold the city together anymore, let alone the country... Fighting broke out everywhere. And then came the sickness."

"That's right, the sickness. Nobody could figure out what was causing it. It started with a rash, which soon turned to ulcers. You lost all your strength, your hair fell out, and you just kept oozing blood and pus all the time. Everyone got the same symptoms. And there wasn't any medicine to treat it. Not anywhere."

"People dropped like flies."

"Everybody was terrified of everybody else. The sick became pariahs, and they were turned out, or even killed."

"People called it the shrivelling disease, but nobody really knew what it was."

"Women couldn't have children anymore, and plants stopped bearing fruit. People and cities and even the land shrivelled up and died."

The pilgrims spoke up one after the other as fragments of memory began coming back to them. Together their voices rolled out from the path like waves of the night and disappeared into the darkness of the forest. Rentarō gradually pieced together a sense of what had taken place.

The cities had grown as their populations increased. Untold numbers of people lost their jobs and were thrown out of their homes. In order to create work and shelter for the crowds wandering the streets, cities expanded by converting the surrounding farm and forest land into developments. They reached into every nook and cranny from mountain to coast. But it was never enough. Then temperatures began to rise. The sun beat down relentlessly. Crops withered, and famine spread everywhere. Like armies of locusts, mobs of starving people swept from one neighbourhood to the next in search of food. Boats remained tied up at dock all along the coast, slowly succumbing to rust. Buildings were torn down, factories shuttered, and store shelves grew bare. Supplies of every kind continued to dwindle – food, clothing, sundries – and soon there was nothing left to take. The only thing growing was the sickness. But medicines had run out. People banded into groups for mutual protection, only to have the climate of fear and hatred tear them apart almost as soon as they got together. Many began seeking refuge in the mountains, thinking they had a better chance of surviving there. That's what a lot of people had done during the war, too. Except this wasn't a battle between nations; it was a contest of everybody for himself, with everybody else his enemy.

"They blamed me for their troubles. They threw stones at me, and tried to kill me."

"Nobody would let me in their group. I had no choice but to leave the city."

"There wasn't anywhere I could stay," the horned woman said, bursting into tears. The child in her arms began to cry, too.

"We had nothing left to our names."

"We couldn't survive in the city."

"The villages wouldn't have us either."

"Our only choice was to travel Mandala Road."

Their excitement at remembering what they'd forgotten had now given way to a heavy gloom.

Leaning on her staff and dragging her tattered robes behind her, Granny Uba approached the pilgrims huddled together on the ground. "The secret is to forget!" her voice rang out. "Simply forget, and the sadness and pain will disappear."

She raised her arms and wrapped her robe around the woman with the baby. Like a mother hugging her child, she held the two inside the folds of her rags for several moments. The others watched with sorrow in their eyes.

When Granny Uba spread her arms again, the woman gave her head a shake and let out a deep breath. "I feel sleepy," she said, and promptly started back toward the huts, rocking the baby in her arms.

While the others gazed after her not quite knowing what to think, Granny Uba began taking them one by one inside her robe. The little flute player, the giant carter, the old man with the rabbit, the man in the string shirt, the one-armed woman – each vanished briefly into the ragged folds of her robe, and when they reappeared they simply said how tired they were or how late the hour was and headed straight for the huts.

When the man who was white all over went by, rubbing his eyes sleepily, Rentarō asked, "So what comes next for you folks?"

"What else?" he said, appearing perplexed by the question. "We'll keep looking for Yakushi."

"But I thought your troubles were over?"

"Don't be silly. How could that be when we haven't even seen Yakushi?"

"But what about just now when...?"

Since he knew Saya wasn't Yakushi, Rentarō broke off. The carter came up and slapped the white man on the back.

"I'm sure we'll find Yakushi someday."

"That's right. And when we do, he'll deliver us from the calamity." The two men walked off together.

Granny Uba had erased their memories again. But that puzzled Rentarō. Wasn't the whole point of the pilgrimage to find Yakushi?

He turned toward the old woman. She was standing in front of the androgynous youth with her arms spread wide to wrap around him. But the youth pulled away.

"I don't want to forget."

She looked surprised, and her arms stopped in midair.

"Whyever not?"

"I don't want to forget," the youth said slowly, keeping his distance. "If I forget, I'll go back to doing the same thing over and over again. Walking up and down Mandala Road, forever and ever. Isn't that right?"

"That is the journey of life. Doing the same thing over and over again. Nothing more."

He slowly shook his head, then turned and walked away. The old woman lifted her staff and waved it at the youth's back.

"Don't be a fool!" she shouted. "There is no other way besides Mandala Road!"

He didn't respond. His quiet footfalls receded up the dark path.

With an angry grunt, Granny Uba jabbed her staff into the ground and spun back toward the huts. Catching sight of Rentarō, she stepped in his direction. He backed away, not wanting to be wrapped in her robe like the others.

"Who *are* you?" he asked. "Why do you keep leading everybody on a wild goose chase?"

"That is my role."

"Role? It's your role to trap these people forever on Mandala Road? I think you're just looking for company, and this is how you get it. You're the one who doesn't want to remember anything."

He stepped forward and tore the scarf from around her head. She gave a hoarse cry. He yanked off the entire ragged robe draped over her shoulders. Beneath it was the pitch-black figure of a person. At first he thought it was simply an effect of the surrounding night. But then he realized he wasn't looking at a human figure at all – only a black emptiness shaped like a person. This wasn't possible. There had to be someone under those rags. Peeling his eyes, he peered harder into the hollow darkness. At long last a form began to emerge. A woman in a kimono. A thin, bony figure with a sharp, pointed chin and two fierce eyes staring at him.

"Yōko?"

"You keep forcing me to remember," she said, her face and her voice both contorted with bitterness. "What you did in Malaya. That disgusting woman." She edged forward. All colour and tone had drained from her cheeks, accentuating her desiccated features. She bared her teeth and continued. "I never wanted to know about your Malayan whore. I never wanted to hear a word about her. So why did you have to bring her home with you? It's made my life a living hell. Anytime you're out of the house, I can't help picturing you with that woman. It tears me up inside to think of you sleeping with her. You've ruined my life. I can't have a single moment's joy anymore."

Extending a dry, scaly hand, she ripped the robe from Rentarō's grasp and threw it over her shoulders again.

"Can you blame me for wanting to forget it all? For not wanting to be reminded? For wishing I'd never known to begin with?"

She began winding the scarf around her head.

He grabbed the loose end. "I never wanted you to suffer, Yōko – not even now. You and the children matter to me, too. But I can't abandon Saya. There's Isamu to think about."

She gave a hard shake of her head as she finished wrapping the scarf.

"Can't we all get along, Yōko? Please?"

"I am not Yōko," came the voice from inside the rags. The front of the robe spread wide, and he saw the hollow darkness within. "I am Granny Uba. I am the one who wipes memory away."

The two far edges of the robe swept through the air to swallow him up.

57

Feeling someone shaking him by the shoulder, Rentarō opened his eyes. He raised his head to find a man with short-cropped salt-and-pepper hair peering down at him.

"Are you all right?" the man asked in a worried voice. "Did you get sick or something?"

He was wearing a patched suit jacket, and had a large basket strapped to his back.

Rentarō propped a hand on the ground and pushed himself upright. Shuddering with cold, he realized his shirt was open in front and quickly began buttoning it up. He saw at the same time how dirty his clothes were, and that he had no shoes.

"You look like maybe you got lost up here and took a fall somewhere," the man said sympathetically, also noticing the state of Rentarō's dress.

He stood up and brushed himself off as best he could. He was on a narrow road winding through a hillside of trees just beginning to put out their first spring leaves. Water burbled somewhere down below. He felt as though he'd come upon a scene he hadn't set eyes on for many months or even years – as if he had been away on a long and distant journey from which he had only this moment returned. But he could not recall where that journey might have taken him. His clothes were filthy, he reeked of sweat, a scraggly growth had sprouted on his face, and on top of all that, the five-tiered baskets with which he made his living were nowhere in sight.

"I have no idea what happened to me," he finally said. "The last thing I remember is setting out on Mandala Road."

"That's exactly where you are. Mandala Road," the man immediately remarked, pointing to his feet as he said it.

But nothing about the road looked the least bit familiar. "I don't get it," he said. "I can't seem to remember anything."

"Ah," the man nodded, as if in sudden comprehension, putting a hand to his forehead. "That happens a lot along this road. People from outside go missing, and then when they turn up again, they don't remember a thing."

Rentarō nodded vacantly. He truly did not remember a single thing. He had a clear image of getting off the train at Awasuno Station and starting up Mandala Road with his baskets on his back, but after that it was all a complete blank.

"Where do you come from?" the man asked.

"Senbashi."

"If you're heading back, maybe we can go together. I'm actually on my way to the station myself, for a trip into Toyama."

Rentarō decided to take him up on the offer. He couldn't very well carry on with a sales trip when he didn't have his baskets. They began walking side by side in the direction of Awasuno.

The man had a light step. "My cabbage crop has been really good this spring, so I'm on my way down to the black market to sell a few heads. Back during the war, price controls meant you could hardly make any money no matter how well your crops did, but these days it's different. Now it actually pays to work harder."

Rentarō looked into the man's basket. Sure enough, it was filled to the brim with cabbages. There were birds singing in the treetops. Warm morning sunshine shone through the branches onto the road. As he listened to the man's upbeat talk, Rentarō's own spirits lifted.

The best idea was to go home. There'd be both good and bad in store for him there, but all he really needed to do was hoist everything onto his shoulders like his five-tiered baskets and keep trudging along. If he just did that, he was bound to get somewhere in the end. He felt himself filling with optimism.

After a while, the narrow track came to a wider road. In the thick grass beside the trail was a stone marker that said "Mandala Road." Rentarō recognized it from when he started out. He remembered only as far as seeing this marker and making the turn. He tried again to recall anything that might have happened after that, farther up the road, but it was all lost in a swirl of green haze that offered nothing to latch onto. Somewhere in the distance he heard a young girl laughing. It was an innocent child's voice, probably calling out to someone. He turned to look, but there was no sign of anyone about.

"Hey, it's this way," the cabbage grower called to him from a few steps down the wider road.

"Yeah, I'm coming."

Rentarō took one last look up Mandala Road as it stretched away through a tunnel of trees, then turned to follow the man in the direction of the station.

58

The sky was red with the dawn. Shizuka saw Isamu to the gate as soon as he'd washed up and got dressed. He wanted to catch the first express back to Osaka.

After making love in the middle of the night, they had fallen asleep in each other's arms. But now, in the morning light, she felt no closer to Isamu than she had the day before.

"Well then," he said with a smile when they were at the gate. "I suppose I'll say goodbye here."

He made no attempt to give her his address in Osaka, nor did he suggest they should see each other again. She doubted they ever would.

What she'd made love to last night was the menhir in the park from her childhood. The penis that had held her like a magnet all these years. Sleeping with Isamu had finally freed her from its pull. But she wasn't sure, yet, what this might mean.

"Goodbye," she said with a bow.

Isamu bobbed his head in return, then set off down the road between the rice fields in the morning chill, his overnight bag swinging in his hand. Shizuka watched him go until he'd grown small in the distance before turning back toward the house.

As she walked past the Volkswagen parked in the driveway, she noticed the figure of a man curled up in the back seat. He'd pulled off the seat cover and tried to wrap it around himself for warmth.

To her astonishment, it was Asafumi. His face was dirty, with the rough beginnings of a beard, and to judge by the patches of bare skin poking from beneath the cover, he appeared to be stark naked.

Why in the world would her missing husband be sleeping in the back seat of the car? What had happened to his clothes? When had he returned? Why hadn't he woken her up?

Then she remembered that she had spent the night with Isamu.

Had he seen them making love? She felt as if all the blood had drained from her body. But surely there were other explanations. The front door had been locked. Maybe he simply decided to sleep here because he didn't want to wake her. He'd removed the key from the ignition but hadn't locked the doors. He probably got back early this morning and figured he'd wait in the car for her to get up. That had to be it, she told herself, as she pulled on the rear door handle.

The click of the latch woke Asafumi. He gave a big yawn as he looked up at her. Without saying anything, he slowly sat up and slid out of the car, holding the seat cover around him. He took a deep breath of the fresh morning air before looking at her as if for the first time.

The look in his eyes told her that he had seen her with Isamu after all. She suddenly found herself standing at the edge of a cliff.

"I've been seeing another man all along," she said, making the leap.

Though not Isamu, there had always been someone else. The moment the words were out of her mouth, there came an exhilarating sense of relief. She realized she'd been wanting to say this for a very long time.

"I know," he said. Yes, somewhere in his heart, he had known. He had been blocking it out by listening to music. He hadn't wanted to see it. Just as his parents had pretended that Saya did not exist, he had pretended that Shizuka did not have another lover.

With the seat cover wrapped around him, Asafumi moved toward the front door. She stayed close beside him.

"What's going to happen to us?" she asked anxiously.

Asafumi paused when he got to the door. "I don't know if I love you anymore," he said.

Shizuka lowered her eyelids as if she'd been prepared for the blow. Asafumi realized she thought it was because she'd been unfaithful.

"No, no, I didn't mean it that way. It's not because you were sleeping with someone else."

"You mean... you didn't mind?" she asked haltingly.

Asafumi leaned back against the door. The sun was beginning to edge across the bare rice paddies beyond the hedge. With the harvest over, the fields looked as if they'd been spruced up in preparation for winter. Asafumi felt a wistful sort of cleanness in his heart as well.

"I minded all right, in all sorts of ways... But when facts are facts, you have to accept them." He paused for several seconds, and there was a note of frustration in his voice when he went on. "It honestly doesn't have anything to do with your sleeping with some other guy. It has to do with me. I realized that I didn't know the first thing about myself. How can a person who doesn't even know himself know whether he loves someone else? There's just no way, basically. That's what I meant."

She caught her breath for a moment, but then said, "I suppose you're right." She looked across the yard at the thicket of trees and shrubs, and her eyes settled on the tree of the dead standing tall above the rest.

"I think I'll go back to Yokohama," she said.

It was like an ice pick going through him. He'd always suspected the day might come when Shizuka would tell him this. It was one of those things he was pretending not to see.

"I'm going to stay here," he said after a long pause.

They held each other's gaze. It was as if they had become the weaver girl and the goatherd looking at each other across the River of Heaven. They were both realizing for the first time just how wide a gap existed between them. And in that instant, everything they thought they had built up together as husband and wife seemed to dissolve into thin air. All they had left was a vast nothingness holding them apart.

The extent of that void began to make Shizuka's head spin, and she looked away. "How about I get us some breakfast?" she said, stepping into the house.

Still holding the seat cover from the car around him, Asafumi raised his chin and let out a long breath. As he tilted his head back, it bumped against the front door with an audible *bonk*.

59

After seeing Isamu off to school, Saya went into the garden. The seedlings were crowded shoulder to shoulder in neat green rows, each rubbing its leaves against the next in the spring sunshine. Saya bent down and began pulling out the little weeds that were also starting to pop up. The smell of fresh soil clinging to the roots warmed her heart.

With such brightness all around her, it felt as if the dark feelings she'd had before must have belonged to a different person. Maybe hatred was something that carried you away into another world. Maybe it took you into the part of the jungle where the evil spirits were. Maybe the moment you tasted it, you became lost in that part of the forest.

What she needed to do was to pull out every shoot of hatred that she found growing inside her. If she kept at it, then, just as vegetables can thrive when the weeds are gone, the time would come when healthier feelings could take root.

As she continued weeding, she hit something hard, and a sharp pain shot up through her hand. When she looked, blood was already oozing from her fingertip. A red drop fell on a silvery object lying among the weeds. It was the finger-hole knife. The crescent blade glistened in the morning dew.

So this was where she had dropped it last night.

When she reached to pick it up, a pale hand emerged from the soil and snatched it by its tiny handle.

With a violent shudder, she jumped to her feet.

The woman from the repatriation boat rose out of the ground like a column of smoke. There was blood running down her neck, and she looked at Saya with hate-filled eyes as she waved the knife in front of her.

You killed me!

The cry was followed by a flash of the blade. The tip tore across Saya's stomach. She straightened, and closed her eyes. A silvery flare burst across the inside of her eyelids.

For several moments, she stood with her eyes held tightly shut, not moving a muscle. A bee buzzed in her ear. Somewhere in the distance she could hear children at play. Then, slowly, she opened her eyes.

The woman was gone. On the ground lay the little knife, with a single drop of blood on its blade. Saya ran her hands over her stomach. She found no sign of a wound.

As she let out her breath in relief, she felt a spasm in her loins and was gripped with pain. Her legs buckled and she fell to her knees. It was a crushing pain that wouldn't let go. She dropped onto all fours. A cold sweat broke out on her forehead. She could feel a small lump being pushed out between her legs, followed by a warm, sticky fluid. Then the pain receded.

Still trying to recover her breath, Saya got to her feet. She knew instantly what had happened. When she removed her underwear, the small bloody mass it held spilled onto the ground.

My baby, she thought, but she didn't have the strength to say it aloud.

Instead of killing her, the woman had killed her child. She felt a surge of hatred swelling inside her.

Before it had time to take shape, she began scooping at the earth with her two hands. Her cut finger throbbed with pain, but she ignored it. When she came to harder soil, she dug at it with the knife to break it up.

Once she had a hole the size of a Japanese pumpkin, she gently laid the blood-soaked lump at the bottom. Next to the child who'd never had a chance to see the light, she placed her brother's knife. Then she pushed the dirt back into the hole.

With her hurried digging and filling done, Saya let out a deep sigh. The bright spring sunshine still warmed the day. On the gentle breeze came the scent of flowers. She sat gazing at the mound of earth in front of her for quite some time, then slowly got to her feet and turned toward the house.

Entering by way of the veranda, she opened the closet and pulled the white drawstring bag from her travel case. It still held quite a few of the seeds she had brought with her from Malaya.

She went back to the garden with the bag and took out one particular seed. It was from the tree of the dead. She pushed it into the soft mound of earth.

"Kesumba is your name," she said.

She sat on the ground and stared at the dark brown dirt. After a time, she realized she was playing absently with the contents of the white bag. The seeds from the Malayan jungle sifted through her fingers, making a faint squeaking noise as they rubbed together.

She listened to the barely audible sound with her eyes closed. *Squeak-squeak, squeak-squeak.* She felt the corners of her eyes growing warm and moist. Then tears traced lines down her cheeks and fell to the ground.

The seeds from the jungle were whispering in her ears. It was the sound of bare feet pounding the earth; the sound of her tribe treading the forest path from one settlement to another. Time would circle round as they walked, and when they arrived at the new place, they would find the trees laden with fruit and the palm huts collapsed. Her people would rebuild the makeshift huts and begin life anew — as if reliving the lives that they'd lived before.

Whoonnng, nnnng, whooo oo-oo-oong.

The song her people sang rose from deep in Saya's throat. As the notes flowed through her lips, they mingled with her tears and fell to earth. Nourished by both her tears and her song, the seed she had planted would soon sprout up. And in time it would rise to stand among the trees of another forest. It would not be a forest where evil spirits dwelled. It would be one where songs and tears flowed.

With her eyes closed, Saya pictured the day when she would walk in that forest yet to be.